STONEWALL I

KEITH KAHLA, GI

The Coming Storm

Paul Russell

St. Martin's Press New York

A version of Chapter I appeared in *American Short Fiction,* and a version of Chapter III in *The Mammoth Book of Gay Erotica.*

Design by James Sinclair

www.stonewallinn.com

Library of Congress Cataloging-in-Publication Data

Russell, Paul Elliot.
  The coming storm / Paul Russell.
      p.   cm.
    ISBN 0-312-20514-7 (hc)
    ISBN 0-312-26303-1 (pbk)
    I.   Title.
  PS3568.U7684C65   1999
  813'.54—dc21
                                                                99-32207
                                                                CIP

10 9 8 7 6

This book is for
Christopher Canatsey
and for
Tom Heacox

COURAGE TEACHERS

Acknowledgments

For their various and invaluable contributions, I wish to thank Harvey Klinger, my agent; Keith Kahla, my editor; Ralph Sassone, Christopher Bram, Jill Rosenberg, Daisy, Sugar Baby in the sweet hereafter; Robert Tatum, Lawrence Schimel, Eric Brown, Darra Goldstein, Dean Crawford, Mark Valentine, Karen Robertson, the late James Lewton-Brain.

The Coming Storm

I

The young man came striding across the threshold of Louis's office with all the vigor and self-possession his recommendations had promised, and though something in Louis's soul paused there momentarily, he dismissed that pause as nothing but a shadow. Tracy Parker's handshake was firm, his smile clear and winning. And scrupulous punctuality, in Louis's book, always boded well.

"Please." He gestured, and Tracy seated himself with the loose-limbed ease of someone who makes himself instantly at home. In deference to the mid-August swelter, he wore no jacket. He'd rolled up the sleeves of his white dress shirt and loosened his tie. His hair, Louis noticed, was in some need of a trim.

"Not to worry," Tracy apologized as if having intuited his interviewer's thoughts. He ran long fingers through lazy, straw-colored locks. "It's as shaggy as you'll ever see me. I just didn't have time to get it cut."

Certainly it was a promising start. Louis dabbed at his brow with a handkerchief and said, "Thanks so much for getting yourself up here on a moment's notice. I hope you won't hold the weather against us. The humidity can really be quite ferocious."

Tracy smiled indulgently. "It's just as bad down in the city," he said.

"I think you'll find the humidity is even worse up here," Louis told him with some certainty. Then, glancing needlessly over Tracy's résumé: "I see you've been doing carpentry work the last few months."

Tracy held out a bare forearm. "How's this for a tan? It's probably the best shape I'll ever be in. At least my body. Though I'm afraid my brain's turned to mush. I get home at night and all I do is watch TV. I can hardly wait to get back to the life of the mind. Slumber of the mind is what I call the last six months or so. I'm incredibly excited. Books and education and learning are what my real life is all about."

"I have to say," Louis told him, "that we were really very interested in you back in April. But unfortunately we only had the one position. Though now, as it turns out, we still have that position."

Tracy nodded amicably. "You've been left in the lurch," he said. Comfortably—or perhaps it was nervousness—he rested his right ankle on his left knee, and proceeded to massage the knob of his anklebone.

Louis was a little disconcerted to see that Tracy wasn't wearing any socks. "Left in the lurch. You could say that," he admitted.

"What an odd phrase," Tracy said reflectively.

Louis didn't follow. He kept watching, with some skepticism, the gap between khaki cuff and black loafer.

"I mean, 'Left in the lurch.' What do you think that means, exactly? Left in the lurch." He mouthed the phrase with relish.

"You've got me," Louis confessed. The curiosity of the young intrigued him.

"Do you ever think what a peculiar language we speak?" Tracy went on. Whatever the cause, he seemed admirably able to generate his own enthusiasms out of thin air. "When I was in college, I studied in Germany for a year. I hardly spoke a word of English the whole time, and what it made me realize was what an amazing language English really is. This crazy, jumbled-up language, not like German, that's so consistent, no exception to the rules. English seemed so alive—like, I don't know, some kind of slithering snake. I don't think the German department ever forgave me, but Germany was definitely an important learning experience for me."

Perhaps, Louis thought with a sigh, the young man would turn out to be something of a bore when one got to know him. This penchant his generation had for saying everything at once. Still, to call English a snake was somehow odd and interesting.

"I have a long-standing interest in Germany myself," he felt he should mention, if for no other reason than to spare Tracy the need to fill him in too fully on what he called his learning experience.

"Have you been there?" Tracy asked animatedly. "I mean, I'm sure you've been there. But a lot?"

It made Louis smile. "Oh, fairly frequently," he told Tracy. "My wife and I. We've traveled all over. Munich, Dresden, Berlin, Stuttgart. We enjoy the cultural offerings, especially the opera. There are some splendid provincial operas, you know. We were in Freiburg—"

"Freiburg," said Tracy. "That's exactly where I was—at the university. Freiburg im Breisgau."

It was Louis's turned to be dogged. "There was a production of *Rosen-*

kavalier we saw four times," he went on. "So fiercely intelligent. And then we were in Berlin later and saw another production, much better singing, the orchestra was magnificent, but the production was a complete mess. No *idea* behind it. That's what you can get in those smaller theaters. Exciting young directors who have ideas. Who aren't running on automatic."

He stopped. He'd been on the verge of saying, "Running on automatic is the problem with most people's lives." But he was wary of seeming to preach. It proved an increasing hazard as the years went by, and there was nothing like the subject of music to draw him out. You should have been a musician, Claire was always telling him—but he had no aptitude whatsoever for music, except as a listener.

"Opera's a bit out of my league," Tracy admitted with a smile. "I think it's definitely an acquired taste."

"Well," Louis teased, "isn't that what education's all about?"

"And I'm always willing to be educated," Tracy affirmed. He smiled broadly, even remarkably, Louis thought; as if a smile could be generous enough to enlarge the recipient as well. He'd seen enough. The spark was there, the earnestness, the enthusiasm. It shone through whatever inexperience might cloud the young man.

Besides, with the semester starting in less than three weeks the position needed to be staffed immediately. He'd been wrong about one candidate already, but proceeding with caution wasn't something he could afford at the moment. That Tracy would take the job seemed a foregone conclusion. Still, he felt he should talk him through one or two things. Youthful enthusiasm could be blind to the broader realities.

"You haven't taught much before," he noted.

"I taught a year in Japan . . ."

"But not American students," Louis cautioned him. "Especially not our particular brand here. The Forge School fills a certain niche."

He was conscious of choosing his words carefully.

"Our students are not exactly, for the most part, what you would call model students. They're quite talented, many of them, but for one reason or another they haven't performed well in their previous schools. Still, they're boys who should go to college. They come from affluent families, they have good prospects out in the world. But they need an extra bit of prodding. Our mission is to make sure they don't damage their futures too much at this stage in their lives. Our job, to be blunt about it, is to get them into college. If I may say so, most of our students suffer from a kind of inattentiveness to their best interests. That's the main challenge: to get these boys to understand their best interests, at least in terms of education. As simple as that. It's not just about getting them into college. It's about teaching the value of education. We're a progressive institution in the best sense of the word. We try to help each of our students find his place and fulfill his potential there. If that interests you, then I'd like to offer you the chance to work with us for the coming year."

He'd been long-winded—he knew that—but Tracy's attention hadn't seemed to flag. The young man furrowed his brow only for a single, inscrutable moment. Then, looking Louis in the eye, his gaze bright and direct: "I think this is something I'd be good at," he said. "I have to tell you, to be honest—I could make twice as much money carpentering, but this is where my life is. I'm sure of that."

So it was done. He could stop fulminating inwardly against the young woman who had so impressed him back in the spring but who had, at the last minute, excused herself with no more than a brief note of apology to say that she had, as she blithely put it, been made an offer she could not refuse by a girls' school in Lausanne, Switzerland.

He'd considered firing off a frank note of warning to that Swiss school, but resisted the temptation. At his age, he didn't need to go ruining crass young lives. Experience had shown that they could manage that quite nicely on their own. And in any event, this Tracy Parker would work out just fine. William and Mary English major, class of 1991, B-plus average, a year's teaching experience at a technical school for young women in Nagoya. How effortlessly he must have won their hearts with his American good looks and easygoing style. And the Forge School, he suspected, would prove no different. The students would adore him, if for nothing more than that youthful charisma for which there was, one regretfully had to admit, simply no substitute.

Louis himself had possessed such a quality once, had held on to it, in fact, for many years. Teaching had been his life, though his abrupt and traumatic elevation to the post of headmaster had effectively curtailed his classroom activities. It was perhaps just as well. With the years, the task of winning over his students had become harder and harder. He could see the suspiciousness in their eyes, their all-too-understandable reluctance to open themselves to this old man. What on earth had he to tell them anymore about their troubled young worlds?

He thus found himself, on this August afternoon of his sixty-fourth year, fiercely envying Tracy Parker the intangible currency of youth he carried so unawares. Twenty-five years old. He had been twenty-five himself when he first started teaching at the Forge School—though he had *not*, he reminded himself sternly, in those days felt himself possessed of any kind of currency, intangible or otherwise. Twenty-five was a terrible age, after all; like any other, fraught with all sorts of anxiety and disquiet.

He moved distractedly about his office, sifting through stacks of paper left over from last semester: obsolete memoranda, reports, notices of one kind or another. Some stacks he shifted from one cluttered surface to another. Would he miss any of them? In a sudden bout of resolve, he took up a batch of pages and, without so much as glancing through them, placed them in the wastebasket.

What a mood he felt himself in! August was a month he survived only by creeping from one air-conditioned refuge to the next. His office, unfortunately, was not one of those refuges: Seldom used in the summer months, it had never been modernized. The large windows lay open to the leafy, listless quad. No breeze stirred through. Out on the sun-dappled lawn nothing moved except for two crows that marched arrogantly up and down. Years ago there hadn't been so many crows, had there? Now scarcely a dawn came when their hideous cries didn't wrest him from his hard-won sleep. Songbirds, he'd read, were disappearing from North America. The noble raptors, also, were all but wiped out. Crows, jays, grackles—only the scavengers seemed inclined to proliferate. The future promised a tough, ugly world all around.

He threw another stack of papers in the trash and, if only to put off the actual exertion a quarter hour more, contemplated the walk home. On fine dry days he loved a brisk walk. Autumns were glorious that way, but in this tropical simmer his body betrayed him. He turned porous; incontinent sweat oozed from him. Whose fine idea had it been, on the Olympian heights or deep in the bowel-dark underworld, to condemn us to the messy, intractable burden of bodies, the sheer tedium of our confinement in the flesh?

He wanted nothing so much as to find himself lying on the sofa in his cool, darkened den—wafted there instantly, effortlessly—and listening to music on the stereo, Brahms or Bruckner, body on hold, mind adrift and yet hyperalert, his attention both compelled and freed by the rigorous structures of sound surrounding him. There was this indolence about him; had he been born in the previous century, he might well have found his way to the opium dens, languishing there as his thoughts roamed extraordinary landscapes. It would have been a danger, certainly. The temptation to dream his life away had always lurked.

A knock on the door startled him. Reid Fallone's broad round face peered in slyly.

It took some effort for Louis to rouse himself from his torpor. "Welcome back," he said. "You survived."

His colleague glided into the office and conspiratorially shut the door behind him. It was a habit Louis hated: as if anybody would be eavesdropping on an empty campus.

"Alas." Reid sighed. "Survived only to return to this benighted exile. Did you know we're to have dinner tonight? Libby spoke to Claire. She said you were over here."

"A headmaster's work is never done," Louis told him with a certain degree of satisfaction. "I managed to fill that position we had open back in the spring."

Reid looked confused. "I thought we'd already filled it. That terrific young lady from Yale. The one who wrote her thesis on Anthony Trollope."

"It turns out she's not coming. It's a long story. But dinner's fine. I'm looking forward to it."

"But that's terrible," Reid went on disappointedly. "She was spectacular. Exactly right for us."

"This young man will be just fine. He certainly seems eager enough." Even as he said it, though, he detected a strain of defensiveness creeping into his voice. Perhaps he had been too hasty. Perhaps he should have consulted Reid before making an offer.

"Another eager young man," Reid said. "Just what we need around here."

"Well, it's done," Louis told him irritably. "For better or worse. But now tell me about Athens. I'm sure you had a marvelous time, as usual. Thanks, by the way, for your cryptic postcards."

Reid sighed grandly. "One never knows what to say. Anyway, I'll regale everybody with the official tales at dinner."

He paused, and suddenly, out of nowhere, Louis was on the alert. He knew his colleague too well. (What if Tracy Parker wasn't, in fact, a prudent choice for the job? One gave oneself away at every turn.)

"I trust your research went well," Louis prodded.

"Oh, the research," Reid said distractedly. Already it was too late. Louis braced himself for whatever would come. "It was fine when I could work. But my allergies turned out to be just awful. The smog and the traffic and everything. And oh my God, the heat. I could go on. I didn't get done half what I had intended. But of course there's always next summer. And I did manage to track down one or two rather obscure items. That in itself, I suppose . . ." He stopped midsentence, both of them perfectly familiar with this line of talk. Reid's research, as he called it, had been going on for more years than Louis cared to count. It was a wonder there were any Byzantine churches left to investigate.

Though safely behind closed doors, Reid glanced momentarily over his shoulder, a reflex that might, in other circumstances, have been comic. Reaching into the pocket of his rumpled jacket, he withdrew a photograph and, without a word, laid it on Louis's desk.

A blond woman in her midforties stared up at him. She had the leathery look of someone who'd squandered years in the sun. Nevertheless, she retained clear traces of her former beauty. A man's white dress shirt had been unbuttoned to reveal the black bathing suit she wore underneath. It was night; the setting appeared to be an outdoor café. In the flash of the camera, her eyes glowed. She looked slightly drunk—or startled, caught at something.

She seemed put out by the presence of the camera, betrayed by it. He assumed Reid stood behind the viewfinder. Her mouth, its smile fading, seemed about to lash out in complaint. Louis felt a surge of squeamishness.

He glanced up at Reid, then back at the photo. He wouldn't touch it. To touch it would be to involve himself in it. And yet he was already involved. This was hardly the first time Reid had burdened him with such a confession in the nearly forty years they'd been together at the Forge School. There had been that awful hour in the midseventies when he'd confessed, his voice brimming with guilt and exhilaration, the summer's escapade with a young woman in Ravenna. He'd sworn Louis to strictest secrecy: No one could know; the information would crush poor Libby. Why? Louis asked at the time. Why have you done this? Reid only touched his heart with his finger- tips, a delicate gesture he'd learned, perhaps, from ancient frescoes or mo- saics, at once so eloquent and absurd that it effectively silenced whatever other questions Louis might have presumed to muster over the years. Be- cause it all happened with depressing regularity: those solitary "research" trips abroad, those end-of-the-summer confessions. Louis felt it his duty to register profound disapproval, but despite the possibility that their friendship had, over the years, perhaps outlived its natural span, he had nonetheless faithfully played his part in the marital deception Reid had pledged him to assist in.

Sighing deeply, with an air of satisfaction—or was it melancholy?—Reid placed his hands over the paunch he'd negligently allowed himself to acquire down through the years. "She heads the American excavation at Pella," he said. "Louis, I really fell for her. I think she might be the love of my life." And he sighed again.

"You don't have to tell me any of this," Louis reminded him.

Reid looked at him imploringly. "If I don't tell somebody," he said, "I'll begin to think it never happened. And it did happen. I was sitting in a café in Kolonaki. She was at the next table. Kept sending glances my way, then long frank stares. I was talking to a fellow Byzantinist about the mosaics at Daphne, and then when I was finished, she came over and said, 'Your English is so good, I thought you must be the leader of the Hungarian team.' Not a trace of a smile. How could I not fall for that? We went right down to her hotel in the Plaka. The afternoon sun was coming in through the windows. She's such a terribly avid person, Louis, so hungry for life. I had the sense of just being—how shall I say?—*enveloped* by her. I was practically floating in the light."

Louis took out his handkerchief and ran it across his forehead. "At least spare me the more gruesome details," he said dryly.

"Oh," Reid told him, "there are no gruesome details. She teaches at the University of Texas—married, alas, with three children. Entanglements, en- tanglements. They joined her in Athens there at the end, which was awkward. She didn't want me to meet them, and obviously I agreed. But can you believe this? When I boarded the plane to fly home, there she was, husband and children too. What an extraordinary coincidence. But I must say we were magnificent: didn't even acknowledge one another. Two perfect strangers. She'll be in Athens for a conference over Thanksgiving, and if there's any way, I'll be there too. The relationship's impossible, of course. She says there's no future. It was a moment, is all, and I respect her for that. I couldn't respect anything else. But the fact is, it happened, Louis."

He reached over and plucked the photo from the desktop. For a long moment he stared at it somberly. All the triumph had gone out of him. He seemed, suddenly, sad and old and tired. "Louis, Louis," he said. "What was I thinking? Why do I do this to myself? I'll never lay eyes on her again."

He bit his lip, and for an appalling moment Louis thought his friend might start to cry. But he didn't. Instead, he laughed.

"Can I tell you?" he said. "We had so much sex I still ache all over. She was insatiable, Louis. She taxed my imagination severely. But I don't think I disappointed her. This old man definitely has some surprises left in him."

Louis wouldn't say anything.

Reid leaned forward in his chair and gripped the edge of the desk. "I feel like I've touched something real, Louis. Body and soul. Sometimes I actually get the feeling there really is some meaning to all this mess we call life. The smile of the divine. And there are other things—but I'll tell you about them later."

Louis did have to admit that—for whatever reason—Reid looked rather perversely radiant, as if that Athenian light, even now, enveloped him. Still, he couldn't resist asking, "And how was Libby's month on the Cape?" Perhaps it was his own failure, a small-minded lack of imagination in the face of some great adventure he failed entirely to comprehend. Nonetheless, he felt an acute itch of guilt about Libby, kept all these years in the dark. And for the sake of what?

Reid, though, appeared unfazed. "Oh fine, fine," he said. He picked up the photo and replaced it thoughtfully in his pocket. They'd not speak of her again, this American archaeologist from the dig at Pella. He'd had his say. Now she was between them; he'd safely housed her in Louis's imagination—where she was free to undergo any number of awful metamorphoses.

"It's good for Libby to pack me off the way she does," Reid said fondly. "Demanding old coot that I am. She loves her summers. She positively flour-ishes in my absence."

He smiled broadly—almost as if he meant those words.

Shielded from the sun's merciless glare by the sunglasses he felt so vulnerable without, Louis walked home feeling disconsolate and violated. How dare Reid barge in like that—not into his office, but into his soul? For the hundredth time, he decided theirs was a friendship he could no longer sustain. But how, after all these years, to end it? He was too vastly implicated, because Reid's secrets really were entirely safe with him. There was that degree of brilliance in his friend's careful organization of his affairs: here he lived beyond reproach; there, well, anything could happen. And with some regularity did. But were Louis, in some mad fit of candor, ever to reveal the sad truth about his friend, no one would believe him. This schoolteacher who delved into obscurest Byzantiniana, who wrote a pompous column called "The Religious Perspective" for the local newspaper, and whom, as a result, the students had dubbed Father Fallone—apparently without irony: he'd conned them all.

Nevertheless, a damning photo had lain briefly on Louis's desk. What other tracks had Father Fallone foolishly left uncovered? Louis couldn't escape the notion that, despite his care, Reid was still playing with fire, the kind that could without warning sheathe one's whole life in irreversible conflagration.

Louis knew all too well about playing with fire. Years ago he should have said, simply, sternly, a scrupulously principled stance, "I don't want to know." But he'd been younger then and full of dangerous curiosity.

He made a mental note to steer Tracy Parker clear of Reid's orbit. There were too many ways of becoming entangled with someone like Reid, and the not-unfriendly word he'd been looking for, ever since their interview, to describe Tracy Parker finally came to him: *guileless.* Perhaps, like Parsifal, a perfect fool.

Now there was an amusing, frivolous thought.

Sweat slid down his sides. He considered taking off his linen jacket and carrying it over his arm, but decided against it. He didn't like the feeling of being unclothed.

At Academy Avenue he paused for the crosswalk light to signal safe passage. Traffic streamed endlessly past, sleek new automobiles hermetically sealed against the tribulations of August. Even through dark lenses, the light off their windshields dazed him.

In some countries, India for instance, men weren't afraid to be seen sauntering along under the shade of an umbrella. Would that he had the courage to put up an umbrella under this unremitting downpour of sunlight. But that had been the trouble with his whole life. A fear that people might notice; people might talk. That was why he found it impossible to imagine a single word of the book he'd fooled himself into thinking he'd spent years preparing for. *Closed Fist and Open Palm: Moral Discipline in the Works of Thomas Mann.* This past summer he had once again cleared a space for it; despite Claire's urging, there had been no European vacation, not even a week on the Cape. Every morning he'd compelled himself, with faultless discipline, to inhabit his air-conditioned study for the three long hours between breakfast and lunch. And nothing had happened. Morning after morning he sat at his uncluttered desk and no thoughts came. He opened the diaries of Thomas Mann at random and read. He brooded over the *Observations of a Non-Political Man* and the "Snow" chapter from *The Magic Mountain*. Idly he wrote out certain names: Nepomuk Schneidewein, Pribislav Hippe, Clavdia Chauchat. This subject he knew everything and nothing about. It wasn't so much that he had no thoughts in his head, but rather that, constipated from years of withholding, they now refused to issue forth.

Certain pages had been written. He kept them in a black notebook, which, one day soon, he promised himself, he intended to destroy.

He remembered Reid once chiding him: "You're so straitlaced. Loosen up, my friend. Life is not a prison sentence." Stupid not to have asked Reid for a lift home in that embarrassing, bright red sports car he drove these days. But the last thing he wanted this afternoon was Reid.

He had always recognized that the path he had chosen would be difficult. He asked no pity, expected no compassion.

A sudden commotion behind made him turn his head. Two boys on bicycles had ridden up. In the roiling heat, they'd taken off their shirts and tied them to their handlebars. As was the fashion among teenagers these days, they wore their outsized jeans slung implausibly low on their hips; the ribbed waistlines of their boxer shorts showed a full two inches.

They were thirteen or fourteen, with aggressive haircuts and earrings in their ears. One had a tattoo on his forearm: a rose or some other flower. Their bellies were smooth and hard, their chests thrown boldly forth against the wide world that was all theirs. He would not give them more than a single glance. There was something too obscene about them, too intimidating.

Feral. He could almost smell it on them.

But already he'd betrayed his nerves. He'd failed to notice that the light had finally changed. WALK, the crosswalk sign commanded imperiously. "Out of the way, Pops," one of the boys told him, while the other made what sounded like a farting noise with his lips as they charged past him with only inches to spare. He watched their naked backs, that interval of shorts between jeans and skin, the motion of their buttocks as they stood on their pedals and pumped furiously away.

No doubt about it. He'd become a relic, something to be thrown away. There was no one else like him remaining in the entire world.

Claire had gone out, and Lux didn't hear him come in; asleep on his pillow in the kitchen, the ancient dog raised his head as Louis entered the room, then heaved himself heavily to his feet. There he stood, unsteady, disoriented. Since his stroke last spring, he listed a bit to the left.

"Hello, old fellow," Louis told him. He bent down to scratch behind the German shepherd's ears. Clouded eyes watched him. "Feeling creaky today?" he asked as he unlatched the back door and held it open. "It's the weather. That's all."

Lux made his way with difficulty down the two shallow steps. He waited a moment, confused, then took a few uncertain steps out onto the grass and squatted down. The outdoors seemed, these days, to overwhelm him.

He'd have to be put down in the fall, before the cold came. They'd decided that. After thirteen years, it was going to prove difficult. Already Louis was severely dreading his own weakness.

"Good fellow," he praised as Lux made his painful way back up the steps and through the door. That long-ago autumn their second daughter had left for college, some loneliness had given Claire the idea of rescuing a dog from the pound. He'd have purchased a purebred himself, but he had given in, and perhaps she'd been right after all. No one could have asked for a sweeter companion these past twelve years.

Rummaging in the refrigerator, he found an end of kielbasa. Lux's tail thumped the floor with something like his old liveliness. Louis had taken to indulging him, this good and faithful dog facing death at the hands of the humans he trusted.

On the counter, Claire had left a stack of mail—sans bills, which she'd weeded out. Through some set of circumstances he could no longer quite remember, those had become her domain quite early in their marriage. He sifted through what was left: a newsletter from their Republican congress-woman, a package from the Musical Heritage Society. The latest New Yorker offered a vaguely displeasing cover, as seemed often to be the case these days, and its table of contents held little of interest. Except for their monthly ritual of the opera, they never ventured into the city anymore; it had become as strange and off-putting as the magazine that bore its name.

At the bottom of the stack of mail a flimsy blue airmail envelope lay. The gaudy stamp advertised itself as Tanzanian. Puzzled—who on earth might he know in Tanzania?—he carried the mysterious communication into his study and seated himself at his desk. He'd always opened letters with an inexpli-cable sense of dread.

Childish, blocklike letters lurched across the page.

Dear Mr. Tremper,
   Probably you won't remember me. I graduated from the Forge six years ago. I was in your tenth grade literature class where we read A Separate Peace. Now I'm in the Peace Corps here in the town of Arusha—hard to imagine! But I love it, I love what I'm doing. We've been building a bridge across a stream where usually the locals have to ford and in the rainy season it floods. It's really satisfying to be helping people like this. I also

tutor adults and children in English. They're really a beautiful people here, the Liguru people.

So why am I writing. Well, the other day I was in this little library the Mormon missionaries run, and guess what I found there? A Separate Peace! So I took it out and read it all over again and I had so many memories. I remember our English class really well, it was a really important time for me. You were the teacher who first got me interested in English, which I ended up majoring in College (Ithaca College). It was the friendship between Finny and Gene I really related to, and the school stuff and all.

Anyway I'd been thinking and I thought I'd just write and say thanks for the help and encouragement you gave me. It's lonely here sometimes. The stars at night are really amazing, though. Maybe I'll try to teach them to read A Separate Peace (my students, I mean!!).
Sincerely,
Robert Wainmark (Bobby)

Louis vaguely remembered the thin-faced boy with big brown eyes who'd kept mostly to himself, sat toward the back of the class, rarely ever spoke. One of those adolescent enigmas one despaired of ever reaching. There'd always seemed something faintly sorrowful about him, some sadness that kept him quiet. His work had been earnest but mediocre. And had he written the occasional poem? Louis wasn't entirely sure, six years down the road, but it seemed possible he'd turned in some vague, obdurate bit of lyric from time to time.

On consideration, he seemed to remember that distinctly. And one of the younger teachers, a dorm adviser, had once mentioned that Bobby had problems with bed-wetting: that too came back to Louis. He read the letter over again, these words addressed to him from Africa, this young man—he'd be around twenty-three now—who'd thought of him on an African night under the lonely shining stars.

Louis was faintly embarrassed that he could recall so little about him. He swiveled his desk chair around to locate the atlas on the bookshelf. Opening the heavy tome on his lap, he perused pinked-tinted Tanzania's cities—Dar es Salaam, Dodoma, Iringa, Kigoma—until he found Arusha in the north, under the very shadows, it appeared, of Mount Kilimanjaro.

He himself had never been to Africa, would never go. The continent held too little interest for him, and far too much in the way of fear. Though northern Africa did beckon in its bleak, unforgiving way. As a boy he'd followed with secret admiration the campaign of Rommel's Afrika Korps, their valiant and thrilling fight.

He read the letter through a third time, then opened his filing cabinet, took out a manila folder, and filed it with a dozen or so similar letters he'd received over the years. What else did one do with an attempt at communication like that? If he were to write Bobby back, what would there be to say? He had answered some of his boys' letters in the past, had even maintained a semblance of correspondence with one or two of them, but inevitably it petered out after a couple of years. They moved on to other things—as they should. Their prep-school teacher, having served his purpose with them, appropriately turned his attention to the latest crop of young minds needing encouragement, advice, lessons in various kinds of fortitude. From time to time, of course, he received stray news: This one had married into great wealth, or that one had earned a law degree, or was practicing medicine. More often, they moved docilely into their fathers' businesses—a fate that had, he supposed, been the point for most of them all along. He didn't mind, and if the Forge School alumni gave generously to the annual fund, he was hardly the one to complain. He prided himself on having few illusions. The world was a complex place, and there were many complex accommodations to be reached with it.

But Africa, the Peace Corps. Such a destination was a distinct rarity among his boys. He found himself oddly pleased with quiet, sad Bobby Wainmark.

Someone was speaking his name.

"Louis," Claire said, quietly but firmly. She bent over him, gently prodding his shoulder as music played—the Bruckner string quintet he'd received in the mail from the Musical Heritage Society. He lay on the sofa, must have fallen asleep; yes, near the end of the adagio he'd grown so drowsy he'd closed his eyes, started to drift, and as happened whenever he first entered that slumbering state, the music had taken on the most deliciously heightened intensity. Melodies ached along his veins. A chord's dissonances melted voluptuously somewhere near his heart. Music heard when half-asleep transformed itself into some nearly shameful language.

He'd forgotten they were scheduled for dinner at Reid and Libby's. Rousing himself from the sofa, he told Claire, "It's the weather, is all. That's what's getting to me."

She had dressed for the occasion: black skirt, white blouse, a colorful scarf thrown about her neck. She loved dressing for occasions; the social moment still mattered to her. He himself had lost that. She accused him, only half humorously, of having grown curmudgeonly while she had soldiered on, still nursing some hope in the possibilities of human interaction. Perhaps it was their respective careers, the different kinds of human contact they allowed. He seldom found himself brooding over the strange fact that she, who never had shown aspirations toward any such thing in their younger years, had gone on in middle age, after their daughters left home, to finish a Ph.D. in English at the state university in Albany while his own benighted dissertation, abandoned so long ago at Cornell, would never see the light of day. Now she taught courses at the community college, and some nights tutored prisoners within the high, gloomy walls of the nearby correctional facility for women. With the years she had grown liberal, even radical. She helped the poor, the desperate, the disenfranchised—those were her very words—find their way into four-year colleges a rung or two below those his own students aimed for.

He supposed he could genuinely admire all that.

As usual, Claire drove. It had been years since Louis had been behind the wheel, and he was no longer entirely certain he could be trusted there. But Claire had nerves of steel. She negotiated the Taconic and the Autobahn with equal ease, and he admired that about her too. The early evening air was still thick and heavy, but the light their Audi sped through had a kind of magnificence about it. Not like that Greek light Reid had floated in—but then he didn't envy Reid one bit. This was his light, the tempered, shifting light countless painters on countless canvases (one hung, in fact, in his office) had tried to still. Except for his years at Cornell, he had lived in the Hudson Valley his whole life.

"You're doing it again," Claire told him. The sound of her voice made him jump.

"What?" he said.

She held up her fist, clenched and unclenched it several times.

"Sorry," he told her. "I didn't realize I was doing that."

"What are you so anxious about?"

But if he was anxious, he had no idea of it. Yet her accusation sounded exactly right. "Oh," he told her, "you know how I get every year before school starts."

"We should have gone away this summer," she told him. "We should have taken those three weeks in Germany."

"I don't think the summer's been a complete waste," he judged. But the truth of it bore in on him. Even the landscape, as they passed the new Wal-Mart that would spell the death of Middle Forge's fragile Main Street, seemed suddenly blighted. He had sat at his desk. Nothing had happened. The summer, like his life, had passed him by.

A developer had bulldozed lots into what had been, at the beginning of the season, a grove of trees. Some miles beyond those suburban ravages, out in the still unspoiled countryside, Reid and Libby lived in the house they'd built when Reid came into his bit of inheritance. At the school, it had caused something of a controversy. Faculty were generally expected to live in faculty housing, either dormitory apartments or, for those married and with families, the row of houses along Academy Avenue. The Forge School was a residential campus. But Reid had been adamant, and Louis, then in his first year as headmaster, had let him have his way. Fifteen years later that moment of weakness still perturbed him. Dr. Emmerich would not have given in. Dr. Emmerich would have maintained faculty discipline. But Dr. Emmerich had died in a rainstorm on a country road at night, and Louis was on his own.

"Reid will be in his Hellenic mode," Louis observed. "Ten to one we're having shish kebab or some such thing."

Claire smiled indulgently at him, as she did whenever she caught him being mean. Weakness and meanness: certainly he had his share of failings.

Still, he persisted. "Too pretentious, don't you think? Inflicting one's vacation on one's guests."

"He's only trying to hold on to something before it slips away," she said. "I think that's perfectly understandable."

He felt duly chastened, but perhaps he had wanted that. She always had large sympathies—and who benefited from them more than he?

Castel Fallone, he had privately dubbed Reid and Libby's dream home. As with most dreams, it perhaps revealed unwanted truths. Behind the grandiose facade lay echoing, underused rooms. Reid and Libby had wanted but failed to produce children, and the house seemed sadly meant to accommodate that nonexistent family. And while Reid delighted in what he pompously called the cathedral spaces—he loved tootling endlessly on his reproduction harpsichord, its busy clatter resonating in the emptiness—Libby had always seemed ill at ease under those vaulted ceilings. She much preferred their dark, cramped cottage on the Cape, to which she fled during the summers when Reid went abroad.

Meeting them at the door, awash in the rose perfume she had been in the habit of dousing herself with for as long as he'd known her, Libby looked flushed, hectic, as if she'd just managed to pull herself together the moment before their arrival. Louis felt fairly certain she had not turned into a furtive drunk on them; it was simply that time and circumstance had taken their toll on a woman who had once been rather beautiful. And summer seemed to have added a few pounds of its own to the weight of years.

"Oh, you're finally here," she said, with a nervous buoyancy that, in turn, made him suddenly nervous. "Reid's fired up the grill. I don't know why he's in such a hurry, but he claims he has an important announcement to make at dinner."

"Libby," Claire complimented her, "you're all tanned. Louis and I look like mushrooms."

"I'm well done is more like it," Libby said. "Stick me with a fork and I'll ooze butter."

For some reason Claire found that funny. She rubbed her friend's arm affectionately. They'd been roommates together at Barnard, and whenever they were around one another they instantly reverted to some impenetrable banter left over from their youth.

He followed the two women through the blessed air-conditioning of the house, silently irked by the truth of what Libby had hinted at the door: They were, in fact, a good half hour late. And he hated people who were late. Clearly Claire had put off waking him as he lay slumbering on the sofa. It was a strange, inveterate incapacity of hers, far too ingrained to stand any changing at this point.

On the terrace in back, Reid looked comfortable in sandals, baggy jeans, a loose white shirt that failed to conceal his girth. He wore a straw hat. Without any success Louis tried to picture him as the conquering Lothario among the lady archaeologists. From a great bowl Reid lifted skewers dripping with marinade and laid them on the fire. Flames flared up, hissing.

So he'd been right about the shish kebabs. He wondered if Claire would notice, but she seemed oblivious to this proof of his acuity.

"The perfect hot-weather drink," Reid advertised, holding up a milky glass of ouzo and water. "The Greeks spent three thousand years perfecting it. I spent all summer drinking it."

"An ouzo sounds delightful," Claire said.

"A martini for me," Louis demurred.

"Ah, the old staple. Some things never change with Louis, do they?" Reid teased Claire.

"Louis is very conservative," Claire agreed.

"I really don't care for ouzo," Louis protested. "I never have. If you don't mind, I'll go fix myself a martini."

"Suit yourself. You know where the makings are."

Busying himself with the grill, Reid wouldn't look at his guest; as he made his way indoors Louis noted the avoidance with a quiet sense of wonder. Was Reid regretting the afternoon's impulsive confession? Certainly such a thing had happened before; after an initial eagerness—even compulsion—to reveal all, he'd withdraw, and an awkwardness would fall between them for a few days. Mentally, Louis upbraided his friend: If you don't want me to know something, then don't tell me. But don't punish me for hearing you out. Surely that was simple enough.

Though Louis knew next to nothing, personally, about sexual regrets, the squeamish morning that followed some sordid night, the thought descended on him that Reid's sudden awkwardness with him might be said to resemble, more closely than one might wish, exactly such a fit of regret.

The unbidden revelation put him in a very damp mood, and he found himself, in Castel Fallone's cool and spacious kitchen, going a bit heavier on the gin than he otherwise might. He took a sip, then another. He knew he shouldn't be drinking alcohol at all in this summer heat: liquor only made him sweat like the proverbial pig. But the promise of an announcement at dinner from Reid had him strangely on edge. He found himself thinking anxiously about that photo, the way Reid's lady friend looked at the camera, her glare at once fierce and hungering. Were archaeologists really such a sex-starved lot as all that? Did pigs really sweat?

Imagining, suddenly, a vast slurping muck of a mudhole, in a mighty swallow he drank the whole of his martini; then, feeling slightly ashamed, he made himself another. Out the window, he could see the three of them on the terrace, Reid holding forth before his appreciative audience. If any of them wondered where he'd taken himself off to, they showed no sign of it. Surely he wasn't jealous. Or if he was, then of what was he jealous?

Another phrase rattled around his head: to seize life by the throat. There had always been something vaguely goatish about Reid Fallone; didn't he, in a sense, devour everything that came his way?

Judging himself sufficiently fortified, he sauntered, fresh martini in hand, back outside. The warm air enveloped him. Reid was waxing apocalyptic.

"I'd sit in the cafés of these prosperous Macedonian cities and feel it all around me in the air: how these people are worried sick about their future. You see on banners everywhere, 'Pray for the Peace of the Balkans.' And well they should pray. This time next year, it's them we could be reading about in the papers, and they know it. Things could happen just like that. Snipers, guns in the hills. Would the rest of the world give a damn? It's why the Greeks are backing Serbia, and I have to say I agree with them. 'Greece: Serbia loves you.' I saw that graffiti everywhere. There're just too many people out there who want to get their hands on Greek Macedonia. The Albanians, the Bulgarians. The Turks."

The last word rang in the air ominously.

Louis had tried to follow it all in the newspapers, but the situation left him confused and depressed. Everything was too entangled, too deeply rooted. What had seized him most was the destruction of the beautiful Ottoman bridge at Mostar. Now *that* had had an awful clarity about it.

"The Serbs have shown themselves to be out-and-out butchers," he said with sudden certainty.

"There's plenty of butchery on all sides," Reid returned just as certainly. "What the Serbs have done is nothing compared to centuries of Turkish tyranny. Islam. That's the real thorn. A Muslim state in the heart of Europe. It's in no one's best interest."

"Except, I guess, those Muslims who already have the misfortune to be living in what you call the heart of Europe."

"The entanglements are tragic," Reid conceded. "And then there's the whole German angle: Germany recognizing Croatia. All those old alliances and memories. The Ustashe and all that. And now the Germans want to send peacekeeping troops—which of course Serbia will never stand for, given what the Nazis did there. Nor will the Russians."

Louis wasn't sure he wanted to know exactly what the Nazis had done. Reid had baited him and he'd allowed himself to be drawn in, only to discover he was at a distinct disadvantage. Reid was the one who had been there, after all. Reid had seen things with his own eyes.

He often felt his erstwhile friend had that particular advantage over him.

With a gesture of resignation, he withdrew, even as Reid announced that the kebabs were done. "I thought," he said, "we'd eat outside. The evening's so lovely." Louis's heart sank. No one, it seemed, minded this heat the way he did. To the west, he saw with some relief, Valhalla-like thunderheads were rising. A storm's sudden violence might just cool things off.

From a sweating tin pitcher, another Greek affectation, Reid poured cold glasses of retsina all round. Raising his glass in a toast, he announced, "To good friends, who are the most important thing to me in the world. And so I want to share with my good friends an important development in my life." He looked at each of them in turn, finally resting his gaze on Louis. And Louis realized that, earlier, he'd been entirely wrong: Reid wasn't ashamed at all. He was decisive and defiant; he challenged them all to find fault with his reckless way of moving through the world. "I made a very serious decision about my life this summer," he continued in a grave, measured voice. "What I've done, I haven't done lightly."

Louis felt his stomach go sour with anxiety. Rather than meet Reid's unwavering gaze—it was as if Reid meant this announcement for him alone—he stared resolutely into his wine. A film of condensation had settled over the surface of the glass. He waited tensely. He braced himself. He thought he could hear thunder in the distance.

"What I've done," Reid said, "is make a conversion to the Greek Orthodox faith."

Louis couldn't have heard that correctly. "You've what?" he said, the words out of his mouth before he could rein them in.

"Face it," Reid told him with a shrug that was suddenly impish, as if the whole thing were some elaborate practical joke. "I've been inching toward this for years."

Libby laughed loudly. "And I was worried you'd been diagnosed with cancer," she said.

Louis glanced at her with surprise. That had certainly never occurred to him, but perhaps it should have. Things would happen to them, after all. Libby herself had already been touched once by mortality's dark finger. The smudge remained to this day.

A sudden memory overtook him—from years before, his one visit to Greece. A monastery, unprepossessing outside, claustrophobic inside, floor-to-ceiling martyrdoms of every imaginable variety, all rendered with grisly relish. Suddenly into that dark interior had flooded a group of schoolchildren. Candles were lit. Under the eager eyes of nuns, they lined up to kiss the icon of the Blessed Virgin, two dozen avid young lips giving adoration in a gesture both greedy and cloying. It was to this that Reid had given himself over.

"Libby," Louis asked desperately, avoiding Reid's eyes, his smug contentment, "really—what do you think about this?"

"I think he's quite serious," she said. She stared ahead with that fiercely distracted look that overtook her features with increasing frequency of late. It seemed unnecessarily cruel for Reid to have exposed her like this, without warning. But she took it admirably in stride. "Not my thing, certainly. But then he's not asking me to do anything. He isn't even asking me to understand, particularly. Are you, Reid?"

"No," he said, gently, almost regretfully, but at the same time with a chilling implacability, "as a matter of fact I am not."

Libby looked at her husband, and then at Louis. She smiled, but her smile was entirely unreadable. Perhaps she was only stunned—as he was—or perhaps truly indifferent. Louis had never in his life understood her. There were times, in fact, when he'd positively feared her incomprehensibility. She was his wife's best friend. Their enduring admiration for one another much predated his own arrival on the scene.

"The Orthodox Church offers a great many things to admire," Reid said, though Louis had difficulty focusing on his sentences. "Not the least is the liturgy's incessant striving for the sublime. Nothing so mundane as human reason encumbers those divine words. It's not about speaking, it's about singing. About mystery and miracle and ecstasy. The intervention of the divine in earthly affairs. A kind of cosmic lightning strike on the terrestrial."

"Ick," Louis felt he had to say. He could only think of the American woman who led the excavation at Pella. What part, he wondered, did she play in all this ridiculousness? Still, the illusion of love had, in its time, led to stranger depravities.

Reid seemed to sense that. "Not all that different from your Wagner, really. What else is *Parsifal*, after all?"

An immediate retort failed him. Thomas Mann had called the opera "a compound of religious impulse, sheer lasciviousness, and sure-handed competence that comes across as wisdom." He'd perused those words that very morning, in his study, in one more futile attempt at work. But surely that assessment was wrong too; surely it missed the point.

Unless it was precisely the point. Perhaps everything, when one came down to it, involved some degree of sham at its heart.

"Does this mean you're obligated to go around kissing icons now?" he asked.

But Reid only laughed his most capacious belly laugh. "Louis," he said. "You sound like I've betrayed you. It's not that I've become a Hindu or a homosexual or anything so dire as that. As I see it, I'm returning to the common roots of our faith. Of all the versions of Christianity available to us, this is perhaps nearest to the original. Don't I remember you once saying, if you were a Catholic, you'd have fought Vatican Two tooth and nail? The mass is meant to be said in Latin, I think you argued—and quite persuasively, too."

He *had* said that. Leave it to Reid to quote him out of context. "I also said, if you'll remember, that you can't be other than what you are. What you were raised to be, that is. In your case—and mine too—once an Episcopalian, always an Episcopalian. To try to be anything else is disingenuous at best." He heard his voice trembling with an anger the situation itself didn't perhaps entirely warrant.

Claire, he could sense, was watching him with great curiosity, even fascination.

"So education is hopeless," Reid extrapolated, his voice cool and measured. Clearly he was enjoying this. "You're saying you can't grow out of anything. You can't transcend your own particular cultural or historical prison."

"You're twisting my meaning," Louis said sharply, hitting the flat of his hand against the table. "You always do that." The impact knocked over his wineglass, which he tried to catch but only succeeded in propelling off the table and, with an explosive shatter, onto the flagstones of the patio. The commotion didn't prevent him from hearing Libby tell Claire, quietly but in all seriousness, "They're very happy to see one another. It was a long summer they spent apart."

The longed-for storm from the west had never materialized. Thick, hazy moonlight silvered the hills. The road was a mirror spread out before them. Under his wife's sure hand the Audi streamed through the sleeping countryside.

As a child he'd loved being taken for car rides at night, being out in the darkness but shielded from its harms.

"I must say, Reid is looking awfully well these days," Claire observed. "Both of them, in fact. Their summers apart always seem to invigorate them."

They hadn't spoken since leaving. The mildness of her tone reassured him. He had thought she was angry with him, but apparently she wasn't, even though his behavior had undoubtedly given cause. Her ability to forgive was one of the things he thought her remarkable for.

"I must say I admire that marriage," she went on. "They've rather sensibly managed to accommodate one another over the years."

Louis was silent. He still felt a little drunk, though it was wearing off, and an unpleasant metallic taste had settled in his mouth. How much did Claire *really* know about those accommodations she so admired?

But it was a subject he wouldn't broach, at least not head-on.

"Frankly, I worry," he said. "They're both getting fat. That's always a sign of something amiss."

He could sense Claire smile at him from behind the wheel of the Audi.

"Moral failing in your book," she said. "Comfortable is what I'd call them. Occupying a fuller space in the world. They haven't been content, either one of them, to stay put. They've both grown over the years. It hasn't always been easy. I think there's a lot to be said for that."

"Fat," he repeated, letting the ugly word hang in the darkness. He was doing it again. He wondered if Claire would have put on more than the modest number of pounds that she had, over the years, had he not been there to steady her course.

"You've really been in some mood all evening," she pointed out. "You were practically impossible back there."

"Reid is such a hypocrite," he told her. "Conversion my ear."

"Changes upset you," Claire diagnosed. "I've never seen anybody who was so heavily invested in the status quo."

"It's not the change," Louis defended himself. "I don't care what religion he professes. It's just the sheer perversity of it. I'd like to think I take religion a little more seriously than that. And did you see how Libby just sat there? She didn't know what to do. I feel so sorry for Libby sometimes."

"Oh, I think Libby knows what's what. She's stayed married to him, after all."

"Talk about a miracle," Louis said.

He felt once more on the verge of something. It would be so easy simply to say what he knew. A few frank words formed themselves in his mouth.

He couldn't do it.

In the dark he wished he could see his wife's face, decipher what she might be thinking. Because perhaps it wasn't necessary to say these things. Perhaps she already knew. How could she not know? And Libby also. People always knew more than you gave them credit for. Perhaps, in the end, no one had any secrets at all.

In which case, perhaps better for everything to remain in silence.

"The miracle," Claire said, "is that *anybody* stays together."

For a moment he let her words lie. But then he felt he should say, "I think we've done pretty well."

"Oh," Claire confirmed, "all things considered, I think the two of us have done remarkably well."

Bobby Wainmark was teaching the Africans to read. "Like this," he said in his flat baritone. Into his mouth he put several tiny silver bicycles. Then, taking Louis by the hand, he led him across an empty stretch of desert dotted with what appeared to be small Byzantine chapels. Great unfamiliar birds, much larger than crows and brilliantly plumed, strutted about on the ground preening themselves. Under the open, star-filled sky, several ebony-skinned African boys lay sleeping on pallets, eyes closed, arms crossed over their thin chests. Bobby moved to the first and leaned over, placing his lips against the boy's lips. Louis could see him transfer into the boy's mouth a silver bicycle. Then he moved to the next and repeated the gesture.

The sight filled Louis with revulsion. "Now," Bobby said in a curiously detached voice when he had finished, "all that remains is to fertilize the egg." He seemed to be wearing some kind of ritual garb involving a skirt, and he made as if to undo it at the waist, was just on the verge of pulling the cloth back, when Louis woke.

He turned on the lamp and slid from under the covers to sit on the side of the bed. Three o'clock. He'd dreamed badly, he knew, but already it had faded. Claire slept peacefully beside him. How could one get to the age of sixty and still sleep so peacefully? Their conversation in the car had not left him happy. Once an Episcopalian, always an Episcopalian, he had once said, leaving out the inconvenient fact, known to no one now but himself, that he'd grown up Baptist and converted to that statelier religion during the tumultuous years of college. It had offered him—at least this was what he had believed at the time—some ideal image of himself. In his heart of hearts he suspected he did not believe in God at all, but only in religion. Its social force, its powers of policing and restraint.

His life seemed to him, sometimes, a geography riven with fractures and fault lines that could only, over time, yield to disaster. And yet the disaster, for some reason, had never seen fit to occur.

Was it a sin to suspect a truth and never to utter that suspicion to a soul?

In the middle of the night, the bedroom seemed small, somehow shabby. There were cracks in the plaster near the ceiling. The dresser was cluttered with photos of Susan and Caroline at various ages. He felt wide awake. A phrase was in his head.

Left in the lurch.

What in fact was a lurch, that one could be left in it?

He felt mildly irked at Tracy Parker for having planted such a thought in his head. Had he known how it would come back to haunt his interviewer in the middle of the night?

He got up stiffly, slipped his feet into slippers, and went over to the closet. Pulling from its hanger his deep blue robe, he wrapped himself thoughtfully in its luxurious fabric. Then he made his way downstairs.

On the desk in his study, the atlas still lay open to the map of Tanzania. So Reid had had a summer mistress, and he had gotten a letter from Africa. In its way that letter had cheered him. It had been the best moment in a day of only ordinary difficulty. But then, for the first time since waking, he remembered his dream with some clarity.

Frowning, he closed the atlas, returned it to its shelf, and withdrew the dictionary that sat next to it.

"Lurch," he read, his finger following the fine print. "From the Middle High German *lurz*, meaning the left hand, by way of the Old English *belyrtan*, to deceive. A situation at the close of various games in which the loser scores nothing or is far behind his opponent. Embarrassment, disadvantage, discomfiture. Obsolete, except in the phrase 'to leave in the lurch': to desert someone in time of trouble; leave in a desperate situation."

Well, he thought as he shut the book, that was a fine and useful phrase if ever there was one. He'd have to remember to enlighten the newest member of the Forge School's teaching faculty when next he saw him.

II

They stood in what must surely be the entrance to hell. The din was tremendous. Cages lined both sides of the narrow room. She could barely manage to look any single creature's way, let alone meet its eyes. Some cringed and whined, some stretched out in piteous displays of submission. A few howled and hurled themselves against the bars.

"Gee," Tracy said.

"I'd forgotten," Claire had to admit. "I hadn't remembered it was so un-nerving."

She'd completely blocked from her memory whatever trauma had accompanied her excursion with Louis to this same pound. Twelve years ago, the building had been brand-new; since then, due to a chronic shortage of funds (YOUR DONATIONS HELP KEEP US ALIVE implored a hand-lettered sign at the front desk), the facility had deteriorated badly. Lemon-yellow paint peeled in strips from the concrete-block walls. Half the drop panels in the ceiling were missing; rust-colored splotches marred the rest. The fluorescent lights buzzed and sputtered.

"It's like walking some kind of gauntlet," Tracy observed. "Only reversed. *They're* the ones in trouble. We're just here for a visit. Now I feel like I want to go home with about ten dogs."

"You could always take two," the attendant said helpfully. Her good cheer was unsettling: barely out of high school, and already inured to the horrors. HI, read her name tag. MY NAME IS CINDI.

Louis would disapprove of just about every aspect of poor Cindi, beginning with the "i" at the end of her name. He'd have felt obliged, on the sly, to mention the unfortunate fact of her weight. It was just as well he'd decided not to accompany them this Saturday afternoon; he'd had work to do, though she suspected what he actually intended was to lie undisturbed on the sofa and listen to the Metropolitan Opera broadcast. He had told her she should invite Tracy to dinner; he was sure the young man was tired of subsisting on macaroni and cheese.

"Is it more ethical to take two little dogs or one big dog?" Tracy wondered aloud. "I really sort of wanted one big dog."

The subject had come up the week before, when they'd had him over to the house for after-dinner cocktails. Finding Lux on the cushion in the kitchen, he'd been won over instantly. He squatted down and gently touched behind the dog's ears. "Hey fella," he'd said. "Good fella."

"He doesn't really respond much to anything these days," Claire found herself apologizing. They were cowards to keep putting off the inevitable. But under Tracy's caress, Lux roused himself. His tail beat the floor contentedly.

"He likes you," Louis said. He stood awkwardly with a tray of martinis. "You have a way with animals. He can tell that."

"I've always been good at interspecies relationships," Tracy told them. "Better than with my own kind." Seating himself cross-legged beside Lux, his careful attentions were extraordinary: He uncovered some old ember of life in Lux and coaxed a surprising glow from it. So that had been her first impression of him: a slim, lightly muscled young man in jeans and a sports jacket communing on the kitchen floor with an ancient German shepherd. He had an unblemished virility about him, a lovely face acne had never scarred. For a moment—she didn't know why—she'd felt an unexpected lump in her throat, the sting of a tear in her eye.

"I've been wanting a dog for a long time," he'd confessed to them. "It's the first time I've been settled enough to even think of something like that."

"You should remember, though," Louis cautioned, "if you stay on here next year, you'll be in a dorm apartment, and there're no pets there."

He was always thinking far into the future. He'd done that for Susan and Caroline: started their college careers before they were out of elementary school, worried about husbands and families before they were in puberty.

"And if you stay here long enough you should think about getting a cemetery plot," Claire added.

Tracy only laughed, which was how she'd intended it. And even Louis hadn't seemed too annoyed, though the look he gave her was familiar. It said, Throw caution to the winds. You'll see what happens. Next year this time he'll be trying to unload a dog on us.

But next year wasn't this year, and for now Tracy was living in one of the houses usually reserved for married faculty with families, the whole huge space to himself and a big yard where a dog would love to run.

Any of the craven dogs in the cages before them, in fact, a whole doomed menagerie refusing, as the poet urged, to go gentle into that good night.

"Cats are in back, through that door," Cindi told them over the frantic ruckus. Without thinking, Claire walked through the metal door and let it shut behind her. That muted the furor, thankfully, but her heart was beating wildly. She'd panicked. She hadn't been able to take it. Some more stalwart self had plucked Lux from the flood lo those many years ago.

The cat room may have been quieter, but terrible drama unfolded here as well. Sensing something was up, the kittens mewed and cried and like little monkeys climbed the wire mesh of their cages. They were showing off, she realized with a shock. They were showing off to her, offering themselves desperately to this unlikely woman who'd stumbled into their domain.

But not everyone was showing off. In some cages older cats sat and would not perform. They stared out hopelessly, aware that they stood no chance in the competition.

Just minutes ago she'd been standing out in the flat sunlight of a late September morning. The maples in the lot across the way were beginning to slip into brilliance. Life had seemed benign, even gorgeous. She had offered to help Tracy pick himself out a dog, simple as that. But all it took was to open a door and suddenly you found yourself in hell.

Somehow this room was far worse than the corridor of dogs. Huddled down in the back of its cage, a gray adult watched her with a sad, unforgiving scrutiny. Despair: that was what shocked her. She hadn't known animals were capable of that. And the gray cat held her; she couldn't break its bleak gaze. She took a step back, then another, till her back was against the cold metal of the door.

With a great effort she pulled it open and escaped to the straightforward clamor of the dogs. She found Tracy directing his attention toward an unprepossessing mutt with beagle blood in its background.

"That's Betsy. She's about four years old, already neutered," Cindi informed him brightly. "Her owners were nice people, they really loved her, but they moved into a condo that doesn't allow pets so they had to give her up. She's a very companionable dog. She's got a quiet temperament."

"Betsy. Who'd call a dog Betsy?"

Claire said, "People who'd get rid of her, that's who."

"And what about that one over there?" Tracy pointed out a black Lab mix that had worked itself into something of a frenzy.

"Somebody found him wandering along the highway. People do that— they drive to another town and let their dogs off on the side of the road to get rid of them. Can you imagine? Normally he's wonderfully self-possessed. They get all excited when people drop by."

Claire found herself hating Cindi, her stoic acquiescence in all this. Yet she herself managed as well; on Thursday nights she tutored prisoners at Greenhaven. She walked into that facility with, if not a clear conscience, at least the sense that she was doing what she could to help.

She didn't think what she saw in their faces was despair—but could she know?

Cindi had let Betsy out of her cage, and Tracy and the dog were inspecting one another with great enthusiasm. "Betsy!" Tracy yelped, and Betsy barked back. Or Betsy barked and Tracy yelped "Betsy!" in response. It wasn't clear who was leading whom.

"I've fallen in love," he told Claire. "This is the one I want."

It wasn't the one she'd have picked, of course. Still, she somehow liked it that he'd passed over the more obvious choices.

"If she doesn't work out, you can always bring her back," Cindi offered.

"I wouldn't dream of that," Tracy said. "I'd go in her place."

Claire could see the remark catch Cindi off guard. A wounded coolness came over her, and she moved off, with what Louis would have called a hippo amble, to gather up from her office the substantial amount of paperwork necessary to release Betsy into the world. A perfectionist of red tape, she filled out form after form with maddening meticulousness. Tracy sat patiently stroking a quiescent Betsy, and at great intervals dutifully signed what was presented to him.

In the absence of visitors, the dogs had quieted down. And in the cat room as well, Claire imagined, though of course she could never know. Wasn't there a law of physics: The presence of an observer unavoidably affects whatever is being observed? The gray cat with the sad, unforgiving glare haunted her. Louis would have a fit if she brought home a cat. He distrusted cats profoundly. Even to see one prowl across the lawn caused him great anxiety.

"Tracy," she said impulsively. She reached over and tapped him on the shoulder.

He looked at her curiously. There was something so open and receptive about him, some mildness in his eyes, the turn of his mouth. He must think her an old woman composed of little more than a series of abruptnesses. She'd called him that morning to say—rather peremptorily, it seemed to her now—let's go see about a dog for you. He needed prodding, she had noted. And he didn't yet have a car—someone would have to drive him. So her intervention wasn't illogical. Though one day in the perhaps not so distant future he'd have a wife of his own to prod his well-meaning intentions into the good deeds he was so clearly capable of.

Back through that gauntlet of beseeching dogs she led him, through the metal door and into the false refuge of the cat room. The kittens took up their miserable show exactly where they'd left off. But like herself, Tracy saw past their antics, saw the older cats without her pointing them out. "Ouch," he said.

She hadn't been sure why she had suddenly wanted him to see this—or rather, had no longer wanted to be alone in having seen this. That was it: she had wanted to see if he would see what she had seen.

To point out one gray cat in particular was entirely unnecessary. It crouched warily at the back of its cage and knew her exactly.

"I can't stand it," she said. "I can't stand knowing all this is here." And she turned and walked resolutely back out the door.

Louis would have been merely puzzled, and perhaps she had put Tracy off as well. But once they were back in Cindi's office—she continued her paperwork with lip-biting concentration—the young man was all brisk, regretful practicality. "It's too bad," he said. "A new cat in the house would really be the end of poor old Lux."

"To tell you the truth, it would probably be the end of Louis as well. Or at least our marriage. He has this loathing for cats which is, well, practically theological."

Her whimsical frankness made Tracy laugh. For better or worse, it alleviated the sting of the cat room.

"I always suspected Louis of belonging to some secret religion," he said playfully.

"He does keep a black book," she said. Which was true; she'd come across it once, on his desk, where he'd forgotten to secret it away. She'd refrained, sensibly, from opening its pages. It wasn't like him to keep a diary.

"A black book," Tracy said. "The gospel according to Louis."

"Well," she told him, "he has to get his strange ideas from *somewhere*." The laugh they shared, abrupt and unforced, sealed their moment of collusion. She imagined how it marked the beginnings of an intimacy between them.

"Stay for some lunch," he urged, as if in confirmation, when she dropped him off at his house. "It's the least I can do to say thanks for all your help."

She considered for a moment, then accepted. She liked the idea of Tracy Parker fixing lunch for her. He had a talent for suggesting possibilities; no doubt it made him a terrific teacher in the classroom.

A shame he found himself exiled to a house on the edge of campus, instead of in the dorms where he belonged, and where students would, she was sure, flock to him for advice and reassurance and the simple pleasure of his company. A shame, too, that circumstances had him channeling those companionable impulses toward a dog.

She held Betsy on the leash while he fished in his pocket for his keys.

"We have to take off our shoes," he said. "I keep house Japanese style."

The door swung open to reveal a large, bare room.

"You should've seen my apartments in Nagoya and New York. They were this big." He used forefinger and thumb to illustrate. "Each thing I own gets its own room here."

It was very nearly true. The living room consisted of a couple of large floor pillows, a stereo set, also on the floor, and two stereo speakers. The kitchen boasted a battered metal table and two flimsy-looking chairs. The dining room was entirely empty except for a stack of books. Through an open door at the end of the hall she glimpsed a futon, a bookcase made of boards and bricks. How different it had looked, all those years ago, when Jack Emmerich had lived here.

"This isn't where you live," she observed. "This is where you're camped out. I'm sure we've got some spare furniture in the attic we can send your way."

It was another intervention, she realized.

"Actually, I like it like this," he told her. "I have this feeling too much stuff would just distract me."

She stood in the middle of the depressingly empty room. "From what?" she asked, genuinely curious.

They looked at one another for what seemed an unconscionable stretch of seconds. "That's a very good question," he said, with a seriousness that struck her as more melancholy than she'd intended to provoke.

They might have said more, she thought later, but just then, her nails clicking loudly across the bare floor, Betsy returned from her exuberant exploration of her new abode.

Lunch, Tracy warned, was leftover lentil soup from the night before. As he heated it on the stove, she sat precariously on one of those flimsy chairs and watched him, in jeans and a white T-shirt, barefoot, little more than an overgrown kid, really, playing house for the first time in his life. He must be quite lonely. She tried to think of a young woman she might introduce him to, but no one occurred to her. Despite everything, she and Louis led a fairly circumscribed life.

Beneath the table, Betsy napped at her feet. Claire hoped she hadn't railroaded Tracy into this.

"I'm afraid all I've got to drink is water," he told her.

"Water's fine," she said.

"I drink a lot of water," he went on. "I try to keep my system flushed out. I stopped eating meat about a year ago, and I can't believe how much better I feel. I could just feel my arteries unclogging."

On the counter she had noticed many brown bottles of vitamin supplements. She'd have to alter the evening's menu.

The soup, when she tasted it, was surprisingly subtle.

"You made this from scratch?"

"I love to cook," he explained. "The secret here is cumin. Just a little, that I add right at the end."

He brought out peppery goat cheese, some crisps, two tawny pears.

Perhaps he wasn't just camped out here. Perhaps he knew exactly what he was doing. There was a kind of luxury to this pared-down life he'd set up for himself, something inherently unsteady but at the same time sure-footed.

As she cut into the ripe flesh of a pear, she said, "I hope I didn't seem pushy this morning. I hope I haven't foisted a dog off on you."

With his bare foot he caressed Betsy's sleeping back. His toes were long and bony. "No, no," he told her. "Motivation was exactly what I needed. My trouble is, I think about things, but then I never put them into action. So this is a good lesson. It's empowering. I need to transfer more of what happens up here"—he pointed to his head—"into reality."

So he was not like her husband at all.

She had fallen in love in her own strange way one rainy evening the day before Thanksgiving on a downtown sidewalk in Poughkeepsie. The year was 1956 and she had graduated from Barnard in the spring, a late May ceremony that also came off in the rain, a fine drizzle differing from this bleak November version only in its warmth, and serving to link the two moments as major milestones in her young life.

Libby had met her that afternoon at the train station, all hugs and kisses and tears-through-smiles, the first time they'd seen one another since Claire's five-month pilgrimage with her mother through the capitals of western Europe. There was so much to talk about, a flurry of catching up, a torrent of words, and then the big news, withheld for various reasons from the voluminous letters Claire had found waiting for her at a succession of hotel desks but now blurted out in the capacious brick-vaulted hall of the station three minutes after Claire's arrival: Libby was engaged to be married, a June wedding to—no surprise, really—the man whose quickly ascending star Claire had been able to trace with little difficulty through the course of her friend's rhapsodic missives.

Though, still, it was shocking. Shifting her suitcase from one hand to the other, she had said, "I'm so happy for you," wondering if her tone matched the words and thinking, So why was that the one thing you couldn't tell me? Did you expect to break my heart or only to tap me, gently but firmly, into my place?

Her heart, she had discovered in the last half year, was of durable stuff. You could test its mettle with a hammer. Europe and distance had further tempered it.

"At least I *think* I'm happy for you," she revised. "When do I meet him?"

"The sooner the better," Libby told her. "In fact, he's waiting for us outside in the car."

"I don't get a chance to prepare myself?" Claire asked with mock dismay. It reassured her to see that she was far calmer about this development than her friend, who'd presumably found that weeks of getting used to the prospect had made her more rather than less anxious.

"I thought I might lose my nerve," Libby confessed. "This makes me extremely nervous right now. This meeting, I mean. You know everything about me, and nothing about him."

And what does *he* know—about anything? Claire wanted to ask, but out of sudden sympathy refrained. Instead she said with some honesty, "Let's say I know enough about you to trust you're making the right decision. How's that?"

"I hope you mean it." Libby clutched her friend's free hand and led her toward the entrance and the black Dodge pulled up just beyond. "Remember, we had a pact. We pledged ourselves to be realistic. The world is what it is."

"The world is what it is," Claire confirmed. "Am I giving you any reason to doubt that?"

"None whatsoever."

She was disappointed that Reid Fallone was not more handsome; even so, he was handsome enough. His gaudy tie impressed her with its sense of adventure; that was the thing she first noticed about him. Beneath that rumpled gray suit, then, lurked a certain wildness. She could appreciate that. She was glad for Libby.

To her he was exceedingly, though not excessively, attentive. There was a poise to his overtures. He jumped from the car to take her suitcase. He shook her hand with warmer enthusiasm than her hand was usually shaken. He was a man who clearly loved women: their gestures, their habits, their legs. That was fine. There was nothing wrong with that.

He taught school, the youngest of three brothers who stood to come in for a certain amount of money at some point in their lives. He was in the first flush of success, she could tell, and pleased to be acquiring a wife as some tangible emblem of that success. Already he was speaking of the family they planned to raise—a brilliant family, she could tell. She saw Libby ensconced in triumphant motherhood, surrounded by her lively brood. The picture formed itself so clearly in her head.

With a single stroke life had changed—her sense of its capacities, its boundaries. They had been roommates together at Barnard during a time when the world was settling in for the long haul of a cold war. The Bomb loomed over everything. Spies and traitors lurked—in friends, family, perhaps even in oneself. So the official story ran. To compensate, the two had invented other lives, a private world meant to augment the stifling, suspicious America that hemmed them in on all sides, and from which, by virtue of their out-of-date qualities—style, sophistication, subtlety, the three Hisses, they called them, after some unfortunate headlines that were dominating the news—they felt themselves hopelessly estranged.

They explored certain avenues of resistance, had once even ventured to a smoky lesbian bar in a Greenwich Village basement, only to retreat shuddering from the grotesques that inhabited that particular gateway to hell. Perhaps for a moment, in a certain light, their world had looked lesbian to them, but that had clearly only been an optical trick, some mad illusion performed with mirrors and scarves. Much more to their tastes were the glittering worlds that unfolded on the stage of the Metropolitan Opera; they even felt at home amidst the male couples opulent in their black ties and tuxedos, though the desire to follow their lead into tuxes never held much appeal for either of them. They were who they were. They found a peculiar comfort in one another.

Then all that fool's paradise ended. They commenced adult life in the warm rain; Claire went abroad for five months of museums and opera; she returned. She hadn't really thought the end would happen quite the way it had, and that surprised her.

No less of a surprise, though, was the discovery of how quickly life could move on. Nothing ended. Only hours later, waiting in line for a movie on Main Street—part of Libby's strategy for the weekend, to head off any possibility of a long chat *à deux*—she found herself taking in the young man who'd been foisted off on her. A blind date, the first she'd ever been on in her life. Libby and Reid had sprung it as a cruel surprise. Or perhaps the intent was only kindness. She couldn't tell. If it was to be a time of momentous changes, then why not allow oneself to be swept along?

It was hardly love at first sight, because he wouldn't look at her. Wouldn't meet her eye. He stood with his hands in his pockets and gazed distractedly off into space. There was nothing, however, to see except streetlights in the drizzle, the occasional car, the anonymous facades of Main Street's shut-up stores. And yet he looked around so peculiarly, as if searching something out. As if trying to see anything but her.

She was far more interested in observing Reid and Libby together than paying attention to this diffident young man. Still, she roused herself to make an effort—even to the extent of boldly taking his arm as he showed their tickets to the usher and they moved into the theater.

Forty years later, the only thing she could remember about the movie was the image of a black-haired man getting out of a car to have coffee at a diner in the desert. Perhaps he was a killer on the run. She couldn't recall. His hair was intensely black, his features handsome and brooding. If she remembered correctly, he wore a black shirt, black jeans. Even the clear blue sky above him seemed dark with foreboding.

Afterwards, they themselves had coffee at the diner down the street, the four of them squeezed snugly into a booth, she and Libby on one side, with Libby facing her fiancé and she facing, finally, her blind date. There was no choice but for him to look at her. There was nowhere else to look. He had fine, nearly feminine features; masculine but fastidious gestures. He possessed the air of someone who kept himself on a short leash. From his high school days of cross country—this, for some reason, Reid had advertised about his friend—something of the runner still lingered. Some love of distance and open spaces, of freedom and solitude. He would not hem one in. She could see that about him.

She could also see that he took no initiative on his own; he was purely reactive. His vagueness was a shield for sharper qualities he declined to let show. Throughout the evening's conversation, he had followed Reid's lead—cautiously, though not without his own leavening of dry wit. They were an oddly matched pair, teachers at the same boys' school, each in his way full of the life of the place, their students' antics, their foibles.

Reid regaled them with tales of the boy they called the Little Lord: a royal refugee from some Balkan kingdom the latest war had erased entirely from the map. His family had escaped to New York with what seemed to be the entire treasury of their country. His sisters had sewn rubies into their undergarments. The Little Lord, Reid intimated, had even secreted an especially large one in a certain body cavity (they all smiled indulgently at his risqué talk). From that particular trauma the poor fellow had not yet recovered. He lived in a constant fear that he would be kidnapped, or even assassinated. None of the other boys were supposed to know who he was, but his upbringing made his aristocratic origins next to impossible to conceal.

The subject of the Little Lord roused her date from his distraction. For the first time he grew animated. He joined in to tell them how the boy's parents sent a limousine up from New York every Friday to retrieve him for the weekend. How the other boys generally wished him good riddance, his behavior toward them was so ineffably haughty and aloof. One afternoon, Louis came out the front of the building to find the Little Lord looking frantic beside the unattended limousine. Having just passed the driver in the corridor, he was able to convey what he assumed would be a reassuring message: the driver had stepped inside to the lavatory to wash his hands.

Wash his hands, cried the Little Lord. Yes, of me!

"He's very sweet, thoroughly miserable, quite lost as a matter of fact," Louis told them in conclusion.

"And without Louis's protection would long since have fled the Forge," Reid added. "His parents think the world of Louis. They invite him down to their box at the opera. Can you imagine? Louis is in heaven. Opera's what he lives for. Or rather, on—like some men depend on their sirloin."

She waited in vain for Libby to volunteer a word about their own opera-going days. Those clusters of young men looking handsome and refined in their black tuxes. She had envied them their world, because so clearly it was theirs. She and Libby were at best strange interlopers, only marginally more at home in the opera house than in that basement bar in the Village. But then the lights went down, they all turned their faces to the golden stage where night after night marvelous worlds unfolded in which nothing or no one was ever too strange to exist.

Perhaps Libby had never understood that in the same way she had. But perhaps, on the other hand, Louis would. She studied his handsome face for signs, and when he caught her staring at him, for a long quizzical instant, the first of the evening, their gazes held fast. In his eyes lurked uncertainty, a question mark. Despite his caution, he gave himself away as one of those refined young men to be found milling about so elegantly and aimlessly during the intermission of *Tannhäuser* or *Lohengrin*, sweet, thoroughly miserable, more or less completely lost.

Then he looked away, and she thought of the way her father, an inveterate angler, hooked sleek iridescent trout in fast-flowing mountain streams. But who had been caught? For a single inspired moment only, she had glimpsed some private life of his come flashing to the surface. Did Reid know, or Libby? And as for herself, was this what was called falling in love, this wayward glimpse of another person's soul? She longed to ask someone, anyone, but of course there was no one. With Libby, she knew, that chance had passed. They would never talk that way again. Once Reid had shuttled the two of them back to Libby's, her old friend pointedly announced her utter exhaustion. A theatrical yawn punctuated her intentions. They had had, in the train station, whatever talk they would have. With stalwart resolve Claire bid her friend good night—and, as it were, good-bye.

But she'd not been in bed five minutes before a knock came at the door, a rap so tentative she nearly failed to register it. A margin of light appeared, widened—a figure slipped into the dark of her bedroom. Without a word Claire drew back the covers to let her in. The night was chill. Outside, the rain fell steadily. Without a word they clutched each other in panic or terror. And was it panic or terror that made her consciously evoke at that moment Louis's thin face, his guarded eyes? It was in his eyes you knew him: that was why he never looked at you. See, she said to herself, I will manage this too. I'm as capable as any of you. Certainly it wasn't the first time she had ever fallen in love. But it was arguably the only time she'd ever fallen in love so purposely.

She woke to find herself alone in the bed, a vast gray dawn breaking, and yet she was not lonely. In her mind's eye she saw, quite clearly, Louis Tremper boarding a train. She saw him, eager and excited, among the crowds at Grand Central—for one always became a different person on disembarking in New York: more confident, more purposeful. He would come calling, or they would meet under the great chandelier at the Met. He would bring her dark red roses and take her to dinner. With one another they would be bold and honest; they would keep no secrets back. He would bring her gently into the future.

Lying bereft in a big bed in the guest bedroom of a house in Poughkeepsie where she knew she no longer belonged, Claire vowed that within six months all that impossible fantasy would somehow be made to come true.

If Louis felt irked by the last-minute substitution of eggplant lasagna for his favorite veal marsala, he'd concealed it admirably. In fact, now that they'd moved from dessert to decaf espresso, he evinced a lively interest in Tracy's dietary practices.

"I don't mean to pry," he apologized. "It's just that I'm curious. This is something that interests me."

"I'm completely game," Tracy said. "Ask me anything. I pride myself on not having any secrets."

She wanted to tell him, Don't let Louis bully you, but decided he could acquit himself perfectly well on his own. She saw with some satisfaction that he wasn't going to let Louis intimidate him. That pleased her. Tracy, she had decided, would make a welcome addition to their circle of friends. And he would benefit from their company as well. His lonely life in that big empty house resonated in her.

"Let me ask you just the simplest sort of question," Louis said. He leaned his elbows on the table and clasped his hands under his chin. "How did you come to this—what shall I call it? This *practice*." He let the word out fastidiously.

Tracy smiled his open smile. He was used to charming his elders. "You mean, was I born to it or did I choose it?"

Louis laughed appreciatively. "You could put it that way."

Tracy leaned back comfortably in his chair. "You could say I'm more interested in the planet than I am in myself. And for the sake of the planet, we just can't keep eating animals. For one thing, there're just too many people. It's too inefficient. The amount of resources it takes to raise one beef cow could feed dozens of people. The rain forests are disappearing so we can eat cheap hamburgers. But that's not the real point. That's just the practical point. The more important thing is this: to eat other creatures like ourselves—it's unethical. That's what we have to realize. There's a continuum between human beings and other animals. As long as we do violence to other animals, we'll keep on doing violence to ourselves. The one feeds off the other."

Louis had assumed his most inscrutable expression. Over the years, his eyes had ceased to give him away. He could stare down anyone. "And you really think the human race is one day going to give up eating meat?" he asked.

Tracy glanced at Claire, then back at his skeptical interlocutor. She wanted to tell him, Louis likes you; he only tests young men whom he likes.

"Well, I definitely think it's possible to change," he said. "The human race has managed to change other destructive practices that for thousands of years seemed okay. I mean, there was a time when slavery was okay and nobody thought anything about it. The Bible even condones slavery. Now basically everybody on the planet agrees that's immoral. And the idea that strong countries can invade weaker countries without a second thought—you can't do that anymore because we've agreed, at least on principle, that's wrong too. And the oppression of women: that's starting to change. The notion that women are inherently inferior to men and that's just the way it is. So yes, I'm very hopeful. I think eventually we'll live in a world where eating animals will be considered immoral, just like slavery or war. It just won't be an option for civilized people anymore."

"You sound like you believe in a utopia," Louis said accusingly.

Tracy was forthright. "I do," he confirmed. "I believe that one day peace and gentleness and love will be the rule and not the freak exception. If I didn't believe in a utopia, I'd have a very hard time going on."

"Fair enough," Louis told him. "But let's take this issue of not eating other creatures to its logical conclusion." He adopted his driest, most precise tone. Claire had nothing to add; she simply watched. Before her eyes, some bond was being formed that had nothing to do with her. It was what men did, or at least the men she kept company with. "Once we exclude mammals from our diet, as you seem to have done, then what about dairy products? Milk, cheese. Yogurt. And what about fish? And if you think about it, aren't plants fairly extraordinary life-forms in their own right? Should we really be eating them? Is it ever justifiable for one life to trample another, even if they're as different as monkey and carrot? All life is life. And what about rocks? What if they're holy creatures? What if lightning is alive? Don't you see where we're heading if we follow your prescription? Eventually, it'll be morally impossible for us to exist at all. So that all your improvements, based on a respect for life, have the end effect of rendering life impossible. Because all existence takes place at the expense of some other existence. That's the hard truth of the universe that eventually you're going to have to run up against."

It was the kind of extreme position Louis loved to take.

"You've got me," Tracy confessed. "I can't argue against your logic."

Louis smiled triumphantly, and Claire thought: the spider and the fly.

But Tracy wasn't finished. "I feel like there's more than logic to the world," he went on. "Which is why"—he smiled as he said it—"I'm still not going to eat meat."

Perhaps it was better, after all, to be the fly. Was Louis pleased with his guest's tenacity? Certainly it was difficult to be a young man, especially around someone like her husband, whose sympathy for young men usually hid beneath such a considerable show of skepticism.

They had driven themselves to a hiatus. To break it, Louis turned to her and wondered, "Shall we finish with a nightcap? Tracy? Some liqueur?"

"Sure," Tracy said. "Why not?" Clearly he knew he had not done too badly.

"I'll get it," she said, and went into the kitchen. From the cupboard she took half-empty bottles of kirsch, Grand Marnier, Chartreuse, Amaretto. She found small, stemmed glasses. She liked this moment, the end of the evening.

At the end of his own drawn-out evening, Lux twitched fitfully on his pillow in the corner by the stove. He was being pursued, overtaken; his waking tremors had begun to follow him into sleep. Louis talked of having him put down, as if it were a moral obligation.

When she returned to the dining room, she found that the conversation had shifted to surprising territory.

"Besides being an educational innovator," Louis was telling Tracy, "Dr. Emmerich was, of all things, a great champion of pork. No one ever called him anything but Dr. Emmerich, by the way. I knew him nearly twenty-five years, and I never once called him by his first name."

She stood in the doorway with the liqueur tray and felt the oddest sense that she was somehow intruding, as if Louis had sent her out of the room precisely in order to confide something to Tracy. He never talked about Jack Emmerich. There had been between them a bond like that of father and son.

"He came from a family of butchers," Louis told Tracy. "His father, his grandfather, all his uncles except one who was, curiously enough, an opera singer. Dr. Emmerich himself owned a pig farm up in Sullivan County. One of the annual school events every fall was a field trip to the farm. As many boys as wanted to go, which usually was close to the whole school. We'd head out on a Saturday morning, spend the day traipsing through the woods, exploring the old Indian Rock on the ridge above the property. In the afternoon, Dr. Emmerich would supervise the butchering of a pig. He'd gather all the boys around and give them a little talk on what they were about to see. He didn't mince words, and he wasn't for squeamishness. People should know where their food came from. He was an avid proponent of hunting— responsible hunting. It could keep people honest. I went with him a number of mornings, never with much success. I was always a disappointment with a gun. His happiest times were out there in the woods on a crisp fall day, especially with his favorite boys. It was a great reward to go hunting with Dr. Emmerich. Whatever game they brought back, the school cooks would prepare. It was a stipulation of Dr. Emmerich's: if you cooked for the Forge School, you had to know how to prepare game. And to roast a pig. He'd have the carcass hauled back to school and the next day he'd preside over a pig roast down by the lake. It was a great celebration. It marked the turn of the year. The blood month, farmers call November. Cool, clear weather after the first frost, leaves falling, the smell of pig roasting on a slow fire. What with kicking a soccer ball around all afternoon, the boys were ravenous. It was a fine tradition."

"Sounds very *Lord of the Flies*," Tracy said.

"Quite the opposite," Louis countered amiably. "See, I'm not at all against your vegetarianism, just as long as it's undertaken with the proper—what shall I say?—the proper *gravity*. In fact, I would maintain that to abstain from meat altogether, and to partake of meat the way Dr. Emmerich would have us partake, not in innocence but in complexity—well, the two paths really amount to the same thing. It's all the thoughtlessness in between that makes a mess of the world."

"Gee," Tracy said. "This vegetarian's almost tempted. Do I get to look forward to a pig roast this fall?"

"I'm afraid that's a tradition that's been allowed to die out," Louis told him sadly. "Nothing like that happens anymore. But here's my wife with the liqueur. What will you have?" And he began enumerating the choices with an attentiveness to detail that would have seemed inexplicable, Claire thought, were one not in a position to understand his agitation.

"I didn't realize it was nearly eleven," Tracy said. "I should probably be on my way. I told Noah I'd get him back to his dorm by eleven."

"A student?"

"Noah Lathrop."

"A sophomore," Louis noted dubiously. "A somewhat problematic sophomore, if I remember his records correctly."

"He's a nice kid when you get to know him. I got permission from his dorm adviser so he could watch after Betsy. I thought it'd be good to let him have some responsibility for something. Give him some confidence. I hope they've managed to bond with each other."

Louis looked at his watch and frowned. He reverted to a headmasterish tone. "Is Brill his dorm adviser? You should give him a call. We try to keep the boys fairly strictly to hours, you know. Tell him you'll be by in, say, forty-five minutes. I imagine Noah can manage one late night." He paused for a moment, as if uncertain; then said, almost offhandedly—he hated rejection—"Before you go, I wanted to play you that bit from Strauss's *Daphne* I mentioned at lunch the other day. The transformation scene. Lovely stuff."

For the briefest instant, Tracy took on the look of a student detained after class.

She hadn't realized he and Louis had ever lunched together. "So has my husband been proselytizing you?" she asked, feeling sorry, in her way, for both of them, Louis with his shy enthusiasms, Tracy who no doubt had ears only for whatever barbaric stuff passed for popular music these days. Perhaps they should actually ask what music he listened to.

"Louis suspects there's an opera connoisseur lurking somewhere inside me," Tracy confirmed. "He says he detects that. Right now, I'd have to say I'm *only* a proselyte."

The word made Claire smile. "Did you make that up?"

"It really is a word," Tracy told her. "Greek. It means 'newcomer.'"

"I'm not sure *Daphne* is exactly what I'd welcome a newcomer with," Claire admonished her husband.

"You're an opera buff too?" Tracy asked.

"I've never thought of myself as a buff, exactly. But yes, I suppose you could say that." Suddenly she felt old and quaint: these two ancient opera *buffs*. Well, then, perhaps they should, after all, turn Tracy into one as well. There was always something sly about any act of education. Eve had learned that in the garden. Turning to Louis, she suggested, "Why not start him off with something more immediately pleasing? Perhaps, oh, I don't know— perhaps *La Bohème*."

Louis sniffed and rolled his eyes.

"He considers Puccini beneath contempt," she explained to Tracy. "Though *I* like it, sentimental simpleton that I am." Then, to her husband, "But there must have been a time when poor Mimi struck *some* chord with you. Before I ever made your acquaintance, of course."

"Never," Louis snorted. "I saw through *La Bohème* when I was fifteen years old. Meretricious stuff."

Tracy looked from him to her. He knew he was out of his element, perhaps uncomfortably so. Nevertheless, she could see how he tried valiantly to keep up his end. "Ten points," he said lightly, forlornly, "for using 'meretricious' in conversation."

Louis made that quintessentially Italian shrug he'd perfected over the years. What can I say? "Now go make that phone call," he instructed Tracy, "and I'll set up the turntable."

She brought in the dessert dishes and espresso cups to where her husband stood at the sink. He'd taken off his sports jacket, rolled up his shirtsleeves. Washing dishes was one of the few domestic chores he professed to enjoy. After an evening of animated conversation, it allowed him to sort things out.

"The eggplant lasagna was very good," he said, scraping the soggy remains of that culinary adventure into the compost bucket she kept for the garden. In honor of their guest she'd set out her mother's willowware, but Tracy hadn't seemed to notice. Louis slipped the fragile plates into soapy water. "Very good," he repeated. "But I wouldn't want to live in Tracy's meatless world. That's what worries me about these idealistic young people: the lives they long for are so depressingly insipid. Just because you pretend the universe doesn't have teeth doesn't mean you won't get eaten in the end."

"They're frightened," Claire said. "It's a very frightening world out there."

Louis shook his head grimly and wiped a plate clean with his sponge.

"But the evening wasn't a bad one, was it?" she asked him.

"Not at all," he said. "I have to confess, I rather like our young man. Even if he is a bit too eager to make a good impression."

"Our proselyte," she teased. "I think we intimidate him. I think he's trying to live up to us."

She wondered if the magnificent music from *Daphne* was running through Louis's head as it was through hers. Perhaps it had not been a bad place to start after all: the hapless nymph turned so gently and ravishingly into a laurel, the music obscuring her voice as leaves and branches and roots thrillingly overtook her human limbs.

But what had Tracy carried away? He'd listened politely, though, it seemed, uncomprehendingly. The language was simply beyond him. She was disappointed; after secretly rooting for him all evening, at evening's close it was with her husband that she once again found herself standing.

"I can finish these up," Louis told her, "if you want to go on to bed. I'll be up in a bit."

His sleeplessness—or perhaps it should be called wakefulness—no longer unnerved her, though for years she'd felt it as a kind of abandonment. She knew now: sleep made him feel too vulnerable, this man who worked so hard every waking moment to compose himself.

In the hallway the red light on the answering machine blinked mutely. A message had come through, presumably while the three of them had been awash in the music of transformation: Louis was meticulous about shutting off the telephone ringer whenever he listened to music. She turned up the volume and touched the Play button.

"Just calling to say good night. Perhaps you're out. I'll talk to you tomorrow. Or call me if it's not too late."

Libby's voice sounded tired but calm. "Too late" simply meant, Whenever you get in. Libby was like Louis in that respect, though different shadows peopled her night, a disconcerting confusion of self that deranged at times the very foundations. Libby's night was a time for flinging oneself against walls, or calling out from upstairs windows to the black sky overhead. There had been messages sent out from that abyss. There would be, Claire was sure, such messages again. But for now Libby seemed to live, however precariously, in the midst of some reprieve.

Upstairs, in their bedroom, she closed the window she'd opened earlier to the afternoon's warm sun. Would Louis remember to shut the windows downstairs? The chill never bothered him as it did her. She thought to call down, but decided against it. There was always that moment in their evenings when, even though they occupied the same bed, they went their separate ways.

Once, she remembered as she undid the brooch at her collar, a call had come through at four in the morning, Libby's voice childlike and sounding very far away, as if from some icy planet circling a fierce dwarf of a star: "Claire, honey, I've decided I'm going to kill myself."

She opened the little mahogany box where she kept the few pieces of jewelry she allowed herself—mostly old, mostly her mother's—and laid the brooch thoughtfully to rest. She slipped off her blouse, inspected it for blemishes, and, finding none, hung it in the closet. She unfastened her bra.

Libby, when she had found her in that immense folly of a house her husband had built her, was dancing alone and naked in an unused upstairs room. Claire had always feared unfurnished rooms, deserted streets, the long summers after school let out; bad things, she knew, happened in empty places. A marvelous night for a moondance, Libby sang along with the tape player balanced on a windowsill. She shook her bare, wide-nippled breast. The sunken scar of her shorn other, nearly two years gone, shone whitish. Her body had grown thick and fleshy, as if her brush with death had made her hungry for life.

On the floor before her, on a single sheet of white typing paper, fifteen or twenty blue pills had been neatly laid out. A tall glass of water caught the light.

Louis had waited downstairs. He wouldn't come up. Your friend reminds me of Medusa, he'd once teased her on a night, years ago, when they had lain together after a rare, disarranging bit of love. Now she could sense him moving about anxiously downstairs. She knew she depended on him absolutely, clung to the slender lifeline his pacing spooled out for her as she lowered herself into the dark well, hand outstretched, to pull to safety her drowning comrade.

She had always imagined, as she stepped into her nightgown, that they would somehow drown together, she and Libby. Instead they had grown old. Their nights grew longer. She imagined tendrils growing from her fingertips, her toes. To become something entirely other than what one was. By no means was *Daphne* Strauss's best opera, but even the least of his scores was a world that could be lived in. Perhaps that was where she took her comfort—in how he filled out the emptiness, peopled it so lushly with notes.

Downstairs Louis was farting. He did that, loudly, when he thought no one could hear. It spoke volumes about the life he led, the ways he hemmed himself in. Tonight he'd reminisced about Jack Emmerich. It was as if one small bit of flotsam had floated up from a submerged wreck. What was Louis like in the privacy of his soul, where no one could hear or see? She wasn't sure she'd recognize him, if ever she were to glimpse that other self who was not, and had never been, her husband. And which was more real, that reserved, courtly, and difficult man she had lived with for forty years, or the unrevealed, sequestered Louis, his farts and shouts never to be visited by anyone? For she was certain that that other life existed; its details might remain hidden, but not the fact of its secret flourishing.

She went to the bureau and touched, as she did every night before going to bed, the framed photos of Susan, of Caroline. She had said to them, You must exist. She had sent them recklessly out into the world, hapless emissaries of her sometime couplings with this man. What truths of their father did they carry? Or, for that matter, of their mother as well? For she had her own share of secret flourishings no one need know about.

Moonlight streamed in the open window she'd shut against the chill. September was marching to an end. Soon she'd switch to flannel. She'd be putting extra blankets on the bed. From the woods behind the house an owl hooted: somewhere on the Forge School's campus that solitary and nocturnal creature managed to survive. Downstairs, Louis farted again.

She hadn't forgotten the gray cat. Had only pushed it to the back of her mind, where it lurked as hopelessly as it had in its cage at the pound. How long, she wondered, would they keep it there before putting it down? Putting it to sleep, as the euphemism went. If she went back tomorrow . . . but she knew, stretching out her limbs under the quilt, the cool smooth sheets, she never would. She supposed they did it by lethal injection, though she really didn't know. Somewhere she had read that impounded animals went on to medical experiments. They had their spines broken, or were infected with lethal agents. Science probed their mysteries in the hopes of bettering the world—or at least of prolonging human life, which was supposed to amount to the same thing.

She had helped Tracy Parker acquire a dog. She had looked a doomed cat in the eye and looked away. She could not bear to contemplate the visit they'd have to make to the vet one day soon with Lux. All this management of life and death. And there was Libby to think about too.

Sleep had always, blessedly, come to her instantly. Sleep was welcoming arms; sleep was the dark cave. Desire for oblivion. She did not fear to name it—and named, it didn't particularly threaten her. It was simply what she lived with, as she lived with any number of things. That daily reprieve from life that guaranteed her life. Everyone made a pact with something or someone. No one escaped. Claire had never considered herself an exception to anything.

III

They sat in an uncrowded First Avenue bar, their fourth or fifth in a chilly October evening of exuberant wandering, and watched, during the occasional lapse in their conversation, two short-haired young men play a game of pool. Dressed identically—jeans, black boots, gold rings in both ears—the two players could have been brothers, even twins, though the way they touched each other suggested that they were lovers.

For some moments Tracy gazed their way in wistful contemplation. To be back in New York was to feel haunted. Though he had been away only two months, the city he had loved and perhaps inexplicably fled and now returned to for a weekend visit seemed strangely unreal compared to the brave new life he had elected for himself in that town of quiet desperation some miles up the Hudson. Turning his attention back to his friend, he said, "Basically I'm staying one step ahead. I teach all day, then rush home and try to figure out what to do tomorrow. It's exciting, I guess, but exhausting."

Devin Shimabukuro toyed with the cigarette he'd extracted from the Marlboro pack that lay between them on the table. "You can't fake it?" he asked.

"They're smarter than you think," Tracy said. "They give me a run for my money. But they're fun that way."

"Want one?" Devin offered the cigarette.

"Why not? I've been living like a saint. It's driving me off the deep end."

"I'm sure you love it," Devin said. "You always had saintly tendencies."

"Get out." Tracy slapped playfully at him from across the table, into which countless patrons had carved their names, frustrations, longings.

"Which I personally have tried to encourage," Devin went on. Flicking his lighter, he held it out. Tracy leaned over to touch the flame with the tip of his cigarette. Devin drew another one out of the packet for himself.

Tracy had always been crazy about the way Devin handled his cigarettes. If he could manage cigarettes half that well, he'd smoke all the time too.

Tilting back his head, Devin blew a plume of smoke from his thin lips.

"You're watching me," he said.

"I know. I can't help it."

Devin half shut his eyelids and smiled at him langorously. His father was courtly Japanese, his mother a fierce Jew from Chicago. The mix had spawned an extraordinary beauty. At twenty-five he was boyish and aloof. An edge of wear was just beginning to show itself in the fineness of his features. He took up his empty glass and forlornly turned it upside down. One or two drops fell into the ashtray. He made his mouth into a theatrical pout. "Another beer?" he wondered.

"You do encourage me, don't you? My head's practically spinning. I'm out of the habit. I'm going to have a splitting hangover tomorrow."

"That's what Bloody Marys are for."

"You," Tracy chastised him fondly.

One of the pool players had moved near them to prepare a shot. He checked over his shoulder to make sure his cue would clear them. Tracy gave himself over to a momentary study of the young man's denim-sheathed buttocks. Did his companion fuck him? He found himself picturing it: the young man bent over the pool table, cheeks spread, pink puckered hole ready to receive his partner, the one pumping away inside the other with brilliant abandon. Desire flickered in him, thirsty and dry. The player tensed and shot, his buttocks clenching in sympathetic spasm. The ball ricocheted against others with a succession of sharp, satisfying clicks.

"I am *such* a bad shot," he complained with a sigh. Resting his hand on his partner's shoulder, he leaned a close-cropped head into the other's neck, and Tracy felt in himself such an uncomplicated outflowing of goodwill toward these lovers or brothers or both that his sudden, inexplicable proximity to tears startled him.

When he looked back at Devin, his friend was watching him curiously. Tracy rummaged in his memory to recognize that stare.

"What?" he said quizzically.

Devin continued to stare at him. His voice was casual and matter-of-fact. He might have been saying anything in that tone of voice, but the dreamy look that stole over his features betrayed him. What he was saying was, "Let's go home and have sex."

"I'm enjoying being out like this," Tracy told him. "Let's have another beer. Then we can go home."

Devin's smile showed his acceptance of that. He stretched his legs out under the table and rested them on the seat of Tracy's booth. He wore pointed Italian shoes so fashionable they were practically ugly.

Tracy didn't resist the invitation. Reaching out his hand, he stroked Devin's thin ankles through his socks. Ankles could excite him. He shook from himself a sudden torpor of desire.

"I have to go piss," he said. "You order."

In the bathroom, the urinal was occupied, and the stall also. The man at the urinal seemed not to have relieved himself in a week, his stream was so copious and unending. A photo collage of men so young they were scarcely out of adolescence adorned the walls. Naked and smiling as broadly as toothpaste advertisements, they all had erections some bit of trick photography had doubled or tripled in size. The effect, initially more comic than arousing, was finally, Tracy decided, more depressing than anything else. With some relief he turned his attention to the condom dispenser whose bulk on the wall hid at least some of that relentless display. He fished in his pockets for change. "That's the idea," said the man of the endless bladder as he zipped and moved over to the washbasin. "Have fun. Play safe. Getting lucky tonight?"

Tracy pocketed the condom and positioned himself in front of the urinal. "I'm visiting an old friend," he said as he extricated his penis from his jeans.

The man considered him frankly. "You wouldn't want to liven things up, would you?"

Once upon a time the man had obviously been quite handsome. Now, stranded in his middle forties, some bright urgency in his gaze betrayed the desperation with which he sought to hold back the ticking clock.

Tracy was almost apologetic. People fell for him. His smile won them over, his brown eyes. He'd never gotten by on that, but it was something he carried with him. And he was still young. He had no doubt how much that counted for. "I haven't seen this friend in a while," he explained. But in spite of himself he felt the unsought stirrings of an erection; his piss came in fitful spurts.

"Old times' night," the man said. "I understand."

He took a slip of paper from his wallet and wrote out a phone number. "You never know," he murmured, and boldly slid the folded paper into Tracy's shirt pocket. "You have, by the way, a very beautiful cock there," he mentioned as he walked away.

From the stall, still occupied as it turned out, came a snort of laughter.

Disconcerted, Tracy zipped up and returned to the booth without washing his hands. Devin had ordered not only beer but shots of whiskey as well. "I'm still celebrating your return to the *cité radieuse*," he explained. He held Tracy's hand in his and stroked it fondly. "You've been away from us down here far too long, lamb chop."

"Who'd have thought I'd end up in exile?" Tracy told him. "I guess it's my own damn fault."

"Upstate," Devin sighed. "I hear there're a lot of prisons upstate."

"Prisons and prep schools."

"Youth must be educated," Devin said. "One way or another. No one said it would be easy, or that the cost would not be great. Some might even consider you a hero, slaving away to make the future safe for"—he paused and threw up his hands—"well, for whomever."

"Safe for the rich," Tracy told him disgustedly. "I'm working my butt off so some superprivileged spoiled brats can get into college and not fuck up their lives too much. The headmaster was quite frank about that when I first took the job. We're making sure the little darlings don't embarrass themselves too much when they step into Daddy's business, which is probably some corporation that ruins third world countries with the stroke of a pen. Only he didn't quite put it that way."

He was surprised to hear himself sounding so sour. He'd perhaps been talking too much to Reid Fallone, whose mordant epithets for his students were legion and, in their way, contagious.

"Face it," Devin told him, "everything's a compromise. We all do it. You think the fashion industry's a vision of socialist utopia? Rich people all over again. They control the world and there's nothing you or I can do about it."

"Let's don't talk politics," Tracy said. He took up the shot glass and downed his whiskey in a stinging swallow. "I'll get too depressed. And actually, some of the kids at the Forge aren't too bad."

"Here's to ignoring reality." Devin raised his own glass. "Or at least softening the edges. And to the boys of the Forge, as you call it—at least the ones who aren't too bad. So tell me, any cuties in your classes? Hot little numbers itching for the teacher to bring them out?"

"Please." Tracy prodded Devin's ankle. "Don't be prurient."

"I'm always prurient," Devin told him. "But I can afford to be. I don't teach them. To me they're just tight little theoretical bodies to be drooled over from afar."

"Yeah, tell me about it," Tracy said. "They're just kids."

"Be honest," Devin cajoled him. "Don't you find there's something really attractive and, well, *moving* about a fifteen-year-old boy?"

"Let's not continue this little discussion," Tracy said.

"But I think I'm on to something."

"You wish."

"I don't know," Devin teased. "I can imagine things getting to be very difficult."

"I think," Tracy told him, "you let your fantasies get a little out of hand. Teaching isn't what you think it is. Anyway, let's get off this subject." He reached in his pocket and took out the condom. "See what I got?"

"Pour moi?"

He laid it on the table between them.

"Pour whomever."

"Only one?"

"You're incorrigible," Tracy told him. He took up the foil pack and replaced it in his shirt pocket. "It's the thought that counts. I'm depending on you to be well stocked. Now let's go home."

Out in the streets, a fine chill rain had begun to fall. "I'm so happy to be here," he had to exclaim. He took Devin's arm as they walked west toward the apartment. "It's just so stultifying up there. Everybody's so straight; they all have wives and kids. Can I tell you? I actually got so desperate I went to a meeting of the county's gay and lesbian group. Sort of a support group with volleyball games and square dancing on the side. It was in the basement of a church. So depressing. There wasn't anybody in the room I'd touch with a ten-foot pole. They all looked so lumpy and depressed, and such bad haircuts. It's from living upstate. It does something to you."

"Get out while there's still time, girl," Devin said. "I didn't want to mention your haircut. I didn't want to hurt your feelings."

Devin's apartment was above an Afghan restaurant. Pungent aromas of cumin and lamb and eggplant pervaded his rooms. His roommate, Frank, was out for the evening, if not the entire night.

"My *selfish* roommate," Devin said. "You'll get a kick out of this. The other night I'm lying in bed jerking off before I go to sleep, and I can hear that Frank's jerking off too. So I say, 'Hey Frank, why don't you just come in here and fuck me while you're at it?' And you know what he says? 'I need to spend some quality time alone.' And it's not like he was making a joke."

"Frank's sweet," Tracy thought he should say, though he agreed: Frank tended to be depressingly earnest. He wondered if he too could seem like that at times.

"He *is* sweet," Devin affirmed. "And look: he left us flowers. He's such a homosexual."

Frank had arranged a gather of lemony gladiolas in a vase on the coffee table.

"Well," Tracy had to observe, "I feel very welcomed."

"Though the place is just a mess," Devin apologized. In a manic burst of energy he moved about the room straightening the pillows on the sofa, the magazines on the coffee table. He took off his thin black tie and unbuttoned the collar of his white shirt. "What a day it was at the office," he vamped. "That is, before I met you."

Tracy stood and watched. They were both at a sudden loss with each other. He hadn't expected to feel awkward, and neither, apparently, had Devin, who busied himself with putting away the dishes in the dish rack.

"Hey," Tracy said decisively. "Calm down. Come here."

He held out his arms; an excitement surged in his chest.

"Hello," Devin said gently, as he came into his arms. Imitating the boy in the bar he'd observed earlier, the pool player, Tracy leaned his head into Devin's neck. There was a pause in music called the fermata, that eye with its raised eyebrow that commanded, Stop here, linger, take a deep breath before moving on. Louis Tremper had introduced him to the word during one of those sessions of after-dinner music-listening that had become something of a weekly ritual. Suddenly he had to laugh, not so much at Louis Tremper intruding on his thoughts at such a moment as the urgent pressure he had become aware of in his bladder. "I don't know why I've got to piss so much," he told Devin, releasing himself from their embrace. "I must have the world's smallest."

The walls of Devin's bathroom were painted black, and there was no mirror over the basin. As he pissed a clear heavy stream he considered how easily, and with what a sense of relief, he'd taken up Forge School's strict regimen. His life there was bare, uncluttered, and if he'd stayed away from Devin's *cité radieuse*—all that aimless energy that was Manhattan, specifically gay Manhattan, its clubs and restaurants and gyms, its ceaseless striving for the chic and the buffed, under the guise of which one's real life, whatever undiscovered thing that might be, frittered itself away—his exile wasn't unintentional. Even now, inside this not unpleasant fermata, all he secretly wanted was to be back in Middle Forge reading a book and sipping a cup of tea. With a shiver of longing that was a little surprising, he found himself missing Betsy and the lovely, clarifying emptiness of his rooms.

He'd arranged for one of his students to house-sit; given him keys, instructions on feeding and walking the dog, free run of the place. Noah Lathrop probably wasn't the best choice, but it was a gamble Tracy'd felt he wanted to take. He'd made light, to Devin, of Louis's welcoming words about the Forge School, but the truth was that he had actually taken them to heart, and he was trying to earn his students' respect, their trust. With Noah, from the very first, he had felt an unspoken challenge that was also, perhaps, a call for help. Here was a kid more chased by trouble than most. His father was the one Tracy had been thinking of earlier, the man who ruined third world countries with the stroke of a corporate pen.

At the thought of Noah, a pang of emptiness spread through him. He saw the boy as he had last seen him, standing in the doorway, having shed the slightly soiled Forge School sweatshirt he'd been wearing when he arrived, gym bag in hand, for his weekend of house-sitting; as Noah had pulled it over his head, his sky-blue T-shirt had ridden up, revealing an expanse of flat belly, the heart-stopping flaw of the navel set tautly in the smooth flesh. He'd rolled the sweatshirt into a tight ball, kneading it thoughtfully as he absorbed one or two last-minute instructions. As the taxi waited at the curb, Tracy resisted the urge to attempt some casual bit of affection—a hug goodbye, perhaps, or that light peck on the cheek Europeans found so unobjectionable. Instead he registered only the immense gulf between teacher and student as Noah, turning, still seemingly preoccupied with wadding up his sweatshirt, mumbled "See you when you get back," and disappeared inside.

Tracy found Devin already stripped and in bed. Unbuttoning his shirt, he folded it carefully and placed it on top of his overnight bag, in which lay, even now, the Halloween present Noah had sprung on him before he left. What to make of that offering, or what he would say about it on his return, he had not the slightest clue, and he realized it was exactly this quandary that he had been keeping at bay since leaving Middle Forge.

He sat on the edge of the bed to take off his shoes and socks. It was late; almost certainly Noah was in bed, his body curled under warm covers; probably he was fast asleep. Tracy shivered in the apartment's chill air as he stood and removed his pants. With comical eagerness his cock pointed straight out in front of him.

Devin's smooth body was warm as Tracy snuggled in next to it. He put his arms around his treacherous friend of many years and pulled him close. He could smell, not unpleasantly, the whiskey and cigarette smoke on his breath. Someone had once remarked to him, "Kissing is like eating a warm peach," and Tracy always thought of that whenever he found himself in the sweet, wet surprise of a kiss with a man.

A little stunned with the luxury of touching another body after so long, he slid his hands along slim, boyish hips till he found what he was looking for. Tracy always teased Devin that his parents had given him the best of both worlds: the slender body of an Asian, the cock of a Caucasian. In the dark of desire, this substantial offering he grasped might almost belong to anyone he chose to imagine. His desire was specific and urgent. "Go on," he told Devin huskily, "I want you inside me."

Devin laughed. "He's passionate tonight," he observed to no one in particular. "Mary, where's that condom?"

Disentangling himself, Tracy reached over to find his pile of clothes. Devin's thumb traced the crack of his ass. His shirt pocket was empty, his pants pockets, too. "I can't find it," he said.

"Did it fall on the floor?"

"Why does this always happen? Can you turn on the light?"

"Honey, you know I'm not going in there without a rubber."

"I don't see it anywhere," Tracy said dejectedly.

"I tell you what," Devin said. "Frank keeps a bowl of the little darlings by his bed. You go in there and borrow one. I'm sure he won't mind."

The air was cold on his flesh. Tracy felt a little silly, traipsing around an apartment naked, his still-aroused cock jutting out in front of him. For a moment there with Devin he'd felt the most delicious anticipation, as if, somehow, it wasn't Devin beside him in the darkness but the pulse of some mad possibility. Now all that fantasy was gone, but nonetheless a strange elation still worked in him. On the nightstand beside Frank's bed, as Devin had said, sat a dainty antique bowl incongruously filled to the brim with foil squares. As he plucked out two for good measure, he heard a noise, footsteps, and then, confused, afraid, turned around to find himself face to face with a quizzical-looking Frank who had just walked in the door.

"May I help you?" Frank said, not so much deadpan as simply earnest.

"Um, hello," Tracy told him, conscious of the gaze that was eagerly taking in his fading hard-on. "I was just, um . . ." He waved the condoms forlornly in front of Frank's face.

"Oh," Devin's roommate said mildly, "you're welcome to them."

"You're a saint," Tracy told him. "I definitely owe you one."

"Anytime," Frank said. His tone was warm and sincere. "And you and Devin have a good night."

Tracy found Devin with a pillow pressed to his face, heaving with suppressed laughter. When Devin uncovered his eyes, Tracy made a fright face—open-mouthed, wide-eyed—and fell into bed beside his companion.

"Perfect," Devin gasped. "Perfect. Now where were we?"

"Jesus Christ," Tracy moaned. "How am I ever going to live that one down?"

"Oh," Devin told him as he moved in closer, "we'll fix that in no time. See, I'm all ready to go. Roll that thing down on me. That's good. Now how do you want to do this?"

Usually he wasn't quite so voluble. "Shh," Tracy said. "Just let me turn out the light." He was surprised by how swiftly desire once again overtook him. Anybody can be anybody, he told himself as he eased his body down onto Devin's, the blunt pain of a beautiful pleasure wedging him open, filling him up, for all the world, he thought, like a delicious flower of fire blossoming inside him. No one is anyone, he told himself with relief as the flaming flower bloomed and unbloomed rhythmically in his flesh. Noah Lathrop was just a troubled boy he happened to know, a problem student he taught, an odd stray flicker of yearning, a phantasm.

Devin always went off to sleep immediately afterward. He had left the radio on low, tuned to a classical music station, which he claimed helped him sleep better. Like the rumblings of an uneasy stomach, thunder obscured its background murmur now and again with its more urgent demands. From the next room came the unmistakable sounds of Frank spending some quality time alone. Tracy lay awake, trying to listen to one set of sounds but not the other, or to both together, or to neither, but his bladder was full again and his mind as wide awake as it ever was. Sex did that to him: opened some part of his brain that usually was still. He could never find sleep till hours afterward. In a kind of alert stupor he lay motionless, unable or unwilling to hoist himself from the futon and stumble through the dark to the bathroom. Once, long ago, he and Devin had woken in the morning to find that someone—they never knew who, and though both playfully accused the other neither would admit it—had pissed the bed. Another chord of thunder added its voice to the quiet business of a piano concerto. He thought about getting up to turn it off, but some bit of tenderness toward Devin made him refrain. At least one of them should sleep restfully.

For years he had played what he called the memory game. Whenever the present, whether through anxiety or insomnia, became too present, he'd consciously cut some cord that bound him to it and allow his mind to drift, rudderless, within a memory. Often he found himself reliving, with undiminished pitch, a certain distant summer of storms. In memory, at least, blistering squalls broke out across the landscape every late afternoon, gray curtains of rain shot through with blue-white snaps of lightning, heart-stopping eruptions of thunder. Then the clearing aftermath, sunsets of fantastic drama. A decade later Tracy could no longer recall the exact details of his initial meeting with Eric, nor trace the slow degrees by which, over two months, they had become friends. He couldn't even remember Eric's last name, an omission of memory that plagued him until he decided he must never have known it in the first place—as if it were possible to be so preoccupied with a person as to miss so fundamental a thing as that.

What he could never forget was the wondrous shock of falling in love. He was fifteen. Emotions he'd glanced at on other occasions and then shunted nervously aside coalesced around this lanky, twenty-seven-year-old costume designer and wouldn't dissipate. August found them together every noon on the lawn in front of the theater where Tracy worked as a summer intern. Shirtless, they'd stretch out in the long grass and take the healing brunt of a noontime sun that gave no clue of the thunderheads it already, in secret, had begun to breed.

"It's because we're so close to the ocean," Eric told him. "The seacoast of Connecticut is famous for its storms." Like much of what he said, it was enchanting if dubious. Hailing from Kansas, Eric was an aficionado of violent weather, its vagaries, its cruel wonders. Once a tornado had passed directly over him as he lay prone in a ditch by the side of the highway, sparing him, but he'd never forget the cyclonic roar, the sudden ear-thumping dip in pressure, the eerie feeling that some ghost of enormous force was treading across his back. He talked vividly and nonstop—they both did, it seemed, in their daily respite together before their tasks took them separate ways, Tracy to help in building a great stage ark for *Noye's Fludde*, Eric to the cramped little costume shop to fashion shining robes for the patriarch and his sons, or elaborate heads of papier-mâché for the fabulous animals the ark would bear to safety.

One thing Eric had let slip, early on in their voluble friendship: how he suspected, despite his girlfriend in Manhattan, whose praises he freely sang and whom he went every weekend to see, that he was probably, all things considered, a bit gay. He reported it casually, the way you might report "I'm a Libra" or "I graduated from Oberlin," both of which were in fact the case. But unlike those other facts, this one possessed Tracy completely. His own fledgling secret, never before uttered, perched on his tongue, tested its new-found wings, but then, despite everything, refused to fly. Before he could say it, they'd somehow moved on to other, safer things. And then day after day passed, and the subject didn't come up again; they talked about Shakespeare and Tennessee Williams and the weather in Kansas and he began to wonder whether Eric had ever confessed such a thing about himself, or whether his own less-than-reliable imagination hadn't spawned those words, the way tornadoes appeared out of nowhere in the heartlands.

Each evening he drove home to his parents' house nursing the unaccountable certainty that he would never see Eric again, that some mysterious reckoning would take him suddenly away, no message left, no good-bye. Storms passed over the house, an old maple in the backyard came down, and once he saw lightning dance like a sprite along the telephone wires. Then the reprieve of blue sky to the west. He flung himself out of doors, walking for hours, solitary, his heart storming without any end in sight.

Nights in particular were torment. No sooner had he shut his eyes than Eric's afterimage, as if imprinted by lightning, swam before him: the loose, vibrant ease with which he carried himself, his teasing smile and liquid eyes, the way he wore his blond hair, fine as midwestern corn silk, pulled back tightly in a ponytail.

By day he found some furtive consolation in studying Eric's half-naked body reclined next to him in the grass: his featureless navel set in a flat belly, the trail of dark hairs that disappeared past the waist of his gym shorts. Often Eric wore an earring in his left ear, a tiny blue-green stud you could miss if you didn't look closely. Other days there was just the hole where his lobe had been pierced, and that was worth examining closely as well.

Every morning Eric brought a duffel bag with him to the costume shop, and at the end of the day he reclaimed it, hoisting it over his shoulder and sauntering off to wherever he spent those nights Tracy would have given his soul to share. Small things made the boy desperate. One morning they stood at the mailboxes and Eric read through a note he'd received.

"You're frowning," Tracy told him.

"Oh," Eric said, "it's just from a guy I ran into last weekend at a party. It's nothing." And folding the piece of paper, he stuck it into his bag. But the words made Tracy burn. That afternoon he excused himself from his stagework and hastened to the costume shop. Eric had told him he and his assistant had to drive into town after lunch to buy some things. No one was around. Sick and excited, he found the duffel bag stashed in a corner. Loosening its cord, he slid his hand inside. His fingers touched soft fabric, underwear and socks and T-shirts. Resisting the temptation to spill the contents onto the floor, to smother his face in communion with all that secret, sweat-sour fabric, he instead extracted the folded-up slip of paper and read breathlessly.

"You're right," was all it said. "I was an asshole. I'm sorry."

Anything was possible, of course, but nonetheless he felt utterly, despondently sure. Something had happened that night, or hadn't happened—but whichever it was, a terrible sense of loss accosted him. With unsteady hands he replaced the note in the duffel bag. In a fit of frustration, he made his way back to the stage. He had the beginnings of a headache, and the incessant banging of hammers as they built the ark seemed to nail the lid on the coffin of all his hopes.

As a child Tracy had been fascinated by an hourglass that sat on the desk in his grandfather's study. Whenever he visited their house in Connecticut, he would sneak into that hushed room, redolent of old books and leather armchairs and pipe smoke (his grandfather and namesake had retired from a New York law firm of legendary prestige). When he inverted the glass, at first nothing seemed to happen. Though a steady trickle leaked through, the level on top hardly changed. Only at the end did all the sand suddenly appear to run out at once.

For a week of performances, *Noye's Fludde* sailed through its deluge to reach safe shore. Who could have guessed, in advance, its odd relevance? When the audience joined in for a final, heaving hymn, tears came to Tracy's eyes. The month had been the most important of his life. Helpless, he watched the vortex open as Eric made ready to return to New York, where he and his girlfriend would be looking for an apartment together for the coming winter, which would, Tracy felt sure, be never-ending.

Those lunches on the sun-drenched lawn turned gray with anxiety. Each day he trembled on the verge of that bold confession he'd spent sleepless nights rehearsing. But each day slipped from him. Then at the last possible moment he found himself speaking. They had shared what was to be their final lunch together; they lay on their backs, shirts rolled up underneath their heads as pillows. No breeze blew; the air was sultry and thick.

"I want to sleep with you," Tracy said. The words sounded dull and impossible. Silence swallowed them up, and Eric only laughed.

"Do you have any idea what you're saying?" he wondered aloud, as if they had both been napping, as if Tracy had spoken incoherent words in his slumber.

"I want to have sex with you," Tracy said. This time the words were clearer; they hung there and refused to disappear. He felt as if he were swimming up from some great drowning depth. His heart beat so furiously in his chest it seemed impossible the whole lawn didn't hear. When he dared look Eric's way, Eric had turned on his side and propped himself on one arm. He was watching him with a soft and unfocused gaze.

"Hey, Tracy," he said gently, perplexedly. "Don't you think you're way too young for this?"

Tracy was on his side now too, facing Eric across mere inches of space, a gap both negligible and infinite, and Eric was shaking his head slowly. "I should have realized," he went on, as if in bemusement—or perhaps it was wonder. "I guess I should've noticed."

Boldly, Tracy reached out his hand. Lightning did not strike. He touched, tentatively, then with growing assurance, his friend's lightly stubbled cheek. He ran his fingers along the jawline he'd longed for a whole month to caress.

"No," Eric told him after a moment, taking him by the wrist and pushing his hand away.

"I thought you liked me," Tracy said.

"Stupid," Eric told him. "Of course I like you. I'm fucking crazy about you."

It seemed impossible that they could be here like this. Tracy couldn't contain himself.

"Then what's the problem?"

"So what's the problem?" Eric laughed bitterly. "You're priceless. The problem is, either way, I'm going to regret this, whatever I do."

"Then there's no problem," Tracy said quickly, afraid to give either of them time to think. He knew all about time. "Better to go ahead and make it with me than not make it with me."

"We both know that's not true," Eric said simply. He sat up abruptly, and clasped his arms around his bare knees. Tracy watched him in profile: that ponytail of cruelly pulled-back hair he'd never seen unloosed, blond sideburn fading out into stubble, the jaw his fingers, unbelievably, had grazed. The space around him, the silence, was inviolable. Tracy had never been so conscious of the sky above the earth, the dangerous clouds that gathered there, the way humans lived beneath such grandeur and threat every moment of their lives. Eric, too, seemed intent on figuring up some incalculable sum.

"What the fuck," he said at last. "Come on, let's get out of here. And just remember"—he paused in slipping his T-shirt over his head—"you're the one who started it."

Tracy's erection made it painful for him to stand up. When he tugged at his crotch to rearrange himself, he saw Eric's gaze flicker there for a moment, darken, and then dart away.

Wordlessly, they walked, past the theater to the edge of campus, then along a busy street lined with student bars and bookshops. They were radiant criminals, unafraid, untouchable, bringing off the greatest caper the world had known. And the world, oblivious, let them pass right by.

Cutting through an empty lot, they entered the woods. It was a place Tracy would never have thought of going. A path took them alongside an overgrown field whose edges were thick with blackberry brambles. On the far side an abandoned house hid among young trees that had crowded up around it. The porch sagged, the windows were broken out, but despite the relentless procession of summer storms the roof still held. It solved a mystery.

"Totally illegal," Eric said, "but what can you do? The rent's unbeatable." His mood had lightened; he reverted to his familiar, carefree self—the self who'd gotten drunk on vodka at a party in high school and let his best friend Charlie pierce his ear with a hot needle.

"You're crazy," Tracy told him. "Wasn't there anyplace else you could stay?"

"Really, it was lots of fun," Eric confessed. "At night there was an owl I could hear. Heather absolutely freaked when I told her about this place."

But Tracy wasn't freaked. He saw the difference between himself and the hated Heather quite clearly. To live like this seemed, at the moment, nothing less than heroic. To roam the world with only a knapsack of belongings; to sleep in fields, in the woods—even in abandoned houses. He himself had longed for great adventures. To visit India, Nepal, Tibet. To meet the friend who'd go anywhere with him, do anything.

"I want to kiss you," he told his new friend of the wide world. Already he could sense the heady air of the Himalayas. He moved toward Eric; their embrace was clumsy. It tumbled them down in slow motion onto the floor. Tracy lay on top and explored Eric's mouth with his tongue.

"You're certainly the precocious one," Eric laughed and pushed at him playfully. But he gasped as Tracy felt his way inside his gym shorts. "Hey," he warned. His cock was long and thick and lazy. Freed from his shorts, it lay flopped over his thigh like a big snake sunning itself on a rock. Tracy raised it up and kissed its bulbous head. He breathed its sweet reek. His lips rested against hard beautiful flesh.

Then he felt Eric take both sides of his head and firmly lift him up. "I can't do this, Tracy" he said. "You're a kid. I can't change that."

"I know what I'm doing. I'm not a virgin," Tracy lied.

"No," Eric said. "I'm not doing this."

It seemed too wildly unfair only to get this far. "Please," he heard himself say. He hated the unmistakable pitch of desperation in his voice. And he was amazed to see there were tears in Eric's eyes. The young man curled his mouth. His brow furrowed up. Unable to speak, he simply shook his head. He took Tracy in his arms and held him, rocked him back and forth for the longest time in silence, tears streaming down his face, Tracy dry-eyed but pressing his cheek to Eric's cheek in his hopeless attempt to make those tears his own.

It was seven years before Tracy saw him again. On a sunny day in June thousands marched down Fifth Avenue beneath banners and placards. Tracy stood on the sidelines and watched. And there was Eric, whose last name he had either forgotten or never known. He beat a hand drum and shouted slogans of desperation and defiance. He'd lost his looks; he was gaunt and bright-eyed, terrible signs Tracy had grown, over the years, to recognize. His ponytail had vanished, all that gorgeous silky hair Tracy had never seen loose now sheared so short he looked practically bald. Tracy was sure it was him:

something in the limber way he moved, the loose way he threw his shoulders back. His lips had kissed those lips—even, for a moment, that big lazy cock that had never gotten entirely hard for him. The sun shone fiercely. Black and white balloons filled the sky. The sidewalks were mobbed with cheering onlookers. Eric banged relentlessly on his drum for the whole world to hear.

Tracy stood on the sidewalk in front of the address he'd been given and tried to find a front door, or a least a buzzer. To his surprise, only the slightest of headaches had chosen to settle behind his eyeballs, in the stiff back of his neck. His anus felt raw from last night's adventures.

There was no door, no buzzer. To the side of the little building a locked iron gate led into an alley, and perhaps that was the way in.

"Arthur!" he called out in frustration, and at an open second-floor window Arthur appeared, smiling impishly, his head wrapped in a maroon bath towel.

"Oh young man," he called down, falsetto. "Yoo hoo!"

"I bet you spend hours leaning out that window," Tracy told him.

"My elbows've worn a bare spot on the sill. See, there's this old Italian woman lurking in my ancestry. Now don't run off. It'll take me a minute to come down and let you in, honeypot."

Someone had hung a bird feeder from one of the spindly street trees, and little gray birds hopped nervously from branch to branch. The overnight rain had caused most of the leaves to drop all at once; they formed a bright yellow skirt on the sidewalk. He was sure he didn't feel the least bit nervous. You're not obligated to go, Devin had counseled him.

Appearing behind the gate, Arthur fiddled noisily with the lock. "Maybe it makes some people feel secure," he said, "but me, I feel like I'm in prison."

"At least the Jehovah's Witnesses don't pester you," Tracy told him.

"No," Arthur said as the gate swung open heavily. "The Jehovah's Witnesses definitely do not pester me."

"Well, they actually came to my door," Tracy said. "They brought children and pamphlets."

"To sell? To give away? What did you do?"

"I was rather proud of myself. They asked me, Do you read the Bible? And I said yes, as a matter of fact I do, and I'm appalled by what I find there. How anybody could worship such a cruel and bloodthirsty God is beyond me. Well, they just turned and ran." Wishing he could have drawn the anecdote out a bit more, he concluded, "I don't think they'll be back anytime soon."

Arthur watched him curiously. "Just hope lightning doesn't burn your house down," he said with a seriousness that caught Tracy off guard. He took Tracy in his arms and planted a big wet kiss on his lips. Tracy let himself be gripped tightly for a long moment; then, as Arthur turned to lead him into the building, he surreptitiously wiped his mouth with the back of his hand.

With a flourish, Arthur threw open the door onto a very small, wood-paneled room. "It's, well, charming," Tracy judged.

"Cozy, I like to think of it as. But my own. Domestic bliss at last. I have no furniture—but then, I have no room for furniture. So it's fine. At least I don't have to put up with roommates. And there're only five steps to negotiate. For that time when stairs start to be a problem."

There was nothing in the tiny room to engage his attention conveniently—no books, no CDs, no personal artifacts at all—so he sat down on the step that led up to Arthur's alcove bed. Regal in his maroon turban of a bath towel, Arthur took the room's single wooden chair and seated himself grandly: hands on his hips, legs crossed at the knees. He'd always been such a queen. For an awkward silence they both studied the extremely worn Turkish carpet on the floor. "You like?" Arthur said at last. "I'll put it in my will. Rescued from a garbage can. You could say I felt an affinity for it."

There'd been Arthur's phone call a year ago, after several months of lapsed contact between them. In answer to Tracy's somewhat surprised "So how've you been?" he'd said mildly, almost apologetically, "I'm afraid I've been having a little health problem," a bad cold he hadn't taken care of until one afternoon he collapsed in the editorial offices of the women's magazine he worked for and had to be spirited to the emergency room. Diagnosing pneumonia, his doctor had remarked tersely, "I suppose you realize what this means."

"Whatever you are," Tracy said, unwilling to take his eyes from the relative safety of the carpet, "I wouldn't call it moth-eaten."

"Always the diplomat," Arthur told him, reaching out across the narrow space of the room to pat him on the knee.

He'd been unsafe with Arthur. In a moment of unaccountable madness, he'd let Arthur fuck him without a condom. They couldn't find any in the apartment, it was late, it was cold out, they were both a little drunk, a little stoned, they were both feeling carried away. "Go ahead," he'd said, "put it in me," and then felt, after a few deep thrusts, Arthur's semen spurt inside him. Afterwards they hadn't talked about it; they'd pretended not to notice it had happened.

He'd always tried to be careful. He could count on the fingers of one hand the times he'd swallowed another man's come. Only twice in his life had he let himself get fucked without a condom, and that other time had been years ago. The thing to do, of course, was to get tested. But it wasn't that he wouldn't do it; he couldn't. Knowing for certain, losing for good the far-fetched possibility that there was nothing to worry about, that it was all in his head, the psychic terror and lifeline of that game he played nightly with his own darker thoughts—all that paralyzed him. And look at it this way, he argued to himself: if your dad, who never smoked or drank, died of liver cancer at forty-nine, then you, who've been fucked in the ass by a cock loaded with deadly virus, could very well live to be a hundred.

He didn't believe that for an instant.

"Let me get dressed," Arthur said, "and we'll go out. One does tend to exhaust, rather too quickly, the meager charms of my new abode. Are you hungry? There's a lovely little restaurant around the corner, which I've managed to make my home away from home."

He stood and slipped his bathrobe from his shoulders. He'd always been skin and bones, but now the skin stretched over those bones was translucent as the parchment on which monks had copied out their hymns to the God Tracy professed to deny. Arthur was wasting away. His ribs really were a cage. Only his cock, that formidable organ, remained undaunted. Horsedick, Tracy had used to tease him. All that was four years ago—in between Tracy had lived a year in Japan, gone trekking in Nepal, read nearly half of Proust and built houses in the Hamptons. The virus didn't care about those things. If it was going to hunt him down, it wouldn't matter how far he ran or how many bargains he made.

For an instant he thought about just giving up; why not surprise them both and go down on that cock with all the abandon he used to muster when they were going out?

Who would that joke be on? he wondered as Arthur, oblivious to all that desperate fantasy, selected from his closet a red-and-black flannel shirt. He pulled on khakis four sizes too big and cinched them together with a broad belt. Unwrapping the towel from around his head, he shook out the longish hair he tinted with a henna rinse.

From the very first it had been madness. Swept off his feet: that was the only way to describe that feeling of being caught up by the wonderful whirlwind this talkative rail of a boy from south Texas, met at a dinner party through mutual friends, turned out to be. At twenty-two, Tracy had never met anybody quite like him. Seven years older and vastly more experienced in the ways of the world, Arthur was game for practically anything, as Tracy found out later that night. He'd heard of a wild time, but he'd never found himself thrown in with such primitive unfettered energy as Arthur brought to bed with him. Naturally cautious to a fault, Tracy had found something inside him whispering yes, and despite his better judgment plunged in.

It turned out to be way over his head. He was disconcerted to discover exactly how much sex Arthur had had in his short life: on the docks and in back rooms and with strangers he'd brought home from the street, anonymous and dangerous and obliterating sex. He loved getting slapped around, or pissed on; he loved, as Tracy would squeamishly learn, taking a fist up his ass. Accosted by two men in a doorway on his way to meet Tracy one evening after work, he'd followed them upstairs and smoked crack, reporting afterward, cheerfully, "My hair felt like it was on fire." His one regret: those two shady characters hadn't fucked him. He'd thought that was on the agenda, and sex on crack, by all accounts, was supposed to give you a truly life-expanding perspective on the world.

Tracy, who'd waited for an hour at the café before finally giving up and going home, listened with something very like terror to this man he'd made the mistake of confessing his eternal love for only two weeks before. Arthur, who was all for love, albeit of a more temporal kind, had confessed back that he himself, unfortunately, wasn't in love at the moment, wasn't sure he *wanted* to be in love right now, didn't think, in fact, he quite had the time for it. Which wasn't to say there wasn't lots of truly fabulous stuff that could happen between the two of them. Tracy hid his hurt and soldiered on, but in only a few more weeks he was ready to understand quite clearly the ways in which he couldn't, whether through cowardice or just plain prudence, rise to Arthur's challenge. At the same time he began to glimpse in this love of his life—beyond the charm, the sweetness, the wit—a certain cold desperation lurking. He'd understood that he had to bail out of this particular whirlwind.

"So," Arthur said, regarding himself in the mirror (he ran a bony hand through his hair to muss it), "do I look gorgeous these days or what?"

"Gorgeous is as gorgeous does," Tracy told him regretfully.

The little restaurant around the corner was the kind of place that had made Tracy love New York. It threatened, in fact, like so many small moments this weekend, to make him fall in love all over again. Hardly bigger than the railway car he'd ridden down in, its tables huddled close. An elbow's length away, three women carried on a lively conversation in Italian.

Their waiter was too quietly beautiful to be either an actor or a model, just one of those boys who, like moths, find their way to Chelsea. He handed them their menus with lovely presence. "So how's your sex life?" Arthur asked. "Oh, not you, honey," he told the waiter. "I mean this one. By the way, Tracy, you should order the trout with pepper bacon."

"I'm a vegetarian," Tracy reminded him.

"Well, I have to tell you, it must be this disease, but all I ever want these days is meat, meat, meat. I think *I'll* have the trout, and with extra bacon if that's possible. *You*, my dear," he went on, "should order the yummy sweet-potato pancakes. And for dessert"—Arthur smiled beatifically at the waiter—"we will both have double helpings of you."

Tracy could only marvel at their waiter's truly wonderful self-possession. Arthur was a regular here, after all.

"See?" Arthur tapped Tracy lightly on the wrist. "You *are* hungry. So back to my question. S-E-X. And you'd better tell me you're getting it on somewhere, somehow, with someone up there in your new home. Otherwise you're just taking up valuable space on the planet."

Tracy laughed uncomfortably, though something like this line of questioning was presumably what he'd come to Arthur for. "Sorry to disappoint," he said.

"Well, I at least thought you and Miss Devin-Eleven would still be getting things on."

"Oh, that," Tracy said, his memory of last night now bleakly clear. "Your typical all-night convenience store" was how Arthur had once described Tracy's friend from college. Between those two there existed a fierce mutual animosity that Tracy afforded himself the luxury of believing had everything to do with him. "Did you know Devin's got a real boyfriend these days? Apparently I'm the last to know. He only told me this morning. It's serious with a capital S. They're thinking of buying an apartment on the Upper West Side. I find out all this, I might add, only after we'd done it every which way. So much for serious."

"My dear, if I didn't know better, I'd say you sound bitter. And anyway, never, *never* apologize the morning after for what your hormones were telling you last night."

"You're right. It's his serious relationship, not mine. Devin and I have been this way with each other for years. I can't imagine it's about to change any-time soon."

"The old friends syndrome," Arthur said. "Tell me about it. What is *with* gay men?"

But Tracy didn't know what was with gay men.

"Surely, though, you're at least *interested* in someone?" Arthur pursued.

"You know," Tracy said brutally, "I don't know if I've ever been all that interested in anybody, to tell you the truth."

Arthur was above being wounded. "Now, now," he consoled. "You always say these extreme things, even when you're not under duress. Or *are* you under duress? There are five gazillion gay men your age out there casting about for husbands right now. It's a seller's market, as far as I can tell. Don't you think," he asked their waiter grandly as a whole trout, smothered in bacon, was set before him, "that this gorgeous man sitting across from me is extremely eligible?"

"Of course," said the waiter without blinking an eye. "And would you like for me to debone your fish?"

"Anytime, anywhere," Arthur told him, and sat back in his chair to allow the young man room for that delicate procedure.

Tracy waited in silence, studying the waiter's beautiful wrists, his hairless forearms, the fingernails that were bitten to the quick.

"You do that very well," Arthur complimented when the task was complete.

"And it's not even my greatest talent," the waiter told him.

Now *there* was somebody you could fall in love with. Though the young fellow didn't seem particularly interested in anything except doing his job. Besides, Tracy had been through all that before. He'd dated beautiful waiters, and they were all the same. Why were the beautiful ones always so vacant? What did beauty matter, anyway? As the beautiful vacant waiter bore away the bones on a saucer, and Tracy and Arthur both followed him longingly with their eyes, Tracy complained, "Does everybody always have to be on the prowl for love?"

"Well, as a matter of fact, yes," Arthur said with great certainty. "Everybody does have to either be in love or be on the prowl for it. It's a rule. I, for example, think I am absolutely in love with this trout. Don't you want even a taste?"

Tracy the vegetarian wasn't, after all, above consuming a bit of fish—or even, God forbid, bacon—now and again, as Arthur knew all too well.

But Tracy shook his head. Suddenly his hangover, which had mercifully been lying low, welled up in him. Feeling not the least bit hungry, he stared at his orange pancakes, so prettily and fatuously decorated on their blue plate with slivers of orange, strawberry, pineapple. "I don't think any of that's for me anymore. I'm not talking about eating meat. I'm talking about other kinds of hunger. Desire. I want to get clear of it all. Maybe it's just the times we live in."

"You mean AIDS?"

"Not just AIDS. This whole gay thing," he said. "Or not even that. This whole relationship thing. The need to be involved with someone else, like you're not complete unless you are. Isn't that a great word, *involved*? Makes me think of puppets with their strings all tangled up together. Sometimes I almost find myself wishing, I don't know, that I'd never gotten into any of it. That I'd stayed on the sidelines and just watched it all."

"What an odd thing to say," Arthur remarked coolly. "You haven't gone and tested positive, have you?"

Tracy's chest constricted in familiar panic. "No, no," he said hastily. "Nothing like that. I'm completely healthy. I'm probably too healthy."

Arthur was still watching him closely. "Meaning what?" he said.

"I don't know. I don't know why I said any of that."

"I see," Arthur told him.

"Meaning, I don't even know what I'm talking about." Tracy drummed his fingertips restlessly on the tabletop. "I'm just totally confused about myself right now."

He needed, he felt obscurely, to show Arthur how unhappy he was, even if that unhappiness wasn't exactly true. He needed, more than anything else, for Arthur simply to ask, "Do you regret having had sex with me?" He needed to erase the simple fact that, despite his best intentions, he and Devin had fucked last night, that he'd allowed it to happen when for the past two months he'd been celebrating his clean break from the city, the entanglements it had come to stand for. That he'd enjoyed it immensely.

Was it possible Arthur knew him well enough to guess all that? Spearing a last piece of trout, he studied it for a moment on the end of his fork. "So you're going to stay out of trouble for a while. Well, good luck with all that. As for me, I'm going to stay where I belong, which is smack dab in the middle of trouble. It's the only place that's halfway interesting."

"I don't feel very satisfied with how I've managed to express myself here," Tracy said.

Contentedly, Arthur pushed his empty plate to one side. "Don't worry. You schoolteachers always have a way with words. I personally think it's been good for us to have this chat. In fact, I would go so far as to say that, these days at least, I think good conversation is really the best form of sex. And we haven't had conversation in so long, you and I. One of those proverbial blue moons. Can I confess something terrible? For a while, before you moved away, I had the misguided impression you were avoiding me. Now wasn't that just plain silly of me?"

"Completely," Tracy lied. "I was incredibly busy with stuff. You know how it is."

"And can I confess something else while I'm at it? Maybe it was for the best if you were avoiding me, because, see, I have this suspicion that you, of all people, have no idea that I, of all people, graduated from the Forge. Isn't that a hoot? Now don't look so shocked. It was years ago, fourteen to be exact."

For a second time in their conversation Tracy felt that tightness around his heart. He wasn't the least bit superstitious. Still, an itch prickled along both his legs, an icy finger ran down his spine.

"You've hardly touched your pancakes," Arthur noted.

"I'm really sorry I didn't call," Tracy told him.

"It wasn't like I had anything really to tell you about the Forge. It's not a bad place, really it's not. What does Quentin Compson say to that peachy roommate of his? I don't hate the South, I don't hate it. But tell me"— Arthur's voice grew reflective—"is Louis Tremper still there?"

Once, years before, as he was about to step into an elevator he had the strange premonition that the elevator was going to get stuck, and that he shouldn't get on. But that was ridiculous, and he'd gotten on anyway, and the elevator did in fact get stuck. He was trapped there alone, in the stifling dark, with no way out, for nearly an hour. Tracy spoke with some care. "Actually, Louis is headmaster there now."

"Too bad," said Arthur. "For him, I mean. I was so hoping he'd moved on. But then why should I be surprised? I mean, once Herr Professor Doktor Gestapo von Emmerich got his claws into you, that was it. Kaput. Trust me, I should know."

Tracy felt the elevator begin to move. "I think Dr. Emmerich died," he said. "I'm not really all that clear on the details, but I get the impression that Louis became headmaster all of a sudden—you know, unexpectedly. I haven't really talked to him about it. I do know that he thought extremely highly of Dr. Emmerich."

"Yes," Arthur said, "Louis did think highly of Dr. Emmerich, unfortunately, and so, at a certain point, did I, and yes, Dr. Emmerich did die, and I personally hope it was a gruesome death. Pardon my compassion, but that man terrorized poor Louis. Had him under the heel of his jackboot from the word go. There are other things I could tell you, but frankly, my dear, I won't. They'd depress me too much. But anyway, you should say hello to Louis from me. I've completely lost touch with him over the years, but I'm sure he remembers me all too well. He was a very important presence in my life there for a couple of years."

How Louis and Arthur might have managed to get along Tracy couldn't even imagine, though all at once, before his eyes, he saw Arthur as he might have been at fifteen or sixteen, however old he'd been when Louis was his teacher, and what he felt was a longing, a loss. Louis had known Arthur when he was still just a kid. Though Louis, on the other hand, would have been exactly the same dapper fugitive lurking behind his sunglasses.

Smiling at some secret thought, Arthur leaned close. "Maybe you should invite me up for a visit sometime," he said. "I wouldn't mind seeing Louis again, after all these years."

The thought made Tracy somehow uneasy, though he found himself telling Arthur that a visit was certainly not out of the question. "Not next week, or anything like that, but sometime, sure, that would be fun. I should have the Trempers over for dinner anyway. God knows I've been over there often enough."

"Louis's famous evenings. Let me guess. After dessert he makes you listen to classical music. See? Nothing changes. I'm glad he still does that. I remember when I was a sophomore, he played me Pachelbel's Canon. It was before that delicious little piece got turned into such a cliché. We sat in the dark and just let the music do its thing. I have to say, it was a beautiful moment. We never had any music like that in south Texas."

For a moment he was quiet; they were both quiet. "I've never forgotten it," he said. Then, after another pause in which Tracy tried to fit together the various, faintly troubling pieces of puzzle whose overall shape he wasn't in the least sure of, "Here you've gone and put me in a mood. So Louis is still married to that dyke, is he?"

"Arthur!" Tracy had to protest. "Claire's been very kind to me."

"Oh, she's very kind to all Louis's young men. Believe me. They're a very devoted couple."

Tracy remembered the day he'd had to wonder, afterwards, for the briefest of moments before dismissing the thought as ludicrous, whether the headmaster's wife intended to try to have an affair with him. "When I was in Japan," he said, perhaps a little testily, "the rumor went around that I was a monk. I mean, they thought I lived in a monastery back in the States. Slept in my coffin and everything. Took a vow of silence. Students get strange ideas. You can't trust everything you hear."

Arthur stared at him intently. "You're not out to anybody at the Forge, are you? Not even to Louis."

"It's never come up," Tracy defended. The circumstances under which such a subject might come up, especially with someone like Louis, weren't immediately apparent to him. "I mean, I've only been there a few weeks. It's not like I wear a sign around my neck. When the time comes, I'm sure the right people will know."

"I think," Arthur observed, "this is part of what's got you worried. The teacher's a fag. You hadn't thought about that beforehand, had you? It was different in Japan. Now you've got all these yummy American boys on your hands. I'd say you're in a bit of a delicate situation."

"No." Tracy was adamant. "I can assure you that that's not it at all."

All the Metro North cars had names: John Cheever, Thomas E. Dewey, James Fenimore Cooper. Maria Mitchell, whoever she was. He boarded the Washington Irving.

Coming out of the long tunnel from Grand Central into the sun, he felt a pang of loss so keen it took him by surprise. Forget Tokyo. No matter how you felt about it, Manhattan was still the center of the world.

Around the edges, though, it was fraying. The train glided through a no-man's-land of looted automobiles, mounds of rubble, whole streets of abandoned buildings, their windows boarded over with sky-blue plywood. At the base of bleak apartment towers sycamores struggled in bare earth, their limbs draped in shredded plastic bags tossed from the stories above. And then in an asphalted lot, five shirtless Puerto Rican beauties were playing basketball in the mild October sun.

There was no denying it. Boys grabbed him. Their loveliness tore him apart. The world was a wonder after all.

For a while he tried to sleep, but that was no good. His brain seethed with the weekend's sensory overload: the spent condom lying on the floor next to Devin's bed the morning after, Arthur's cheerful enumeration of his various symptoms, the array of pills he was taking. In the seat behind him, a man and woman talked back and forth to one another with dull, mechanical constancy. Their voices weren't loud, but as if having haplessly discovered the frequency of their broadcast, Tracy couldn't seem to tune them out. He hated couples who'd been married so long their lives had settled into what amounted to little more than a stupor. Did anything mean half as much to them as a momentary glimpse of boys without shirts playing basketball meant to him? What would they make of his razor-sharp ecstasies—or, for that matter, the terrible anxieties a twenty-five-year-old gay man these days had to fight down every minute of his existence? All the probabilities were that he'd be dead at half their age.

For a moment he was on the verge of remembering something important, but then the couple behind him resumed their dreary exchange of nothings, and the memory, whatever it had been, went behind a cloud. Desperate to sever himself from their voices, Tracy rummaged in his bag and pulled out *A Separate Peace*. He was surprised anybody still taught it, but there it was on the syllabus Louis had given him at the beginning of the term for English II. He could barely remember a thing about it. A prep-school kid with a crush on his best friend. Kind of suspicious, really. But it might prove interesting to teach—the challenge being, of course, to get his students to think about all that without seeming to steer them too intently. Arthur had been at least partially right: the last thing Tracy wanted, at this early point before he'd sufficiently settled in, was for his class to be able to write their teacher off as a fag.

Though maybe, he thought, he should give them exactly that chance. Maybe it would do them some good. They were so terrified of being little faggots themselves that they were afraid even to touch one another for fear of their motives being mistaken. That was one of the things that had surprised him about the Forge. Told that he'd need to supervise some athletics, and remembering his own high school days, he'd looked forward to the innocent pleasure—well, maybe not so innocent—of the locker room, only to discover that virtually none of the boys would even set foot in there. After the period was over, they hightailed it back to the privacy of their dorm rooms to shower and change.

Suddenly the memory that had failed him earlier returned at full wattage. Funny what difficulties the mind, left to its own devices, could hedge on. For most of the weekend he'd managed to put Noah's so-called gift almost completely out of mind.

"Something to entertain you on the train," the boy had said, presenting him on his way out the door with what seemed to be a partial roll of toilet paper wrapped loosely around an unsharpened pencil whose eraser end was capped by a rubber jack-o'-lantern's head. "And Happy Halloween," he'd continued awkwardly.

Seeing there was writing on the toilet paper, Tracy had started to unroll it; but Noah grabbed his wrist. "It's for the train," he admonished with a nervous, inadvertent laugh. "No fair peeking."

He had an unhumorous way of smiling. His eyes would narrow to slits, the corners of his mouth pull back tensely. He looked more grim than amused, and it worried Tracy about him. He knew so little about this boy, his inadequacies, both academic and emotional, the various troubles that dogged him. What he did know, or at least had come, during the last month, to sense with some certainty, was that Noah represented a special kind of challenge. But the nature of that challenge, and whether he would prove at all adequate to it, completely eluded him. Certainly his Japanese students, those well-behaved and inviolable girls, all giggles and at the same time possessed of a really sublime earnestness, had been straightforward compared to this American boy who offered him toilet paper and a pencil.

He hadn't waited till the train. Deposited some half hour early by the taxi—Louis had warned him they were highly unreliable—he'd sat on a bench in the bleak Metro North waiting room and unscrolled his present. On the individual sheets of toilet paper, one sentence per sheet, Noah had written in felt-tipped pen that bled almost illegibly:

> *i wonder what he looks like when he's asleep*
> *i wonder what he'd look like with a beard*
> *i wonder if he likes it here*
> *i wonder what he was like in high school*
> *i wonder if he likes us*
> *i wonder if he lets anybody get to him*
> *i wonder if he ever gets depressed*
> *i wonder what he'll be doing in ten years*
> *i wonder what he thinks he's doing now*

Following was a crude caricature of an alarmed face—wide eyes, open mouth, hair on end—along with the cryptic caption, as if he'd been reading ahead in his assignments (though that seemed rather uncharacteristic of him):

> *help me finny i'm drowning*

Out over the river, rippled, shale-gray clouds were moving in from the west. The surrounding hills grew somber, the waters darker. He would not think anymore about Noah. Though he had this sudden, distressing feeling. The word floated in his head: *subcutaneous*. It was so sudden, so unexpected. How had he let someone get under his skin like that? Devin had been almost too right: there *was* something moving about a fifteen-year-old boy. Not so much the individual boy himself, but rather some quality that attached itself to him, the simple fact of his youth, the territory he was passing through. Some light that shone about him that made him, for a moment, crazily special. How strange that you could fall so hard for that trick of light. And what, when you fell, did you want from it?

Idle thoughts. There wasn't anything he wanted from Noah, unless—and this was the startling thought that occurred to him as he watched the sullen plain of the river out the window—what he wanted was not to be seen through. He paused, testing that discovery, its plausibility. *i wonder what he thinks he's doing now*, Noah had written with sly aggression. Was it true that that was precisely what he feared, some threat by Noah to see through him? To catch him unawares at something he himself was too dense to see. To unnerve him. From the very first his casual glance had said, almost contemptuously, I know you. And he had been attracted to that. Yet what did it mean, to be known? And why on earth should he care?

Once, when he was in college, a boy had stopped him on a path and given him just such a look. He was only a kid, thirteen or fourteen, but Tracy, suddenly, was uncannily aware that sex, its hunger and lure, lay somewhere in that look. Unnerved, he'd hurried on, gaze averted but spookily certain that if he paused to glance back, that boy would be standing there looking after him. Safely in his dorm room, he'd flung himself on his bed and, in a fit of desperation, saying to himself, "You're crazy, you're crazy," even as his imagination spun thrillingly out of control, masturbated furiously.

Shifting uncomfortably in his train seat, he tried to concentrate on the landscape passing outside the window, the river's flat shallows where birds skimmed in the dimming light. Painters had sought these shores. On the wall of Louis's office hung a very minor production of the Hudson River School: a limpid twilight, oxcart fording a broad stream; the Catskills drowsing in the pearly distance.

Out in the river, an oddity caught his attention: a series of ramparts and crenellated turrets set on a small wooded island. He'd seen those ruins on the way down; they caught his imagination, an inexplicable romantic folly out there interrupting the ordinary run of scenery. Who had built it, and why? He'd craned his head to catch as much of it as he could before it passed by. And this time too: flitting past the train windows, in an instant it was gone. But it had broken, thankfully, his somber reverie. He reentered the droning frequency of the couple behind him.

"Somebody," the old lady was telling her husband, "really should get out there and tear that thing down. It's a terrible eyesore. And somebody might get hurt."

Betsy's boundless enthusiasm ambushed him at the front door. Drooling and slobbering, deliriously happy, she desired him as no one, it seemed, had ever desired him. She kept leaping up to put her paws on his thighs. "Hey," he told her, "I missed you too." In the empty living room he could see Noah rousing himself from what appeared to be a nap on the sofa.

"Jesus, what a racket," Noah complained.

"Fit to wake the dead," Tracy told him.

"Well, I guess that would be me." Noah stood and stretched. His drab short hair was disheveled from sleep, and he combed through it with splayed fingers, to no particular effect. Barefoot, he wore gray sweatpants, a blue flannel long-sleeved shirt, untucked and half buttoned. Used as he was to seeing his student in regulation blue blazer and red tie, this casual dress—mufti, he supposed it was—struck Tracy as oddly intimate. "Your dog, by the way, is a whore," Noah observed matter-of-factly. It took Tracy, still puzzling about *mufti*, off guard.

"How so?" he asked seriously.

"Well, the instant you were gone, she transferred all her affections to me. One hundred percent." Kneeling, Noah encircled Betsy in his arms. "Didn't you, girl? You didn't think about him one bit."

Where his shirt fell open, Tracy couldn't help but register smooth skin. Still thrown a bit by Noah's antics, and half hoping, guiltily, for a glimpse of nipple, he asked, "How do you know what goes on in her head? She may have been secretly pining for me the whole time."

"You can believe anything you want," Noah said. He held Betsy's head and peered into her eyes.

We're not really fighting over the affections of a dog, Tracy thought. We're doing something else. But he wasn't exactly sure what that something else was.

He didn't really know Noah at all, he felt with a pulse not unlike nausea. He wasn't sure he wanted to know him. He wasn't sure he even liked him.

But the die, it seemed, had been cast. He'd made his overture of friendliness; in the form of Betsy he'd handed Noah responsibilities he couldn't now easily withdraw. To draw back would be a gesture of cowardice.

Abruptly dropping the subject of Betsy, Noah leaped to his feet. "I have to tell you," he said excitedly, "I think this house of yours is haunted. I kept thinking somebody was hiding in the closet, but then I'd look and nobody was there."

"Get out of here," Tracy told him. He considered, for the briefest of moments, making the obvious joke, but decided that would be distinctly unwise. Instead, he asked, "What on earth did you have for dinner?" Kneeling down, he in turn nuzzled with Betsy—who did seem promiscuously eager for any affection that came her way.

Noah only shrugged. "I'm just telling you," he insisted. "I think this house has secrets. I think things happened here."

Shaking his head in bemusement—he'd never lived in such a welcoming house—Tracy tried to humor Noah. "All old houses are like that," he said. "More things used to happen at home. Babies got born. Old people died. Did Betsy notice anything?"

"She's just a dog," Noah said.

"Well, dogs have incredibly fine hearing. There's this whole world out there that only dogs know about."

"I think Betsy's maybe not the smartest dog," Noah judged. "By the way, you got some messages on your machine."

He was disconcerting, the way he veered abruptly from this to that. Attention deficit disorder, according to his files. He took Ritalin for it. They were a remarkably doctored-up bunch, these Forge School students. Still, as Noah glided over to push the button on the answering machine—Tracy was about to say, "That's okay, I'll listen to them later," but it was too late; the tape was already rewinding—something in his movement, the purposeful way he sailed through space, chest out, head bent, gripped Tracy with surprising force. There was a moment in late boyhood when shambling awkwardness and long-limbed grace came together in tune. Noah rang with that clear pure pitch, and Tracy felt, gazing at the boy who stood by his answering machine, shifting his weight from one foot to the other as the first message began, something very much like awe.

"Oh, hello there." A tentative, cultivated voice spoke from the tape. "Louis Tremper calling. Claire and I wondered if, perhaps, you might care to come by this Friday for drinks and dinner, but I see you're not in. Well, I'm sure we'll run into one another on Monday, but I hope you'll be available."

Noah watched him. He had presumably heard all this already. The machine beeped and the next message, which Noah had presumably also heard, began to play.

"Hi sweetie," a high, musical voice sang out. "It's . . ." There was a pause, in which Tracy hoped, absurdly, the machine would cut off. But it didn't. "Arthurina. As in . . . *Queen* Arthurina. So lovely to have seen you. Hope you had a fabulous trip home. You know, I've been thinking, and I would definitely really really love to come see you, the sooner the better. And good luck with staying out of trouble. So many ephebes, as they say, and *so* little time. Call me soon."

In other circumstances the coincidence would have been interesting, even propitious, but Tracy felt himself redden as if an accusing finger had been pointed his way.

But what did it accuse? Noah was nonchalant. "That's all," he said. "Only two. Do you want me to save them?"

"Yes," Tracy said. "I mean, no." Did he owe an explanation? "An old friend," he said lamely.

"So will he come up and visit you?" Noah asked. It was impossible to tell whether he was interested or only making conversation. He was inscrutable that way. Then, without waiting for an answer, he changed the subject. "You should buy a television. I went crazy without a television here. How do you stand it? What do you do at night?" He paced restlessly up and down the bare room.

"Oh," Tracy said (thank God, he thought, for attention deficit disorder), "there's this bloody old woman who comes out of the closet, and we sit and talk."

"Fuck off," Noah said lightly. "You're too weird."

"Me?" Tracy said in mock surprise, both relieved and disappointed to leave the subject of Arthurina safely behind.

It made Noah smile; this time there was even a hint of humor in his eyes. "You're weird because you've got nothing in your house," he proclaimed. "There's a ton of things you need to civilize this place. I should've made you a list."

As if to show the extent to which his house-sitting had gained him some stake in the house, he flung himself back down on the sofa and, grabbing a pillow, held it to his chest. "Before your friend comes up to see you, we should go shopping," he said. "I'll help you fix this dump up."

"I sort of like it like it is." Though he wondered if that only meant there was something depressingly lacking about his inner life.

"You mean—empty," Noah told him. "Ghosts *love* empty houses."

"Oh yeah?"

"Well, I mean, wouldn't you, if you were a ghost?"

"I have to think about that one," Tracy told him. There were perhaps worse things to contemplate than spending some Saturday afternoon at the shopping mall with Noah, looking for various furnitures that might keep away the ghosts. It might even be interesting, educational.

Though it might also move things a next step in a process he should perhaps call a halt to while he still could. Before him flitted the crazy image: Noah and Arthur meeting one another. It was simply impossible. He had way too many different lives going on at once.

"By the way," he said distractedly, to get his mind off that troubling thought, "thanks for your Halloween gift." Releasing Betsy from his attentions, he looked forthrightly at his house-sitter. He hadn't thought he was even going to mention it.

Noah squeezed the pillow as if he wanted to force life into it. "I guess I was kind of bored," he said. "I'm great at procrastinating."

"Well, it was very, uh, creative."

"Yeah, yeah," Noah said flatly. "About as creative as my asshole."

Tracy scrambled to conceal his surprise. "You kids have such foul mouths these days," he joked, though inwardly the words sent a sharp thrill through him.

"Sorry," Noah apologized, as if it were a belch or fart that had slipped out. "It's just a saying."

What could Noah possibly know about assholes? Except that he had one—whose secret particulars Tracy, in spite of himself, had no choice but to contemplate inwardly.

"Kids these days are stupid as dogs," Noah went on. "But then you know that. You're the one who has to teach us."

But Tracy was unwilling to pursue any of that any further. "Look," he said, for fear of spoiling the acute, unlooked-for pleasure he'd already got, "I think you've gone and hurt Betsy's feelings"—a betrayal that wasn't strictly obvious from the way she lay, content, on the bare floor between them.

"Aww . . . Betsy," Noah crooned. "Light of my life." He released the pillow he'd been hugging to his chest and reached down for the top of her head, stroking her delicately for a minute. Her tail wagged madly and Tracy thought, All this affection, for the dog, the pillow. But none, apparently, for him.

Instantly he chided himself for that stupid thought, even as Noah said, relinquishing Betsy with a regretful sigh, "I should probably be getting back to my dorm. Believe it or not, I have to try to do some homework tonight."

"That's the spirit," Tracy told him heartily. But as Noah disappeared into the bedroom to gather his things, he felt both relief and disappointment. He was suddenly, depressingly, conscious of invisible lines circumscribing him all around, unmarked boundaries it was unwise, even downright dangerous, to cross.

"So now," he said as Noah, hair newly combed, shirt buttoned, sneakers the size of motorboats on his feet, reappeared in the doorway with his gym bag of belongings, "tell me honestly. Did you really see a ghost in my house?"

IV

Beneath the bleak fluorescent lighting of study hall, where thirty of them hunched diligently over their work, Mr. Brill somehow managed to grade papers at his desk in the front of the room and keep watch at the same time, his sinusy breathing audible, like a slippery fish hauled up on deck and gasping.

No distractions: that was key. In Noah's dorm room there were way too many things to lead him astray, variously collected rocks and seashells and wasp nests whose contemplation could fritter away an hour of valuable study time before he even realized it. Particularly alluring: a foot-long fish fossil from Wyoming his dad had sent him on his fifteenth birthday. Its fifty-million-year-old skull and backbone, its delicate fins and scissored tail, all lay precisely etched in the undulating sandstone. He could daydream about just about anything except, unfortunately, algebra. Nothing made him feel stupid like numbers made him feel stupid. He'd rather count all the bones on that fish.

From time to time, his voice bored and slightly bullying, Brill punctuated the quiet with more than just his breathing. "Mr. Delson," he called out, his ancestor no doubt closely related to that fish from Wyoming, "let's stop dreaming about ice cream cones, or whatever it is you're dreaming of."

In the back of the room, somebody suppressed a snicker. Brad Delson sat, lost in thought, idly licking the tip of his ballpoint pen. Supposedly it was all for their own good. Since Noah had been at the Forge, his own habits had definitely improved: his academic tutor was cautiously pleased by his progress, and his English teacher said he'd really liked some of his more off-the-wall compositions, the ones he usually got Ds on in other classes. Go figure. But then, none of the other teachers at the Forge wanted you to call them by their first name the way Tracy did.

"Mr. Laskii-Meyers," observed Brill, hardly bothering to raise his eyes from the page he was perusing, "I thought we weren't going to have any more fantasies about Jerry Garcia. The long strange journey is, alas, over."

On second thought, Brill wasn't so much a fish as a monkey, a baboon with his orangutan wife and chimplike children and an obsession not with bananas but with model trains. He'd commandeered the basement of Goethe Hall to lay out his train sets, miles and miles of track, miniature villages and tunnels and hills. The school's worst losers all flocked to the Miniature Railroad Club like moths, and though Noah had been down to Gorilla Brill's private domain only once, when all the newcomers had gotten dragged down there on a tour, those gloomy, cavernous basement rooms, originally built as bomb shelters (at least that was the rumor), had unaccountably spooked him. The doors were reinforced steel, huge concrete pillars supported the ceilings, there were two underground levels rather than one, and reputedly the shelters were still stocked with canned goods dating from the fifties. He hadn't seen any supplies when he was down there himself, but Joey Pinnavaia had lifted a few and displayed them, bulging and rust-spotted, along his windowsill. Forty-year-old green beans: now that was something that could set you thinking. When the big one came, Noah hoped somebody remembered to bring along a can opener.

Anyway, it was stupid to think you could survive a nuclear war. He tried to imagine what it would be like to be cooped up with no light or fresh air. Claustrophobia was no pretty thing. He'd go insane. He'd attack people with his bare hands.

When they ran out of food, what were they supposed to do? Eat one another like those people whose airplane crashed—where was it, the Andes?

There he went again. *Tom is six years older than Mike. Five years ago, Tom was three times as old as Mike. How old is each now?* There was no hope for it. He read the problem in his algebra book six times in a row and still didn't have a clue how to solve it. Trains looped through it. A bomb exploded. An airplane crashed in its midst. He'd read somewhere that the thumb was the tastiest part of human flesh.

One more time he tried to focus; then, with a sigh, he gave himself over to his unruly thoughts.

Across the aisle, Christian Tyler was reading a music magazine he'd slipped into his notebook. With silent envy Noah watched the collage of photos and text that enlivened its pages. Chris was reading a tribute to Kurt Cobain.

It wasn't completely by accident that he'd picked a seat near Chris, though he was careful to make it look like one. There was something weirdly fascinating about a kid who'd inexplicably, over the course of a single summer, undergone a change so radical the Federal Witness Protection Program would have been proud of the results. Six months ago, flashing his good-boy smile, speaking bright nervous words that didn't say a thing, Chris had been totally forgettable. Active in the Boy Scouts, the Catholic society, the drama club and school newspaper. Never in trouble. On weekends his mom picked him up, took him home to Connecticut. But then summer came and maybe he'd gotten struck by lightning, because when he came back in September, not only had he shot up a couple of inches in height without, it seemed, gaining a pound; not only had he gone and dyed his hair lemony yellow and started wearing his clothes in some kind of purposeful disarray; but something deeper and stranger had happened. It was as if some other completely different creature inhabited his body. From coiled like a spring he went to limber as a willow tree, and his voice too, this loud, teasing singsong that made people nervous to be around, like he knew something funny on you but wasn't telling. Gary Marks started calling him the Fatwa—who knew why, exactly?—but it stuck. In a bathroom stall a warning one day appeared, scratched into the metal: CAUTION: THE FATWA LIMBO DANCES. Nobody even said the name Christian Tyler anymore, just the Fatwa.

Everybody stayed their distance, and Noah too. The Fatwa didn't seem to care. He strolled down the hallway with his head held high. Nobody roomed with him. Maybe it made sense: the school wasn't about to put anyone else in the Fatwa den. Still, it didn't seem quite fair—the best room on the hall, a double big enough it could've been a triple, and nobody but the Fatwa bouncing around in there, maybe crazy. Who knew? People always had one kind of animal or another inside them, but if the Fatwa was carrying one, it was an alien from some completely different planet, something both scary and alluring in a dangerous sort of way. As for his own animal, Noah thought it was probably a rat, like the wet slick-backed thing he'd seen climbing out of the school lake one day.

"Mr. Lathrop, Mr. Lathrop."

With good-natured mockery, Brill was calling his name. "Take your leave of whatever heavenly ladies are dancing in your head and come rejoin us here on good old planet Earth."

Though nobody laughed, he could feel his face flash crimson. *You'll pay*—he tried to laser the thought into Brill's reptilian mind, but of course that was a mind too dense to get it.

As for his own mind, he guessed his concentration wasn't safe anywhere. The least little thing could send it off. He looked back down at the page—*James is twice as old as John, but four years ago, he was three times as old as John was. How old is each now?*—but not before stealing one last look at the Fatwa, who kept reading his covert magazine with the kind of concentration Noah could only envy. From time to time he brushed a lock of lemon-colored hair out of his eyes.

· · ·

The summer he was twelve was the summer he discovered the woods, a state preserve that abutted the gated development, Forest Haven, where his dad lived in a style befitting a man whose offices were four floors down from the top of the World Trade Center. The woods had been there all along, of course, but he never fully grasped that till the day he found a way under the boundary fence, a gap of nearly a foot where kids or animals had tunneled under. It was easy to pull yourself through, though he always imagined, halfway under, that an alarm would go off in the development's entrance booth, the guard would push a button, and metal teeth would clamp down, skewer him right at the waist. He'd still be alive but helpless, nothing he could do, which was sort of exciting in a way to think about, till you remembered dogs would come and tear at your flesh, crows would peck out your eyes, ants crawl into your mouth and up your asshole—probably there was some tribe in the Amazon who tortured people like that. Then in the next moment he'd cleared the fence and stood in the open, for all the world like a prisoner who'd just broken from Sing Sing. With a silent cry of relief he flung himself into the mysterious safety of tall trees and tangled underbrush.

A creek had gouged its way among stony hills. In sweet-smelling glens ferns grew six feet tall, and if you followed the creek half a mile, a nearly bottomless pool nestled amidst big mossy boulders. August sun filtered through the trees. On his favorite flat rock he stretched out in dappled shade. Lie still enough long enough and the forest, forgetting you were even there, went about its business without any longer noticing you in its midst. Invisible things came to the surface. The whole air was full of . . . presence. At such moments the woods were *his*, the way his thoughts were, or his dreams at night. He never met a soul there.

There was a complicated kind of insect singing, a shimmer of heat. Birds hopped from branch to branch. Ancient warmth radiated from the heart of the boulder he lay on, passing through him on its way to becoming air and sky. In the deep pool, nearly past seeing, big fish swam silently.

At the pre-Forge prep school he attended, that exclusive Massachusetts joint that was his dad's and before that his granddad's alma mater, he'd had no friends. From time to time someone drifted into his orbit, but something always happened—a fit of fury, a scuffle in the dirt, a bloody nose or ripped shirt, sullen silence. Nobody lasted. He wasn't lonely. More than people, it was things that interested him. He collected the feathers of birds, cicada shells, smooth pebbles from the stream. On the rock beside him, a dragonfly with iridescent blue wings perched motionless for a full minute, two minutes, three. Fifty million or so years ago in this same spot those wings might have been ten feet across. He felt himself shrinking till a Jurassic dragonfly hovered over him, its stinger poised to go right through him. But did dragonflies have stingers? Instead of a giant dragonfly, how about a hunter walking through the woods with a rifle. How about a silent, silver spaceship landing, slender beings with dark liquid eyes emerging from its hatch to take him inside, stick him with metal probes, put implants in his teeth, a chip in his brain.

The flat rock was warm. The dragonfly was still flitting about, its blue sheen alien, shockingly beautiful. He felt slightly sick. Nobody was there. Nobody would come for him.

One afternoon a few days before, in the backseat of his dad's Lexus, he'd found a cigarette lighter, not the plastic kind but an old-fashioned, satisfyingly substantial rectangle of metal. Its heft in his pocket made him feel grown-up, serious. What more logical thing to do than build a fire?

From the forest floor he gathered a mess of branches, then loaded them down with leaves. He'd send smoke signals, or maybe spear a trout in the stream and grill it over hot coals. Chanting loudly, he'd strip off all his clothes and dance around the roaring flames. When he flicked the lighter, a pale ghost of a flame wobbled in the breeze, but the leaves, to his dismay, wouldn't catch. They smoldered without burning. When a slip of actual fire appeared, it was a sickly child clinging to life. It nibbled the edge of a leaf and disappeared. Even the acrid leaf smoke seemed to have no heart for rising, but instead clung close to the ground.

Then he noticed that the pale flames were spreading along the ground as well. It wasn't alarming, but it also wasn't what he'd expected. A circle gradually widened.

He could put it out. He had no doubt of that. He'd built his fire by the edge of the deep pool for that very reason. Still, for one or two minutes, maybe longer—afterward he wasn't so sure—he watched that circle of fire with calm curiosity, the way he watched spiders' webs on dewy mornings or the water for lurking fish. And then without a single moment of transition he was more scared than he'd ever been.

The fire had a life of its own, and there was no stopping it. He tried to stamp it out, but when he lifted his foot, the fire sprang right back in place. The more vigorously he stamped, the more that seemed to urge it on. He scuttled to the creek, cupped his hands, sloshed handfuls of water back in the fire's direction to a hiss of steam, a smell of wet ashes. But the flame had taken on a healthy orange complexion. It didn't roar, but let out a low murmur, crackling and fidgeting as it ran eagerly along the ground, pausing here and there to scale the finger-thick trunk of a sapling or burst from a green bush.

He ran. Following the creek back the way he'd come, he stumbled, fell, picked himself up to run some more. His heart was pounding, he'd scraped his knee on a rock, a branch had stung him on the cheek. Finally he rested, looking back where he'd come. Opaque with leaves, the forest had swallowed the fire completely, gulped it right down into its immense green belly. A strange sense of relief came over him. He walked along calmly. When he came to the fence he followed its graceful curve, touching with his fingertips the smooth metal spikes, the rough brick piers, all that comforting solidity. Beyond, he could see the roofs of the houses that fence protected from harm. At the gatehouse to Forest Haven the guard recognized him and, smiling, waved him past.

All that August afternoon bitter smoke hung over the neighborhood. It crept in through windows tightly shut against the humid summer heat. It infiltrated the air conditioners. People stood outside on their lawns. A helicopter flew low overhead, sirens wailed, the roads clogged with fire trucks from surrounding towns. Men reeled long hoses from their trucks, sucked the pond at Forest Haven half dry when the pressure in the hydrants gave out. They carried shovels and axes into the woods. Several, overcome by the smoke, the heat, were carried away in ambulances. The fire burned thirty acres.

Through it all, Noah slept soundly. His dad and stepmother were away; he had the big house to himself. He'd never slept so well, a slumber profound as hibernation. Deeper and deeper he burrowed into the snug, sheltering den of his bed, covers thrown over his head, pillows muffling any sounds of the world, his brain shutting down, his body turning itself off. Was he in there for only hours or whole days? He dreamed no dreams, just lay in a dark, merciful blank. When at last he crawled out of that refuge, he felt rested but weak. In the kitchen he made himself pancakes, drenching those golden roundlets in butter and syrup and grape jelly. He poured himself a tall glass of milk.

Venturing a cautious peek out the window, he saw that nothing had changed. The sky was clear blue, the clipped lawns emerald; generous sunlight sheathed the wealthy neighborhood in a further embarrassment of riches.

One of the better players on the Forge's not-too-terrible soccer team, Tim Vaughn was a clean-cut, laid-back junior from Albany who, in the free half hour before eleven-o'clock lights-out, liked to sit around in his boxers and shoot the shit with whoever stopped by, usually Gary Marks, Patrick Varga, and Kevin Motes, teammates who lived on their hall. As roommates, Noah and Tim got along with a minimum of friction, both being fairly skilled at keeping out of the other's way. In the general scheme of things Tim wasn't a bad ally to have.

At the end of the day, the Fatwa was frequently on the soccer team's collective mind. Down the hall, the door to the Fatwa's room was, as always, shut tight. He would slip in and out, but they hardly ever saw him; he never seemed to venture into the bathroom or the shower; on weekends he took the train to Manhattan, and nobody knew what he did there. The mystery of him down the hall, behind that closed door, drove them wild with a mixture of contempt, curiosity, and outright hostility. None of them, it seemed, had any clear memory of him from the previous year, though about his drastic transformation they had any number of theories. Tim Vaughn thought it was a brain tumor. Patrick Varga had heard his father was a millionaire who lived in Singapore, but that the Fatwa had never met him. Kevin Motes argued that the Fatwa was just a freak, pure and simple.

"He tried to kill himself," Gary Marks insisted. "He tried to kill himself because he knew he was a faggot. He looked in the mirror one day and realized, Oh my God, I really am a faggot. I have got to do myself in. Wouldn't you try to kill yourself?" No one was more inflamed by the idea of the Fatwa than Gary, who was the aggressive, sometimes too aggressive, star of the soccer team. Some nights he'd actually go down the hall to the Fatwa's door and knock, saying in a loud voice when there was no answer, "Masturbation alert! Masturbation alert! No jerking off in the dorms. We know you're in there. We know what you're doing. Crank the rocket down and come out with your hands up." Once, desperate at his failure to get a response, he'd stormed back to their room and, in what struck Noah as one of the oddest spurts of energy he'd ever witnessed, scissored a beaver shot out of one of Tim's many porn magazines, scrawled the words "Fatwa's Mouth: Candid Portrait" across the top, and slipped it under the Fatwa's door. But even that provoked not a word in response; it was as if, to the Fatwa, his tormentors didn't even make it across the threshold of his attention.

That had been last week. Tonight, Gary sat at Tim's desk and guarded the mysterious J. Crew shoe box that contained, he announced portentously, "the final solution." The others clamored to know what was inside, but Gary was determined to remain the master of the situation. "I declare the citizens' tribunal of Goethe Hall officially in session," he said.

Noah was adept at tuning out when he wanted to. These were Tim's friends, not his. He'd retreat to a far corner of his bed, letting the others commandeer the chairs and crowd around the room's other bed, where Tim sat cross-legged, occasionally scratching at what must be a very persistent case of jock itch. Nobody seemed to mind that Tim's roommate tuned them out. Noah was the kind of person they could take or leave. Perhaps the kind of person the Fatwa had been, back when he was simply Chris Tyler.

Spiral notebook propped against his bent knees, a pillow supporting his back, Noah ignored Gary's maunderings. An idea had been itching at him all day, and he scribbled furiously. When he got a story urge, there was nothing to do but grab a pen and write. Otherwise it was too much like getting a hard-on and not jerking off; the feeling you were left with was sour and uncomfortable.

THE THRUWAY MUST GO THRU
by Noah Lathrop III

Chapter 1

Once their was a grandma & she lived in a big old white house in the
woods. She had a garden of cucumbers & tomatoes & onions & squash.
She had four cats, a dog (beagle), a racoon, two squirrls & one skunk,
all very tame. She lived happily ever after, except—

One day a man from the Government came. He said, I'm very sorry
but your house is in the middle of where the new Thruway has to go.
So you'll have to move.

Grandma had lived there her whole life & she had no place else to
go. Her children & grandchildren lived in a city far away.

I'm so sorry, said the Government man.

Well, I wont go, said grandma.

The Thruway must go Thru, said the Government man.

Grandma took her broom & said I'll swat you. Now leave me alone.

I'll be back, said the government man.

If you come back I'll swat you, said grandma. Can't the Thruway go
somewhere else.

No, said the man.

Can't it go around my house.

No, said the man.

Can't you build a bridge over my house or a tunnel under my house?

No, said the man, The Thruway must go Thru.

Chapter 2

The next day Grandma looked up. There was a black hellicopter flying
in the blue sky. Go away, she said, but the hellicopter wouldn't go away.
It flew above her house all day long. It scared the animals. It's
chopper blades made a wind that knocked down all the vegetables.

Chapter 3

The next day the Government man came back. Now, he said. The
Thruway must go Thru.

No, said Grandma. The Thruway must not go Thru. And she picked
up her broom.

Okay, said the man. Open fire.

A bullet zinged by Grandma and hit her dog (the beagle). Oh no, cried grandma.

That's just the beginning, said the man.

Zing, zing, zing. The cats fell over, & the squirrls & the racoon & the skunk.

Chapter 4

Grandma cried & cried. She took her shovel & buried her pet animals. Then she heard a roar. Looking up, a great bulldozer came toward her through the woods. It made this huge roar.

Get out of the way, shouted the Government man on the bulldozer.

At the last minute Grandma jumped out of the way & the bulldozer smashed her house to smithereens. Their was nothing left just a heap of junk. Then the black hellicopter came & dropped a bomb on the heap of junk & that was that.

Oh no, said Grandma. Even her broom was smashed to smithereens.

The Thruway must go Thru, said the government man.

She looked up & here came rode graders and ciment-mixers and steam rollers.

Out of the way, they all yelled.

No way, she said. The Thruway will Not go Thru.

Yes it will. They rammed into her with the bulldozer & then the steamroller rolled over her & the ciment-mixer crushing all her bones till there was nothing left.

Chapter 5

Well, said the Government man. Good work. Job well done. Cash bonusses for everybody. Now I will go Home & take a shower.

Noah had written it all down so fast his hand ached. He felt feverish and excited. At the top of the page, under the title, he wrote in block letters A TRUE STORY (FOR CHILDREN). He crossed out the word "beagle" where he'd written it and put in "cocker spaniel" instead; then, remembering his mother had a cocker spaniel, he wrote "labbrador." He didn't know why he'd written "beagle" in the first place. Or why, in fact, he'd written any of it.

Reading his story through made him feel faintly nauseated. In his desk drawer, in a folder on which he'd written *Read This and Die*, he had a whole pile of stories, some starring himself, others about various kids at school, still others made up totally from scratch. Once he put them away, he could never bring himself to look at them again, though it crossed his mind that he could maybe show one to Tracy Parker sometime, just to see what he'd say. His teacher already thought he was weird, Noah could tell, but he also had a hunch that Tracy sort of liked weird kids. "I value your weirdness" he could almost hear him say, and it made him laugh to himself.

Could Tracy have been a weird kid himself growing up? Noah tried to imagine, but all he drew on that one was a blank. Tracy Parker was like a shut door: you didn't know anything about what was going on in there. It frustrated him, the way the Fatwa's shut door frustrated Gary and the others. Or no—it was different. It wasn't the principle of the thing, but something else. I feel like you're trying to get to know me, he told Tracy in his head. But then you won't let me get to know you. You won't let me in. But he wasn't sure he even wanted in. What did people want with each other, anyway?

Mr. Parker, you're a challenge, he admitted, but then reminded himself, sternly, not to go having these imaginary conversations in his head. Lately he'd been doing that with the Fatwa as well, and it just messed you up, something else as bad and pointless as jerking off. Not that he'd been too successful in cutting down on that habit either.

Gary Marks, in the meantime, had become quite animated. Leaping from his seat, he clasped the mystery shoe box to his chest. "Oh excuse me," he said in a mincing voice. Standing in place, head held high, lips pursed, nose in the air, he did his best to mimic the Fatwa's striding walk. "Oh please, Mr. Tremper, can I kiss your ass like the little faggot I am? Please, Mr. Tremper, I don't want the other boys to talk to me. I don't want them looking at me the way they do. With their . . . their . . . their eyes of desire. And most of all, I don't want them messing with my secret in the shoe box, which I carry with me everywhere." His audience whooped with laughter. "God, he gives me the willies," Gary concluded disgustedly.

"So what's in there anyway?" Patrick coaxed.

"Yeah, Gary, let's see the money shot," added Tim, his hand busy at his inner thigh. Gary had worked them all into a palpable excitement. Even Noah felt, if not stirred, then at least—and in spite of himself—interested.

Gary teased the shoe box's lid open an inch or so, then closed it back. He was reckless and a bully, which were no doubt virtues on a soccer field. He held his more sensible friends in the big rough palm of his hand.

"Here I am," he narrated, comfortably back in his own voice, "walking along, minding my own business, and guess what? I hear this loud thump and I look over, not five feet away . . ." With a flourish he slid the lid fully off, and tilted the shoe box so they could all see its contents. A pigeon lay snugly inside, its body limp, his pink eye still wide open and staring.

"No way," Tim said.

"The fucking thing just dive-bombed right out of the sky. Thunk. Dead as a doornail. Missed me by that much."

"I can't believe you went back and got it," Kevin said. "A motherfucking dead bird. That's really fucked."

"Don't worry, I've got plans for this guy. Don't you think he looks rather gay—I mean, for a pigeon? I can tell he wants to go party with his little friend. The two of them are going to have just a gay old time of it tonight."

Tim, apparently, was hesitating. "Not a good idea," he cautioned. "He'll know we did it. I don't want my ass fried over a stupid pet trick."

"Ten bucks he won't say a word about it." Noah pretended to reread, with immense concentration, the stupid story he'd written. The two friends bet on nearly everything: test scores, ball games, even whether this song or that one would play first on the radio.

"Fifty," Tim said grimly.

Gary looked pained. "Oh man, you know I don't have fifty bucks."

"Twenty, then. Since you're so sure you're going to win."

"Go for it, Gary," Patrick said.

"Okay then, twenty," Gary said. The power Gary had over his friends, especially Tim, who was usually pretty smart about things, interested Noah a great deal. How was it that he felt so completely immune? Gary was a handsome guy, funny in his way, but clearly this was one seriously disturbed dude; either his friends didn't notice or secretly they liked that about him, his manic ability to go right to the edge without any fear of the consequences. He'd been expelled from his last school, though no one on this end of things seemed to know what for.

"Everybody heard that, right?" Gary said. "Twenty smackeroos. Noah," he called out. "Did you hear? You going to be my witness?"

"Yeah, yeah, I heard," Noah told him. He made a point of concentrating on his spiral notebook, the hectic words on the page. The stupid steamroller rolled over and over the stupid old woman, crushing her bones. His lack of talent made him sick.

"Mr. Fatwa, here we come," Gary said in a comical, high-pitched voice as he lifted the limp pigeon from the box.

"Oh man," Kevin said. "That's really fucked."

The bird's shimmery head lolled to one side. Gary regarded his trophy. "God, it's an ugly motherfucker," he judged. "Well, one ugly-ass bird deserves another. Come on, dudes. Let's do it."

Holding the pigeon in mock-flight before him and buzzing softly between his lips, Gary shuffled from the room, Kevin and Patrick in close attendance, Tim rolling his eyes at Noah but bringing up the rear nonetheless.

Noah rolled off his bed, stashed the pages of his story in the *Read This and Die* folder, and went to the open door. He could see them gathered, down the hall, in front of the Fatwa's room. A burst of stifled laughter, a giggle.

"Hey, I know," Gary said in a stage whisper. "Somebody get some string." Then, more loudly, loud enough to be heard through a closed door, "Hey, Noah, you got any string in your room?"

Noah didn't say anything; regretting he'd even set foot in the corridor, he held his palms out to communicate neutrality. Businesslike, Tim turned and stalked back to the room. He moved past Noah without acknowledging him, as if embarrassed, and Noah, standing aside to let him past, felt suddenly sorry for his roommate, who rifled noisily through his desk drawer, finally pulling out a ball of jute; then he overturned onto his desktop a water glass filled with miscellaneous items—paper clips, rubber bands, pencils, the thumbtack he wanted.

Seeing him provisioned, Gary gave a thumbs-up from down by the Fatwa's door. From his vantage Noah watched the four boys huddle close over the bird, Gary quickly forming a noose and sliding it over the neck. Then, to a flurry of giggles and "shhs," he pressed the thumbtack into the door's soft wood and leaped back. His friends high-fived one another jubilantly. The pigeon dangled from the door.

Noah felt a sharp, mean stab of pleasure—not at the dirty deed, though there was a strange, vicious excitement in that. Maybe the Fatwa was a mystery, and Tracy Parker too, but Gary Marks was way too obsessed with faggots, Noah thought with cruel satisfaction, to be anything but a faggot himself.

He waited, heart racing, for the hunter who was coming through the trackless woods, a bestubbled man with weird, bright eyes and a beak like a bird's. He wore a red hunter's cap and carried a shotgun, and yelping beagles ran before him, frothing with excitement, fanning out over the ridge. Someone had tied him down to that boulder; he couldn't free himself, and after a few moments he didn't even try. He just waited patiently, full of excitement himself, for the dogs that would tear him to pieces, the hunter who would shoot him full of holes. It never hurt. It just felt odd, the way your stomach did on the roller coaster at Six Flags. The waterfall made a noise like the mockingbird that sometimes perched outside the dorm window, a warbling song that kept twisting back on itself, a never-ending loop, and it seemed to him that maybe the water was being recycled too, there was a pump at the bottom that brought it back to the top so that it could pour over the lip of the falls once more.

Beneath his thighs the sheets were warm and wet. *Fuck*, Noah breathed soundlessly. He'd gone and done it again. This was supposed to happen when you were a kid, a flaw you were supposed to outgrow; instead, unfairly, in his adolescence he'd grown into it.

Fortunately, Tim was a heavy sleeper. His steady, resolute breathing hung on the verge of a snore. More than anything Noah dreaded waking his roommate during one of his middle-of-the-night tasks, and though that terminal embarrassment hadn't yet happened, one of these nights it was bound to. Easing himself from bed, moving stealthily in the dark, he stripped off his shorts, then carefully peeled back the soaked sheets and wadded them into the special hamper he kept in his closet. He took off the plastic undersheet, replaced it with a fresh one, spread new sheets out over it.

He could never sleep after one his accidents. Pulling on a clean pair of gym shorts and T-shirt, he padded barefoot down the hall to the bathroom, pausing at the Fatwa's closed door to note that the pigeon had disappeared without a trace. Despite telling himself he was entirely innocent, he nonetheless felt remorse at the thought of the Fatwa behind that door, listening to his tormentors do their work, then in the quiet aftermath slipping out to survey the damage. What rage or loneliness or fear had the Fatwa felt as he carried the pigeon to the trash can, or outdoors to dump it under a bush, or wherever he'd quietly disposed of it?

The dorm was utterly still but Noah's nerves were dancing. And of course his bladder was empty. Still, for several minutes he stood in quiet misery before a cold urinal, breathing in its sweet reek of disinfectant. Behind him were three toilet stalls. A hint of something dreadful tickled along his spine. He stuffed himself back in his gym shorts and slowly turned around. Two of the doors were swung wide open, but the middle one was shut. He took five soundless steps till he stood before it, then taking a deep breath, he briskly shoved it open.

Nothing. Empty.

CAUTION: THE FATWA LIMBO DANCES warned the grafitti etched above the toilet paper dispenser.

Why did he feel so unhappy, freaked out in the middle of the night? It was more than just pissing his bed, more than just the sorry stuff with the Fatwa, though the perfect thought occurred to him: when he got back to his room, the pigeon would be hanging from his and Tim's door. He trod the corridor slowly, lengthening out the suspense of not knowing, wondering if perhaps it would more than anything else relieve him to see the dead bird justly returned to its perpetrators. But nothing like that, alas or fortunately, had happened; there was only the half-torn Star Fleet Academy decal that had been on the door when they moved in, and the rarely used yellow message pad, its short red pencil dangling from a string.

In the room's dark, shored up by Tim's adamant snoring, he managed to find his sneakers without crashing into anything. He pulled on a sour-smelling sweatshirt. Slipping out the dorm's emergency door—its alarm, unbeknownst to the dorm adviser, deactivated since the first week of school—he stood on the steps and breathed in the cool night air. Track was supposedly his sport, since they all had to have a sport at the Forge, but he was the worst member of the team by far—it was a joke he was so bad—and Coach Smith usually didn't care when he missed as long as he had an excuse. He'd been smart enough to make a photocopy of the note Tracy had written for him one day, so he could copy the handwriting. He felt a little guilty taking advantage like that, but there were several times when his ability to do a passable forgery of Tracy's signature had already come in handy.

He ran leisurely, taking long springing steps and enjoying a kind of weight-lessness. Street lamps lit his way along the path that ringed Sunrise Lake. Otherwise the campus was dark, its buildings abandoned to slumber. He hated the Forge, its rules and monotony, the losers who went there, himself included—though to be honest, he didn't hate it any more than he'd hated every other school he'd ever been at. It was just school in general he hated, the way it made him feel stupid and desperate. I could run away from all this, he thought, just go and never come back. The literal possibility made him smile.

Though he wouldn't get away with it at fifteen any more than he had at eleven or twelve or thirteen at that school in Massachusetts he'd hated so much. He could flee to the steppes of Central Asia and still his dad would track him down, lift him up like an errant chess piece, put him back in his correct place on the board. Then the game would go on as if exactly nothing had happened. Believe me, I have my ways, was his dad's chilling phrase—not about tracking anybody down; rather, some business he was trying to do in some tenth-rate African country nobody else wanted to touch with a ten-foot pole. That much a twelve-year-old Noah had taken in as he stood in the door, sorry now about barging into a living room he'd thought was empty, his dad shooting him that glance that said, Why not make yourself scarce, buddy? His dad's golf partner A. J. was sitting on the sofa and laughing but trying not to show it because the African guy, for all his broad smile, was looking pretty miserable—and Noah had gone around for days after trying out that phrase, Believe me, I have my ways, mouthing it a dozen times in an hour but never quite getting his dad's dry, careful way of saying it, so cool unless you thought it was directed at you, and then it might be seriously scary.

At night the campus was rife with the secret life of animals after dark: deer, skunk, raccoons, possums. In the woods on the other side of the lake an owl hooted richly, on the lookout for small victims below. Noah liked running in the midst of all those fleet-footed rogues and scavengers of the dark; he felt a satisfying burn in his thighs, his calves, the healing pump of endorphins to his brain. Up ahead, in the wedge of light beneath one of the street lamps, he saw a figure, probably the old security guard who made his ineffectual rounds at night. As Noah slowed his stride, prepared to veer off into the dark, a surprising creature came bounding his way.

"Hey Betsy," he said. "It's me." Out of breath, he stood his ground as she clamored at his waist with her front paws.

"Oh, now I see," Tracy said. Silhouetted against the light, he held Betsy by a leash he'd let unspool as far as it would go. "You two arranged this little tryst beforehand. I wondered why she was so urgent to go out."

"I told you not to bring him along," Noah chided the uncomprehending animal who continued, ecstatically, to dance around him. The in-love-with-Betsy routine, begun as a joke but now settled into habit, felt a little weird, though if Tracy was into it he supposed he'd go along as well. He felt strangely nervous to have run into his teacher like this, and even Tracy seemed a little concerned.

"But seriously," he asked Noah, "are you supposed to be out so late? Or did you decide to run away from school?"

Noah laughed; if only Tracy Parker knew. "I thought I'd run away from myself," he said.

"Now that's funny. What a beautiful night for it," Tracy told him.

But did Tracy even guess how beautiful it was? Only if you'd burned a forest down could you truly tell how full to the brim a night sluicing among the trees could be. Then Noah's body tugged him back to the fact of himself and he rubbed at a sharp little ache that had sprung up in his left calf. "Actually, I couldn't sleep," he said, conscious of the momentary flicker of Tracy's interested gaze in the direction of his leg, the fleeting animal satisfaction of having been noticed. "I was trying to tire myself out," he added.

Tracy seemed to consider that. "Don't let me keep you," he said, turning his briefly strayed attention back to Betsy, who was noisily foraging something in the leaves by the side of the path.

So that was how easily his teacher dismissed him, as if he were nothing special after all. A bitter pang flared in Noah: maybe he should just leave the inscrutable Tracy Parker to walk his damn dog in peace.

"Or you want to walk with me?" Tracy went on, casually erasing that flare as easily as he'd provoked it. "I was going to make a circle around the lake." He spoke as if there was nothing out of the ordinary about them running into each other like this, but maybe that was how he lived. Maybe he seized whatever came his way, Noah thought, like his dad's pal A. J., the jail time he'd spent for some trouble or other, and when he got out he'd said, "Watch me. I'm gonna grab this fucking life by the balls and not let go." That was down in South Carolina; he'd taken them flounder fishing in his boat. After only three months of freedom his tan was already leathery and deep, his smile triumphant. There was a mad invisible bull raging inside him, bucking and snorting and stamping to get out. He'd taken Noah aside and said, "Buddy, let me tell you, this is exactly what we've got." Indicating the horizon with a broad sweep of his arm. "So use it. Use it all up."

That magnificent desperation: the hungry, proud, remorseless animal. Was Tracy Parker like that as well?

With his teacher he walked in silence, whether awkward or comfortable Noah just couldn't tell. He tried hard to listen for the animal inside Tracy but couldn't hear a thing. Either there was nothing there, which was spooky, or if there was anything, it was crouched down, lying in wait. Figuring he was already trespassing, he decided to take a chance. "Hey Tracy," he said. His voice sounded shrill and unconvincing, but he wanted to see the animal, if only to glimpse it through the thicket. "Did you freak about that package I gave you last week?"

He knew he was a jerk for asking, but Tracy didn't say anything. Perhaps he'd completely forgotten already. Perhaps someone like Noah Lathrop III made no impression at all. If he picked up a phone this instant and called A. J., his dad's interesting and momentarily interested friend would no doubt say, "Who?" Under the right circumstances even his own dad might say that to a son who bore his name's legacy so stumblingly through the world.

"Did I freak?" Tracy said at last—slowly, like he was thinking it over. "No," he answered himself, drawing out the "o." "I was just . . . well, curious, is all."

Noah had no aptitude for thinking strategically. All the tests he'd ever taken had told him that. Like a rat in a maze, he threw himself headlong down this passage or that, crashing abruptly into dead ends, returning endlessly to the same point of no return. Once again he struck out blindly.

"Curious about what?" he asked.

"Well," Tracy said, "I'm just not used to being interrogated. Especially by a roll of toilet paper."

Noah hadn't considered that. At the time, he'd somehow thought the toilet-paper aspect was a good idea—more humorous than anything else. But then he'd had lots of good ideas that turned out to be fucking terrible.

"There wasn't nothing else to write on," he apologized lamely. "Sorry if you got offended."

"I wasn't offended," Tracy said mildly. "Not at all. I was interested."

Did he wish Tracy had a little of A. J.'s crazy bull raging inside? But his teacher was so careful, so temperate. Perhaps there was no wild and risky thing in the world he wanted more than anything else. Perhaps he was just the nice, concerned adult he pretended to be. Cut to the chase, Noah thought. Otherwise they'd walk and talk all night.

"So when are you gonna answer my questions?" he asked bluntly.

Tracy stopped on the path and turned to him. Once again, as if whatever might get said could be so illuminating, they stood in an island of light thrown down by the street lamps. "The answers," he said, smiling so handsomely that Noah thought, Be careful, I could come to hate you, "the answers are yes, no, yes, no, yes, yes, and maybe. Now what do you really want to ask me?"

Failure, that familiar feeling, settled all around Noah. "I don't know," he mumbled.

When did you first know you were a fag? he wanted to ask.

Or, If you *are* a fag, then what exactly do you want from me? And what am I supposed to get from you?

Tracy stood watching him. He had a good strong jawline, a super chin; he should be a model or an actor. And he must be thinking thoughts in that high forehead of his, but nobody ever let you know their thoughts. They were too afraid you'd use it against them. That was what was so depressing. For just once, two people standing in the middle of the night should be able to say what was on their minds, no matter how weird or fucked it was.

"Do you think . . . ?" Noah said, but then, afraid, he hesitated. It really was incredibly hard, wasn't it, to try to talk to another human being. Not the free kind of talk that happened around the dorm room but talk that cost you, talk you staked not twenty dollars but your life on.

"Yes?" Tracy still was studying him. No, Tracy Parker was longing for him. Probably he was dead wrong, but he felt it anyway, strong and disquieting and attractive. That night in South Carolina, when he and A. J. had sat out on the pier after everybody else had gone to bed and his dad's friend admitted he'd drunk too many cocktails: the bull was raging then, for sure. Surprised, Noah had brushed away—more than once—that insistent, roving hand, the sloppy lips and aggressive mouth, till it became a sad kind of game between them. Does my dad know this about you, he'd wondered with what he hoped was contempt but suspected might be more like awe. Never in his life had he felt the strong beam of longing directed his way before, how it trapped you in its scary glare, stopped you dead in your tracks.

Would he welcome a roving hand if it came his way right now? Summoning up all his recklessness, he asked, "Do you think people are afraid to say what they really think?"

Tracy Parker remained imperturbable, seemingly preoccupied with the beagle at the end of the leash straining to nose around in yet another smelly patch of mess she'd sniffed out. "Probably," he said. "Most of the time." His voice turned wary, he shifted his stance—and suddenly, just like that, the wave of longing that might have been passing through Tracy Parker was gone, vanished up into the night like a tease of starlight. Or was Noah looking in the wrong place? Because he had the strangest feeling it was still there, only ducked under cover, prudently out of sight but lurking very near, ready at any moment to return.

Tracy had bent down to wrest from Betsy's mouth a wet hunk of tree branch. "Nasty," he said, while Noah watched the top of his teacher's head, where the indifferent streetlight caught in his brown hair. I'm the water-logged rat trapped in the maze, he thought. Funny that a whole encounter that could go nowhere had started out with him running. Already they were on the far side of the lake. The path curved back toward the campus buildings. Believe me, I have my ways, his dad had said, and though it had only been some businessman from Africa in way above his head, his dad had completely meant those words.

Noah spoke quickly. "We're all gonna die," he said. It wasn't what he'd thought he was going to say, but a powerful desperation had seized him.

"One day," Tracy amended philosophically, though the wariness in his voice raised itself up a notch. They were all going to die, and in the meantime would stand here talking and talking till it happened. But even talk would be okay, Noah thought, if they could just talk about what was in his head that he couldn't get any other relief from. If they could talk about the Fatwa, about Gary Marks, about a dull gray pigeon dangling from a string against the dark wood of a door.

Very probably he was totally wrong about Tracy Parker.

"I can't believe it," Noah said again, the desperate animal in him talking out loud. His voice was almost a shout. "We're all gonna fucking die." If you couldn't talk, at least there was this. He loved it—the surprise of shouting like he did, how wild it was. And with that he was off again and running. Even Betsy was too startled to follow. A strange elation carried him like the wind. He thought he heard Tracy cry out after him "Wait!"—but instead of stopping him in his tracks, it only made him run that much faster.

V

On a downtown sidewalk a woman lay dead. Pooled blood made an odd halo around her head; a trickle ran down into the gutter. She wore a dark sweater, a light skirt. At her side a string bag spilled onto the pavement two loaves of bread, three or four cucumbers, one tomato. Knowing full well the danger from snipers in the hills above the city, she had made a foray out to buy food. Her face registered grim resolve, as if even in death she looked forward to no less than she had had to face in life.

Louis folded the paper so that he would not have to look at the news from Sarajevo, and set it on the kitchen table as he went about his morning ritual.

Claire allowed herself few luxuries, but breakfast in bed was one of them. It had started years ago as a joke, a frivolity. After nights that were by turns awkward and tender, mornings had presented a problem for the newlyweds—what to do with themselves? Before marriage, Louis had always taken a particular satisfaction in making his own breakfast, and finding himself one morning up and about earlier than usual, and at loose ends, he had hit upon the idea of surprising his new wife. She had received the breakfast tray with a bit of irony—he supposed that was expected, even necessary—but did little to conceal the real pleasure it gave her to be waited on like this first thing in the morning. He always thought of something he'd once read: if you pray regularly and consistently, eventually you will believe. The success of their marriage, not only its survival, but its flourishing, had been built to a great degree upon the quiet, humble exercise of certain forms of prayer.

On the stove, water boiled in two saucepans. Into one he dropped a cool white egg. The other he poured into the teapot, where her favorite tea, delicate oolong, lay waiting. For himself, strong coffee percolated in the clever little machine on the counter (a gift two Christmases ago from Susan, his eldest). From the toaster he plucked crisp slices of bread, then resumed preparation of the fruit salad he devised nearly every morning from the bounty to be had at the local supermarket (he was thinking of that poor woman in Sarajevo). This morning he cut up cubes of watermelon and honeydew, sliced an apple and a peach, tossed in a few red grapes. He drizzled the whole with honey and a spoonful of brandy. Macédoine, they called such a salad in Germany: from Macedonia, that volatile Balkan mix. Dividing his more harmonious macédoine into two bowls, Louis set one on the breakfast table, next to the newspaper, and the other on a tray. The timer dinged on the stove, and he removed the egg, its innards, he hoped, still mushy the way Claire liked them. A little silver eggcup, one of a pair picked up at an antiques fair, received the pleasingly perfect oval. His own breakfast never included an egg, and though he somewhat disapproved of Claire's daily craving for one, at the same time he enjoyed adding this extra touch to her meal, as if to distinguish it from his own more spartan repast. He couldn't help but feel, secretly, just a little virtuous.

She was awake and sitting up in bed; more than that, she was already at work, her practice being to grade four or five student papers before rising. How she could stand that, first thing in the morning, was beyond him, and it struck him as another example of her truly remarkable devotion to the drudgeries of her work. Paper grading, when his own routine had included that odious prospect, was something he'd tended to put off till a herculean effort would be necessary to get through the daunting pile that had accumulated. A bad work habit, and less than ideal pedagogy, the endless production and consumption of student prose being, he supposed, a necessary evil, though one that Socrates, for example—no shirk of a teacher—had managed to dispense with altogether, and with no apparent detriment to the education of his articulate flock of pupils. Louis thought he would be all for a back-to-the-basics drive in education: a teacher, an olive tree, a bit of midday wine (the ancient Greeks had watered theirs down to keep their heads lucid), and, last but not least, six or seven eager and receptive youths seated at one's feet. It still disappointed him that he had found modern Greece, the one time he'd visited it, so unlovable, its landscape bleak and forbidding, its cities and villages a disillusioning overlay that—for all practical purposes, and those of a dreamer as well—effectively obliterated nearly every trace of its classical predecessor. Even the Greeks themselves these days were virtually indistinguishable from the Turks and Slavs whose invasions had all but absorbed the noble Hellenes of ancient times.

"I came across something that will amuse you," Claire said, looking up at him with a smile. "Let me find it. I should compile a book. It would be very funny and just too sad. Oh, here it is. 'It's a doggy dog world.'" She spelled out the offending phrase.

"Pretty good," he told her, setting the tray on the bed beside her. "A doggy dog world. That's really very good. I should tell Lux, in case he doesn't already know—though I suspect he does."

Her reward for all those conscientiously marked pages, he knew well, would be a few chapters of a murder mystery. Then, often still in bed, she would work diligently for a couple of hours on one of the essays that, unlike himself, she occasionally finished and, to his mild chagrin, published in this or the other feminist journal. Of course, teaching only part time did free her from the consuming worries of a job like his: the distracting case of Christian Tyler, for example; also the undeniable fact that Goethe Hall would need to be reroofed before winter set in, an expenditure he had altogether failed to foresee when putting together the year's perhaps too-thinly-cushioned budget—and these just two of many problems bedeviling his mind this morning. Despite all that, he had the nagging suspicion that such responsibilities had really nothing at all to do with his writerly constipation.

"You have your class tonight," he said, not so much a question as merely a statement, a confirmation of what he knew perfectly well to be the case. But it was how they spoke to one another in the mornings. There was some sense of order to be found in reciting each other's schedules.

"I'll be gone before you're home," she told him. "I'll leave your dinner in the oven before I go out."

"Fine," he said. "You're all set then?"

She nodded as she poured her tea. What was the curious word he had heard from Tracy the other day? Enabler. It was the language of pop psychology that Louis particularly despised; nonetheless, it came to him now that perhaps, in such small moments as these, this was precisely what they had been for one another, he and Claire—enablers.

In the kitchen, seated before his toast and fruit salad, he unfolded the newspaper and could not resist studying more closely the photo on the front page. Death fascinated him. He knew it was a fascination one should resist with all one's heart, a temptation resolutely to be looked away from, and yet he felt the overriding compulsion to look. The photo had, after all, been printed for all the world to see, and though it was somehow shameful to print such a thing, to assail unsuspecting people over their morning coffee, at the same time he was glad they had done that, whoever had made the editorial decision. It was certainly no more shameful than what happened daily on the streets of that beleaguered city. Before this corpse he felt a terrible wonder. What bound people together was so fragile, he thought as he paged through the rest of the paper, and their barbarity so enormous.

Yes, he thought. The savagery would arrive here as well—not tomorrow, perhaps, but the day after tomorrow. And when it came, it would come quickly; it would take everyone by surprise. A sniper would pick him off as he stooped to retrieve his morning newspaper from the floor of the front porch. He could see it so clearly.

Now, now, he told himself. It was all too easy to let one's thoughts roam unduly first thing in the morning. It could trigger a funk that might last the whole day. For several minutes he concentrated on a dull article about the county's recycling woes. But just as he was congratulating himself on his self-discipline, a small item at the bottom of the page caught his eye: EX-TEACHER CONVICTED ON SEX COUNTS.

Despite his better judgment—and yet he had something of a professional responsibility, didn't he?—he read on. A highly respected teacher at a New Hampshire prep school (of far more distinguished lineage than the Forge School, it must be said) had been arrested some months earlier for trying to lure a twelve-year-old boy into his car. Now a jury had convicted him on more than three hundred misdemeanor counts of possessing child pornography, fifty-three felony counts of exhibiting child pornography, and one count of attempted felonious assault. For each misdemeanor charge he faced a maximum of one year in prison, and up to seven years for each felony.

Like a whisper, some ghost sensation passing through him, Louis felt an unaccountable surge of something not unlike panic, no less powerful for being utterly groundless. Why on earth should he feel even a hint of such a thing? He had never in his life come remotely close to any act that could, by the farthest stretch of the imagination, be construed as having a connection with such derangement as this. The scant details the article offered were bizarre, pathetic.

> When he was stopped with the boy and questioned by police officers, he was wearing a T-shirt emblazoned Camp KYO and carrying a knapsack containing more than 500 photographs, mostly of naked people. The bag also contained a pumpkin mask and a handwritten price list titled Pay Scale for Pumpkin, which listed dollar figures along with acts like "allowing pumpkin to lotion you."

Louis did not like to think too much about such a person. And yet— certain dark fascinations the mind fixed itself on, unable to resist. When he put down the newspaper, he found himself staring once again at a woman lying dead on a sidewalk in Sarajevo.

• • •

Even before he stepped into the office Louis could tell that Eleanor Oster-houdt was in a state. Ostrichlike—had her last name somehow influenced the association that always sprang to mind?—she sat behind her desk in a black turtleneck with a gold crucifix pinned to the throat, pink wool sweater draped around her shoulders (he had never seen her, even in the warmest of weathers, without it), and with furious concentration enjoyed her cigarette.

Smoking was against the rules, of course. No one was allowed to smoke on campus, and the headmaster's office, of all places, should abide by that sensible legislation. Nonetheless, with a slow, luxurious intake of breath the headmaster's secretary sucked smoke deep into her lungs, held its exhilarating toxins inside herself for a full ten seconds, then with great reluctance released the spent pleasure.

Louis mustered his most insinuatingly cheerful voice to wish her "Good morning." She looked up at him, eyes narrowed, so he amended his greeting: "Or perhaps not so good."

She held out to him a piece of paper.

"I know, I know," he said guiltily. "It came in yesterday afternoon after you left." Just as well she'd had to go for her doctor's appointment; he wouldn't have relished her receiving in person the offending document, a petition from the awkwardly titled Coalition of Concerned Students Un-leashed Concerning Cancer, or COCSUCC, as their more-to-the-point acronym announced. Behind the sophomoric joke—whose high spirits, boys being boys and all that, he easily forgave—lay a deadly serious complaint. How disheartening students were these days. Of course it was wrong for Eleanor to "pollute the environment and cause unacceptable risk to the health of all concerned." Louis had tried to explain to yesterday afternoon's delegation of rosy-cheeked lads that Eleanor was a colorful relic from a by-gone era, a time when smoking, believe it or not, was simply a given, a fact of life. In those long-vanished days, one smoked or did not smoke, he told them, but no one paid the slightest heed one way or the other. It was clear they found that very hard to believe. How to tell them that what mattered was not Eleanor's habit of smoking, and the infinitesimal risk it might cause to anyone but herself, but rather her much vaster habit of loyalty, her almost fanatic devotion to the school? That pardonable hyperbole of Jack Emmer-ich's, "Without our dear Eleanor, the Forge School would cease to exist," had more than once, over the years, revealed itself as literal truth.

It took him a moment to realize that the paper Eleanor held out to him was not, in fact, the petition from COCSUCC, but rather her resignation.

"This will not do," he said simply.

"The time has come," she told him. "I've outlived my usefulness here. I'm a liability."

"Ridiculous," he countered. "You'll never outlive your usefulness here." Though he realized, even as he said it, that one day, sooner rather than later, she would in fact retire. She must be close to seventy. Her health was bad; smoking had ruined her lungs, her heart. And where would he be—where would the school be—when that happened? Reluctantly he had to admit that it might be time to begin to think a little more about the future; if, that is, he wanted to ensure that there was to be a future for the Forge School's venerable legacy.

"Now put that away," he told Eleanor. "This is just nonsense. I'll take care of it with no more ado."

He'd find Doug Brill, whose heavy hand, Louis had no doubt, lay behind all this, even as that acronym had been smuggled right past his ever-vigilant gaze.

Like some terrible mark of punctuation, she stubbed out her cigarette in the ashtray. "If it keeps up like this," she observed dryly, "we might as well be living in Russia."

"Oh," he said. "Russia. My impression is that people in Russia smoke and drink to their hearts' content."

"I've got my passport somewhere," she went on. "I even own a fur hat. Maybe I'll emigrate. By the way, your nine o'clock appointment is here," she told him.

He had utterly forgotten his nine o'clock appointment, put it right out of his head.

Seated in one of the office's two seldom-used armchairs, Christian Tyler did not seem particularly ill at ease, and Louis hoped that he, likewise, gave off no sense of edginess. Considering the circumstances, he felt it somehow inappropriate to give even the appearance of hiding behind his fortress-like desk.

"And how are we doing?" Louis asked.

"Okay," Christian told him. He sat with his legs crossed at the knee, his dangling foot shaking with what Louis hoped was nervous energy and not nerves. Though he tried hard to be approachable, he knew that some of the boys found him—his manner, his age—intimidating.

"The room situation is better?" he asked gently.

"Much better."

"And the other boys on the hall?"

Christian merely shrugged. There was an odd distance inside him, as if he were undertaking some calculated withdrawal from the world, shrinking into a protective space he had discovered inside himself. Louis wondered if this withdrawal would grow more pronounced with time. *He's not sick yet,* Christian's father had assured the headmaster. *It may be years before he actually takes a hit from an opportunistic infection.*

The question Louis had asked himself innumerable times was this: what would Jack Emmerich have done with a boy who tested positive for HIV? But his mentor's guiding light, usually so steady, on this occasion proved too faint to steer by. He was on his own.

The case had unfolded over the summer. Some routine blood work had revealed certain anomalies in the boy's white-cell count, which had led to further tests, and eventually to the shocking diagnosis. He was only sixteen. Louis had not pressed for the details, God forbid. But he had found himself unexpectedly moved by the long and surprisingly honest letter Christian sent him in which he expressed a wish to return to the Forge School in the fall. He detailed the intensive therapy he had been in, the rather daunting regimen of medicines his doctor had put him on. "All I want is to try to pursue a normal life," he'd written. "Whatever that might be for somebody like me with a death sentence." His father had concurred, making a special, unaccompanied trip to the Forge School to argue his son's case, and though Louis had hesitated—he had any number of concerns, obviously—the tall, dapper man in an expensive Italian suit seemed, as he sat in Louis's office on a thundery summer afternoon, so devastated by recent events that it was scarcely possible to deny either him or his son their wish.

To be honest, Louis had had some difficulty remembering Christian Tyler exactly. Neither physically nor mentally outstanding, he was one of those students who tended to blend in. Reid had taught him, however, and without knowing all the details of the case, which Louis had promised to keep confidential, vouched for Christian as "the great unremarkable middle ground."

Louis was thus shocked, when the first of September came around, and before classes had even commenced, to see striding across campus a Forge School student he had never to his knowledge laid eyes on before. In regulation jacket and tie, the boy sported a yellow flip of dyed hair so defiantly unnatural-looking that it could only be intended as an affront to the world at large. Having learned on previous occasions that certain rebellious fads had a way of spreading like a contagion through the student body and thinking to nip this particular one in the bud, Louis charged over to the young man with a stern "Excuse me."

"Dr. Tremper," said the offending student. "I've been meaning to come by your office." He enunciated the words carefully, as if already fairly certain of their effect. It had been such a peculiar moment. Louis had never, to his knowledge, known anyone with HIV, and this encounter, happening so unexpectedly, stopped him dead in his tracks.

The boy was no beauty. Acne marred his cheekbones. Up close he had that teased, artificial, effeminate look one used to associate, when Louis was growing up, with obvious pansies. In ordinary circumstances Louis would have been revolted, and yet he found himself, standing face to face with Christian, instead inexplicably touched by something he could not, at the moment, quite pin down; for the rest of the afternoon that unnameable sensation nagged at him, and it was not until sometime later that he realized what a strange chain of association had been triggered by the encounter: how, in the elevator of the hotel on the Lido, Gustav Aschenbach, cast by chance into a close encounter with Tadzio, notices that the Polish boy's teeth are brittle, unhealthy looking. In a passage Louis had often perused with curiosity, Aschenbach thinks, "He is very frail, he is sickly. In all probability he will not grow old." And then Mann adds something strange and imponderable: that Aschenbach finds himself reassured, even gratified by that thought.

But of course, Christian Tyler was hardly anything like a Tadzio, and Louis certainly was no Aschenbach. Nevertheless, call it pity, or tenderness, or perhaps even awe, some completely unexpected emotion had been awakened in Louis. There was no evading it. This boy would not grow old. He would die before his time. That fact held the normal rules in abeyance. And as the semester progressed, Louis discovered that it gave him a not entirely virtuous sense of pleasure to bend or even ignore certain regulations for Christian. It was, of course, perfectly within his jurisdiction to make any arrangements he wanted, though Doug Brill did grumble a bit, and Louis suspected him of occasionally turning a blind or at least myopic eye toward some of the mischievous goings-on in his dorm, pranks that under other circumstances might not appear particularly egregious, but that seemed to Louis, bound to his silent knowledge, inordinately cruel.

Louis knew Christian could get sick at any moment. And then what? With relative certainty he told himself, He's only got two years left here; he'll live to finish his time at the Forge School.

But then what? He tried to imagine the unimaginable prospect of life ending so soon.

"Look," he said, "if there's anything you need—anything I can do—please don't hesitate to be in touch with me. You'll do that, won't you?"

"Sure," Christian told him. "Like I said, I'm doing okay. I'm just trying to focus on my schoolwork. I get a little depressed, but I have my medicine." He forced a smile. Unlike Tadzio's, his teeth were quite perfect. "Thank God for Xanax," he said.

"Sigmund Freud," said Reid, leaning back in his chair and placing his hands over his capacious belly, "makes a really marvelous claim somewhere. According to the master—and who are we to doubt him?—children's curiosity about sex is really nothing less than their sexuality itself. That's how integral it is to their very being. And furthermore, sex-curiosity is the basis for the curiosity children show about everything else. It's the root of everything."

Having just joined the conversation already in progress between Reid and Tracy at the faculty table in the cafeteria, Louis fastidiously unfolded his napkin and waited for whatever bombast was to follow.

"But now here's something interesting," Reid went on, undeterred by his friend's arrival. "As Freud sees it, this overwhelming sex-curiosity is fundamentally at odds with the social ideals of education, because if children are curious to know all about sex, adults, on the other hand, insist that children need to know about something else—namely, what Freud calls Higher Culture. And why is that? Why, in order to distract them from what they are really interested in. Namely, sex. In other words, education teaches children to lose interest in what matters most to them. In order to make curiosity acceptable, something else has to be added to it, and that something is what we call education."

"That's fascinating," Tracy said gamely, and Louis thought, as he prodded with his fork the rather sorry-looking lump of salisbury steak on the plate before him: why on earth has Reid been reading Freud? But then he was like that, an omnivorous reader. One never knew what he was going to dredge up next.

"For Freud," Reid summed up grandly, "the search for knowledge, even in its purest, most disinterested form, is at base what you might call sexually inspired."

"Oh please," Louis said testily, accustomed as he was to these pronouncements lobbed his way, like ineffectual missiles, in a years-long campaign to sow doubts. Nevertheless, that distasteful newspaper article from earlier in the morning intruded into his thoughts in a most annoying way.

Reid laughed his obscene belly laugh. "Louis resents my intellectual promiscuity," he explained to Tracy.

"I resent your tossing around scurrilous half-truths. Thank God we've gotten out from under Freud's shadow, and not a moment too soon."

"Freud, my dear friend, still has much to teach us. The poet Auden called him the dark healer."

Why, Louis wondered, did Reid always feel he had to identify his references for the unwashed masses?

"The dark healer," Tracy mused. "That's very good." Louis noticed that his wise young colleague had packed his own lunch—cheese, an apple, a wedge of dark bread—rather than submit to the cafeteria's regime. As headmaster, he doubted he had that option. It would set a bad precedent. With fortitude, he plunged into a meal that, he reminded himself, never tasted quite as dreary as it looked.

"And some truly frightening lessons they are," Reid added. "But now I must go and educate the little darlings. Get their minds off sex and on to the truly important things, like religion and grammar and the attractions of wayward molecules for one another. Oh, there I go again. Never mind."

And taking up his tray, its heavy plate licked clean, he was off. Tracy laughed and shook his head. "What a trip," he said. "I'm really starting to like Reid."

"He's got a brilliant mind, no doubt about it," Louis said tersely, "but frightfully undisciplined."

"You two've known each other for years, haven't you?" Tracy asked, picking up his apple and examining, as if for blemishes, its shiny skin. "The other day he was telling me some story about how both of you came to the Forge School at the same time."

Louis felt that twinge of anxious embarrassment he often felt whenever he learned that someone had been talking about him. What had Reid been saying anyway?

"You actually met on the train, is that right?" Tracy went on eagerly. "And you didn't have any idea you were going to the same place till you actually got there. . . ."

"Is that what Reid told you?" Louis asked. He watched, a little squeamishly, as Tracy sank his teeth into his apple and chewed loudly. It was certainly true after a fashion, Louis thought. He had been so young then, so full of high foolish hopes, and he had felt liberated by his decision to take time off from the rigors of his dissertation, all his prodigious mental efforts having failed to yield any more than a scant few pages. Even his dissertation adviser had noticed, with some concern, the mental strain he had been under. A year's teaching job would provide a salutary break, and there was no doubt in anyone's mind that he would return with renewed vigor and enthusiasm. Taken in perspective, the prospect of teaching a lively handful of prep-school boys for a year qualified as something very like a lark.

There are a few scattered moments in one's life when everything seems possible. Perhaps that is why he struck up a conversation with the stranger seated across the aisle from him on the train to Middle Forge that morning. Talking to strangers was not something he normally indulged in, but there was something about his traveling companion that appealed to him, some sense that this was hardly a person to spend his time in fusty libraries, and yet Louis could tell, just by chatting with him about the weather, the scenery along the Hudson that passed by their windows, that he was educated, knowledgeable about a wide array of subjects. His profile was noble, there was a quiet fervor in his eyes. Louis was charmed; he was, as he said to himself at the time, quite taken.

"Quite a coincidence, really," Louis told Tracy.

Perhaps, had he known they were both bound for the same destination, he would have acted differently, been more circumspect. But that had been part of the marvelous sense of freedom he had felt that particular morning, suspended between the old, hemmed-in certainties of Cornell University and the new, uncharted possibilities of the Forge School. Though he seldom rode that train anymore—whenever they went down to the opera, Claire drove, her foot heavy on the gas, her hand steady on the wheel—Louis still retained a romantic fondness for that stretch of river and shore, associated as it was with some ineffable sense that life could be lived after all.

"Reid said you were great buddies from the word go," Tracy prompted him. " 'Bosom buddies' is the phrase he used."

"Well," Louis said, surprised and not a little touched. "I'm not sure I'd go that far." What with one thing and another, it felt like they had been estranged for so many years. But it was undoubtedly true that he and Reid had almost instantly managed to strike a chord with one another, though its precise key, and whether it was major or minor, remained subject to debate. And it was entirely to Reid's credit that he had shunted aside, with great gentleness, those youthful enthusiasms when it became awkwardly clear, for the sake of everyone concerned, that they must necessarily remain without issue.

"He thinks the world of you," Tracy said. "He credits you with keeping this place running."

"I met my wife through Reid's good offices," Louis said, realizing that it might very well sound like a complete non sequitur. "For which I am eternally grateful," he added. And wondered: did the phrase "youthful indiscretion" mean anything these days? He had been no older than Tracy at the time, though he couldn't imagine he had ever felt so young as Tracy seemed to him now.

He tried to think what young men did these days, left to their own devices as they were. He knew next to nothing about Tracy's life—his friendships, his loves, whatever they might be. Did he know what it was like to have a bosom buddy, as Reid so quaintly called what had been, at the time, a friendship very serious and, to be truthful, not a little frightening?

He might have been on the verge of asking, only Tracy, stashing his apple core inside the brown bag he'd brought his lunch in, said, "Well, I suppose I too should be off to educate the little darlings."

It made Louis wince; he didn't like that phrase the impressionable Tracy had picked up from Reid one bit.

Not until late in the day, after missing him in the cafeteria, then later at the copy machine, did Louis succeed in catching up with Doug Brill. He was skulking about in the faculty lounge, New York Giants mug in hand. Louis had never known anyone to skulk so; he imagined how even in church—that depressing little red-brick building on the outskirts of Middle Forge that

Doug attended with fellow enthusiasts, as Reid mockingly called them—whether standing to sing a hymn or on his knees in prayer, he probably still skulked. For a single irreverent moment Louis saw God—Doug Brill's white-bearded Father in Heaven, not his own considerably more complicated and amorphous deity—looking down from on high and commanding, in a deep and resonant voice, "Thou shalt not skulk in the house of the Lord thy God!" He wondered about that word, *skulk*. A bit of Viking argot lodged in the language, relic of old coastal raids?

It was his worst fault, and again he caught himself red-handed—not wondering about words, but judging others. But then Doug Brill had asked to be judged. Without a second thought he'd hurt Eleanor Osterhoudt's feelings; there were some transgressions, in Louis's book, that could not be overlooked.

"May I have a word with you?" he asked curtly.

"By all means," Doug told him confidently, helping himself to that pungent brew that passed for coffee, courtesy of Eleanor's ministrations. The audacity, Louis thought.

"Then let's step in my office," he said. "Please, after you."

Settling into the seat Christian Tyler had occupied hours earlier—would he sit there if he knew?—Doug Brill looked at him with exasperating seriousness.

Without pausing for second thoughts, Louis plunged in directly. "I'll not have this," he said, handing the petition to Doug. "You should be ashamed of yourself."

With an expression of mild interest, Doug Brill scrutinized the document. "I don't understand," he said.

"You're not familiar with this little masterpiece of student prose?"

Doug, still skulking, moved uncomfortably in his chair.

"Well," he said. "I may have seen it. I certainly had nothing to *do* with it."

"Meaning?"

Brill looked at him innocently. Louis thought about the man's mouselike wife, his brood of sickly-looking children.

Perhaps Brill was thinking of them too. "With all due respect, sir," he said cautiously—it infuriated Louis to be called sir—"and this is not to cast any kind of aspersions at all, but some of us believe the headmaster's office is not setting a good example for the rest of the school with regard to the smoking issue."

Louis felt certain: were Doug ever to discover Christian Tyler's secret, the stalwart man would go ballistic, as the curious saying went. Louis imagined the young man's head splitting apart to reveal an armed warhead where his brain should be. Nothing proved more clearly that he'd made the right decisions regarding the boy.

"Talk straight to me here," he said. "Tell me what's going on."

Doug set his coffee mug carefully on the desk and clasped his hands together in a show of thoughtfulness. "Some of my athletes were talking," he said. "We've got a discussion group, sort of a Christian support group, and they were talking about ways to make life better on campus. It concerns them—frankly, it disheartens them—to see some of the kids going over to the other side—the other side of the lake, I mean—to sneak a smoke in plain view of everybody else. It's like they're flaunting it. And then to see an administrator . . . well, it's just that we've got to be role models for these kids, not confuse them."

"So you encouraged them to put together this little petition." Louis was dying to call attention to the acronym, but thought better of it. Perhaps things weren't so serious after all; some kids having a bit of fun at the coach's expense.

"I thought it might be good for the students," Doug said. "Educational."

Louis had learned to be suspicious of the word *educational*. It covered, after all, a multitude of sins. "And for Eleanor?" he asked. Then, since Doug seemed to have no answer for that, he continued: "The Forge School is a community. And one of the compacts by which any successful community endures—any organism, for that matter—is its ability to live at peace with itself. For the greater good, we've all got to learn to live with each other's personal foibles."

Doug did not look at all convinced. He took a long sip of his coffee, then said grimly, "The health of our students is at issue. That rises above personal foibles, I would think, sir. And besides"—he played his trump card—"didn't Middle Forge just recently pass an ordinance making it against the law to smoke in a public building?"

"Perhaps," Louis said.

"No, sir," Brill reminded him. "It did. Period. End of story."

Louis sighed. He hated certain kinds of logic. "You're right," he said. "You're absolutely right."

He reminded himself that this was a man for whom winning was everything. Against great odds, Doug had taken the soccer team to the finals three times in the last four years, and since soccer had been one of Jack Emmerich's great loves and Louis was committed to continuing the school's excellence on that particular playing field, he'd made himself close to indispensable. Out for his own brisk constitutional, Louis saw him run past every morning—ten miles a day, Doug boasted. Perhaps he'd been the clumsy, overweight kid in school, the butt of jokes and playground bullying, and in response had made himself through sheer will into the capable athlete that he was. And was that not wholly admirable? Nevertheless, there was something self-satisfied in his fitness that made Louis uneasy. Perhaps the two of them were not as different as he might like to believe. There was, objectively, no reason in the world to dislike Doug Brill. He stood for all the right things. Even his militant stand on smoking was clearly, painfully, in the right, and

Louis felt a sudden twinge of anger that Eleanor's habit had, in a sense, held his office hostage. But of course that was his great weakness: loyalty to his friends had always come first, a loyalty that, truth be told, sometimes blinded him to larger issues. He was well aware of that. It had happened before.

"Doug," he pleaded. "Please be reasonable with me here. We both know Eleanor. We know she's set in her ways. I haven't told anyone else, but this is almost certainly her last year with us. Chances are she'll be retiring in June."

He knew very well it probably wasn't true, but he also knew it might placate Doug, who, having been wounded more than once by Eleanor's tart tongue, would in all probability prefer the prospect of her leaving for good in six months to her indefinite reprieve as a reformed smoker.

"You'll see to it that all this goes no further, okay?" he said sternly. He knew that people like Doug responded well to authority. "You'll talk to your students, calm them down. Their concerns are legitimate, obviously. But it's a complex world out there. I have many more important things on my mind than smoking. I am counting on you to defuse this for me. Do you understand? I have great faith in you."

Doug sighed. For a moment it seemed he might be weighing the consequences of further dispute. Louis hated being heavy-handed like this.

"I'll speak to the issue at Assembly next Wednesday," he continued. "We'll work things out. You just keep the simmer from becoming a boil, okay? I'll appreciate that greatly."

He would fashion a general statement about the school's smoking policy. He would urge everyone to care for their health. Come September Eleanor would still be around, smoking like a steam engine, and the tiresomely unimpeachable Doug would be back to visit him, sitting in this very chair, angry and bitter—and rightfully so—at having been betrayed. Nothing would have been solved, only made worse. He could already see it, and yet he did not have the will, at the moment, to offer Doug anything more than he already had. This was how one made implacable enemies. He was simply not cut out for the steady work of fortitude, which had come so effortlessly to Jack Emmerich in crises great and small. How strange that he had spent most of his life doing something for which he was really not very well suited.

On those evenings when Claire taught her Introduction to Writing by Women, she would often relocate, after class was over, to the diner across the street from campus, where she would continue the conversation for another hour or so with some of her more committed students: harried working mothers, overweight and resentful secretaries, joyless lesbians. Louis thought he could imagine those sessions all too clearly, Claire drinking cups of decaffeinated coffee while the others indulged in slices of those poisonous pies that turned endlessly in the brightly lit display carousel. Likewise the endless rehearsal of the grievances of the misfortunate, which seemed to constitute so much of what passed these days for intellectual life at the college level, and which Claire seemed to find unaccountably exhilarating, even, in her words, "empowering." The kin, perhaps, of Tracy's "enabling." Not that he begrudged for an instant Claire's getting out into the world, her belated discovery of her considerable talents as a teacher and scholar.

What he did begrudge, just a little, was being left to knock about the empty house two evenings a week. Prey to all sorts of stupid anxieties and doubts, he forsook his usual books and music. He sipped more scotch than agreed with his stomach. Turning on the television, he sat in a stupor before its empty visions. The mullahs of Iran, he'd read with a great deal of sympathy, had outlawed satellite dishes in an attempt to withstand the inane tide of what passed for popular culture in the West.

It was with those dreary alternatives in mind that he had first broached his proposal to Tracy. The young man had been so kind, after that first evening at their house, as to signal his pleasure in having made the acquaintance of *Daphne*, that tale of a woman confused by desire, torn tragically between the terrible love of a mortal and the terrifying love of a god.

"I think I never really got into classical music because I never had anybody to explain it to me" was what he'd said—Louis remembered the sentence exactly—and since there was nothing Louis liked better than, as Tracy put it, explaining classical music, he'd decided to set about redressing that unfortunate omission in his junior colleague's education. It was hardly the first time he'd taken on himself the role of musical guide. As an adolescent, on long summer evenings when other boys played stickball in the streets or chased after girls, he would call his parents into the living room after dinner and make them sit quietly, together on the sofa, while he positioned a stack of heavy seventy-eights on the Victrola. For two heavenly minutes the scratchy force of a Beethoven symphony filled the room's dim air. "There's the main theme in the violins," he'd point out, resisting the undignified urge, occasionally yielded to in private, to actually conduct the music with expressive hands, wildly flailing arms. "And now the horns come in, and the cellos, and in a second it's going to shift into minor."

"Yes," his father told him patiently. "I think we can hear all that."

But did they hear it the glorious way he heard it? That was his fear: that without his intervention, these moments of great beauty might slip away unremarked by the world at large.

All too soon the music ended in a hissing of empty grooves.

"I think that's enough for now," his father would say, even as the next disk made ready to drop onto the turntable.

"There's more," Louis would say hopefully. "That's just the beginning of the first movement." He dreamed of one day ushering his parents—who, in

the right mood, could enjoy music a great deal, especially the chamber concerts sponsored by the Germania Association before the war, unfortunately,
canceled such opportunities—through the intricacies of an entire symphony. Then they would understand not only the music's tumult and loveliness, but the tumult and loveliness that lay unexpressed in his own young
soul.

If the memory made him wince these fifty years later, especially as he had
proved so deaf, at the time, to the unruly noise of his parents' marriage
splintering all around him, he nonetheless recognized that the impulse that
had first stirred in those evenings of erstwhile musical appreciation had never
left him. His educational aims might remain more or less intact, but his
methods, fortunately, had long ago ceased to be quite so crude.

This particular evening he had decided, after consideration that had filled
the greater part of the afternoon, on some songs by Schubert, a few selections
from *Die Winterreise*. His intent was to play Tracy several different recordings
of each song, so that he might begin to hear the interpretative gestures a
singer can bring to a piece of music. Pulling the first record from its sleeve—
the venerable Dietrich Fischer-Dieskau, accompanied by Alfred Brendel—
he positioned it carefully on the turntable. He had resisted investing in a
CD player as long as possible, predicting, wrongly enough, that that technology would turn out to be a short-lived fad.

Tracy was late—already it was nearly fifteen minutes past the hour. Pacing
restlessly around the den, Louis rearranged the pillows on the sofa, checked
the audio equipment, double-checked to make sure the porch light was on,
all the while feeling a sickening sense of panic and regret. He'd run into
Tracy in the corridor after classes had finished and offhandedly reminded
him, "See you at eight, right?" just to make sure. Tracy had smiled at him
forbearingly, in a way that hinted, were one inclined toward anxiety, No need
to remind me; I'm perfectly capable of keeping my appointments. Louis had
rebuked himself for that parentlike slip—though now it perhaps turned out
that such a reminder had, in fact, been in order.

Waiting, he thought, was the most miserable condition a man could find
himself in. His whole life, he had been waiting for one thing or another.

For a second time the doorbell rang, though, as if by listening for something too intently one could miss it altogether, he had not registered the first
ring until he had heard the second.

"I'm really sorry I'm late," Tracy apologized. His face glowed healthily from
the brisk evening air, and when he smiled, it seemed to Louis that all the
unbounded, virile optimism of youth itself was present. In an instant, those
fifteen minutes of worry were forgiven. "I was on the phone, and I completely
lost track of time."

But hard on the heels of that relief came an odd emptiness. Who had he
been talking to? Louis realized, with a sense of longing, that he really knew

nothing at all about Tracy's life outside the routines of school and the occasional musical evening. Presumably he had friends—down in New York, no doubt. He had mentioned, once, having gone away for the weekend. Might there not even be a love interest somewhere in the background, a young woman, perhaps, a lively young professional in publishing, say, in magazines, an alum of William and Mary like Tracy himself, a girl he'd known practically forever? Louis tried to picture their life together, but failed utterly. This figure who stood before him seemed bravely independent, unattached, mercifully unsullied. Parsifal, he had once thought, and he smiled to himself at the memory of that early impression.

Over a subdued flannel shirt Tracy wore a handsome sports jacket. During the past month and a half, Louis had noted with approval the young man's adoption, even on occasions like this evening when it wasn't strictly necessary, of what could be considered adult attire. That he still looked a bit as if he were playing dress-up only added to the charm.

"Well," Louis told him, "I hope you're ready for a bit of music. Would you care for a cocktail?" He always asked, and his guest, disappointingly, always demurred.

"I'll just have a glass of water," Tracy said.

"As you wish," Louis told him, while pouring himself a real drink. He could make a very small scotch last quite a long time when there was serious music to be listened to.

Once the lights were dimmed, they were ready to begin their journey. How much should he say by way of introduction? Reluctant to overburden Tracy with useless information, at the same time he knew how important it was to set the scene. Self-consciously he cleared his throat, then began his bit of narration.

"When he wrote *Die Winterreise*, Franz Schubert was in the final year of his brief life. He is said to have told his friends, 'I have composed a cycle of dreadful songs for you.' *Schauerlich*. Do you know that word? 'Dreadful' in the sense of exciting dread. I think you'll hear that quality quite clearly. In this first song, listen to the music's deliberate pacing, like footsteps. Listen to the way the voice darkens." Handing Tracy a German/English lyric booklet, he lowered the needle into the groove and sat back. A woeful descending figure in the piano, the wanderer's sorrowful tread. Then Fischer-Dieskau's sonorous, lovesick baritone.

A look of serious concentration settled onto Tracy's features; a bit of a frown perturbed his forehead, behind which an alert and agile brain would be processing the raw data of sounds into music. But what music did Tracy hear? Certainly it was not the same as what he, Louis, experienced, who had heard this song many times and under many circumstances. How he longed to convey the depth and darkness these notes had acquired over the years. But perhaps, already, a similar process had begun in Tracy. In the future, whenever he heard this music, he would perhaps think back to this first occasion on which he had encountered it. And what, exactly, would he think? *Die Liebe liebt das Wandern*, the singer lamented. *Gott hat sie so gemacht.* Yes, it was true. Love *did* love to wander; that was how God, in his cruel and infinitely jesting way, had made it. And as for Tracy, what loves had he known in his brief life?

Louis thought he could hear from Tracy an audible murmur. Likewise, he found himself rather more moved than he had perhaps intended, and decided, rather than risk disrupting the mood with some remarks on Fischer-Dieskau's splendid vocal technique, to let the winter's journey continue.

Through four more songs, then, they sat in silent communion—until Tracy, in the pause, stretching mightily, said with an embarrassed smile, "I hate to do this, but can we take a break? I need to go pee."

Instantly their fragile pact was shattered. Tracy often interrupted their musical evenings like this; bladder control was not the young man's forte. Through the bathroom door, Louis could hear the sound of his vigorous stream, so unlike his own fitful efforts. Then, without warning, an incongruous memory seized him, an image he thought he'd successfully laid to rest long ago: his mother, her eyes dark and wide, her hair disheveled, repeating over and over in a flat, measured voice, "I see clearly now, I see everything clearly now," words that had excited in him, an adolescent of fourteen, such dread, words clairvoyant and absurd, for what had she seen so clearly that it had blinded her mind like an explosion of light?

"Now that's better," Tracy said cheerily, returning to his seat with a small dark spot, Louis couldn't help but notice, just visible on the front of his khaki trousers. But if Tracy felt better, Louis suddenly felt far, far worse. It was as if his mother stood, incorporeal but icily intact, there in that room so many years after her trouble, like a raging torrent, had carried her helplessly away from them all. So, she seemed to say. You too. Your father's son.

"These songs are really kind of amazing," Tracy enthused. "I've never heard anything quite like them."

"Yes, they are quite remarkable," Louis agreed, wondering if the truly remarkable thing wasn't Tracy's ability to banish ghosts, mothers, the dread doubt that always hovered close. "But I think," he went on, "we should listen again to 'Der Lindenbaum.'" Though not, as he'd originally intended, in another performance. Fischer-Dieskau did a particularly fine job with that gem. When its final, innocent-sounding but not-so-innocent notes had ended, Louis lifted the needle and set it aside. Tracy looked up from the translation booklet he'd been following along in.

"I'm curious," Louis said. "Tell me, what do you hear? Talk to me about this song."

Taken off guard, Tracy looked a little alarmed.

"It's not a test," Louis hastily reassured his guest.

That made Tracy smile. "Well," he said slowly, prolonging the word in his scramble to formulate something, "speaking as a proselyte"—and again he smiled—"I'd have to say that there's something going on here. I mean, under the surface. Things aren't what they seem to be. This linden tree that's offering him rest—there's something that scares him about that."

"Yes," Louis said, pleased with the direction of Tracy's groping sentences. "And do you hear how the music works with the words to accomplish that? How the shift into minor in the middle of the song leaves its traces even after we return to major at the end of the song? There's a sinister tenderness to that word *Ruhe*. It's not just rest and repose it offers—"

"No," Tracy said simply. "It's death."

Earlier, in a moment of doubt, Louis had seen himself as he might appear to the young man: fussy, pompous, an aged pedant harping on obscure and even alarming obsessions. But now he told himself he needn't have worried. Without having to be prompted, Tracy had understood. Was there anything more reassuring? That, after all, had been what drew him as a young man to Claire: her ability to intuit those moments he feared might be lost on others. That had been Jack Emmerich's gift as well—it had been his genius. This small circle of the elect. Anchorites, guardian monks charged with preserving intact their precious hoard down through the long twilight. Wasn't it Jack's much-beloved poet who had said, "Marvels this day cannot grasp / Are rife with the fate of tomorrow?"

The room was quiet all around them. From the kitchen, Lux on his mattress heaved a loud, profound sigh, almost a groan. It might have been comic, but neither of them took it that way.

"When I was in Japan," Tracy said, "I learned this word—*hakkanai*. It's the cherry-blossom thing—beauty that only lasts for one brief moment. And the sadness that comes from that, but it's a thrilling sadness. I don't really know what I'm saying."

And neither did Louis, exactly, but he felt very much the spirit of what Tracy was trying to say. The moment itself was everything. It had its own formidable eloquence. Lux sighed again from the kitchen, and this time the effect registered on Tracy as comic after all.

"My thoughts entirely," he said. "Just one big long sigh. Maybe I'll take you up on that cocktail now."

"Scotch?" Louis asked, both surprised and pleased.

"Sure," Tracy said. "Sounds good."

As he stood at the kitchen counter, refilling his own glass and resisting the temptation to give Tracy an extra large splash—in celebration of what, exactly?—Tracy's voice came to him from the den. "By the way, you'll be so proud of me. I actually went out and bought my first classical CD the other day. That Schubert sonata I liked so much."

"The B-flat opus posthumous," Louis said.

"Who'd have ever thought?" Tracy told him, accepting the amber-filled tumbler Louis offered him.

"Did you want ice?" Louis asked.

"No, no," Tracy told him, sipping appreciatively, "this is just great as is." Louis was all at once acutely conscious that Claire's class had been over for some time now, that her session at the diner never lasted more than an hour: sooner rather than later he would hear the sounds of the Audi in the driveway. It was silly, superstitious—or perhaps only selfish—but considering how well the evening had gone so far, he felt he would just as rather Tracy be gone by then. Tracy, however, perhaps under the inspiration of the scotch, was intent on declaring himself.

"One thing I realize," he said a little grandly, "is, all the music I grew up with—most of it was just crap. I mean, I listened to what everybody else listened to. What they fed me on the radio. But it was stupid. It was junk. But I never knew anything else. So I feel like you've given me a gift." He raised his nearly empty tumbler. "Thank you," he said gracefully, thrillingly. It was enough to make Louis think of beautiful moments that would not last. But Tracy wasn't through. "I have to tell you," he went on, as if confidentially, "I think I'm really starting to like this place. I didn't know whether I would, at first, but I'm starting to really feel at home here. Like maybe I fit in."

"Oh, I think you're a very good fit for us," Louis assured him.

"There were certain things I thought I wasn't going to like—little things, like how the students all have to wear coats and ties to class; how there's this strict code. But I kind of see the point. It's bigger than just the Forge, what it stands for." Louis winced at the familiar shortening of the school's name; Tracy had picked up the usage, no doubt, from the students, who liked to make the school sound more like a high-walled, forbidding prison than the studious community of scholars it strove to be. He considered gently correcting the young man, but how to do that without seeming stern, even humorless? So he decided to say nothing—it was thus, exactly, that traditions crumbled—as Tracy continued, his voice gaining in intensity, "In Japan they've got this ancient culture, it's so strict and formal and beautiful, but then everywhere you turn, it's like this American sickness is invading everything. You start to hate it. I mean, I felt ashamed. Growing up with it, you just don't notice. And it's the same with our students. They don't have any choice—it's what they're born into, all these stupid computer games and the junk food and the clothes and sneakers. All the stuff they think is cool. But they're just victims. I mean, they don't know any better. They don't even know how to think about it. Am I talking too much?" he asked, suddenly self-conscious.

"No, no," Louis told him. "Please go on."

"I have this ideal, I guess, of what it means to be educated. How to be loyal to the beautiful things. I have this image—it's almost exactly the opposite of everything our society makes kids into. All this ugly stuff, this loud stupid bullying that passes for cool. I'm sorry, I'm just going on and on here."

And perhaps he was, but listening to him earnestly chatter on, above and beyond whatever Tracy was striving to find words for, Louis realized something he had only dimly thought about before. He hardly knew this young man, really, and certainly Louis had no intention of retiring anytime soon—his health was good and, more to the point, the Forge School was his life—but ten years from now, fifteen, mightn't he be permitted, if only for a moment, to entertain the possibility that one day in the distant future, Tracy Parker might be the headmaster of the Forge School?

"I agree with every word you've said," Louis told him gratefully. "It delights me to hear someone of your generation say such things. Let's say it makes me feel less . . . I don't know"—and here, surprisingly, he found himself thinking of Eleanor Osterhoudt, of Christian Tyler, of a nameless woman facedown on a sidewalk in Sarajevo—"Perhaps it makes me feel less stranded."

The house was quiet. Tracy Parker had gone; Claire had returned. Now she slept peacefully upstairs; Lux slept fitfully downstairs. Everything was in its place and Louis was in his study, at his desk, his notebook open before him. Not since the fruitless summer had he pulled the notebook from its hiding place at the bottom of his desk drawer, but tonight he felt a beguiling intoxication—the effect, no doubt, of the evening's stirring music, its heady conversation. It was as if a door had opened: not *into* but *out of*.

He reached up and took down, from its shelf, his much-perused copy of *The Magic Mountain*, and turned to the chapter in which Hans Castorp discovers the pleasures—some surprisingly perilous—to be had from listening to the Berghof's newly acquired gramophone. It had been no accident, of course, that he himself had chosen to introduce Tracy to those late songs of Schubert; it had been, rather, a test, which the young man, happily, had passed more splendidly than his teacher might have hoped. Though Louis had to wonder: to what extent had he led Tracy to those insights his pupil for the evening had so marvelously articulated, and to what extent had the young man arrived there on his own? Did one learn or was one shaped? Hadn't Plato made that distinction, between the fruitful seminar and sterile indoctrination? As for his own insights, had not Mann gently seeded him with every single observation he himself had offered, this evening, about that lovely, disquieting song? "One need have no more genius," Louis read,

only much more talent, than the author of the *"Lindenbaum"* to be such an artist of soul-enchantment as should give to the song a giant volume by which it should subjugate the world. Kingdoms might be founded upon it, earthly, all-too-earthly kingdoms, solid, "progressive," not at all nostalgic—in which the song degenerated to a piece of gramophone music played by electricity. But its faithful son might still be he who consumed his life in self-conquest, and died, on his lips the new word of love, which as yet he knew not how to speak. Ah, it was worth dying for, the enchanted *Lied*! But he who died for it, died indeed no longer for it; was a hero only because he died for the new, the new word of love and the future that whispered in his heart.

The words stirred and troubled Louis. What new word of love had Mann indicated with such careful obliquity? What scene of beguiling intoxication did that shut door swing slowly open to reveal? Putting aside *The Magic Mountain*, he took up his pen; then, a remarkable thing, he began feverishly, as if possessed, to write.

VI

The only male student in Claire's Introduction to Writing by Women was a thin, harassed-looking young man named Tim Veeder. When she had asked them all, on the first day of the semester, to write down on a piece of paper what they hoped to get out of the course, he'd scrawled *A date. (Just a joke!). Really—I want to see how the other half live.*

"Perhaps we should talk," she had told him at the end of the next class, unsure whether this was the right course for someone like him. He'd assured her that absolutely, positively, it was, and that he would love to come to her office sometime and chew the fat but he was very, very busy this semester. He was working two jobs. At the time she'd felt vaguely relieved, but now he sat before her in the cramped cubicle she shared with two other part-time faculty. The day was pleasantly warm for late October, and to take advantage of this last lingering taste of summer Tim had dressed in a Metallica T-shirt, cutoff jeans, and enormous high-topped sneakers he wore without socks. Straight black hairs, vaguely repulsive, covered his skinny legs. Perhaps everyone, men and women alike, should have to shave their legs, Claire thought. Perhaps legs were never meant to be flaunted at all. Nevertheless, she could not keep her eyes from wandering their way.

He talked in fitful spurts, intent, apparently, on spilling not only his own but his entire family's history to her. "My mom," he said, "she didn't want me to do this schooling thing; my dad either. You know—waste of time and money. But I said to them, it's different times now, you've got to get an education to stay ahead. Nobody ever went to college in my family so they all think I'm weird, the weirdo in the family, you know. And I guess maybe I am. It's not like I did so great in school, but not terrible either. One of my teachers, Miss Davidov, said I should go on, and I thought, hey, I'm all for broadening my knowledge. I mean, I always read books on my own and that kind of thing. *Atlas Shrugged*. Now there's a book for you. Did you ever read that one? I read it twice."

"I haven't actually ever read that particular one," Claire told him. "I tried to read one of her others."

"Yeah," Tim said enthusiastically, "when I can find the time, I want to read all her stuff. She's great. Did you ever think of maybe including *Atlas Shrugged* in this course? I mean, it's written by a woman and everything."

She considered the possibility of tackling that one, but instead she asked, "So how is the course going for you?"

"Oh, I'm getting a real kick out of it," he fired back, and she had the disheartening sense, not only from what he'd just said but from everything she saw of him in class, that he was understanding absolutely nothing. Everything he said—and he tended to speak at great length in the classroom, and with great assurance—seemed to her dead wrong, as if, perversely, he took every argument as its exact opposite. It was a terrible thing to admit, but she'd already more or less written him off in a kind of triage. There were too many others in the course she had to try to save.

There was one matter, however, she had to broach with him. "If I don't call on you sometimes," she said, knowing he noticed how there were days when she ignored his impatiently upraised hand for half the class, "it's because I'm trying to let other people have a chance." No need to be confrontational, she thought. No need to alienate him completely by pointing out what a typical male bully he was. And yet the point did need, somehow, to be made.

"I understand," he said. "No problem. My friends all call me motormouth anyway; that is, the ones that don't go calling me motorhead." He grinned as if it were a joke he expected her to get. "But I'll be honest with you," he went on. "It's frustrating not to be able to talk sometimes. And if other people aren't going to speak up, well, I mean, what can you do?"

"One thing you can do," Claire explained patiently, "is give those people a space so that they can find their voices. It's not easy. Women in this culture often have a very difficult time asserting themselves, and I think we all have to be very conscious of gender privilege. Speaking is so often a male prerogative. That's why—"

"It's just the way I am," he said, and not even defensively. "It's in my genes."

"Or perhaps it's a cultural thing," she suggested. "Perhaps it's part of your acculturation as a man to be competitive and aggressive."

"You should see my sisters," he said. "My sisters are practically the same way."

"Have they ever thought of going to college?" Claire asked mildly.

Tim made a disdainful sound. "Are you kidding? Making babies is all they do. I say, whatever makes you happy, I'm cool with that. They both got husbands."

Was it true that men never listened? That they never *had* to listen? She wished she could get her hands on those sisters of his, just for half an hour; their version of their lives would undoubtedly differ from their brother's fond account. But of course they would never get near the college; circumstance had already doomed them to a life of thoughtless fecundity.

But where was the harm in that? she chided herself. She had read the feminist arguments for "reproductive rights," how women must be allowed not only to choose *not* to have children, but to choose to have them as well. She wondered, sometimes, how good a feminist she really was, since to be honest she looked with some horror on the prospect of a world over-run by the illiterate and unwashed—since those were the people whose right to have children was being voiced by such arguments. Was she, at heart, an elitist who would, under the right circumstances, look the other way if the government issued a one-child–one-family policy? And yet she herself had brought two daughters—well cared and provided for, one might add—into the world.

She had come to feminism—as to so much else—late in life, while study-ing for her Ph.D. at SUNY Albany. A lesbian professor with close-cropped hair and ferocious learning, having seen some gleam in a forty-five-year-old headmaster's wife making her uncertain return to the academy, had pushed Simone de Beauvoir and Monique Wittig her way. The former Claire had read with enthusiasm, the latter with great skepticism and not a little incom-prehension. She remained, in certain ways, for all her feminist stance, the person she had always been, though she took pains to keep that hidden from someone like Tim Veeder, who would only use her complexities against her. A hypocrite, she thought gloomily, steering herself back to her student: he was asking for clarification about the next paper assignment, which, due to his two jobs ("grease monkey by day, burger flipper by night"), he was doubt-ful about being able to complete on time.

"Take an extra week," she told him wearily. "But then it really does have to be in."

"*Yes*," Tim said, and he clenched his fist triumphantly in a most unagree-able way. "You're the greatest, Mrs. Tremper. Sorry," he corrected himself with a grin as he bounded for the door. "*Ms.* Tremper." The last thing she saw were those hairy legs of his.

"Don't worry," said a husky voice. A large black woman glided into the narrow office. "*I'm* not asking for no extra time."

"Hello, Sharia," Claire said, always a little disconcerted when students who'd been waiting outside the door made it clear they'd heard everything that went on in the previous conference. "How've you been?"

"I seen better." She slumped herself down into a chair that seemed ill-designed to carry her weight. "Shaquilla's been sick this week, and I don't know what's up with Mikal."

"Sorry to hear it. Is there anybody else waiting for me out there?"

"Not so far as I know."

Claire did a quick calculation: could she afford to skip out on her office hours fifteen minutes early? "I don't suppose you'd have any interest in going to get some coffee," she said.

"I could do that," Sharia told her.

"Then let's," Claire said. She stuffed some papers in her briefcase and was ready.

She wondered, as she often did, if this meant she was playing favorites. And what if she were? Men played favorites all the time and no one minded. Nevertheless, she felt guilty about Tim Veeder, the way she'd dismissed him, granting him that extra week on his paper because, frankly, she didn't think it would make any difference.

If there was one student in the class to whom Claire directed her teaching, it was this thirty-five-year-old mother of five who worked six nights a week mopping floors at the hospital and by day managed a full load of classes. Sharia's manner was wary, jaded, fierce. She had the worst teeth Claire had ever seen. But her mind, Claire had managed to discern through the grammatical nightmare of her essays, was bracingly bitter and clear.

What a pair they made as they sat in the bleak student center canteen and sipped bitter coffee from white foam cups, this prim-looking, silver-haired white woman in black, her colorful neck scarf affixed by a silver brooch, and across the table a very large black woman in slightly soiled pink sweatshirt and pants and broken-backed house slippers. No one paid them any particular attention—at four in the afternoon the place was pretty much deserted—and yet Claire felt a surge of defiant pride to be seen sitting with Sharia Washington. But wasn't that racist, always to be thinking, This person is white, this person is black? Not black, she reminded herself; a person of color was what one said these days—though, of course, twenty years ago such a phrase would have invited a punch in the face.

Feminism's rigorous demand, by which she tried to live these days, was this: that she undertake to examine all her unconscious assumptions, painful—and never ending—as that task might be. Growing up, she had known no black people, though they had stood silently at the margins of her everyday awareness, silently performing the little tasks that kept the world humming along. They had been like those household gadgets one took for granted. Was it ever possible to put the ways of one's past entirely behind one, however well intentioned one might be?

"I've got a complaint," Sharia said.

"Yes?" Claire said mildly, both inspired by her student's earnest quest for knowledge and a little fearful of her directness. So far, she felt, she had lived up to the daily challenge Sharia posed; but she also felt, with awful certainty, that the day would come when she would fail her student, simply by turning out to be exactly who she was, a privileged white woman unable fully to surmount the perspectives of her race and class and age.

Sharia rummaged in her book satchel—it was a child's satchel, perhaps one of her daughter's—and brought out a battered copy of *A Room of One's Own*. "This white woman makes me so mad," she said. "The other night, I had to throw her book against the wall."

"Oh dear," Claire said.

"Can I tell you what I hate about this woman?" Sharia went on. Claire knew she was smiling wanly, ready to bear the brunt of whatever was to come.

"First of all, I hate the uppity way she talks." Sharia tried out her best upper-crust British accent. " 'This claret is rah-ther too too disagreeable,' " she mimicked. " 'And the mutton—simply revolting. La-di-da-di-da.' How'm I expected to listen to a woman who talks like this? Girl, get off your high horse and get your hands dirty like the rest of us. She don't know the first thing about working for a living. And you show me a house with a room of your own when you got five kids running around and I'll show you Buckingham Palace. She needs to get her feet on the earth before she can even start talking to folks like me."

Of all the feminists, early and late, it was Virginia Woolf who spoke most fervently to Claire's heart, so she chose her words with care, reluctant to say anything that might offend and yet unwilling to leave her idol undefended.

"One has to," she began, then found herself rephrasing so as not to sound too like Virginia Woolf herself. "You have to make allowances for the particular time and place a writer grew up in. Certainly Woolf has her limitations, but she also had her vision, and we need to try to see what was revolutionary about the vision without getting too distracted by the ways in which she very much remained bound by the limitations of her time."

Sharia looked highly skeptical.

"She's rich, she's white. I don't see what she's got to complain about."

"She's a woman," Claire said. "She never was able to go to university like her brothers because women weren't allowed. She never had a chance at half the education that's available to somebody like you. In fact, she'd probably say, Sharia Washington's getting a college education, which opens up all sorts of doors and possibilities I never had. So what is Sharia Washington complaining about?"

Had she gone too far? Sharia had a sullen look on her face—but then, she usually had a sullen look. Delicately, amiably, Claire tried to backtrack. "All I'm saying is, it's a historical document. You can't expect it to be more than it is. But without the insights of women like Virginia Woolf, we couldn't have gotten where we are today. In a sense, it's part of Woolf's success that we're now able to perceive her shortcomings. Because of the tools she gave us, we're able to go beyond her. *And,* I hope, we're able to look back with critical distance and judge her contributions clearly."

"I don't understand why we can't just take the damn tools and move on," Sharia said. "Why we got to spend so much time looking back and making excuses? It's like earlier, when we were reading about Susan B. Anthony and that other one, what was her name?"

"Elizabeth Cady Stanton," Claire said with a sinking heart. Was Sharia going to repeat her brilliant but disruptive diatribe from last week's class? She'd even managed to cow Tim Veeder that particular evening.

"Yeah, those two uptight old ladies who were all against giving black men the vote after the Civil War 'cause they were worried what it would do to the cause of white women getting the vote. So yeah, I know, you say the argument's the same there too, we have to make allowances. Well, allowances in your book are excuses in mine."

"I wish you weren't so dismissive," Claire said boldly. The last thing she wanted was to alienate Sharia. At the same time, it was condescending not to hold her to the highest intellectual standards. Sharia deserved at least that much from her teacher, but how to convey that? "If I've learned one thing, it's that the unfortunate thing about life is that everything's mixed. There's no absolute good and there's no absolute evil. There's just a lot of confusion. Even Hitler had some good traits. Just as, I don't know—say Abraham Lincoln—had his share of bad traits. The Emancipation Proclamation was as much for political reasons as for moral ones."

"Making excuses," Sharia muttered.

Frustrated, Claire tried one last time. Unlike Louis, she'd never been good at arguments. They wore her out; they upset her. In the early years of her marriage she had watched aghast as Louis and Reid went at it for hours at a stretch, till it seemed they could never be friends again. Yet the next day, there they were, no harm done. "Look at it this way," she said. "The people who owned slaves, back in the nineteenth century, most of them considered themselves decent, upstanding, God-fearing Christians. They honestly didn't think what they were doing was evil. So were they evil? It would be easy to say yes, that owning slaves made them evil. But they didn't go around thinking they were evil. They thought they were doing the right thing."

"But they weren't," Sharia said. "And so they were evil. If I was to kill somebody, even if I thought it was a good thing, it'd still be wrong no matter what I thought."

"And yet we sometimes say that killing is justified. Look at war. The death penalty."

"Owning another human being is never justified, however you look at it."

Claire was not winning this; in fact, she suspected she was only confirming Sharia's absolutist thinking. And perhaps Sharia was right. Perhaps it was due to a sort of moral laxity on her part that Claire had let everything become so clouded.

"Think about it," she said, seizing with desperation on something Tracy had said once in one of his conversations—arguments, rather—with Louis. "A hundred years from now, society may well think that killing and eating other animals is evil. Everybody's seen the light, and they're all vegetarians in the twenty-first century. And they look back on us in the twentieth century and say, How could they not have known that it was wrong to eat meat? How could a whole society have been so evil? But of course we don't go around thinking of ourselves as evil. And yet the future may think we are."

"That's silly," Sharia said. "There's nothing wrong with eating meat. We have to eat meat. It's part of nature. You can't compare eating meat to owning slaves. They're two totally different things."

"We see it that way now," Claire said forlornly, wondering just how fatuous Sharia would find a young man like Tracy who did, when you came down to it, have everything, everything going for him. "But the slave owners thought it was natural to own slaves. So what if we're just as wrong about what we think is natural? What if the future judges us just as harshly as you're saying we should judge the past?"

"Then I guess we'll just have to take our lumps," Sharia said stoically.

"But do you really believe that?"

"I'm too tired to know what I believe," Sharia admitted with a sigh of exasperation. "I'm just registering my protest against Virginia Woolf."

Claire made herself smile. "Protest accepted. But I do hope you'll go on thinking, being engaged by the things we read. And we'll be getting to more modern writers, black women writers, women of color, before too long. Angela Davis, Audre Lorde. Toni Morrison. Women I think you'll like."

"I better," Sharia said suspiciously, "because so far I ain't liked much of anybody."

"You will," Claire said hopefully. "Trust me."

In the greenish light of the empty pool she felt deliciously anonymous. No one ever knew her at this hour, her favorite of the day, that lull between five-thirty and six when, team practices having ended and the boys gone off to dinner, the Forge School's gym was almost completely deserted. Three times a week she came here to swim her thirty minutes of lengths before heading home, pleasantly reinvigorated, and three times a week she marveled that she had missed out on this pleasure for so much of her life. As a girl she'd been too self-conscious about her thin frame and giraffe-like limbs to enjoy the pool's near-nakedness. Only after having reached an age when she no longer particularly cared whether anyone stared at her body, because in fact she had reached the age when no one ever did, had Claire been able to forget herself and find enjoyment in swimming.

At sixty hers was not, she knew, a body she need feel particularly ashamed of, having gardened assiduously for years, and of course for three weeks nearly every summer she and Louis had done their strenuous walking tours of Germany and England. She did not regret having grown old; age quelled so many of the little disturbances one had imagined were simply part of the package.

Water lapped hollowly against the sides of the pool, and in the gym's rafters a pigeon cooed, its call soothing, even enchanting. Was it trapped? Should it be rescued? She wondered if she should alert Louis. From the locker room came the bright voices of boys amplified and echoing like a rougher version of plainchant sung in a cathedral. Pushing off from the side, she swam the crawl, breathing between both right and left strokes as she had recently trained herself to do. Flow, she thought, it was about bodily flow, and indeed, at some point, on her four or fifth traverse of the pool's length, the water seemed to welcome rather than obstruct her passage. After twenty lengths she pulled up, more winded than she might have liked, to see that a young man she had not noticed before stood at the opposite edge of the pool, a figure in black trunks, not a boy but a young man, arms crossed over his chest and looking, perhaps, a bit bewildered—though without her contacts she could not make out clearly the expression on his face. Nevertheless, an odd thing happened. He waved to her.

"Claire," he called out. "Hi." With that, Tracy Parker dove into the water and swam her way with clean, powerful strokes.

It flustered her a little; had he been watching her as she swam? Or had he only recognized her the same instant she had laid eyes on him?

"What a pleasant surprise," he told her, bobbing beside her, water-darkened hair slicked down almost into his eyes, skin glistening with beads of water. He had not yet lost his summer tan. She clung to the side of the pool and felt the full force of his friendly smile. He did not scrutinize her, for which she was thankful, though she found herself casting glances his way: there was something vaguely stirring about being next to this naked flesh. His upper arms were admirably muscled, his chest broad and lightly etched with hair. She felt no ludicrous stab of desire—those days were too distant—but she did feel appreciation, the old fleeting joy of being young.

She was happy for him, happy in his existence here among them at the Forge School.

"Is it always this deserted?" he asked.

"At this time of day, yes. It's a great secret. Isn't it lovely?"

He seemed, however, a bit disappointed. "Don't you get spooked?" he wondered.

That had never occurred to her. Though perhaps it *was* odd to relish as she did her time alone in this expanse of water so uninflected with anxiety that it could almost seem, as she swam, a loving extension of herself.

"Well, there's certainly no danger of colliding with anyone," she told him humorously.

"Oh," he said, perhaps also humorously, "I don't mind the odd collision now and then. But don't let me interrupt. You were doing laps."

"A few," she said.

"I'll swim with you if you don't mind the company."

"I'd be delighted," she told him.

She took it slowly and deliberately, feeling not the least bit self-conscious—put, in fact, entirely at ease by his presence beside her, and though clearly Tracy could have pulled effortlessly ahead had he wanted, instead he seemed to prefer being companionable to burning off calories. She thought of dolphins running alongside ships at sea, at once serious and playful; she thought of Louis traipsing loyally beside her on those long, peaceful rambles through the Black Forest, the low hills of Swabia, the Thuringian highlands. If Louis's possessiveness toward their new friend sometimes irked and even—dared she admit this?—hurt her, she now felt content. She would have her own friendship with Tracy, on her own terms. Let Louis ply him with opera and scotch late into the night; at the moment she thought she much preferred the frank communion of a swim with the young man. And perhaps this would be their mode with one another. She allowed herself to imagine, as they moved silently together through the unimpeding element, some brisk fall afternoon when they might drive out to Jack Emmerich's old farmstead, still held by his sister, and take the steep path to Indian Rock, where a vista of the Neversink Reservoir and the hazy blue range of the Catskills beyond waited to reward the winded climber.

They had done ten lengths together, which made, for her, thirty in all. The blood coursed pulsingly in her veins; her strong heart was feeling grateful. Yoked to her cumbersome pace, was Tracy getting impatient? Louis, she knew, would have covered twice as many alpine miles in her summers had he not had her in tow, though he, like Tracy now, had slowed his pace to accommodate her. In any event, her exercise time was up; Louis was no doubt lying on the sofa, listening to *All Things Considered* and, if the day had been particularly trying, as most days seemed to be, seeking refuge in a scotch.

Remembering that they had concert tickets for later—though there was plenty of time; she had only to reheat the quiche she'd thrown together this morning, before heading over to school—she told Tracy, "That's all for me. Louis will be wanting his dinner soon. Then we have to make an eight-thirty concert in Poughkeepsie. It was very nice to see you."

"An unexpected pleasure," he said, seeming nonetheless mildly distracted.

"This is my regular time to swim," she mentioned hopefully. "Maybe we'll run into each other again."

"I hope we do," he said, his gaze fixed in the direction of the door. She looked that way, but could see nothing other than two boys wearing the bright red Speedos of the Forge School swim team. Presumably it had been their voices, boisterous yet oddly musical, she had heard from the locker room. Was there a home meet later tonight? she wondered. Uninterested as he was in sports, Louis usually made a point of attending home games whenever possible. Which had he forgotten, the swim meet or the concert? She worried, lately, that he paid less attention to things than he used to, retreating more and more frequently into the consolations of his music.

The boys' voices, unpleasantly loud and boastful, more like crows than pigeons, disrupted the gym's calm, and she could not but feel unkindly intruded upon. Tracy, however, seemed to study them with curiosity, as if they were some strange species foreign to these parts. And indeed, she had often remarked to herself, adolescent boys often seemed foreign, not only to others but to themselves as well, betrayed into these new, ill-fitting bodies they could hardly recognize as their own. Like colts they gamboled about, eager but graceless. She felt sorry for them; the only thing good about the awkward age was that one mercifully grew out of it soon enough.

As she climbed from the water, a little reluctant to leave its shield, Tracy made no movement to follow, nor had she expected him to. "I think I'll stay in here a bit longer," he told her. "Say hi to Louis for me. And enjoy your concert."

It occurred to her that he might enjoy accompanying them at some point in the future. Perhaps they could treat him one of these days.

"Is there a meet tonight?" she asked him casually, nodding toward the boys.

Tracy looked at her blankly. "I don't know," he said. "Why?"

"I was just wondering," she told him.

As she passed the two boys who stood bantering with each other, all long-limbed, hectic flesh and very nearly obscene in those microscopic Speedos of theirs, it was as if she were completely invisible; they did not look her way at all. No matter; neither did they interest her in the least. But as she glanced back, on an impulse, toward the pool, she could see that Tracy was staring at the two swimmers with an intentness that might almost, at first glance, and absurdly, be mistaken for longing.

. . .

Valiantly, as if a symphony were a house one had to build from the ground up, the orchestra sawed and hammered its way through Brahms, the task proving, despite the handsome young conductor's heroic attempts at encouragement, just beyond the grasp if not the reach of the Mid-Hudson Philharmonic. The music making that resulted was both exhilarating and sad to hear in the ornate, half-empty hall of the Bardavon Opera House in downtown Poughkeepsie, and Claire reminded herself, not for the first time during the evening's all-German program, how important it was to support the local arts.

Of course there was the Metropolitan Opera, and the New York Philharmonic, and the many world-class orchestras to be heard at Carnegie Hall, and of course she would not miss those occasions for anything. Nevertheless, Claire could not shake the notion that her own life, in its way, curiously resembled the Mid-Hudson Philharmonic's plight. Like those provincial opera companies in places like Ulm and Freiburg and Nuremberg whose passionate, rough-edged, colorful productions she and Louis used to arrange their walking excursions around, the musicians laboring ardently before her on stage tonight had all her sympathies, for like them she could glimpse the highest peaks glittering in sunlight, and like them she herself struggled somewhere creditably in the ranks of the second-best. As she had learned at Barnard, then relearned years later in SUNY Albany's graduate program, others would always, and effortlessly, surpass her. Never had she suffered from the illusion that things would be anything but challenging for her. Perhaps that was the difference between herself and Louis, whose rigid posture in the seat next to her signaled his mortification at the butchering some of his favorite music was subject to this evening. At Cornell, both as an undergraduate and as a graduate student, he had been brilliant—everyone had said so. The possibility had never occurred to anyone, and certainly, she suspected, not to Louis, that he might fail to achieve great success and recognition in the hallowed halls of academia. He would be a great authority, a world-renowned scholar pronouncing solemnly and profoundly on the accomplishments of Schiller and Goethe, Stefan George and Thomas Mann.

And it had all come to nothing. Taken as a whole, of course, Louis's life was hardly a failure. The Forge School was a noble enterprise, after all, and he had certainly acquitted himself admirably for the last fifteen years as its headmaster, had kept the school going in difficult times, had even seen it prosper. Nonetheless, Claire knew he felt himself a failure, his dissertation wrecked on the shoals of his own perfectionism, his whole life shadowed by that foundering. She often had to wonder what might have been, as he himself apparently wondered as well, sitting for hours alone in his study, even now, thirty years after the eclipse of his hopes, with his beloved volumes of Mann, his black notebook in which, from time to time—at least this is what she surmised—he jotted various inspired nocturnal observations that would never coalesce into a manuscript capable of withstanding the bleaker scrutiny of daylight.

The symphony had reached its difficult finale: for a moment she caught the orchestra stumble, teeter precariously on the brink. Beside her, Louis flinched in palpable discomfort. If he judged others harshly, she reminded herself, it was because he judged himself most harshly of all. And miraculously, as if her husband had borne the brunt of their disappointment for them, the musicians recovered. The brass blazed brilliantly if raggedly. The strings swam upward in a stirring rush of noise. Like a charioteer trying to rein in his runaway steeds, the conductor flailed about excitedly, though it was clear the galloping orchestra, and not he, was in charge. It didn't matter; scrappy with exhilaration, orchestra and conductor crossed the finish line more or less together. Beside her, she could tell, Louis was judging all this abysmal, even shameful—Louis who could not put a word to paper though he had tried. Who had even sacrificed their latest summer to the attempt.

And yet, when the applause began, hearty and sustained, Louis applauded as well. "Bravo," he said quietly, so that only she could hear. The conductor, who had ducked out as soon as the final chord had ceased, returned, his arms open wide, gesturing gratefully to the orchestra that had almost fumbled and then so stupendously recovered. The hall was delirious, though whether the congratulations were for the orchestra, the conductor, or for themselves for having so bravely submitted for the last two hours to the onslaughts of culture, was difficult to say. And what would Sharia Washington think, seeing her teacher likewise worshipfully applaud the music of these dead white males? Could it be that something so simple yet unalterable as her love of Brahms would sadly mark the limits of whatever friendship might be possible between the likes of Claire Tremper and Sharia Washington? If she could imagine, with pleasure, Tracy Parker's face lit by this music, she held out no similar hope for Sharia. And perhaps her embattled student of color was right—perhaps it *was* shameful, in a world where people fought and starved and died appalling deaths in appalling numbers, to spend fifty dollars to listen to a hundred-year-old exercise in high-bourgeois entertainment.

The applause had died down. Always there was this moment of confusion, even disappointment: what to do next? Mechanically Claire rose—saying to herself that Brahms was not Wagner, that Brahms, German to the core though he might be, could scarcely be accused of helping to make possible the twentieth century's carnage—and gathered up her jacket as the lights went up and everyone else (there was not a black face to be seen among them) began to file from their seats.

"I must say, I thoroughly enjoyed that," Louis told her as they emerged into the lobby.

"I'm surprised," she told him. "I thought they played rather badly." Then, remembering his soft-spoken "Bravo" as he applauded, and realizing how tart her appraisal had sounded, she added hastily, "Though they certainly showed spirit."

"They certainly did," Louis agreed. "More than enough to go around, really. Not exactly Herbert von Karajan and the Berlin Philharmonic, but in the end they won me over. Brahms was partial to small orchestras like this, you know. Especially the one at Meiningen, where Hans von Bülow conducted. Less than fifty players, only ten or so first violins. So we may be hearing, in a concert like this one, something of what the composer originally intended. In fact, when von Bülow premiered the Fourth, Brahms rejected his suggestion that they augment the strings. He didn't want a Vienna Philharmonic sound. He knew perfectly well what he was after."

As Louis dutifully recited what he had no doubt cribbed from *Grove's Musical Dictionary* earlier in the day—he loved preparing himself for a concert, and for the opportunity to educate his wife afterward—Claire half listened contentedly; she could tell that her husband, who took her arm as they left the Bardavon and headed toward the parking garage, felt a happiness that all too rarely descended on him—though whether he expostulated on Brahms and the little orchestra at Meiningen because he was happy, or was happy because he had the opportunity to expostulate, she could not say. She felt a sudden swell of gratitude toward Tracy Parker, who listened so patiently to Louis's enthusiasms, and whose attentions had allowed her husband, she felt, an extended spell of happiness in the weeks they had known him. She had not seen the need to report her own altogether pleasant poolside encounter with the young man, for wasn't it precisely these little omissions that had made life possible between Louis and herself? Despite their deeply ingrained habits with each other, they still found it in themselves to be, on occasion, genuinely surprising to each other. She who had been so certain Louis was in misery, listening to all that hectic playing: now *she* was the one who voiced reservations about the music making while he practically sang, he was in such agreeable spirits. And so they went with each other, back and forth, and at the best of times, as she saw it, their relationship assumed the character of a deft, thoughtful, courtly dance whose pleasures, over time, had not been at all insubstantial.

Driving at night, the tantalizing lure of freedom: she loved that. She and Louis had never traveled in the United States, which was not to say that they had not paid visits to their daughters, wherever fate or choice had taken them over the years, Arizona, Missouri, California, and now that Susan and family had moved to Alaska they were no doubt destined to see that state as well. But they had never roamed their own country the way they roamed the back roads and walking paths of Germany and Austria and Switzerland, leisurely and aimless voyages of discovery that had formed, through the years, an archipelago of happy memories—a wandering life altogether apart from their sedentary existence in Middle Forge, disconnected from it the way dreams are from waking existence, an intermittent life that perhaps made its more continuous counterpart possible. On a clear night like this, behind the wheel of the Audi, Claire felt that, just once in her life, she'd like to head west on the open road. Not the busy interstates but the old forsaken highways. The romance of all those world-lost little towns, the great dusty middle states, the high shelf of mountains, the sunset bath of the Pacific.

It had been years since her husband had gotten behind the wheel of a car. He'd been quite an inattentive driver in his day, and so it was perhaps not a bad thing that he had seen fit, not long after he became headmaster, to take himself off the road voluntarily.

She did not mind. Her only demand had been a modest one: if she was to do the driving, she insisted that they invest in an automobile of quality, and though she knew how much Louis had hated to spend the money, he had nonetheless obliged.

Strange to contemplate how any single moment might begin a new life, for had she never taken over the driving she might never have acquired the sense of independence and capability that had led her back to school, first in an evening class at the community college called, appropriately enough, Auto Maintenance for Women, then a master's and Ph.D. program at the state university and thence, in a not unpleasing circle, back to the community college to which, in her way, she would be forever grateful.

South of Poughkeepsie, much of Route 9 was a depressing gauntlet of fast-food restaurants and strip malls, but after Fishkill the clutter thinned, and for the last couple of miles before coming into Middle Forge the road led through a lonely stretch, one of the last open sweeps of farmland not yet ruined by development.

A pale half moon hung in the sky; some stars were out. The Audi hummed along smoothly, powerfully. They had the road to themselves.

"I'm trying to remember," Louis said, "the name of that conductor we heard do the Brahms Second in Stuttgart. Do you remember? It must have been in the mid-seventies. I believe he was Romanian. I can't for the life of me remember. It was quite an extraordinary performance."

"He had an unpronounceable name," Claire told him. "That's why you can't remember. But yes, I remember that performance very well."

But what did it mean to remember a performance? She could really remember nothing, twenty years later, except the impression that it had been remarkable. Exactly why it had been so, she could not begin to say. For a moment she was on the verge of posing that question to Louis, but then she did not, since she had learned that such speculative topics were best left alone between them. She could only conclude that he'd always been a bit of a sexist that way. He and Reid could joust for hours and no doubt such speculative talk was a great deal of the pleasure that accrued when he and Tracy Parker spent their musical evenings together, but between herself and Louis such abstract arguments invariably seemed to turn personal.

The lights of an approaching car dazzled her from her reverie. Reflexively she clicked off the Audi's high beams just as the other car dimmed its own, and in that instant, as if from nowhere, a large white form suddenly appeared directly in front of the car. "Oh," Louis said as she drove her foot hard into the brake pedal. The tires shrieked their protest, the car shimmied, stalled out, and abruptly came to a dead stop. What struck her in the moment after was the utter stillness, as if everything held its breath and then, in the next moment, let out a great sigh of relief.

"What was that?" Louis said.

"I have no idea," she told him. "I don't think we hit it, whatever it was."

"No," he said. "We didn't hit it. But I wonder if that other car did."

On the other side of the road, nearly across from them, the oncoming car, one of those bullying sports utility vehicles that she loathed, had skidded off the road and into the shallow ditch alongside. A man emerged. Claire lowered her window. "Are you all right over there?" she called to him. "I'm going to pull off onto the shoulder so we don't get rear-ended." She restarted the engine and steered the Audi out of the path of traffic.

"Did you see that?" the man asked. He leaned in through the window, a good-looking man in his mid-thirties wearing a Penn State sweatshirt.

"It looked like a dog," Louis said. "Only it was rather too large."

"It sure wasn't any deer," the man told them. "It looked like a horse. That's how big it was. A small horse."

Claire was sure it had had fur and a snout, whatever it was. The moonlight on its coat had gleamed silver.

"It looked white to me," she ventured. "A large white wolflike animal." She doubted it had been anywhere near as large as a small horse—though Louis was right: it was really too big to be an ordinary dog. She had had the impression of speed and purposefulness, as if, in its magnificent and harrowing passage, it had scarcely noticed them.

"Is your car stuck?" Louis asked, leaning across her to address their fellow driver. "Do you need help?"

"I think she's fine," said the man. "We were all just lucky there."

"Well, drive carefully," Claire told him.

"Same to you," the man said.

Her surge of adrenaline was subsiding; she felt more spooked than any-thing else. It had been very close; whatever the creature, they had very nearly hit it. She eased the Audi back onto the road, but could not so easily ease herself back into a sense of complacency as her eyes scanned the dark un-folding fields for the moment that was always poised, when you least ex-pected it, to be upon you.

VII

Fishing in his pocket for change, the boy brought up a handful of coins, which he counted out, one at a time, from his open palm onto the counter where he'd tossed a pack of gum. Entranced, Tracy stood too close behind and scrutinized, recklessly, the blond down feathering the back of a slender neck, the uneven shag of a hairline. When the boy turned his head slightly to the side, Tracy caught the heart-stopping beauty of his profile. Or perhaps not quite beautiful, his nose a bit too large, eyes too sleepy, but nonetheless radiating a secret magnetism, an irresistible force. At fourteen or fifteen, unconscious grace suffused some boys' every awkward move. This one, neither the most miraculous nor the least, wore a loose-fitting mustard-colored shirt, tails out, sleeves rolled to the elbow, baggy maroon jeans, a leather thong around his neck from which dangled—Tracy shifted his stance in order to observe more closely—a small stone arrowhead. He was no Forge student but rather a townie, and Tracy felt overtaken by a delicious, involuntary spasm of lust he did not attempt to quell. He was allowed this, wasn't he? In the last couple of months he had learned, around boys he knew, such scrupulous circumspection; now, in the presence of this stranger whose path his was free to cross, he defiantly welcomed lust's troubling, exhilarating intensity.

What to do with beauty like that, all the energy and perplexity that was adolescence? Where did he live, this boy? Who were his friends? What did he think about? More than anything, Tracy told himself, all he wanted was the impossible—to strike up a friendship, discover some common ground. To speak a language that was as intimate and free as certain dreams, saying darkly, thrillingly, My cock inside of you. Your come in my mouth. Already in that dream he was easing his new friend out of those hip, baggy jeans, exposing smooth young flesh to the surprise of cool air. He focused on the boy's slim, tight hips; with the tip of his tongue he tasted an asshole's bitter, forbidden mystery.

His gum paid for, pocketed, the boy turned abruptly to leave, and Tracy took a sudden backward step out of his way. For an instant their eyes met, but it was nothing. The boy hardly registered him at all.

Regretting his reflexes—how pleasurably their bodies might have collided—Tracy hefted his plastic bottle of seltzer onto the counter and pulled out his wallet. "No," he impatiently told the woman behind the counter as she fumbled to extricate a plastic bag from its companions in the pile on the counter, "I don't need one." If he hurried, he might still catch a final, visionary glimpse in the parking lot.

"I'm sorry, sir," she said. "I have to put that in a bag for you. Store policy." With maddening persistence, the thin, static-charged sheets of plastic clung to one another and would not let go.

He gave up and let her have her way. If only she knew how, like those Siberian miners who, in order to recharge certain vital elements in their sun-starved bodies, periodically bask in treatments of ultraviolet light, he had been infused with a life-giving force. Touched, as it were, by lightning.

When he emerged from the convenience store the boy was nowhere to be seen. The bicycle left crumpled on the sidewalk, which he had observed on entering, likewise was gone. But that was fine. He recalled the precious image to mind, testing its mettle, reassuring himself he'd succeeded in saving the boy up in order to expend him later, at his leisure, while soaping himself in the shower or lying in a drowse on his futon.

At twenty-five Tracy's mind was already a honeycomb of sweetly preserved images, icons of longing to be brought out and celebrated like those saints who had saved cities from plague or conquest: that ambiguous kid he'd encountered on the path at William and Mary, a blond adolescent who used to kick a soccer ball in the street below his room in Freiburg, the dark-haired stunner in the Stuttgart train station he'd followed into the men's room and casually positioned himself next to at the long porcelain urinal trough, watching with racing pulse that uncircumcised young cock empty itself of a fierce golden stream, holy moments he had tended faithfully through the years.

When he got home, the light on his answering machine was flashing. As always these days, whenever he saw he had messages an inexplicable panic seized him. Had someone died? Had he been fired? Had they finally tracked him down?

He frequently had to remind himself that he had done nothing wrong. He had never done anything wrong.

"Do you know who's the meanest drag queen in town?" Arthur chirped. There was a long pause. Unidentifiable music, perhaps opera, played in the background. "Amanda Reckonwith. Get it? You should give me a call as soon as you get the chance, otherwise I'm going to have to march up there and slap you silly. Seriously—I want to tell you about my latest step in regaining control of my body."

What did Arthur mean? For an instant, hope flashed, then faded. It was his third and most pointed message this week, but Tracy found himself unable to return the call. He despised his panic, but let it master him nonetheless. As long as he didn't talk to Arthur, he could pretend the diagnosis had been a mistake, a hallucination—even some ghastly prank his friend had decided to play on him. The alternative was impossible to come to terms with, though he'd certainly tried. He'd made himself face the facts, and the facts made him very desperate. If Arthur really was dying, then the odds were that he, Tracy Parker, who had shared bodily fluids, as the literature so dispassionately phrased it, was following only a few steps behind. Too astonishing for words, and yet, inside his body, he could detect from time to time—what? A whisper or a shadow he couldn't put his finger on, but that stalked him nonetheless, unnerving in its occasional decision to manifest itself when least expected. Just the other night he had dreamed he stood in his living room. Every step he took sent ripples undulating across a floor suddenly spongy with rot. Water oozed between the boards; through gaps he could make out, underneath the whole house, a horrible abyss of foul black water into which it seemed he might sink at any moment. In his dream, that fetid swamp had been there all along, but he hadn't known, or he'd known but chosen to ignore it, and he felt both dread and a disquieting sense of recognition, as if it were his body and not his mind that had chosen to dream this dream.

If there was anybody to talk to about this, then it should be Arthur. Tracy felt, all over again, a stark, unassuagable fear. Perhaps later he would call. Perhaps tomorrow.

"Betsy," he said, surprised at the inadvertent note of urgency in his voice. Ever alert, she bounded toward him with all the hope in the world, and he thought that, if he could, he would change places with her in an instant. "Come on, girl," he commanded, "let's you and me go out for a walk."

The day was warm and lovely, the campus's maples ecstatic with color. Like their human counterparts, certain unruly trees seemed on the verge of bursting into flame, they were so vivid, while others clung stubbornly to the green of summer. And which was he? On the lake, under a pale blue sky thin enough to crack open with a light tap, muscular Canada geese rested from their southward flight. His walk carried him, without his quite realizing it, in the direction of Louis and Claire's house, and he stood on the sidewalk before it, gazing with something like envy at its reassuring solidity, the secure and respectable lives flourishing behind that sturdy facade of white-shingled siding and dark green shutters. Behind a low hedge of yew, Claire's front garden sang its swan song. A few last, straggling rose blossoms, some dark-hued chrysanthemums. Nothing was sadder than a flower garden in autumn, he thought, remembering the unchanging austerity of those Japanese compositions of conifer and stone he had visited in what seemed like another life. Those gardens, perhaps, had avoided heartbreak.

Someday he'd like a garden of his own. Perhaps it wasn't too late to stick a few daffodil bulbs in among the overgrown shrubs that surrounded his house, though beyond that he'd feel too shy about tampering with the yard's neglected state. He was living there only for a year, after all, given ample notice that, were he to remain at the Forge a second year, he'd almost surely be assigned an apartment in one of the dorms as residential adviser. All that was something he'd have to think about, though Louis talked as if it were a foregone conclusion. He had come to sense, from time to time, the barest hint of certain expectations beginning to hem him in.

The toot of a car horn startled him from his contemplation. Smiling, Claire waved his way as she maneuvered the Audi into the driveway.

"Hey," he told her as she emerged from the sleek gray machine whose trunk, simultaneously, popped open. She was surprisingly well dressed for what appeared to be an ordinary Saturday afternoon shopping trip. "Betsy and I were just admiring your garden."

"I'm afraid there's not much to admire," she told him. "It's rather the end of it."

"No," he said. "It's very pretty this time of year. Can I help you with those?" He pointed to the bags of groceries in the trunk. "Here, I'll carry. You take Betsy's leash."

"That's very kind of you," she told him as they made their way into the house. Music filled the rooms. "Louis is undoubtedly around here somewhere. He never misses the Metropolitan Opera broadcasts. Louis," she said loudly. "Look who dropped by."

The music lowered, and Louis appeared in the doorway, looking slightly discombobulated, a strange fish hoisted up from some great, densely pressured depth.

"I was just passing by, really. Betsy and I were out for a stroll. I got tired of grading papers," he added, though that was not strictly true. So far he'd spent his day avoiding them with considerable success.

"Always a pleasure to see you," Louis said in his courtliest vein. And he did seem genuinely pleased.

"Don't let me take you away from your music."

"Perfectly all right," Louis assured him. "I wasn't caring for it much anyway. *The Queen of Spades.*"

Tracy had gotten so used to the older man's sharing music with him, offering it on a platter, as it were, artfully arranged and presented, that he was a bit disconcerted to realize that there were other musics Louis might, for whatever reasons, choose not to share with him. He regretted that the radio had been turned down so low that *The Queen of Spades* was, for all practical purposes, inaudible. The regret even surprised him. But he was relieved to detect no residual awkwardness between them. During their last evening together, after an hour of listening to Schumann, their talk had wandered far afield, into a murky realm where, increasingly, Tracy had had the sense that he no longer quite knew what was being talked about, either by himself or his host, as if at some point their words had begun to veil rather than reveal their thoughts.

He had felt suddenly depressed, on the verge of simply announcing to Louis, "There's something about me you really should know." But he had said nothing, and Louis, who had also, it seemed, been on the verge of saying something—though what he might have been about to utter was certainly beyond Tracy's guess—likewise deferred. Nevertheless, this moment they had arrived at, each from his own trajectory undoubtedly very different from the other's, seemed to offer, Tracy felt very strongly, at least the possibility of their moving onto an altogether different footing with one another.

They had not taken that step, sitting instead in silence until Louis averred that he was very fatigued, there was nothing quite like Schumann to fray one's nerves, and Claire would soon be returning home from her class. Some sense of delicacy on Louis's part ordained that their sessions be finished before Claire arrived. Tracy had walked home through the chill night air feeling vaguely frustrated, trapped, dissatisfied with himself. He should have told Louis this simple fact about himself before, and now, suddenly, it was too late; at some point their acquaintance had shaded over into something more confidential, something like friendship. It was now a thing that could be betrayed. And though there had been no discernible moment when it had ceased to be one thing and become another, nevertheless what had been left unsaid in the transition must somehow now remain unsaid—or at least could not be said without consequences graver or more unpredictable than Tracy was prepared to face.

Escaping his New York entanglements for the solitude of the Forge, he had not at all intended something like this to happen.

"Are you thirsty?" Louis asked. "Did Claire offer you anything?" Betsy was eagerly sniffing at Lux, who had hardly stirred from his pillow in the corner. She stuck her feet out, curved her spine submissively, and let out a bark more craven than friendly.

"Betsy," Tracy warned. The life of dogs, even when it happened in full view, was essentially mysterious.

"It's still a bit early for a cocktail," Claire reminded her husband.

"I can't stay," Tracy apologized. "But maybe Betsy would like some water."

As Claire turned on the tap, an arc of water, like the proverbial leak in the dyke, jetted from the side of the nozzle and splattered the rim of the sink.

"I was going to fix that, wasn't I?" Tracy told her as she set the brimming bowl in front of Betsy, who, her disappointment at Lux's indifference seemingly forgotten, lapped greedily. "Did you ever get a chance to buy those washers?"

"Only where did I put them?" she wondered. At a loss, two fingers tapping her chin, she looked around the kitchen, then plucked a small paper bag from atop the refrigerator.

"Excellent," Tracy told her. "Looks like we're in business. Now let me get under here and shut the water off."

Taking apart the faucet—"See how these washers are totally shot?"—he felt Louis study him, his habitual pose of detachment failing to mask both his helplessness at such tasks and his grudging admiration for such a handy young man. Because that was what Louis saw, Tracy felt sure. Not someone who dreamed of boys and their assholes but a fellow who was well versed in carpentry, who taught school, who could fix leaky faucets. It was too depressing.

"There," he said. He reached under the sink and twisted the valve, then turned the faucet on and off. Water came just as it was meant to. He drank bottled water himself, never from the tap, having read that Middle Forge's municipal supply, drawn from the Hudson, was contaminated with PCBs. Though it struck him as funny: here he was, almost certain to die young, and he worried about the possibility of cancer twenty-five years down the line.

"Sweet," he said, a term any red-blooded American carpenter might use. Louis could barely restrain his praise. It was as if Tracy had saved the two of them from starvation or worse. "Good job," he murmured. "Fine work."

"How can we thank you?" Claire asked him.

"Really, it's nothing," he said, all at once aware that there might be something faintly patronizing in their gratitude. Nevertheless they were, he remarked to himself, in fact now in his debt.

Abruptly Claire left the room, only to return in an instant. "Here," she said with that trace of brusqueness with which she sometimes disguised her more generous impulses. "I've far more bulbs than I know what to do with. I always order too many, and by the time fall comes I never have the time to put them all in."

"Or the space," Louis added.

"He criticizes the profusion of my garden," Claire said. "His own tastes are more formal. Sometimes I think he'd prefer one of those Japanese gardens. You know, stones and raked sand. One or two neatly clipped shrubs."

"No, no," Louis said. "You've a very nice garden. I never criticize it."

"But you did just now."

"That's not true," he said. Then, turning to Tracy, he continued: "Claire resents it that I hardly lift a finger to help. I tell her that's all just as well. I have a black thumb. I'd leave my mark everywhere."

"Ridiculous," Claire told her husband, though Tracy thought it possible she might actually feel wounded. Why did he spend his time with these bickering heterosexuals in the misery of their little marriage? Deep down, where the darkest truths tend to congregate, he despised heterosexuals. At least that was his occasional, skittish suspicion.

"Now take these," Claire said briskly, pressing the bag of bulbs into his hands while he thought, fiercely, I've got to get myself a boyfriend. "Narcissus 'Haweri,' a nice bright yellow. Rather small. They'd look lovely under the shrubs in front of your porch."

But he would never have a boyfriend. He would instead sicken and die. And what if he didn't carry the disease? What if a simple test could lift this dark cloud?

If I have it, he told himself, I don't want to know. And besides, I'm sure I do have it. So what good would knowing do?

"Any special instructions?" he asked, gratefully accepting those knobby, misshapen nodes from which, in six months, improbable life would spring forth.

"Daffodils," Claire told him, "are very nearly infallible."

It was thus with a resolute sense of hope mingled with the sadness underlying everything for him these days that he knelt in the warm, late afternoon sun and, using a screwdriver from his toolbox instead of the trowel that was ideally called for, scooped a series of holes in the sweet-smelling earth beneath the rhododendrons. One by one he nestled his bulbs in snugly for their winter's sleep, then filled in the dirt that Betsy, ever willing to play a new game, occasionally tried to paw away.

"Don't you go digging these up," he admonished her. She looked at him with dark, unfathomable eyes—was it ridiculous to see intelligence there?—then interrogatively pawed the ground once more. "No," he said firmly, but something had caught her attention. Without warning she started from him and dashed toward the street. He glanced up to see Noah cutting across the lawn. Boy and dog caught one another up in a tableau so perfect it might have been choreographed. At least somebody was in love, Tracy thought.

"Looking for buried treasure?" Noah asked him. Betsy had left dirty paw-marks on the thighs of his faded jeans.

"Sorry about that," Tracy said.

"Who cares?" Noah told him. "Tell me you're not, um, planting flowers."

"Well, actually . . ." He grinned, looking up at this boy who might well be some kind of buried treasure himself. "Does this mean I've lost all your respect?"

"Oh, that happened a long time ago," Noah said lightly—a little too lightly, Tracy thought. Did kids have any idea how easily their words could wound? But perhaps it was true, what he said. Perhaps that was exactly what allowed them to joke with each other like this, playfully, without harm.

"I didn't think you were around this weekend," Tracy said. "Weren't you going to the city?"

"Just didn't happen." Heaving from his shoulder the knapsack in which he carried his schoolbooks, Noah sat down on the steps to the porch. He wore no socks. His ankles were bony but beautiful, like his wrists, his jaw.

"This place is so deserted on the weekends," Noah observed, rubbing sleep from those eyes of his that seemed perpetually sleepy.

"Some of us like it that way," Tracy told him, though he wondered just how true that might be. What, on the other hand, was undeniably true was the sense of calm that all at once settled over him. Just sit by me like this, he thought, his bulb planting done, his gesture of hope. Just keep me company.

And as if reading his thoughts, Noah said, "You don't mind if I hang out, do you? I brought some books to study."

That was the altogether pleasurable rhythm they had fallen into. Noah would skip out on the cafeteria two or three nights a week and stop by for dinner, conversation, perhaps a bit of quiet study while Tracy did his own work. Technically, Tracy supposed, it didn't break any rules, and so he hadn't particularly discouraged the practice, his only stipulation being that Noah should arrive and depart as discreetly as possible lest any of the other boys— or anyone else, for that matter—think he was somehow playing favorites. Besides, he was selfishly pleased with the arrangement. If the healthy meals he served, a far cry from those overcooked dishes he'd had the misfortune to sample once or twice in the cafeteria, offered Noah a certain kind of nourishment, the exchange was by no means one-sided.

"I don't mind at all. Why not stay for dinner?" he urged. "The only thing I have to do is get some papers graded."

"My paper?"

"Well, a whole bunch of papers. It'll take me an hour, an hour and a half."

"Then I'll just sit in the living room and read," Noah said. "You won't even hardly know I'm there. Maybe I'll take the Bets out for a spin."

"The Bets," Tracy tested as he led the way indoors. "I'm sure it'll grow on me."

Although his impulse was always to cut straight to Noah's essay before reading anyone else's, as if it alone were much-awaited news from the front, Tracy always resisted, saving his favorite's as a reward for having worked through the rest of the stack. He'd asked them this week to be creative, to write about a relationship between two very different people, an assignment he thought of as a bridge between the book they'd just finished, *The Adventures of Huckleberry Finn*, and *A Separate Peace*, which they were about to start. After two hours of reading good and not-so-good attempts at fulfilling the assignment, he could at last treat himself to the reward he'd stashed away.

Joe & Me
by Noah Lathrop III

Every day when Grandma went out to pick apples Joe & Jelly stayed in they're bed at the top of the house. It was cold and rainey out & they didn't want to get up so they stayed under the covers & they could listen to the rain on the roof which they liked. Joe & Jelly were exactly alike. If you looked at them you couldn't tell who was who, it was like looking into a mirrer. Their teachers got them confused & even their Grandma got mixed up sometimes (actually, lots of the time). They had many adventiures including the time they explored the cave. They liked exploring, only they liked sleeping under the covers where it was warm even better.

Hey Joe, Jelly said.
Yea, Jelly told him.
Are you sleepy?
Yea.
Then let's sleep some more.
So they snuggled down in the bed. Grandma was still picking apples outside, like she always did. In the rain, because it rained all the time there.

Joe & Jelly's dream

Their in this rowboat out on a lake & it was still raining, so the rowboat is filling up with water & their practically swimming with the fishes.

Hey Jelly, there's this island.
Yea. Let's go over to it.
So they went to the island, but what they don't know is, it isn't a real island, it was only in there dream.

Let's build a fire, Joe said.

Yea.

So they did, only it wasn't a real fire, it was only in their dream too. But that was okay, it was still a worm fire, only not warm enough, so they kept getting closer & closer to it til finally they were so close there skin caught fire, & even though it was just a dream they were all burning up, their arms & legs & bellies & even the hair on theyre head & just when there trying to put each other out they wake up.

We go in the bassement

They didn't even know there was a bassement till one day they saw this door and wondered, Where does that go? They thought maybe they weren't supposed to, but they went down their anyway, and what they saw in the dark was Bones piled up to the cieling. Human Bones.

This is kind of wierd, Jelly said picking up a Bone that had been picked clean.

Hey Jelly, I have something that might surprize you, Joe said.

Yea?

I'm really your Father, see. When your asleep I come down here & play with my collection of Bones. See, these are very valluble Bones, but I can't tell you why just yet. But one day you will know.

At the sound of Joe's deep voice Jelly was really scared. He hoped it was a dream but he penched himself & nothing happened. Oh no, were his last words.

I told you so

Joe went walking down the street eating an apple. I saw him coming but I didn't think anything of it. I saw him all the time.

Hey, he said. Don't I know you. I think we have the same hands, same legs, same eyes, same hair.

Oh no, I said penching myself.

The End

Could this be how a Picasso or Rimbaud had first expressed himself—genius bursting forth like a colt, all long-legged and clumsy? Tracy never knew what to make of Noah. But what he did know was that this frisky imagination arrested him, excited him, made him dream. *Excellent!* he wrote. *Your imagination is compelling and mysterious.* But somehow that did not seem entirely right. The piece was a mess, all misspellings and sloppiness. But wouldn't Rimbaud have been trashed by his cautious teachers? Wouldn't Picasso have provoked worried frowns?

Yes, go ahead, Tracy thought. Be crazy, be divine or daemonic, as the case might be. The thought was arousing—literally so—and as he registered his reaction he felt a squeamish sense of blasphemy, aware as he was how Noah sat in the next room and unsuspectingly read, or struggled through, his homework assignment.

Of course, Noah was no Rimbaud or Picasso by any stretch of the imagination, and the depressing suspicion overtook Tracy: that a less interested mind than his would see in his favorite student's feverish scribbling only the evidence of arrested emotional development of the type so easily diagnosable by a competent therapist, Dr. Maurer, for instance, the Forge's resident shrink whom Noah despised so bitterly, and perhaps with good reason.

I hope you've been seeing your writing tutor regularly, Tracy wrote. *This piece is marred by numerous sloppy errors.* He paused before the grade, considering A-plus for a desperate instant, then writing a perhaps too-generous B-minus. Putting away the finished stack of papers, he stretched and went to find his young genius.

Noah was in the kitchen. Tracy stood unnoticed in the doorway and watched with curiosity how, sitting at the table, one leg pulled up under him, he picked through a pile of variously colored M&M's he'd poured out on the tabletop. The finely sculpted head, half turned away from him, seemed truly classical in its features. What strange god had taken up habitation in this temple? What obeisance did he demand? Feeling suddenly a little too much like the devotee before a shrine, Tracy coughed once, gently, to signal his presence.

Noah looked up. "I don't like the brown ones," he explained with no trace of surprise. Between the boy's beauty and the dull words he spoke lay a nearly unbridgeable chasm.

"Don't they all taste the same?" Tracy asked, acutely conscious of the absurdity of love.

"Yeah, they do. But I still don't like the brown ones. They look like rabbit droppings."

Tracy had to laugh. Just let me kiss you, he thought. Let me kneel before you and fellate you in praise.

"What?" Noah said in all seriousness.

"You're funny," Tracy told him, though poking fun was the farthest thing from his mind.

Noah only shrugged, continuing to sort through his candy, and Tracy found himself fighting back an attack of terrible emptiness. You poor kid, he thought plaintively. I could take you away from all this. In Tokyo last year, he had visited Yasukuni, the Shinto shrine dedicated to the teenage kamikaze pilots, a space so pure and austere it had made him ache with longing. Country at Peace, it was called. He wanted to sweep Noah up in his arms and transport him instantly to that sacred precinct. But why? Why, of all things, had he suddenly thought of that place dedicated to the futility of dead boys? They had lived brief lives of fire. They had not sorted through M&M's. Perhaps that was it: he wanted Noah to breathe, just for a few precious moments, that otherworldly air. Then perhaps he'd see how stupid it all was, this life he led. How M&M's weren't worth discriminating about one way or the other, how he was caught inside a whole system of stupidities that were quietly pulling him under, though he couldn't know it, only perhaps have an inkling from time to time, which was the part that was so sad, so terrible. Love was like death that way. He wanted Noah to have the capacity to be filled with awe. But the boy was entirely unaware. He concentrated on picking out the brown M&M's and setting them aside.

Tracy resisted mightily the urge to drape his arms around him, trail his lips lightly across the top of that close-cropped skull, whisper, "I want to save you"—meaning, perhaps, only "I want you to save me"—a plea he nonetheless did whisper, if only in the silence inside himself, where the sound of those words echoed hollowly, the way voices do in the great empty space of a cathedral.

"So I read your story," he told Noah as they sat down to their dinner of steamed kale with garlic, glazed carrots, and potato-and-onion pie. As usual, his guest at first ate cautiously, but then with more enthusiasm, though Tracy wondered if he'd be happier with a burger and fries. "I liked the writing in it," he went on. "The whole thing was very hallucinatory. Haunting."

"I wasn't very happy with the way it turned out," Noah volunteered. "I had some ideas but, I don't know, they didn't really work."

It was endearing, really, to hear him speak seriously of his piece, the labor that had gone into it.

"What do mean by *work*?" Tracy decided to probe. They were back on the legitimate footing of teacher and student.

"Do you know the Brewer Twins?" Noah asked him casually.

"The who?" Tracy hadn't run across anyone by that name at the Forge.

"These two brothers," Noah explained. "I found them on the Internet. They're models, I guess. I mean, they're twins, of course. They look identical. You can't tell them apart. There's this one shoot where they're just horsing around, wrestling with each other, that kind of stuff. So that gave me the idea. Like, if you had a brother who was totally identical to you, and everything you wanted to do, he wanted to do too, like a mirror. It's weird, but sort of in a good way. They're fun."

Tracy tried hard to follow. "So you're saying your piece is about these Brewer Twins? Are they really named Joe and Jelly?"

"No, I'm making all that up. I don't know shit about them. I mean, I just saw their pictures on the Net is all. I got interested in them. Like I think too much."

"You saw a ghost in my house," Tracy reminded him.

Noah laughed appreciatively. "You wouldn't believe the shit I've seen."

"Well," Tracy said, "try me sometime. Would you like some more pie?"

"It's good," Noah told him. "I mean, for vegetarian. I never ate anything fresh growing up. Processed foods all the way. Fresh stuff still tastes odd to me. I miss the chemicals. But you should write a cookbook or something. You could make a mint.

"But let's talk more about my story. Do you have any suggestions how I can make it better? Do you think I can publish it somewhere?"

Tracy was at a loss. Five-paragraph essays he could offer some pointers on, but how to touch something like Noah's? How to tell him it was exactly what it was, an artifact dredged up from some profoundly deep well? As for publishable . . .

"I think, you know, just keep writing stuff," he said vaguely, aware that he was undoubtedly, at that moment, failing some important test. "The more practice you get, the better."

"You think so?" Noah said, a little skeptical, but not nearly as skeptical as he might have been, and Tracy wasn't sure whether to be disappointed or relieved that the boy hadn't challenged his fraudulence.

"Absolutely," he said as if he believed it. "Practice makes perfect. Do you want to help me clean up here?"

"Sure. But first let me step in the bathroom. Onions don't always agree with me. They go right through, you know? Like—whoosh."

Tracy began to fill the sink with warm water and suds. He could easily have waited to do this little task till Noah went back to his dorm for the night, but he enjoyed the illusion of domesticity. They could never live together, of course, but for a few idle hours here and there it was fun to pretend.

And speaking of fun, who were these Brewer Twins? One of these days he was going to have to get Noah to show him what he knew about this Internet—the World Wide Web, which sounded as if a great spider held the planet in thrall. Already he was beginning to feel distressingly antiquated, and he was still far too young, he hoped, to be left behind. Nevertheless, it was a persistent worry: between himself and his students, already, a gulf yawned. Ask Noah what music he listened to, what books he read for pleasure—or, more to the point, what video games he played—and the answers would no doubt confound. And without a concerted effort it would only get worse. How did someone like Louis feel, living daily among boys he no longer had the smallest capacity to understand?

Noah was taking a long time. The image blossomed involuntarily—the boy perched, pants around his ankles, on the toilet, a long ribbon of shit streaming from his anus. Immediately Tracy dispelled the psychic violation. And yet, he told himself, he was innocently interested in every conceivable thing about Noah, who had, after all, caught him off guard a couple of weeks ago with that phrase "creative as my asshole," a moment as memorable, all things considered, as any in his nearly twenty-six years.

Lost in his reverie, relying on habit's autopilot to scour the dishes and place them in the drying rack, he was thus utterly unprepared for the sudden attack.

"What the fuck?" he half shouted, his heart seizing up for a breathless instant, only to realize that Noah—whether in retribution for Tracy's less-than-helpful comments about his story or perhaps just frisky after his shit—had leaped onto his back and was clinging to him, arms wrapped around his neck and legs around his waist.

"Gotcha," he said, his hot breath on Tracy's neck.

"Hey. What's this? No mugging the teacher."

"I'll show you mugging," Noah said. "This is how the Brewer Twins do it."

Tracy dipped one shoulder and Noah slid off him. But the boy wasn't ready to quit. He planted himself in front of Tracy, feet spread apart, a strange grin on his face, ready once again to pounce. A classic stance, Tracy thought. He hadn't suspected Noah was so aggressive, a trait undoubtedly inherited from his father, though perhaps channeled into less subtle forms than international commerce. He could call it off right now, whatever this antic little outburst was, but he didn't. Instead he crouched in his own attack mode, which he'd learned from the dozens of television westerns he'd grown up on. They were both actors now, and they circled around each other all in fun, while Betsy, alerted by the commotion, stood in the door and watched curiously, unable to decide whether to flee or join in. Humans were such mysterious, unpredictable animals, after all.

"Hah!" Noah feinted. He stamped his feet and Betsy barked once, loudly. "Get him, Bets," he urged, but the dog just stood looking from him to Tracy and back, her breath ragged with anticipation, her dark eyes eager but confused.

"Hey, no fair calling on reinforcements," Tracy warned.

"Who takes you for all those great walks? Who sneaks you dog biscuits?"

"Don't listen to him," Tracy commanded, glancing Betsy's way in the same instant Noah chose to spring. They clambered together briefly, arms locked, then Noah used his shin to catch Tracy behind the knee and they both came down in a tangled mass on the stunningly hard linoleum floor. Seeing her chance, Betsy leaped into the fray. "Every man for himself and Betsy against everybody!" Tracy shouted. They all three rolled around, grappling, grasping for purchase, both humans laughing and Betsy ecstatic. She danced among them, nipping lightly, pausing to stand off and bark now and again at the delicious spectacle of human animals finally become themselves.

It took Tracy several moments to register that he was holding Noah's body tight against his. Where the boy's shirt had come untucked and ridden up, an expanse of smooth torso offered itself to his touch, and Tracy, careful to seem aggressive rather than caressing, slid his hands along silky, rib-rippled flesh. Delicately he cocked a knee between Noah's legs—which gripped the invader tightly. Could he feel the rounded cap of a knee cradled against his balls? When Tracy had wrestled as a kid of fourteen, fifteen, the squirming, grappling contact was always charged, always sexual. But then he'd been a burgeoning little queer at fourteen or fifteen, already certain beyond his years. Other boys, presumably, wrestled for other reasons.

Noah was wrestling to win.

Giving up, getting it over with—he realized, sadly, he had to call a stop to this foolishness—Tracy rolled over onto his back and let Noah straddle his stomach triumphant, hands gripping his wrists, pinning him to the floor, blissfully unaware, Tracy hoped—or did not hope.

"Now I've really gotcha," Noah bragged. "You're in real trouble now."

He was breathing heavily. His face loomed.

"You know what we used to do in my old school when you lost a fight like this?"

Tracy shook his head.

"Close your eyes," Noah ordered him. His tone was gloating, certain. "Go on," he said. "Shut them. You have to do what I say."

With a sinking feeling Tracy knew—even as, helpless to resist, he closed his eyes—that he'd gone way too far, let them both go way too far.

"Okay," Noah said, transformed into a figure of commanding confidence, "now open your mouth."

"Don't get weird on me," Tracy admonished.

"Don't worry. Trust me," Noah urged.

Against all his better judgment—Here goes nothing, he thought to himself, here goes everything—he opened his mouth. In that first instant what he felt was the strangest, most unidentifiable sensation. Something wet and viscous had landed in the back of his throat. He jerked open his eyes to see

Noah's face hanging close above his and he realized: the boy had loosed a dollop of warm spittle into his mouth.

"You spit in my mouth," he accused furiously, hauling Noah off himself and sitting up.

Noah seemed hurt, even perplexed. "I told you, it's what we used to do on the playground."

Tracy made spitting sounds, though he did not, in fact, expel Noah's spit from his mouth, instead going through the motions as a sense of shock and wonder spread through him. Fluid from Noah's body was in his mouth, it was even now, as he swallowed, down his throat, inside his body. But what did it mean?

The only safe, easily available response was outrage.

"That's way out of bounds," he said sharply, aware at the same time how little that encompassed anything like his actual response. Nevertheless, the sentence did the work it had to do.

Noah sounded offended himself. "*Sorry*," he shot back. "I was just goofing on you. Don't get so bent out of shape."

"What am I supposed to do? You don't exactly go around spitting on people. What were you thinking?"

And what kind of signals had he been sending?

"I said *sorry*," Noah repeated—as if he had, somehow, merely forgotten himself, reverted to some other time and place: kids on the playground, as he himself had said.

Alone of the three, Betsy had no qualms about their game. She wagged her tail excitedly and barked for more.

"Hush," Tracy said impatiently. "Sit. Lie down. I said, lie down. Good dog." Obedience school had been only a qualified success, but Noah also seemed chastened, ready to lie down on the kitchen floor as well.

"Okay," Tracy said firmly, the teacher, the adult, conciliatory but at the same time setting limits. "That got a little out of hand. Enough horsing around for one evening." But beyond his soothing words, he was genuinely frightened. He wondered if his hard-on had shown. He was too afraid even to glance at the boy, afraid he'd see evidence there too of animal excitement. Or perhaps he wouldn't, and he didn't know which would be worse. He realized he shouldn't have said "one evening." Enough horsing around forever. "It's getting late," he went on briskly. "You should get on back to your dorm before curfew. And I've got stuff to do. I've got to return some phone calls before it's too late."

Maybe it looked worse—as in more suspicious—to push him away like this, but Tracy was too keyed up to think through the alternatives.

"I'm sorry I got out of line," Noah said. "I was just kidding around."

"No, no, that's okay. It was an accident," Tracy told him, hoping a lie might somehow make things better. Whatever else it might be, wasn't spitting in somebody's mouth vengeful, a gesture of contempt? "It was nothing. Forget about it. Now go on home. I'll see you in class on Monday."

Taking his expulsion better than Tracy had feared he might, Noah obediently gathered up his books and stuffed them into his knapsack. The real power here, Tracy thought darkly but with some satisfaction, as he watched Noah docilely do his bidding, is still all mine.

Or was it? Noah seemed, in his way, entirely unfazed. "Hey," he said, pausing at the door to punch Tracy kiddingly on the arm. "It was real."

It certainly was real, Tracy thought, reeling from the impact not of that light punch but the other intoxicating collision of their bodies. It had exactly the kind of unreality that guaranteed just how real it had been. He was so stupid, though whether it was in letting something like this happen or not letting it continue was impossible to say. There was no way not to be stupid here, and stupidity, the instant Noah was safely out of the house, put him in a panic.

What if it somehow got around? Who knew what kids might brag about, because that thought did occur to him, that what Noah had been after, in his show of domination, was some kind of bragging right. How he'd bested Mr. Parker. Mastered him. That would certainly be worth telling his friends in the dorm about.

You never knew. In this situation, especially, as Tracy was discovering with each passing shiver of regret, you couldn't know a damn thing.

I've had my fair warning, he said to himself firmly. It's over. In the future, he'd be strict. He'd curtail Noah's visits, try to get them back on a more seemly footing.

But in his fingertips the memory of Noah's skin was startlingly alive. What if, instead of outrage, he'd had the presence of mind to draw Noah's face to his, tasting those pouting lips, seeking with his tongue the wet insides of Noah's mouth? Then where would the outrage have been? It shocked him to discover that he was actually trembling. Had there been any liquor in the house, he might well have considered pouring himself a drink; he could use one of Louis's generous scotches right about now.

It was early, only ten o'clock; in all probability, Arthur Branson was still awake. With his less-than-soothing cup of chamomile, Tracy settled cross-legged onto his futon, at whose foot Betsy, the evening's too-brief excitements behind her, curled in what he took to be contented sleep, though the occasional tremors running through her sleeping body made him wonder what restlessness she might be dreaming away. Was she running away from him in her dream, longing for some state of independence he had no ability to grant her, having freed her from the pound into a new kind of servitude, which, grateful and benign though it might be, was servitude nonetheless? Dogs and their masters. She had been a lark, an accidental current whose flow he had simply let himself be carried by, and he remembered how he had felt mildly annoyed with Claire, after the fact, for her brisk efficiency in getting him to the pound before he could have second thoughts. Did she manage everything in life that effectively, even ruthlessly?

With sudden resolve, he reached for the phone and dialed. "I've just had the strangest experience," he would say. Or he would say nothing. Arthur, my dear friend, please be there, he thought wildly.

"Oh," Arthur yelped on hearing his voice. "And I thought I was going to have to come up there and give you a spanking myself."

"I've been really, really busy," Tracy apologized.

"But now I've got you," Arthur told him. "So I bestow my forgiveness. I've just been dying to talk to you. Want to hear my news?" Without pausing for an answer, he charged on, announcing in a grand voice that brooked no resisting, "I went and got my penis pierced."

So it was not to be about protease inhibitors or miraculous misdiagnoses. Tracy felt a sudden, desperate disappointment. "And I'm in love with a boy," he wanted to say, as if all desperate measures were somehow commensurate. But he said nothing. He let Arthur chatter on, grateful, he supposed, to be distracted like this.

"I met this woman at a party the other night, this brainiac lesbian, you'd hate her, but anyway, we got to talking and it turned out she had her nipples pierced. So I said, Well, can I see them? And she pulled up her shirt for me right then and there. Those crazy lesbians. But then it got me to thinking. There's this piercing store in Chelsea I walk by all the time, so I just thought, You know what? I'm going to go do this. You'd be so proud of me. I marched myself right over there the next morning and said to the boy behind the counter, Excuse me, do you do genital piercing? It turns out, he'd just gotten it done himself, and he was *very* pleased with it."

Feeling somehow resistant to all this information, Tracy thought he should say something to indicate he was still on the line. "So did he show it to you?" he asked.

"Of course. He had just a lovely cock, and it looked quite beautiful with a piercing though it, I must say. Very exciting. So we looked through his catalog at all the different possibilities, and then I decided on one. It's called a Prince Albert, don't ask me why. Take a couple hours and think about it, the boy at the store told me. Just to make sure. Then come back this afternoon."

"And you actually went back," Tracy said. Why did Arthur's exploits always bring his lurking prudishness to the surface?

"Of course I went back. I could hardly wait. He was very professional. He took me through the procedure step by step. Then he did these breathing exercises with me. When he decided I was ready, he took this long Q-Tip and stuck it up my urethra and held it there for about five minutes to let the anesthetic take effect. And the whole time I'm sitting there thinking, Golly, I'm really going to do this."

Just hearing the details was making Tracy squirm, but his penis, powered by some other source, stiffened with excitement.

"So he takes out a pen," Arthur went on—clearly this wasn't the first time he'd narrated the story—"and he marks the exit hole on the underside of my dick, then he slides this hollow steel surgical tool up my urethra and lines it up with the exit dot. The needle goes through the tube, then once the hole is made, the jewelry goes in, he aligns the ends with a pair of pliers, puts the ball on, and voilà, my cock is now a work of art. Why are you laughing? Is this making you nervous?"

"Yow," Tracy said delicately. "Didn't it hurt like hell?" he asked.

"Nope. Didn't feel a thing. It was a really dense anesthetic. But there was a lot of blood. I had to wear this surgical glove on my dick for thirty-six hours."

"And then what? What does it feel like? *Can* you feel it?"

"When I've got my pants on, I can. I mean, I'm conscious of it. Right now I'm lying here fiddling with it. My new plaything. I can't keep my hands off it."

"Have you jerked off?"

"Not for about a week I didn't. I thought, Oh my God, it'll explode. But then I couldn't stand it anymore, and I thought, Surely he'd've warned me. It's hard right now. How about you?"

"Actually," Tracy admitted, "I am."

"Gosh. I wish you were here to play with it. I can't wait to come up there for a visit and let you see it."

"Well, you should definitely come up," Tracy said in spite of himself, all the while stoking the fires of his five-alarm cock. It was safe to talk. One could talk all one wanted. One could imagine anything at all and be perfectly safe. "Say I'm putting my lips to your cock right now," he told Arthur in a voice whose hoarseness surprised him. "I'm wrapping my tongue around the head. Can you feel it? My tongue's playing with Fat Albert."

"Prince Albert," Arthur corrected him. "Nice slip. And yes, it feels great."

"Now I take your whole fat cock in my mouth. I go all the way down on it."

"I'm holding the back of your head," Arthur said. "I'm pumping my cock in and out of your mouth. I'm knocking against the back of your throat."

"Yeah," Tracy told Noah, "fuck my mouth," as the boy's cock, presumably neither so fat nor mutilated nor deadly as Arthur's, shoved in and out with eager violence.

"Okay, sweetheart," Arthur whispered. "I'm almost there. I'm going to come in your mouth."

"Do it," Tracy told the boy of his dreams. "Cream in my mouth. Blast my throat with it." He was almost there himself.

And then he was there. And Arthur, a hundred miles away, he could tell was there as well. And in his dorm room, sound asleep, Noah Lathrop felt what invisible shock waves pass through his undreaming body?

He always felt a profound desolation after he came, as if one's hopes and desires for anything were proved to be only illusory, the heat of the moment. As if nothing, however coveted, once gained, was worth anything. What had happened with Noah, that unforeseen misadventure so secretly longed for, ruined everything.

"Well, I have to say . . ." Arthur's bemused voice summoned Tracy back to himself. Pensively, he daubed his fingertips in the white semen cooling on his belly. "With Prince Albert here, right before I come, the feeling is definitely more penis-intense than it used to be. Sleep well, darling. I'll talk to you soon."

VIII

So," the Fatwa told him, looking around with a frankly envious gaze, "I guess this is some place, isn't it?"

"I guess," said Noah, suddenly aware of the room's brash opulence. Why he'd invited this person to his dad's apartment on a Saturday afternoon wasn't entirely clear to him. By coincidence, when he'd arrived at the little station in Middle Forge to catch the New York train, he'd seen the Fatwa standing by himself and smoking a cigarette, the only other person on the platform, and after a moment's hesitation he'd gone over to him, struck up something like a conversation. Not that the Fatwa was either very talkative or very friendly.

Of course, Noah thought, the Fatwa probably hated him. That would make sense. The Fatwa probably hated all of them on the hall, and why should Noah be any different?

The Fatwa eyed him suspiciously, blowing out a thin line of smoke quite deliberately and staring off at the cars in the parking lot, the spindly little trees that had lost all their leaves, the frowning hills on the far side of the river. Noah had followed his gaze, wondering exactly what the Fatwa saw when he looked at that scene: whether it was the same as what Noah saw, or whether the different things that had happened to two people in their lives changed what they saw when they looked at something. And what had they talked about? Only a day had passed since that auspicious encounter, but Noah couldn't remember. It wasn't that he'd been trying to attach himself. The Fatwa was the one who'd said, when the train finally pulled in and they got on board, "You want to sit together?"

On the whole, he supposed, the most interesting parts of the conversation had been those that had happened in his head. His new friend put on his headphones and stared out the window for most of the trip, while Noah constructed various exchanges between them, discarding one after the other till he had the slightly discomfiting realization that, though he might, for whatever mysterious reason, want to talk to the Fatwa, he really had no idea what they might talk about.

Only when they'd stopped in the tunnel coming into Grand Central, the lights flickering out, the train in complete silence and darkness, did any real conversation happen. "So what are you down for?" the Fatwa, now just a disembodied voice, had asked him. "What sins are you indulging?"

"Visiting my dad, I guess," Noah had told him, adding, as if it were merely an afterthought, "mostly just hanging out. We should get together."

"That's right. It's classic," the Fatwa told him as the lights in the car winked back on. "Never say a word at the Forge, then best friends in the city."

It was wounding, obviously, and meant to be. But then the Fatwa surprised him. He fluttered his eyelids—a disconcerting habit—and said, sounding weary, as if this wasn't a fight worth having, "Sure, why not? Like, maybe, tomorrow afternoon. I'll bring some weed. We'll go from there."

It wasn't an appointment he'd exactly expected the Fatwa to keep; nevertheless, he'd stayed at home, fielding phone calls for his dad, who had been expected to be back already, but whose arrival from Kazakhstan or Kyrgyzstan, Noah got them confused, accrued delay after delay until, according to the latest phone message from Heathrow, which Noah had listened to from the warmth of his bed but decided not to pick up, he was no longer expected till the evening, when there was supposed to be people over, a party of some kind. But for now, midafternoon, here was the mysterious Chris Tyler moving warily about the apartment's spacious living room, sizing up with cool interest the collection of antique Buddhas on glass shelves along the wall, the mellow old Persians on the floor, not least of all the truly fantastic view, from the balcony, of Central Park in hazy Indian summer sunlight, a forest in the heart of the city waiting patiently, Noah always imagined, till the day came when it could retake the island of which it had been dispossessed. Because he hated New York, really—its hive of humanity, all their futile industry, their joyless pursuit of pleasures. The only place he liked was the prehistoric solitude of the woods, and from those, by his own hand, he'd been expelled forever. The forest, he told himself sternly, gave no second chances.

"So what's your old man do to deserve a dump like this?" the Fatwa wanted to know.

"He's in business," Noah said.

The Fatwa looked amused. "Just business?"

"International business ventures," Noah revised. Kazakhstan or Kyrgyzstan, somewhere over there. He dreaded the party scheduled for later—in celebration, he presumed, of one more dubious deal his dad had closed on, one more inexperienced third world capitalist about to learn some free market lessons the hard way—but though he had half a thought to skip out (the caterers were to come set up at seven), that wouldn't make his dad very happy, and he'd learned, over the years, that whatever it took to make Dad happy was what you did. Like everything else, a therapist had told him once, being an only child comes with its share of responsibilities, of which he was reminded every time he signed his name. Grandfather, father, son. If he felt the weight of that "III," looking like nothing so much as the pillars of a ruined and roofless temple, at the same time he never for an instant considered omitting it from the carefully printed, childlike letters that passed for his signature.

"Well, gee, my mom only sells real estate," the Fatwa said. "She'd pass out if she saw this place. But enough idle chatter. Let's get stoned. My morning buzz is starting to wear off, and you don't want to see this boy without his makeup. It's not a pretty sight." He laughed, a nervous whinny that trailed off abruptly, self-mockingly, as he reached into the pocket of his khakis to extract a small pipe and a plastic bag. Noah reminded himself that the Fatwa was a freak. Everyone knew that.

"Can we smoke in here, or is out there more, uh, prudent?" asked his guest, glancing over his shoulder at the balcony.

For an instant Noah wasn't even sure what the right answer was. He'd never smoked pot, even disapproved of it, and had, in fact, completely forgotten that weed had been part of yesterday's promise.

Together they moved out into the warm sun. Two chaise longues, hideous things, reclined side by side, and they lowered themselves onto the brightly striped cushions. The Fatwa fiddled intently with his pipe, packing and lighting it, then drawing in a deep and grateful breath. When he finally exhaled he seemed steadied, back on the secure footing he'd been without since his arrival at the apartment. He inhaled again, less urgently, and yet again, and just when Noah had started to hope he wouldn't offer, the Fatwa contentedly passed the pipe his way.

"You smoke a lot, don't you?" Noah said, reaching out to take the small metal pipe he'd told himself he wanted no part of. He held the silver object, looking it over curiously, his nostrils bitten by the sweet scent. Only for an instant was he tempted; then a pang of revulsion set in. He handed the pipe back, confessing as he did so, "My dad's a bit of a coke fiend. As are all his so-called friends," an admission he'd never made to anyone before, not even his therapist, though what he hadn't told his therapist, as a point of fact, could fill a book. "So I stay away from the stuff," he went on. "Drugs of all kinds. Booze too. You could say I'm quite old-fashioned."

It made the Fatwa laugh out loud—which, in the middle of his toke, turned into an explosive cough.

"That's so twisted," he said, grimacing, wiping a tear from his eye.

"Sorry to disappoint you," was all Noah could think of to say. He had no ideas, other than the idea that lying with the Fatwa in the warm sun wasn't too bad. Whatever he'd wanted to prove, maybe he'd already proved it. He could get someone's attention. He always thought of himself as someone yelling "Hey, hey" into the wind, waiting for the wind to notice.

"And to think I brought the really good stuff," the Fatwa told him. "Oh well, my friend's not going to miss it."

Noah considered for a moment the information he'd been given. "Your friend?" he asked, conscious of making a decision to embark on a certain kind of conversation. But then, wasn't that what he'd wanted in the first place, to slake his curiosity about various things?

"My friend who I visit down here," the Fatwa told him. "He's a doctor. Old guy—just turned forty. The most interesting thing about him is, he once had an affair with Rob Lowe. At least that's what he claims. He's got practically every photograph of Rob Lowe ever taken, including the parts of the videotape they never told you about. Strange guy, but we get along just fine. He's got the money, I've got the charm. Actually, he's got the charm too. Yeah," he said, nodding, as if reassuring himself on that score, "he's really got way too much charm, come to think about it."

Okay, Noah thought, here we are, and far more quickly than he'd expected. He tried to sound as casual as he could, though he wondered if, by sounding too casual, he somehow betrayed himself. Because it was either a big deal or it wasn't, or maybe it was both at the same time—the point, however, being moot since the question, which was the question he'd had all fall, the question he'd failed to ask Tracy Parker that night a couple of weeks before, had already left his mouth and, in fact, the Fatwa was already answering: "Yeah, I'm queer as a three-dollar bill. So what?"

Just like that, it was done. Noah wouldn't look his way, but why should he, with all the park, its ailing forest and trampled meadows spread out before him, and of course the sky, that perfect, perfect blue marred only by one extremely interesting jet trail, which, if you watched it, could be seen slowly to move toward the horizon, its clear line gradually growing ragged, beginning to dissolve.

"I just wondered," he said evenly. "I mean, I kind of thought so."

"Yeah, well, so there we are. And you?"

Noah knew that the Fatwa, comfortably reclined on his chaise longue, was staring his way.

"I'm not really into that kind of stuff," he said, his eyes intent on the blemished sky.

"No booze, no drugs, no mad gay love. You really are old-fashioned."

"See, it's what I told you. I'm a disappointment all around."

That the Fatwa didn't immediately answer made him wonder, not for the first time, whether that might really be the case. But if he was a disappointment, well, he was also disappointed. The last thing he wanted was to have his questions turned back on himself. That was no fun at all.

"So," he said, desperate to right the situation, "how did you first know about yourself? That's something that's always interested me. Sexual orientation." Though he spoke the phrase carefully, with scientific detachment, he could hear how his voice sounded more strained than he would have wished.

"I just knew," said the Fatwa. "That's how it is. Either you know or you don't."

"I see," Noah said.

"Just like you know you're straight. It's the same for faggots."

"I really hate that word," Noah said. It was one of his dad's words: "Don't be a little faggot," his dad would say to someone he was disappointed in.

"Yeah, well, get used to it," the Fatwa told him. "It's what I am. By the way," he added, as if this conversation interested him not at all, "do you have any juice or anything? I need some sugar. Do you mind if I go raid the fridge?"

"Go right ahead," Noah told him. He was surprised to find himself suddenly so unsteady, trembling even. Don't be stupid, he told himself. We're just talking. But the trembling wouldn't go away. He suppressed a hiccup that arrived out of nowhere, but then another came, and another, the kind of hiccups he got when he was nervous. He held his breath but they tapped up from inside him insistently.

Brimming glass of orange juice in hand, the Fatwa reemerged onto the balcony. He paused, midstep, to take a long gulp. Making no move to sit down, he looked down at Noah strangely.

"What?" Noah asked.

"You've got the hiccups," he observed wistfully.

"Duh," Noah said.

"Here, drink some of this." He held out his half-full glass, but Noah shook his head. The Fatwa, however, was not so easily dissuaded. Without a word he sat down on the edge of the chaise longue so that his hip was touching Noah's leg. "Really," he said. "Take a long drink." His eyes, staring straight into Noah's, looked blurry, but not just from the pot. A phrase floated into Noah's head: the eyes of desire. It made him want to laugh, but instead another hiccup surfaced. Though he was absolutely right, it turned out. Setting the glass on the balcony's wide ledge, the Fatwa said softly, "You're really cute, you know. Has anybody ever told you that?" His hand crept up Noah's thigh.

"I told you I'm not into that stuff," Noah warned him, but he knew his trembling body told the Fatwa a different story.

"You're shaking like a leaf," the Fatwa said. "You don't have to be so nervous. I just want to kiss you."

You shouldn't be surprised, Noah told himself. You shouldn't be angry. You set the trap, and look who got caught. He'd known for a long time that he wondered way too much about things. What guys did together. What it would be like. The curiosity that killed the cat. Back in the summer, on a dare with what he thought of as his dark side, he'd even worked up the courage to buy a plastic-wrapped magazine off a newsstand on the street. *Men in Heat #7 XXX All Male Action.* The Pakistani vendor didn't even blink when he handed over his money. Forbidden purchase in hand, he'd scurried off to peruse the glossy pages in private. What he saw, especially in the spread "Swim Practice," where a blond teenage beauty only a few years older than himself paired off with a handsome, dark-haired athlete somewhere in his late twenties, repulsed and amazed him, the most horrifyingly lovely images he'd ever laid eyes on.

He'd known all along that something like this would have to happen. It was what you got, playing with fire. It was why he'd spoken to the Fatwa in the first place. Everybody knew the Fatwa was a faggot, and maybe to a faggot like him Noah Lathrop III *was* cute. How convenient, Noah thought, and then he thought, in that seemingly endless instant before the Fatwa's lips actually touched his, that no one had more contempt for the faggot freak who lived down the hall than he did, and that was why he was here right now, on his dad's balcony, letting the Fatwa lean down to kiss him. He wanted to know exactly what it was like. How bad it could get. He was the one who'd burned down the woods, after all.

The Fatwa's lips closed over his lower lip, more a gentle tugging bite than a kiss. If he wanted, he could stop this, but he found he did not want to stop it. He was interested by the sensation of the Fatwa leaning over him, his smoky intimate breath, the awkward angle of the chaise longue. He did not close his eyes, though he noticed that the Fatwa did. Presumably this all meant something else to him. The tongue surprised him, a mobile wedge of flesh slithering into his mouth, running over his teeth, his gums. He tried to block its invasion with his own tongue but discovered that was exactly what made a kiss work, their tongues fighting each other, hard to tell who was in whose mouth when.

The blood seething in his eardrums irritated him, and when the Fatwa's long bony fingers started pawing the front of his chinos, closing greedily around his excitement down there, he grabbed at the offending wrist to try to steer it away. But the Fatwa's hand, having found what it wanted, was undeterred. Drowning in the attention, Noah tried to come up for air. Was it a signal? Breathing hard, the Fatwa broke off his kiss to concentrate on undoing the buttons of Noah's pants. Noah hardly had time to wonder before he felt the astonishment of himself exposed to the air. "Lovely," the Fatwa said, and then dove instantly toward his captive prey. Noah let out an involuntary groan. The pictures in *Men in Heat #7* had only conveyed so much visual information. There was no way they could convey the particular information of this, the swoon of it.

"Bedroom," he heard the Fatwa murmur huskily, his voice muffled, as if coming from sleep, as if desire settled a drowse on you impossible to disentangle yourself from, as impossible as getting out from under the warm covers on a cold, rainy morning. Taking Noah's hand, the Fatwa clumsily pulled him from the chaise longue, the two of them almost falling back onto the cushions, which wouldn't necessarily have been a bad thing, Noah thought, still blurred and dizzy from all that tongue, the wet warmth of that mouth as it closed around his blood-thick flesh, the absolute power he had been made to feel—as if, at that moment, he were master of the world, or at least of Chris Tyler, that formerly shy, nondescript kid from Connecticut who right now couldn't get enough of what Noah had to offer. And it struck him that this was the first time in his fifteen years he'd ever felt, completely and unambiguously, without any shadow of doubt, that what he had to offer, even if only for the flurried moment it lasted, was something that somebody else absolutely couldn't live without.

Under the punishing torrent of hot water, the fiercest the state-of-the-art shower could deliver, Noah stood shivering. Steam-wreathed and seemingly oblivious to his erstwhile partner in crime, or at least folly, Chris Tyler soaped himself thoroughly. Sharing a shower: another first, Noah supposed, regarding with as much indifference as he could muster the tall bony body of his mortal enemy. The Fatwa sputtered contentedly, allowing the streaming water to rinse away the suds he'd lathered up. Then, with a decisive gesture, he abruptly shut off the flow. Grabbing a towel, he dried himself vigorously and wrapped the towel around his waist. Unable to snap his fingers and make the Fatwa simply disappear, which is what he would have preferred, and having no better ideas, Noah followed suit—as he had done, he realized, since the beginning of this madness some hour before. That reassured him, somehow. He had taken no initiative; he had simply been there, allowing what was meant to happen to happen and then observing it objectively. The scientific method.

"Well, that was all very nice, I must say," the Fatwa announced after throwing himself down on the bed. "And you got rid of your hiccups. Christian's patented cure. I could make a fortune. But now"—he yawned contentedly—"what I feel like is a nap."

Nice? Noah thought. Was that what it was—nice? He didn't feel so nice; he felt like he'd been thrown off a cliff and hadn't yet hit the ground below.

Chris, however, prattled on. "I thought you weren't into that stuff. For somebody who's not into it, you throw a pretty good fuck."

"I've got an open mind," Noah told him grimly. "I'll try anything once." He had the vague sense that they should have been using a condom, but of course it was too late now. He hadn't even thought of it—or, to be more precise, by the time he'd thought about it, one surprising moment shading into the next, they were already too far gone in what they were doing to call a halt. It wasn't like he could suddenly have claimed a time-out in all that seamlessly evolving activity.

"You knew exactly what you were doing, didn't you?" the Fatwa said. "I mean, when you came up to me on the platform yesterday. You were just using me to find out some things about yourself."

"You had your fun," Noah told him, at once hating and approving his indifferent, dismissive tone. He had taken a seat in a chair in the corner of the room, from which unplanned vantage he could see up Chris's towel to where his cock, still substantial even at ease, lolled about on top of the loose sac of his balls. Even though he was glad he'd been able to resist actually putting his lips on that thing, the fact that he was still, on some level, way too curious about what it would be like to suck dick irritated him. More than that, it seriously disturbed him. Was it true that, in his heart of hearts, he was a fag just like all the rest of them?

"Yes," Chris said quietly, even drowsily, as if a nap really were what he wanted now, "I certainly did have my fun." For a minute or two he lay silent, eyes closed, spread unself-consciously on the bed while Noah told himself, severely, not to despise this person who had quite justly accused him of taking advantage. Just get him up, get him moving. Get him out of the apartment. "Don't even think about going to sleep," he was about to say when Chris's voice startled him.

"I heard you that time," he was saying. "I was in my room. I know you were there. I know you were part of it."

For a moment Noah had no idea what he was talking about.

"The day your friends hung the pigeon on my door," Chris went on, eyes still closed, as if, by talking in his sleep, he could uncover certainties his waking brain failed to know. "I heard you out there with them," he said. "I heard your voice."

It's not true, Noah wanted to tell him. But in a certain sense it was, in fact, true. As he knew too well. He'd gone along. He hadn't done a thing to stop it. But the real truth, the complicated truth—that his own situation was precarious as well; that he hadn't wanted to risk compromising it to come to the aid of someone he didn't even know—how could he even begin to explain *that?*

"I didn't know you then," he said lamely.

Chris sounded stern. "Well, now you do. Now you know me very well. But as I think I said before, this isn't the Forge, so it doesn't mean anything.

What about when we're back? What about then? Are you going to know me then?"

More than anything, Noah hated being lectured to. He knew that what he had to say would sound cruel, but he had no other choice. "We'll see," he said curtly.

Chris opened his hazel eyes and looked at Noah. "Would it just be too surprising if I told you I understood?" Noah could manage to return his gaze for only a few seconds before having to look away. "Believe it or not," Chris continued mildly, "I know all about confusion. So don't feel bad."

He sat up on the side of the bed and looked around. "My, my, we're a messy couple," he observed. Unfurling the towel from around his waist, he reached down to retrieve his boxers, the white tangle of his shirt. "Throw me my pants from over there, will you?" he asked.

Noah dressed as well. It made him happier to be back inside his clothes. Chris stood at the window as he finished buttoning his shirt. "You know," he said in that same reflective voice he'd used earlier when he fingered Noah on the pigeon incident, "people think Kurt Cobain killed himself because of drugs. But he didn't. He killed himself because he had AIDS. The papers never printed that. It got all hushed up. And you know who else has AIDS? Michael Stipe. And Rob Lowe's brother. How do I know this? My doctor friend. He knows the people who know. Can you imagine if that got out? What it would do . . ."

Why was he saying this? It made Noah vaguely uneasy. He reassured himself that he'd had his unprotected dick in Chris Tyler's ass only about thirty seconds, all told—well, maybe a little more, but not much. AIDS wasn't something he exactly liked to think about, except when he needed a plague to wipe out nine-tenths of the population so the cities could fall into ruin and the forests grow back and swallow them up.

"Well, see you, as they say," Chris told him at the door. For an instant Noah was afraid the tall, strange boy might try to give him a hug or kiss or something, but obviously Chris knew better than that.

"Yeah," Noah told him carefully, coolly, though not without respect. "See you."

He shut the door behind him and reminded himself how easily, all in all, Chris had let him get off. He hadn't had to suck cock and he hadn't gotten fucked. He was still intact, his orifices unviolated, which meant the afternoon's insanity was something he could either pretend happened or didn't happen, but either way it didn't really change anything if he didn't want it to. He'd satisfied his curiosity, and the cat had not been killed. The chances were quite excellent he'd never be tempted to do anything like this ever again.

• • •

As if it were only another ordinary evening at home, international business-man and frequent flyer Noah Lathrop, Jr., lately returned from halfway around the world, mixed himself a martini in the monogrammed silver shaker he'd inherited from his father, the original Noah Lathrop, a man too con-cerned with his Hartford bank ever to travel at all, except for two weeks to the Cape every year like clockwork. Noah III sat at the small table in the kitchen and watched his dad add a drop of vermouth, shake Tanqueray and ice, a ritual precisely and lovingly performed. His dad approached his poisons as if they were holy, administering himself doses of alcohol or cocaine the way mountain Baptists take up rattlesnakes, emerging from his self-inflicted ordeal stronger and purer than before. Noah had never known his dad to suffer anything remotely resembling a hangover.

From the living room came the lively noise of the party, his dad's inner circle—the lawyer Roger Baldrick and his coke-fiend wife; Jean, the tough, chain-smoking Vassar graduate who worked on Wall Street and raised horses on her farm in Millbrook; Max Cohen, who also worked on Wall Street; Gunila, his dad's fiancée and soon-to-be third wife; and of course A. J. Grif-fiths, whose southern-accented voice boomed out distinctively—as well as others Noah didn't know, people who came and went, who used his dad and got used in return, who were expendable whether they understood it or not on a festive night like tonight.

He'd followed his dad into the kitchen on purpose, but, as usual when the two of them were alone, found himself at a complete loss for anything to say. He had learned long ago that idle questions like "How was your trip?" or "What was it like over there?" did not even elicit answers. His dad didn't do small talk—he reserved his speech for more important matters—and Noah had the distinct and queasy feeling that he was about as unimportant an item as could be found on his dad's crowded agenda. He'd been eight when his parents divorced, his only vivid memories of those years being the large hedge at the back of the property that had a hole in it where he spent hours playing by himself and hiding from the world; a red pedal car he'd loved; an alarmingly vivid dream of a peacock standing in his room, at the foot of his bed, slowly fanning open its tail, which was covered not with iridescent spots but with real, staring human eyes; finally, an antique Chinese lamp his mother threw at his dad but missed, the lamp hitting the wall instead but for some reason not shattering, something so miraculous-seeming that it stopped, if only for a stunned moment, their quarrel in midshout.

"So how's school," his dad said, a statement rather than a question. He concentrated on the more important business of pouring his martini from shaker to glass without wasting a drop. He had just flown in from some unimaginably exotic or sordid city in Central Asia and nothing about him was changed. "There's something lacking in your dad," his mother told him once. "He's incapable of being touched by anything."

"Fine," he told his dad. "School's fine. Not much to report." It was the first time they'd seen each other since the start of the semester.

"Well, that's good. Want one of these, buddy? It won't kill you."

Noah shook his head. Raising the glass to his lips, his dad sipped gratefully. "I had to come a long way to get this baby," he said.

Later, Noah knew, there would be cocaine as well. He had to admire his dad's huge stamina even as its extremes sometimes unnerved him. The man slept four hours a night at most, his life an unbearable expanse of wakefulness to his son, who absolutely depended on long blank stretches of unconsciousness, easily sleeping fourteen or fifteen hours a day when allowed, craving those episodes of oblivion so much that he felt vaguely cheated if, on waking, he could recall a dream that had inserted itself into his otherwise empty slumber. Those dreams were mostly tedious and threatening. Only the other night a large bald black man standing next to him on the subway had been trying to prick him with a tiny concealed hypodermic needle, and he'd thought on waking, Maybe, like Tim and Gary, I'm a racist after all, and I'm just fooling myself. But who said dreams didn't lie as much as anything else? He'd had any number of annoying dreams lately, none of which he particularly wanted to take credit for.

"Shall we join the party?" his dad suggested, as if it was stupid for the two of them to be stuck in the kitchen alone together. For an instant Noah wanted to say "Wait," but clearly his dad was right: there was no reason. "Have you talked to Gunila?" his dad said as they moved into the living room. "I expect you to, you know."

"I haven't really talked to anybody. I sort of have a headache."

His dad stopped and looked at him. "I've been on a fucking airplane for the last two days and you have a headache," he said, not in anger or contempt, but just as an observation. Then he simply turned and walked over to his friends. Surprisingly close to tears, Noah bit his lip, remembering with a sting of shame his one trip out of the country with his dad and then-stepmom Kendra, years ago, a weeklong vacation in London where a humiliating bout of traveler's diarrhea had forced him to stay behind at the hotel the whole week, and his dad's quiet fury, as if Noah were somehow to blame for this failure of his constitution.

What had happened this very afternoon, here in the apartment, struck Noah again full force. Was he consciously trying to anger his dad by flirting, however tentatively, with the unthinkable? Because if his dad ever knew . . . The clearest image came into his head: just as he had once done when a car had crippled a deer in front of their house in Connecticut, his dad stood calmly and loaded a bullet into a pistol, ready to put out of its misery the wounded animal that was his son.

He forced himself to go straight to where Gunila stood, elegant in black, her blond hair falling to her shoulders, the same color as the champagne in the flute she held in one hand and contemplated rather than sipped. If he talked to her he could avoid—or at least postpone—A. J., whose predations he could already feel broadcast around the room. Whether he liked Gunila or not wasn't anything he felt he had to make up his mind about. Clearly she'd been made to understand that if he was part of the baggage that came along with marriage to his dad, he wasn't a very big part, nothing she'd have to trouble herself over. She seemed grateful for that, as if she owed her recusal from stepmotherhood to his own delicate renunciation rather than his dad's intention—and he'd been perfectly explicit about this—to start a new family after the false hopes that had been raised and then dashed by the disappointingly infertile Kendra.

"Noah," she said. She held out her free hand to him, and he took it, relieved that she didn't want a hug or kiss, happy to maintain this cool, adult formality. "But you've grown." She looked him up and down. "Do you hate it when people say that?"

"I don't know," he told her. "I don't think I'm growing anymore." At six feet, Gunila was four inches taller than he. Only twenty-five, she'd come to New York from Stockholm as a model with the Ford Agency, but now, for reasons he was more or less completely incurious about, she was a spokesperson for Stolichnaya vodka. What that meant, exactly, he had no idea. He imagined her jetting around to different cities and giving speeches that began, "On behalf of Stolichnaya vodka, I wish to take this opportunity to address a matter of great concern to all of us here: the parking situation downtown. Stolichnaya's position is that there should be adequate parking for everyone. And furthermore, all children should be forced to attend summer reeducation camps. And their parents should drink vodka with every meal. Not any vodka, but Stolichnaya vodka." A few months back he'd written a story: "The Adventures of Gunila, Stolichnaya Spokesperson to the World."

Meanwhile the Stolichnaya Spokesperson to the World was asking him exactly the same question about school his dad had asked, and he was telling her exactly the same thing: "Fine. School's fine." Relieved that he'd mastered the art of cocktail conversation with such ease, he was blissfully unprepared for what came next. In that slightly accented way that she had, Gunila asked, "And are you dating?" She peered expressively into his face, as if to ferret out some truth.

"Um, well," he said defensively. "There's just guys at the school." The antique Buddhas lined up against the wall seemed to watch him, even the haunted Buddha on the left, the one he sometimes caught eyeing him, as if to say, We know your secrets, Little One. *Should* he be dating? Sometimes he'd tag along with Tim and his gang to the mall to hit on girls, but that wasn't exactly dating, and besides, it never came to anything. Though Gary

Marks claimed, through smirks and innuendos, to be seeing a girl he'd met at the mall, whatever "seeing" her meant. "The Forge isn't co-ed or anything," he added, realizing his face and ears had flushed with embarrassment.

"Oh, I didn't mean you had to be dating your schoolfellows," she said humorously. "Surely there are ways to meet girls."

"We have mixers," he explained. "There's this other school, Partridge Academy, it's in Middle Forge, where my school is. It's a girls' school. There's a sort of tea in the afternoon once every couple weeks. Either at our school or theirs." What was the point of mentioning that the couple of times he'd trailed along with Tim and his crowd it had seemed pretty farcical, the boys in their red ties and blue blazers, the girls in whatever, everybody sitting around sipping tea and stuffing their faces with cookies and not having much of anything to say in such an artificial situation. Then afterwards, back at the dorm room, hanging out with Tim and Gary and everybody going, "Yeah, that Heather Christianfeld, oh man, I could really get into doing her. And did you see the hooters on that redhead by the window? Yow!"

"And there're these volunteer clubs too," Noah went on, aware how inexplicably hectic he was sounding. "They work with Partridge Academy on projects, like, they visit old-age homes, that kind of stuff." The sort of activities he might actually consider doing if he were a really good person who could get off his ass.

"So yes," he concluded, a bit breathless, having satisfied himself that what he asserted was in fact true, "there's always ways to meet girls." And if he managed to inject a certain knowing slyness into his voice, what was the harm in that?

The Buddhas smiled serenely, mysteriously, unmoved by any of this. "See?" Gunila smiled back at him with her own knowing slyness. "I thought so. Ah, A. J.," she said more loudly, beckoning him over. He held a heaping plate of food in one hand, a glass of iced tea in the other. He'd put his napkin and silverware in his shirt pocket.

"I need more hands," he said.

"Noah and I have been having a wonderful chat. It seems he's become quite the ladies' man at his school up there." She said it as if the Forge were somewhere past the Arctic Circle.

"Like father, like son," A. J. quipped. Did he have any memory at all of that night in South Carolina? Noah was afraid to scrutinize him too closely, lest he reawaken anything better left forgotten. A. J. had, by his own admission, been very drunk.

Suddenly claustrophobic, and focusing on A. J.'s laden plate, Noah said, "Food. That looks like a good idea," and fled for the buffet table the caterers had set up in the dining room. Shiny metal bins held spicy-smelling Indian food: yellow rice, mercurochrome chicken pieces, unidentifiable lumps in mustardy brown sauce, cheese cubes in spinach. Too many of the dishes looked like one kind of shit or another, and he thought back queasily to the dark matter on himself when he'd pulled out of Chris Tyler's butt. Hot, acrid nausea rose in his throat. He hugely, hugely regretted the afternoon. *The Fatwa:* in his mind, he spit that word out like a chewed-over husk from which everything had been extracted.

About one thing, though, Chris had been exactly right: they'd used each other. They'd used each other the way you might use a coffee grinder or a washing machine—to get the job done. But what job had that been, exactly? What had needed to get done besides releasing some spunk, a job your own hand could manage just fine? He didn't feel any different now than he had before, though the tip of his penis stung, as if it had been dipped in something it wasn't too happy about. He'd sat in the Jacuzzi's scalding heat for nearly an hour, trying to soak away all traces of their encounter, but his flesh wasn't a sheet of paper from which could be erased back to nothing the black marks of words, sentences, paragraphs. Scrub and soak as he might, something awful and obscene remained barely legible.

It had been a momentous event, no doubt about it, nearly as momentous as that evening at Tracy Parker's a week ago when he'd felt so paralyzed, so hemmed in by their polite back-and-forth that he'd had to do something, anything, to change the way things were. Not that it had been for the better—just as this afternoon had not necessarily been for the better—since, despite Tracy's perfunctory protestation to the contrary, Noah had clearly freaked his teacher out. Tracy had gone out of his way to be scrupulously, ridiculously correct with him in the days since, never once looking his way during class, feigning urgent business elsewhere once the hour was over. No more "Drop by for dinner if you feel like it" or "Do you want to house-sit Betsy?"

Perhaps I don't like you so much anymore, he thought bitterly, hesitating before the trays of food and the dark-faced waiter in an ill-fitting suit who stood awkwardly behind the table, ready to be helpful, asking himself, with as much irony as he could muster, Had he really fantasized—idly, perversely—about sucking Tracy Parker's dick? Or worse, had he really made a point of imagining, so vividly it made him shiver, the words Tracy would say to him, low-voiced, dusky with desire, their faces so close he could feel the warm, sweetly sour breath in his mouth, "Noah, I think I want to fuck you. Do you want me to? Is that what you want me to do to you?" Even now he felt a swoony rush in his chest; the horny beast stirred, took on a life of its own down there in the lair of his pants. Well, he mused, trying to back away from those thoughts as best he could. That was very disturbing. So much for testing the waters.

"The chicken is very good. Tandoori," said the waiter. Noah barely nodded. He did not want to get fucked by Tracy Parker or anybody else. And yet the dark lure dangled before him, those bleating sounds of pleasure he'd wrested from the Fatwa, that joyful yelp of pain hinting at some inner mystery he thought, with acute desperation, he couldn't live without knowing.

"Sir?" the waiter asked politely. With his hands he indicated the tandoori chicken. In a fog, Noah reached for the tongs and poked around in the pile of red-dyed animal parts. But who was he fooling? Getting fucked by Tracy Parker was about as likely as waking up one morning on the moon. The guy had drawn the lines very clearly, and when Noah had tested them, even just a little, he'd found himself promptly and in no uncertain terms rebuffed. Probably he'd never go over to that house again. It's just as well that it's finished, he thought. Good riddance. It had been a stupid thing even to think about. But all at once he felt completely hollow inside, done in by a misery reminding him, stridently, that the only reason he could even stand the Forge was Tracy Parker, simple things like walking over to his house, knowing he'd be invited in; cooking dinner together; sitting around in that living room and feeling no pressure to be anybody except who he was. Feeling nervous and safe at the same time. And he'd gone and ruined it. Burned it down in one thoughtlessly premeditated moment.

"Well, Noah," said a voice that lengthened out the second syllable luxuriously. Back for second helpings at the buffet table, A. J. had found him. Noah stood, empty plate in one hand, tongs in the other, stalled at the unappetizing alternatives before him.

"Now I don't usually like real spicy Indian food, but this is mild," A. J. extolled. With great enthusiasm he ladled yellowish rice onto his plate, heaped it with bright red chicken legs and dark cubes of lamb. "I've never been to India. Never had the desire. But your daddy's been. He told me the most marvelous story having to do with six women and a busted steamroller, but for the life of me I can't exactly recollect any more than that at the moment. He ever tell that story to you?"

Noah shook his head. A. J.'s gaze seemed friendly, uncomplicated. He'd never know, would he, what the old lech remembered or didn't remember about that night on the pier. Maybe he'd only been joking and Noah hadn't gotten the joke. Or maybe he'd been testing him. Maybe his dad had put A. J. up to it: "Say, A. J., why don't you find out if my son's the little faggot I think he is. Would you do that for me?" Because of course A. J. was married, he had three daughters, why on earth, drunk or sober, would his roving hand end up on Noah? Tonight, fortunately, the old drunk seemed to be sticking to iced tea. With a fine disgust Noah watched his father's friend make short work of a skinny chicken leg, sliding his lips along the naked bone to suck it dry.

"The young gentleman is having a bit of trouble deciding," the waiter said sympathetically. Noah found himself yearning as never before for one of those cool green salads Tracy Parker would never make for him again. "Excuse me," he said to A. J., and to the helpful waiter as well. He laid his unused plate carefully back on the stack. "I feel a little ill. I'm going to get some fresh air." And turning his back on his erstwhile admirer, he walked over to the sliding glass door, pulled it open a crack, and stepped out onto the balcony.

The chill air made him realize he hadn't lied: he really had been feeling ill in there. Like a big blank canvas, like merciful sleep itself, the park gaped, a dark hole in the middle of the teeming city, though hardly empty itself, rampant in fact with whatever reckless creatures, human or animal, ventured forth only under cover of darkness. It would happen at night, he thought, the leafy heart of the forest, embattled, shrunk to a few acres surrounded on all sides by the encroaching enemy, suddenly bursting forth, vibrant, unstoppable, filling the streets with strong saplings overnight, vines climbing the skyscrapers thirty, forty feet a minute, flowering bushes sprouting from the cracks in the walls of apartment buildings whose occupants lay scattered about, felled by a swift silent plague a hundred times more deadly than AIDS. Excited by the prospect in his head, he leaned forward against the balustrade as if to view from above the work of vengeance begin in the streets below. Someone had left a half-full glass on the ledge; inadvertently he almost knocked it off. Beside the glass lay another object which, at first, in the darkness, he couldn't identify, not till he picked it up, held it in his palm. The Fatwa's dope pipe. His half-drunk glass of orange juice. Both forgotten in the recklessness that had ensued; neither retrieved afterward.

What was inside him would never go away. What had happened would never not have happened. He moaned in distress, thinking for a moment to fling the dope pipe off the balcony, into the darkness, perhaps even land it in the ground zero of the park if he put enough shoulder into it—where, perhaps, it would spark the revolution. But instead he slipped it into his pocket, neither an ill-gotten souvenir nor a sober reminder; an excuse, perhaps, to do that scariest of things: actually talk to the Fatwa once he got back to the Forge. Look him in the eye and say: Here, this is yours. Say: I'm not a bad person, no matter what you might think.

He didn't know how long he'd stood there. It was late. Traffic on Fifth Avenue started, stopped, started again. In the park, beneath the orange-gray sky, men went looking for sex with other men. He knew about that. He didn't want strangers; he wanted one specific person. Behind him he heard the sliding glass door open. Expecting A. J.—it would have to be A. J.—he didn't bother to turn around. Life was full of A. J.s and Fatwas and never enough Tracy Parker.

"So here's where you've been hiding yourself." He felt a large hand on his shoulder, smelled the bracing reek of gin. "Fuck Ashkhabad. What a joy to be back in New York."

"I wasn't hiding," he said defensively. "I just needed some air."

"For your headache," his dad said without sarcasm.

"Yeah. That. How's the party?"

"Over. Done with. I threw the bastards out. No, actually, I'm just zonked. I must be getting old. I spent three weeks in that fucking cesspit shitting myself raw. Hey, you remember that time in London." He laughed. "Now it's my turn. Man was not meant to live on cucumbers and melons and week-old lamb. So what do I do? I drag my sorry ass back here with a big fat contract in my back pocket and I find out my associates, in my absence, have been shitting me as well. Fine. Everybody shits everybody in this world. Money is shit. Power is shit. Love is shit. Women are shit. No, actually," he revised thoughtfully, "women aren't shit. Women are cunts."

Martini glass in hand, he sat down on one of the chaise longues. Noah hardly knew what to say. It was his dad after cocaine. His words might be angry, but he spoke in that calm, indifferent voice Noah had heard earlier. That was what made the things he said all the more horrifying: that they weren't said in anger. They were just his observations, rendered with the same scientific objectivity Noah occasionally prided himself on achieving. "It's true," his father went on. "Gunila is a cunt. Kendra was a cunt." He ticked them off on his fingers. "Your mother, Noah, was a cunt. It's really not their fault. They were born that way. But you want some advice from your dad? Put your dick in them all you want, but if you think you can do anything more than that, if you think you can trust them or believe in them, you're just fucked. Do you understand what I'm saying?"

Noah was glad for the darkness. "Yeah," he said wearily. "I hear you." It was as if his dad's drunkenness or wrath, his cocaine blood rush, had spread contagiously to him as well. He looked at his dad and thought, A faggot gave your son a blow job right there where you're sitting. And your son let it happen, he wanted it to happen, because your son is a little faggot who thinks way too much about what it would be like to have a cock up his ass, who's fascinated by that thought and just as scared of it happening as you would be. Who's really pretty freaked out right about now, he's so curious as to what it would be like to get his tight little virgin ass fucked by Mr. Tracy Parker he fucking can't stand it.

"Well," his dad said. He struggled to rise from the chaise longue, and for an instant Noah thought of extending his hand to help. But then his dad was on his feet, albeit a little unsteadily. The miles had caught up with him. The melon and week-old lamb. The shits and cunts of the world. "I'm calling it a night," he said. "I'm fucking done in. But it was good to see you, buddy. You certainly put the charm on our Stolichnaya spokesperson. That's good. For better or worse, she's going to be your stepmother."

"Dad," Noah said tentatively. He rubbed his neck, tender where the Fatwa had voraciously sucked on him. In his pocket he felt the dope pipe. The Fatwa's glass sat inches from his dad's own martini glass.

His dad looked at him with what suddenly seemed like impatience. There was nothing to say, and Noah said it.

"Nothing," he said.

IX

Remembering Jack Emmerich's classroom visits—unlike his own, entirely unannounced, a hawk swooping down on its prey—Louis felt himself strangely intimidated rather than intimidating, a wary interloper as he settled, promptly at nine A.M. and as inconspicuously as possible, into a desk in the back of English II.

He'd barely needed to make the suggestion—merely breathed it, so to speak, over lunch in the cafeteria one day—for Tracy eagerly to take him up on it.

"Okay," Tracy said to the fifteen boys of the class, "today we have a visitor. You all know Dr. Tremper. Just pretend he's not here." Invisible by fiat, Louis knew them as well: dark-haired, dyslexic Joey Pinnavaia, whose father was a prominent Long Island restaurateur; Adam Kozlowski, the son of a high-profile lawyer and, by dint of an unfortunate history, now presumably behind him, of substance abuse, a year older than the other boys in his class; Shade Laskii-Meyers whose complicated and unorthodox family situation Louis had never quite managed to sort out; sweetly clueless Benjamin Cannon; Tim Vaughn and Gary Marks the athletes and David Valentine the chessplayer; Mike Choi from Singapore, who, it was said, could answer any question one might have about the school's computers, not that Louis himself had even a single one.

Seating himself casually on his desktop, Tracy plunged right in. "In some ways the main event of the book comes early on, right? When Gene jostles the branch of that tree and sends Finny falling. And everything else spreads out from there, the repercussions. And so it seems like maybe we want to ask two questions: one, why did Gene do what he did, and two, what does he learn from it?"

It had been several years since Louis had taught *A Separate Peace*: Bobby

Wainmark's class had been perhaps the last time. But he remembered quite fondly and well the enthusiasms that slender volume could engender, the ways it could touch even those boys who might seem unreachable. It was about their lives, after all, the kind of lives they lived unbeknownst to the adults around them. Among these very students in Tracy's classroom there were friendships, rivalries—some known to all, but others completely private, passions that flared invisibly, fruitlessly, though perhaps never entirely to subside.

"So I don't get it," said Shade Laskii-Meyers in his mellifluous baritone. "If they're best friends, then why would he go and do something like that? You don't do that to your best friend. You don't push him out of a tree. It doesn't make any sense."

"They weren't really friends," Tim Vaughn said adamantly. "They were mortal enemies. Only Finny didn't know that. He trusted Gene to be his friend, but Gene was a total creep."

"I don't agree with that," Shade said. "Definitely they were friends. They were like this." To illustrate, he gripped his hands together firmly, powerfully.

"Let's look at the text," Tracy reminded them. "Let's find quotes. Remember, we're interested in what the book actually says, not what we want it to say. Remember to mark key passages when you read."

Books fell open, pages were flipped. A concentrated air of study all at once pervaded the classroom. Louis was impressed. He liked the sight of all those bent heads, the palpable sense of intellectual eagerness. How he missed being in the classroom on a regular basis.

"I've got it," Shade volunteered. He was something of a beauty, though a bit vacant-eyed. His hair could have been neater. Till his father intervened, he'd lived on a women's commune amidst the redwoods with his mother and his sister Rainwater. He'd made an admirable adjustment to the social and academic rigors of the Forge School.

"It's where Gene says, 'The war would be deadly all right. But I was used to finding something deadly in things that attracted me; there was always something deadly lurking in anything I wanted, anything I loved. And if there wasn't, as for example with Phineas, I put it there myself. But in the war, there was no question about it at all; it was there.'"

"Good," Tracy said. "So what's that saying?"

"Well." Shade frowned in concentration. "It's saying he was both friends with Finny but also his enemy. Like, he loved him but, underneath everything, there was this war between them."

"So let's talk about the war," Tracy said. "What war is it, by the way? The larger war, I mean."

"Vietnam?" Benjamin Cannon put forth tentatively.

"Earlier," Tracy coaxed.

"It's World War Two," Gary Marks said with eye-rolling impatience.

"But it's also just any war, isn't it?" Tracy suggested to them. "In some ways it doesn't really matter which war it is."

Vindicated, Benjamin nodded vigorously.

"The war's like a symbol," Shade proposed.

"Very good," Tracy said. "What do you think it symbolizes?"

With a prolonged, indeed painful creak, the door to the classroom swung slowly open. Looking as if he'd just woken up from a very deep sleep, Noah Lathrop mumbled, "Sorry."

"Fashionably late once again, I see." Tracy spoke banteringly, at ease with his recalcitrant student. But perhaps Louis misgauged his tone. Something mocking flickered in Noah's eyes that made Louis think, with sudden alarm, that the boy was going to tell Tracy—in the simplest possible terms, and in front of the whole class—"Fuck off." It was as if those shocking words had already been uttered and hung, palpable, in the air of the classroom.

But instead Noah said, with a faint shrug, "Somebody's got to set the trends around this place."

It was uncanny, though, how absolutely certain Louis was that Noah had thought those violent words, even if he had held back from actually saying them. He had seemed to hear them so clearly, the way shepherds had perhaps once been assailed by voices as they tended their flocks in the fields.

But no one else had heard anything like that. They took it all very differently. "Oversleeping is not what I'd call a trend, exactly," Gary taunted, his voice the confident, bullying voice of the soccer field, the locker room. The class roared with a laughter that wasn't so much nervous as, simply, genial.

"You wish," Noah shot back sharply. At sports Louis knew him to be listless, worse than mediocre.

"Okay, okay," Tracy said. "Enough of that, you two."

"I wasn't feeling well this morning," Noah concluded in a more subdued tone. "I stopped by the infirmary."

"And I presume they gave you a note?"

"They forgot," Noah mumbled, to more exaggerated eye-rolling from Gary.

"Well, you'll bring one by later, right?"

Noah's shrug, once again, seemed to Louis to border on insolence. It was all he could do to restrain himself from saying something. For the first time since class had started, Tracy glanced his way, his gaze both bemused and slightly humorous; then he turned his attention back to the latecomer. Gingerly he urged him up to speed. "We were talking about the war, what role it plays. What it's a symbol of."

"The war in the book?" Noah said. He dropped himself negligently into his seat.

"Right," Tracy told him.

As if it had all at once come to him, Shade announced to the room, "The war is real life. It's just all the things that happen. It's not soldiers and guns and bombs. It's just"—he searched for the right word—"it's just . . . stuff."

Perhaps it was because he came from California, or perhaps the class genuinely appreciated his efforts: in any event, Tim Vaughn gave him a friendly thumbs-up. David Valentine nodded vigorously. Benjamin looked as if he was trying very hard to follow what Shade had said. It was a moment for coming together, and Louis felt somehow pleased—for the class, for Tracy.

But then Noah spoke. "I don't think so," he said sourly, peremptorily. "Look at the end of the book. War's the easy part, whether it's the enemy or, as you say, just *stuff*." He spoke the word with some distaste. "At least in a war you know who the enemy is. It's when there isn't any war that it gets all complicated."

Shade looked at him blankly, though his voice was not unfriendly. "What do you mean?"

"Let's look at that passage," Tracy urged, a little forlornly, it seemed to Louis. "Go ahead and read it," he told Noah.

"I don't like to read out loud," Noah averred.

Tracy was unfazed. "Adam," he suggested, "why don't you read it?"

Adam Kozlowski looked as if he'd been ambushed. Louis's theory was that drugs slowed you down permanently, something nobody bothered to tell these kids.

"You mean the last paragraph?" he asked. Tracy nodded patiently.

In a flat, uncomprehending voice he read out, " 'All of them, all except Phineas, constructed at infinite cost to themselves these—' "

"Mah-jee-no," Tracy helped him along. "It's French."

" 'Mah-jee-no Lines against this enemy they thought they saw across the frontier, this enemy who never attacked that way—if he ever attacked at all; if he was indeed the enemy.' Tracy, what's a Maginot Line?"

Louis could never get used to students calling their teachers by their first names, an unproductive bit of familiarity if ever there was one. It was a practice he'd always discouraged. Had he failed, he wondered, to mention that to Tracy?

"The French had this system of defenses," Noah said. He spoke with brusque, even arrogant, authority. "They were so convinced the Germans couldn't get through, they didn't realize all the Germans had to do was just go around them and then screw them from behind. But the Maginot Line's really not the best image here. For what the book's trying to say, I mean. Because if you look at what it says, it's not the Germans you need to worry about, or anybody else: it's you. You're the enemy. You're the one who's going to defeat yourself. That's what Gene does. He doesn't kill his best friend; he kills himself. And when he goes to the funeral he doesn't cry, because you don't cry at your own funeral. He even says that. Everybody commits suicide, one way or another." He spoke quickly, passionately. There was an unattractive dogmatism to his points.

From Benjamin his words elicited the involuntary exclamation, "Oh, that's not true."

"That *is* kind of a depressing thought," Tracy said. "But aren't you sort of overstating things? Doesn't Gene learn *anything* at all useful from Finny's example? I mean, he does go on to write the book."

But Noah, it appeared, had had his say. He shrugged vaguely, and slouched back in his seat. He let the discussion surge on past him.

"You have to make your own peace with the world," Shade offered. "That's what he learned. Phineas was the example to him. How you have to get over your hate and envy and competitiveness and stuff. You have to accept who you are."

Shade certainly knew how to earn his keep. Still, what Noah had said hung unpleasantly in the air, a chill that wouldn't dissipate. Louis was irked. He glared at Noah but the boy didn't notice. The class had lost his attention. He closed his eyes as if he wanted to make them all go away.

"I think," Louis said when the last of the students had filed out the door and he and Tracy were alone, "that you perhaps give that character a bit too much leeway." But then, regretting he'd spoken in such haste, he added, "Not to say it wasn't a superb class. I thought it was very . . . deft. You were skillful at bringing the students into the discussion. It's just aggravating, a student like that. Does he always come to class late?"

"Noah has this thing about mornings," Tracy said. "The irony of it is, in many ways he's the smartest student in the class."

"That was certainly less than obvious."

"Well," Tracy backtracked. "Smart. That's a hard word to define."

"Don't coddle him," Louis said sternly. "I know it's easy to get distracted by the problems some of these boys have. But it's important to be strict with them. Set boundaries. The school does have a counselor, after all, and I think Noah sees him with some regularity. I believe, in fact, he's required to."

"I don't think Noah likes him very much. Actually, he's told me that they really don't get along at all."

"I can't really imagine him getting along with much of anyone," Louis said, more stiffly than he'd intended. "But that's for the two of them to work out. I must say, though, he was dead wrong about that book."

"I thought he was being rather subtle," Tracy said.

"Dead wrong," Louis affirmed with a tone of certainty guaranteed, he hoped, to settle the matter once and for all. "And one other thing, just in parting: perhaps it's not the best idea to have the boys go addressing you by your first name. I'm not sure that establishes the proper authority in the classroom."

He wasn't happy with himself. He admitted that. The situation had called for some delicacy, and instead he'd ridden roughshod over Tracy's inexperience. He'd come down much too hard. As if to punctuate his distress, snow clouds gathered outside his office window. By nightfall there would be sleet, freezing rain, some kind of ungodly mess. Claire had called to tell him she was coming home early.

Fruitlessly he replayed his postmortem with Tracy, softening the edges, toning down his strident certainties.

"It's far too early in the year for snow," Reid announced, materializing in the doorway and startling him from his remorseful meditation. "Here I'm supposed to fly out on Wednesday evening, and the gods are toying with me. They're just jealous. You'll never guess what a deal I got on tickets."

Louis could only stare at him gloomily. Airline tickets were one of Reid's drearier obsessions; he prided himself on being able to ferret out the most implausibly cheap fares to anywhere in the world. It struck Louis as absurd. Here was a man with considerable funds at his disposal who would nevertheless opt to fly Haitian Air to Chicago by way of Port-au-Prince if it could save him a few dollars. Who found himself, with great regularity, aboard airplanes, usually under the imprimatur of some highly impoverished government's national airline, whose ashen-faced stewardesses, before takeoff, marched up and down the aisle offering free shots of vodka to any passengers whose nerves needed a bit of bucking up.

This particular trip sounded, in comparison to some of his jaunts, positively straightforward. "Air Pakistan, the London leg of the New York–Karachi flight," Reid cataloged joyfully. "Then I've got a shamelessly inexpensive seat to Warsaw. Lot Air—it's almost as if they're paying me for the honor of my company. From there it's a Bulgarian carrier to Thessaloniki, and then good old Olympia to Athens. All for less than it would take to fly from here to Detroit, not that anyone in their right mind would want to fly to Detroit. I'll be back in New York Sunday night."

Louis could only shake his head gloomily. "I can never quite believe you do these things."

"I told you, it's a professional meeting," Reid averred. "I have obligations to my field."

"You have far too much energy for your own good, is what you have."

"No," Reid said. "What I have is a chart inside my head, just a straight line, actually, pointing in both directions, and you know what it says in both directions? Eternity. Infinity. Nonbeing. Nothingness. And in the middle of the line there's an infinitesimal little dot, and above the little dot it says, This Is Your Life. I think about that all the time."

His sudden earnestness took Louis aback. How could such candor not unnerve one at eleven o'clock on a Tuesday morning in the middle of November? "And the Greek Orthodox Church?" he found himself wondering.

"I'll try anything," Reid admitted. "And furthermore, I'll give it a serious try. See: I'm a faithfully married man. I'm an adulterer. I'm a devout Christian who is terribly afraid that there's nothing at all out there except empty space. So there you have it. Nothing but a bundle of contradictions. You, on the other hand, have always struck me as a creature of admirable consistency. I never know how you manage."

And of course, with that, Reid had fingered him exactly. Outside, a cold wind was blowing up a spell of chaotic weather, but in here, his office, everything was warmth and order. If the actual situation were exactly the reverse of that, what did it matter? Louis could only feel a certain solid satisfaction at hearing his success thus confirmed.

"You have my blessing," he said generously. "Though I must say, I wouldn't trade places with you for anything."

"In three days I'll be standing in front of the Parthenon. I'll be making love in a little hotel in the Plaka to a woman I love. I'll be drinking retsina and feasting on grilled calamari. I'll be alive."

He had not thought Reid would remember—and, true to form, he hadn't. But what did that matter? He would mark this day privately, as he had for the past fifteen years. They tended to honor very different pasts.

In a world where everything changed, the Heidelberg on Main Street had managed, remarkably, to persist. He hardly ever went downtown anymore, though there had been a time in the sixties when he and Jack were quite the regulars at the thriving brauhaus. Entering the restaurant's dark warmth from the chill of the street, he couldn't help but push aside, like those heavy protective curtains guarding the portals of certain European churches, a vague feeling of guilt, as though he'd neglected some civic duty. Noon on a weekday, and not a soul stirred in the place except for Ilse-Marie behind the bar. Since he'd last been here she'd grown larger, ruddier; these days her curls' platinum luster was plainly dyed. Her accent, however, had not changed one whit since she'd arrived in this country.

"Professor," she greeted him affably. "*Grüß Gott.*" She seemed to take his long absence from the premises as a matter of course.

"*Grüß Gott,*" he answered, though "Professor" always made him jump a bit.

Hunting trophies stared at him solemnly from the walls. He could not now recall which of those antlered beauties Jack had been responsible for, and though Ilse-Marie would undoubtedly remember, Louis decided he would not ask.

With barely a glance at the still-familiar menu, he ordered a schnitzel and, after a moment's hesitation in which he debated whether a drink at noon might undo him, a bottle of Dinkelacker.

It wasn't just the weather, which grew more somber by the hour. He didn't like being the only customer in the Heidelberg; he felt scrutinized, even accused. Seldom did he so long to find himself amid a noisy, gregarious crowd, one that might keep a cook safely occupied in the kitchen, behind those swinging doors through which Ilse-Marie had just carried his order. He dreaded gruff, blustery Wolfgang's inevitable emergence from back there. For years, a tattered billboard on the side of the old brick pharmacy down the street had sported that jovial, cleaver-wielding likeness: The Wurst Butcher on the Block. And as if on cue, Wolfgang did emerge, his hair sorely thinning, his face gone thick and gray with age. He'd had cancer surgery, Louis remembered.

"Wie geht's, wie geht's?" Wolfgang wanted to know. He slid into the booth opposite. His hands were big and powerful, his nails scrubbed clean.

"Nicht so schlimm," Louis told him. "It's good to see you looking so well."

"Getting too fat and too lazy," Wolfgang lamented. He gestured around the empty room. "I got nothing to do all day. Maybe I should retire. But you want to know a secret?" He leaned conspiratorially close. "It would kill me to see the *Schwartzen* take this place over. When I first opened here . . ."

It occurred to Louis that he'd have perhaps been better off skipping lunch entirely and heading straight to the cemetery. He should have grabbed a bite with Tracy in the school cafeteria, his presence gently reassuring the young man that, all minor qualms aside, everything had really gone quite splendidly in the morning class.

Or better yet, why hadn't he thought, in the interests of investing his colleague further in the institution for which he toiled so diligently, to ask Tracy to accompany him as he paid his respects? Several times now the young man had seemed curious about the Forge School's past, its venerable traditions, its ineffable ethos. Well, it was too late now for that. Another time.

Fortunately, through the Heidelberg's front door burst a party of five, hectic young men in suits, lawyers probably, or insurance men, since those were the only two businesses left on Main Street that employed young white men in suits.

"Got to go," Wolfgang said apologetically. Louis had the feeling they had been on the verge of a more complicated conversation than he had the nerves for. He was apologetic in return as Wolfgang shook his hand (he'd forgotten how powerfully that hand engulfed one's own). "It's awfully good to see you. I'll try to stop in more often." He wished his tone of voice didn't so clearly betray him at such moments.

"*Ja, ja,*" Wolfgang told him. "I know why you're here today."

If that was so, he was doubly relieved that a longer conversation had been averted. He had to admit, sadly, that, although he continued faithfully to go through the motions of grief, the real grief had long since dwindled to little more than a benumbed whisper inside him.

"Thank you," he told Wolfgang sincerely, "for remembering."

As Ilse-Marie set a rather drab-looking plate of schnitzel before him, he could only admire her own lack of desperation. It was clear: in another year the Heidelberg would be gone. Was this how the Germans had soldiered on, against impossible odds, in the final days of the war? As a boy he had followed the newspaper and radio reports as the Allies from the west and the Soviets from the east closed the noose around Berlin. To watch that magisterial city, great dove-gray prince of Europe's heartland, battered and burning in the final throes of its *Götterdämmerung*, raised him to a fever pitch of vengeful excitement that was nonetheless shot through with a heart-stopping and entirely traitorous grief. He was fourteen. At night he lay in bed with his shameful secret. He had given himself over to the enemy's spell. His were, at least in theory, the loose lips that sank ships, his the hands that gave aid and comfort to the ravening scourge. In the quiet of his soul he had mouthed certain words he knew to be terrible, bitter words: *Luftwaffe. Wehrmacht. Blitzkrieg.* How had that happened? A stirring novella read at an impressionable age, some concerts sponsored by the Germania Association of Poughkeepsie, a waiter at the Mountain Brauhaus in the Shawangunks, a veritable Siegfried, blond and bronzed, who had caught his imagination one evening as he dined with his parents, long before he had reached the age when he might be expected to be attuned to such things, and whose image had burned for days like a votive candle lit at the altar of a cult scarcely to be named. It was a mystery as awful as the changes happening to his body, the regrettable habits he had, against all his self-respect and restraint, recently indulged himself in under the covers at night.

But it did not quite end there. In the victorious summer of defeat that followed, during which all eyes turned to the Pacific (to whose fate he was entirely indifferent), Louis had worked his first job. At the Mohonk Mountain House, that grand and rambling resort, fantasia of wood and stone and mossy shingles, he operated the ancient elevator that deposited guests on their appropriate floors. Among the visitors sojourning there for two weeks in August, while atomic bombs fell on Japanese cities, a certain mild-eyed, distinguished gentleman compelled his attention. Day after day he ferried this man, his wife, and his grown daughter to and from their third-floor suite. They were Germans, Louis had deduced from their conversation; refugees, no doubt. They exuded a curious mix of pride, courtesy, and warmth that Louis found attractive but mysterious. The man in particular, with his clipped mustache and austere black-rimmed spectacles, his thinning gray hair and habitual bow tie, seemed at once weary and prodigiously alert. Like a king who has renounced his throne, he allowed himself to be led by his wife and daughter, and yet it was he, clearly, who remained royalty. Who were they? In the elevator's confines, Louis was acutely conscious of a gaze resting on him momentarily, then drifting away only to return, in the briefest of glances, several times during their short ride. Something stirred in him; he had never felt so scrutinized, seen through, calmly disassembled. And yet at the time, despite his quiet young sense of outrage at the liberties this gaze took with him, the impression overtook him that, along with everything else, some strange homage was somehow being paid the lowly elevator boy who dutifully guided the machine to a soft stop at the third floor. But how could that be? Only on the morning of the German family's departure did Louis learn the strange truth: none other than the famous writer Thomas Mann had, for the last weeks, graced the resort with his presence. The uncanny coincidence shivered down Louis's spine. The war had ended. Germany had been laid low in defeat. He knew that Thomas Mann had fled that benighted country, that he had become a vociferous opponent of the evil he saw there; still, Louis couldn't help but mysteriously conflate the author of the classic novella that had so stirred his soul when he'd read it earlier that year with a noble enemy whose capacity for evil, as the great writer himself knew all too well, was so strangely and fatefully linked to its capacity for good.

The Heidelberg's schnitzel proved completely tasteless, even after he squeezed wedges of lemon along its leathery flank, and in any event, he didn't seem to have much of an appetite. Seeing Ilse-Marie busy with her lively tableful of lawyers, he folded a twenty under his half-empty mug and, slipping quickly and unobtrusively into his overcoat, slipped equally quickly and un-obtrusively out the door.

Business had almost completely abandoned Main Street. That had been a camera store; and there, where barbaric grafitti adorned the boarded-up windows, Valley Stationery; and past that, the old Lenape Grocery with its wooden floors and wooden Indian. They'd all been open that afternoon he walked down this street fifteen years ago, an interlude of glorious Indian summer, temperatures in the eighties, the world so vivid with late autumn color it seemed ready to jump out of its skin. One moment he was basking in all that, and the next, sudden as a flash flood in a narrow canyon, a cold surge flowed down the street. Never in his life had he felt anything so peculiar. Within ten minutes the day's character had changed utterly. Clouds engulfed the sun; a chill rain began to fall.

It was later that evening that a knock came at the door. Outside, he could see a police cruiser parked against the curb. The shy young officer held his hat in his hand. The rain had brought down all the bright leaves. "I'm afraid I have some tragic news," the officer explained.

How he hated the way everyone misused that word, *tragic*. So very few things were, technically speaking, tragic. The thought prevented him from entirely grasping what the officer told him.

The cold front had borne down from Canada, picking up moisture over the Great Lakes. After a long dry spell, rainwater mixed with the residue of oil on a road's asphalt surface to form a film, a treacherous slick. It had happened earlier in the afternoon, up in Sullivan County. Jack had been driving back from his farm. Behind him, Louis felt Claire put her hands on his shoulder.

The cemetery lay on the north side of the Reformed Dutch Church, whose sober bluestone facade dominated Middle Forge's commons. Ancient locust trees, now barely more than hulks, rose bare-branched from amid gravestones on whose worn faces the name Emmerich was a strongly recurrent theme; Jack's forebears had come to the Hudson Valley nearly three centuries ago.

At a pay phone on the corner, two young black men took turns talking. Louis noted them just as a precaution. Their gestures looked languid and playful, but a sixth sense hinted at the casual inclination toward violence lying just below their easy laughter.

"Let me stand at your verge, Chasm, and not be dismayed." Louis spoke the old words quietly. He scattered them as if they were flowers. With those mystical lines Jack had introduced him, so many years ago, to the Secret Germany he had already, as a boy, intuited. His first year at the Forge School, they'd sat late into the night sipping kirsch or Jaegermeister, and Jack would read aloud to him from the austere and voluptuous hymns of Stefan George, or they would listen in silence to Schubert and Wagner and Bruckner. Afterward they would talk—wonderful talk, grave and ardent and idealistic. Those nights had been, in a sense, Louis's real education, a legacy carefully passed his way.

One night, listening to Richard Strauss's *Metamorphosen*, those somber variations composed after the Allied bombing of the composer's beloved Munich Opera House, Jack had broached, almost hesitantly, the terrible heart of the matter, observing, "It is entirely possible that what we witnessed in those years was the triumph of a morally good but utterly banal culture over a terribly compromised and corrupt but vastly more beautiful one." Jack's words had made Louis vividly remember, of all things, Betty Grable—those legs, those buttocks, that pert and fetching glance over the shoulder. WIN IT FOR ME, BOYS! she called out invitingly from propaganda posters impossible to ignore. At fourteen, he had nursed his skepticism in silence. There was a war on, and who if not Betty was helping the cause? But all the while he had dreamed, in his solitude and darkness, of the Secret Germany no Betty Grable would ever sully.

It was as if a covert signal had passed that evening between the head-master and his newly hired teacher. Something in Louis quickened. They were comrades in a secret war to save those grave and beautiful things worth saving from the irrepressible vulgarity that had, as Stefan George had darkly declared, trampled down every inch of earth from equator to pole. They both had known, without ever needing explicitly to say it, that that secret and noble war was what the work of the Forge School, in its obscure way, was all about.

Along the empty street an old woman trundled a shopping cart loaded with soda cans. The two young black men, Louis noticed, appraised her as well. But she was tough as a root, an ancient inviolable turtle. They could see, in a glance, there was nothing there for them. He, on the other hand—this old white man in a tweed jacket and overcoat, umbrella in hand and still thinking of Betty Grable, of the bombing of the Munich Opera House, of Jack Emmerich, who had never married—he was without doubt the more plausible victim. For the moment, though, tethered to the phone booth, his potential assailants remained at a safe distance; he would leave if they started to walk toward him.

Had Jack been lonely in his bachelorhood? The school was his life, he'd always said, the education of boys, and Louis had never had cause to doubt the absolute truth of that claim. That had been in the days before people asked questions of every innocent thing, before this relentless need to name, to label, to categorize. People had understood that life might be rich, com-plicated, ambiguous. And about Jack's life, especially as seen from the per-spective of nearly two decades, there had undoubtedly been rich and complex ambiguities, the specifics unknowable from this distance and yet, paradoxi-cally, from this distance clearer than they had been up close.

Reid, for one, had had his moments of wry speculation—Jack's overnight camping trips at Indian Rock with his favorite students, gossip easily dismissable—but then Reid had never fully appreciated the scope of Jack Emmerich, his vision and ambition. Father Fallone might well be the Forge School's reigning genius, but there were musics he had long ago shown he simply could not hear. But perhaps, for all concerned, that was just as well. Certainly it had averted some misunderstandings of a personal nature that might have occurred had he been more—how should one put it?—finely attuned.

In his head the long descending figure from the *Metamorphosen* sounded grievingly. Was there any piece of music more profoundly sad? What is gone, it said with no trace of consolation, is simply gone. The tombstone spelled it out so bluntly. 1921–1980. LET ME MOUNT TO YOUR HEIGHT, SUMMIT, YET NOT BE DESTROYED!

The black men had finished their drug deal, or whatever tricky negotiation they had been undertaking on the phone. They stood alert, as if casting about for what to do next. As for himself, there was nothing more to be done here. He had paid his respects. He had honored his dead. Teacher, fallen comrade, old friend. He was not about to offer himself up.

Ruined for the afternoon, too restless or distraught in heart and head to accomplish anything, he should have simply called it a day, gone home early. But something warned him of the dangers of falling into that habit. The slippery slope was everywhere.

He would take a walk instead. After three in the afternoon the school's center of gravity shifted. Irving and Cooper, the two classroom buildings, emptied out, the boys dispersed to the gym or the playing fields for athletics or to remedial sessions with their academic tutors. When classes were in session he purposely avoided wandering through those halls unless he had specific business; he worried it might look as if he were on the prowl, spying and keeping tabs, which was the farthest thing from his mind.

The empty classrooms had a calming effect on him. He enjoyed imagining what went on there, the work that was accomplished. Each room had its own personality: in one, maps showing Greece in ancient times were pulled down over the blackboards. In another, where Robertson taught biology, carefully tended cactuses covered the south-facing windowsills. Thornhill's math classroom was hung with complex and beautiful geodesic models she'd had her students design and make.

The door to Tracy's classroom was ajar, and he was intrigued to see Tracy at his desk. Perhaps he was marking papers. The sight of a young man busily at work stirred something in Louis. Glad for this fortuitous chance to encourage him once more about the morning's class, Louis rapped lightly on the door frame.

He stopped midway through the door. Tracy was at his desk, to be sure, but he was not alone. Quite casually, hands in his pockets, one leg dangling, Noah Lathrop sat on the edge of the desk.

They both looked up at him—not with alarm, but certainly with mild surprise.

"Louis," Tracy said.

"Hey, Dr. Tremper," Noah echoed. "We were just talking about that class you were at today."

A harmless bit of information, exactly the kind the headmaster might be expected to want to hear. He'd volunteered it, though, just a little too quickly. There was something about this picture Louis didn't like. But what that could be, other than the fact of their both being here at this particular hour, when the classrooms were generally deserted, he didn't rightly know. And what, for that matter, was he himself doing here?

"Please don't let me interrupt," he managed to say, even while observing to himself some ease they had with each other, some intangible level of comfort, nothing in particular he could put his finger on. Then, thinking back to the tensions, even the hostility that had been so palpable between them in the classroom, at least on Noah's part, he felt profoundly confused.

"He's all yours," Noah said, with what Louis supposed passed for a smile from him. "I'm gonna go now. Bye, Mr. Tremper. See you later, Trace."

Louis turned to watch him slouch toward the door. A sudden, unprofessional impulse shamed him. There was no evading it. He never took sides against students, but toward Noah he felt a visceral antipathy. His last-minute application had been a catalog of difficulties, both scholastic and social. A more accident-prone youngster Louis thought he'd never seen. An arm, a leg, a collarbone: half his young life, it seemed, had been spent mending one bone or another. Louis could never shake the suspicion that some people, whether consciously or not, called the storm to themselves.

In the end, he had yielded to the wisdom of the admissions officer. Noah's father, after all, was a man of far-reaching power and influence, and such men were usually exceedingly grateful when their sons effected the impressive turnaround the Forge School promised and, more often than not, delivered.

Louis decided he would say nothing more about the subject to Tracy. He'd had his say. And about first names, too.

Tracy, meanwhile, was smiling bemusedly and shaking his head. "So, I'm all yours now," he said. Then, gesturing toward the window, the quad across which they could both see Noah making his way, "I see it's really starting to come down out there."

Large wet flakes were indeed coming down. Already the lawn was daubed with white. You're making far more of this than need be, Louis chided himself. Still, he could not get out of his head the irritating diminutive Noah had bestowed on his teacher. Not the word itself so much as the fact that Tracy had failed to call him on it. His initial impression had been correct. There was something about this picture he didn't like. One did not give one's life to an institution like the Forge School without, over the years, acquiring some intuitive sense of things.

The kitchen floor was spattered with drops of dark blood. For a moment his heart stopped; then he saw the note on the fridge. One of the polyps in Lux's ear canal—for the last year an intractable source of misery to the poor beast—had burst, and Claire, braving the storm, had spirited him off to the vet to have the ear cauterized. Her mission of mercy made Louis uneasy. Though Claire was a perfectly skillful driver, the vet was some miles away, and he had registered, walking home, how the streets were starting to get a bit tricky. Some days the temptation to yield to superstitions was stronger than others. He would try hard to resist. What he would not resist was the temptation, equally strong this evening, to pour himself a comforting scotch.

Whenever he found himself left alone in the house, he felt dangerously unanchored. Even as a child, when his parents would go out, he'd feel freed from some scrutiny. But that freedom brought not release but emptiness. Anarchy raised its seductive head. He could do anything; there was nothing that was not allowed. He'd march around the house singing at the top of his lungs. He'd get into the pantry and icebox and taste bits of everything. He'd go through his parents' closets and drawers, and afterward feel soiled and disgusted. Joseph Conrad had no doubt been right to observe that the presence of the policeman around the corner is the only thing that keeps us civilized.

A companionable marriage certainly did wonders in working one through the treacherous spots as well. For this, he was eternally in his wife's debt. Sometimes it took an absurdly great effort of the will just to continue to function normally. Even having a drink alone was sometimes a bad idea.

On the kitchen counter lay the day's mail: a circular from the local hardware store, a letter addressed to his wife. He'd seen the envelope's tiny, torturous handwriting before; whoever it belonged to had been writing Claire with great regularity over the past several weeks. The strangeness of that occurred to him. Though she had developed professional contacts over the years and hardly lacked for friends and acquaintances, Claire seldom received mail of the old-fashioned kind.

The envelope was slit open across the top, but Louis resisted the urge to gratify his curiosity. It wasn't as if he'd ever, in forty years, suspected Claire of dabbling in anything untoward and he certainly wasn't about to start now. No doubt she'd tell him, one of these days, about her eager new correspondent.

Settling perturbedly onto the creaking old leather sofa, he turned on the television to try to locate a weather report—that, after all, was a normal thing to do—but the various channels had moved on from their local to national news broadcasts, and he had long ago ceased to watch those corporate-sponsored entertainments. On the public television station, however, a conversation caught his attention. A prominent conservative critic was interviewing a journalist who had written a prize-winning book about the former East Germany. Smartly dressed in a dark blue suit, the young woman spoke precisely, articulately, though her voice was curiously dispassionate. "Consider the case," she said in her clear staccato, "of Olga Schmidt, an East German activist who, with her husband, had worked actively in the peace and environmental movements. After the fall of communism Olga campaigned to have the files of the secret police opened, and ultimately she was successful. As she read the Stasi file on herself, a several-hundred-page-long chronicle of her life as a dissident, she came gradually to a realization. Amid the minute and mostly irrelevant details were certain pieces of information about herself that were so intimate that they could have been known to no one but herself and her husband. For weeks she carried this secret knowledge, but finally could bear it no longer. When she confronted her husband with her suspicions, he acknowledged that, yes, he had indeed informed on her—not just once but regularly, for years in fact. But he insisted that, in doing so, he had betrayed neither her nor their shared ideals. He had seen himself, in fact, as furthering their dissident work by opening up important channels of communication with the Stasi, by allowing them to see the extent of the people's discontent."

Louis sipped his scotch, mildly intrigued by the predicament—betrayals always intrigued him—but at the same time wary. Clearly the journalist had recited this anecdote countless times before. He thought, idly, that he should have stayed to chat with Tracy instead of seeming to flee. Though on the other hand, he cautioned himself not to invest too much in someone who might well prove a disappointment to him in one way or another.

"That's an amazing story," the critic effused. He was pompous though probably harmless. Louis usually avoided his program. "And you see this as somehow"—he cast about for the word he wanted—"*exemplary* of life under communism?"

"Oh yes, absolutely," the young woman told him. Her black bangs made her look rather severe, though perhaps that was the look she intended. "Complicity under communism wasn't between people but *within* people, like the veins and arteries inside the body. It makes no sense to talk about victims and collaborators, because all too often they were one and the same. It happened every day, under every conceivable circumstance. Take something so simple as a third-grade teacher instilling in her students the ideals of the socialist state. Without educating its children in how to think, the state cannot perpetuate itself. That third-grade teacher was as much a collaborator as any informer who turned in his neighbor or coworker."

"We're talking about a tragic situation," the critic said. He drew out the adjective with exaggerated effect. "But fortunately, we're also talking about a system that brought about its own inevitable collapse. The corrupt state that the Stasi tried, through its nefarious means, to prop up is simply no more."

"I would certainly say that a long nightmare is over," the young woman agreed.

"Well," said the critic, who seemed very pleased with his guest's performance, "I must say it will be fascinating to see how the people of the former East Germany manage to come to terms with their new freedoms, freedoms that we take so much for granted under capitalism and democracy."

"That will be the challenge," said the young woman. "Will they successfully play ball in the rough-and-tumble world of the free market, or will they be left behind?"

What was truly fascinating, Louis thought, was the level of self-deception people were capable of. Or was it really something far worse? A carefully calculated mendacity. She had done very well by her book, this young woman. She had won prizes for it. She had been amply rewarded by those in power. Surely she was not so naive or clueless as to think that she stood free of the metaphor she herself had so neatly described.

Suddenly he wasn't so much fascinated as furious. "Idiots," he said aloud to the ghosts on the television screen. Then more forcefully: "Moronic bastards." Those two collaborators understood perfectly well how their jobs—like everyone else's except, perhaps, that impervious old woman he had seen earlier with her shopping cart—entailed nothing less than propping up the State.

In disgust he flicked off the set. Who were they trying to fool? He was an educator, after all. He knew all about inculcating values. Hadn't Aristotle noticed two thousand years ago the importance of schooling people to feel joy and grief at the right things? Hadn't he held that true education was precisely that? Veins and arteries. "I have news for you," he said to the blank screen, the empty room. To the prize-winning journalist and the conservative commentator and Reid Fallone and, yes, Tracy Parker also. The former East Germany hardly had a monopoly on complicity. Life's every moment caught one out in one form of it or another.

From the driveway came a familiar sound strangely deadened by the falling snow: an Audi's engine shutting off, a car door slamming shut. Lux's jubilant bark of homecoming. Just in time, he thought with relief. Just in time. He would try to compose himself for the evening. He would try to play the game—it was perfectly, even deadly, serious after all. He would try to stay calm while doing so.

X

"My body is a temple," said the svelte young woman in the black leotard and tights.

"My body is a temple," repeated the fifteen middle-aged women sitting cross-legged on the floor.

"My body is the dwelling place of God," said their leader, her voice mellifluous and soothing.

"My body is the dwelling place of God," they all repeated.

Claire's legs had gone to sleep. They always seemed to do that. She dreaded the moment when Rachel would command them to rise, to stretch, to bend. She knew she was sure to fall right over.

"When God is in her temple," Rachel told them, "then any woman can accomplish anything she wants."

Claire tried not to giggle, because she suspected that Libby took this all somewhat seriously. Still, it was vaguely distressing. They were two grown women, after all, with good heads on their shoulders. They should know better than to go in for some kind of prepackaged Eastern mysticism. She herself no longer believed God dwelt anywhere at all. The body was an organic machine, period, and God was a figment of its fitful imagination. But the physical exercise, never mind what mumbo jumbo it came wrapped in, was undoubtedly good for her. She gained ten pounds every winter when her garden lay out of reach under its blanket of snow; if yoga could see her through till spring, then she supposed she was willing to put up with it.

When she and Libby emerged from the storefront gym into the pellucid December sunlight, she felt that both of them radiated a pleasant well-being. The organic machines that carried their precious consciousness might be approaching, if not dusk, then at least the late afternoon, but the gears and plumbing and engines still seemed to be in working condition.

Their after-yoga custom was to lunch at Sara's, the health-food restaurant located in the same unprepossessing strip of stores. They sat at a window seat that looked out, through the plate glass, onto the parking lot, the busy street beyond. The restaurant's walls were a soothing gray, its floor a smart checkerboard of black and white linoleum. They both laughed about how, left to their own devices, they'd be skinny as rails. It was their husbands who kept them yoked to such fattening diets. But while Louis somehow stayed trim on his meat and potatoes—a long-simmering resentment against the world can burn off more calories than you might imagine, Claire joked to her friend—Reid piled the pounds on. He had no resentments. He was capacious in every way imaginable. "I do worry about him," Libby confided. "Let it all hang out, they used to say, but this is getting a little alarming. At least I'm trying to exercise, watch my diet."

She had ordered the salade niçoise, her usual, while Claire opted for the grilled seasonal vegetables, under which lurked a comforting lump of polenta. Since Tracy Parker had appeared on the scene, she'd been experimenting with meatless meals.

"Reid is definitely a man of many appetites," Claire agreed.

"I just hope it doesn't kill him," Libby said darkly. "He's in such a whirl-wind these days. His blood pressure's way up. And he's off to Crete for Christmas."

"No," Claire said.

"He claims he's hiking the Samariá Gorge. Huffing and puffing it is more likely. Of course, whatever he's really up to, he's not going to tell me about it in advance. He's too afraid of looking foolish."

Claire considered that scenario. "Do you think he looks foolish anyway?" she wondered.

"Oh, I'm sure we all look foolish, in our way. You know me. I'm quite content for him to have whatever he wants. He showed me pictures of her after he got back from his conference at Thanksgiving. I suppose you could say she's rather fetching, in a harried sort of way. Definitely not my type. She's an archaeologist, of course. American, from Texas."

For weeks they would talk only in the blandest of terms. But then on certain days—the weather, the confluence of planets and stars, who knew the explanation?—a lovely honesty opened between them. They had never kept secrets from each other.

"I sometimes fantasize," Libby went on, "there's this whole circuit of academics who save themselves up for affairs during their foreign vacations."

"As if what goes on over there doesn't count back here," Claire observed.

"Well, it doesn't, does it?" Libby said, perhaps a little tartly. "Anyway, you know how I simply loathe Greece. I hate that whole part of the world. I feel so out of place there. So . . . gratuitous. I remember we were in this village once, and an old man asked us, quite explicitly, Why are you here? What are you looking for? Reid took it all as one big joke. He just laughed. But I asked myself, What *are* we looking for? And I realized I didn't know. Or that's not it: I realized that whatever it was I might be looking for, I shouldn't have to go all the way to some broken-down village in Greece to find it. And that was it, for me. Whatever Reid wanted to do with his life, whatever it was he was looking for, well, that was just fine. I didn't begrudge him that. But I had other things to do."

She had, in fact, taken up painting. Nothing pleased her more than to set up an easel and spend the day in solitude, contemplating whatever scene lay before her. Her watercolors from the Cape, from around the Hudson Valley, softened the cold walls of their cavernous house. In her own modest living room Claire had hung a handsome watercolor Libby had done: Claire's garden with lavender and the old rugosa rose "Blanc de Coubert" in pale bloom. She cherished this glimpse of her beloved flowers through Libby's eyes, their blooms bobbing bravely above shadows slightly more ominous than any she had seen the sun cast in her real-life garden.

"I sometimes wonder what I'd have done if Louis had ever had an affair," Claire mused. "But it's a moot point. He never did. He never will."

"You almost sound disappointed," Libby observed.

Claire was silent for a moment. "Looking back on it all, I just wonder . . ." But she wasn't sure what she wanted to say. "I just wonder if I might have felt less, I don't know, guilty, if he'd gone off and done something or other. I wouldn't have been so afraid of having my own shortcomings discovered. But no. My husband the monk."

"And my husband the satyr," said Libby. "Which one do we think will get to heaven?"

"You mean, which one made his pact with the devil? That's an interesting question, isn't it?" But since it was a question she didn't, at the moment, have the stomach to pursue, she tried changing her tack. "Have I told you, speaking of the devil, about our new young man? Or maybe Reid's mentioned him. Tracy Parker—the new teacher at the school. Louis is quite taken with him."

She had grown rather fond of him herself over the course of the semester: generous, good-humored, perhaps a bit too nice for his own good. And lamentably naive; she had the awful suspicion he was incapable of comprehending the particular place he occupied, at least for the moment, in Louis's imagination. Or that Louis's innocent enthusiasms invariably ended in disappointment of one kind or another.

"Does it ever make you wonder?" Libby asked.

"You mean about Louis? I used to wonder all the time," Claire admitted. "He's undoubtedly the classic sublimated homosexual." She was able to say it simply and easily. "Does that bother me? Not one bit. I just wish he understood himself a little better. But men are such strange creatures, really.

I think most of them would rather we weren't around, at all, so they could just spend time mooning over each other. Hero worship and all that stuff."

"Not my husband," Libby reminded her. "Reid really doesn't like men very much at all. Never has. It's why Dr. Emmerich could never work his magic on him. No, he just puts up with men. It's women he thoroughly loves. That's why Emmerich would never have chosen Reid as headmaster. Not that Reid ever cared one way or the other. I always wonder, though, considering all their differences, how Reid and Louis ever managed to become so close. It's a mystery. But strange to think, if it wasn't for that, you and I wouldn't be sitting here right now."

That was true enough, Claire thought. It was a possibility she had glimpsed one rainy evening years ago. "Where *do* you think we'd be?" she asked in all seriousness. She didn't regret marrying Louis, even if it had been Reid rather than she who'd mattered to him at the time. She'd had her own reasons, after all, hardly less complicated than Louis's. Now, having made those choices, having lived that life, she found it difficult, even impossible, to imagine what other life might have been hers.

Libby seemed unable to imagine herself anywhere else as well. "See?" she deflected Claire's question. "There we go, talking about our men. I'm quite sure they don't get together and talk about us like this."

"I wonder what they do talk about."

"I'm sure I don't want to know," Libby said with great certitude.

"Hey, Ms. Tremper," intoned Tim Veeder, emphasizing the "Ms." "Got a minute?"

"Only," she told him, without looking up from the paper she was marking. "I've got to end office hours early today." Perhaps she was mistaken, but it did seem that her least favorite student had lately taken to haunting her life. Not a week's office hours went by without his confident appearance at her door. He seemed oblivious to the chilly reception his teacher bestowed on him, but had he ever gotten anything more than a chilly reception from anyone? She felt guilty, despite herself, though there *was* the matter of the notes: Post-its left on her door, greeting cards in the mail, Happy Halloween, Veterans Day, Thanksgiving, Thinking of You, No Particular Reason. The matter of the notes had begun to weigh heavily on her mind.

"I had some questions about this week's reading," Tim informed her. He settled uncomfortably into the chair before her desk. "That book we read. I don't know. Something about it really bothered me."

"Essay," Claire corrected, knowing that Tim would still be calling it a book when they discussed it in class.

"Essay," he repeated as she reminded herself dutifully that no one in his family had ever been to college. That his achievement was, in its way, as remarkable as Sharia Washington's. "What really bothered me," Tim went on, "is, well, I don't really know how to say this, so I'll just say it. She's a lesbian, isn't she?"

Claire knew she had taken a chance in putting Adrienne Rich on the syllabus, even this late in the semester, when she had hoped, somehow, the class might be ready. She certainly hadn't planned the course with Tim Veeder in mind.

"I thought the essay made that fairly clear," Claire said tersely.

"Don't get me wrong," Tim argued. "I'm not against the lesbians. It's just that, I feel like if I was in the room with her, she wouldn't even notice me. She wouldn't even want me to be there in the first place. And that just bothers me. I mean, I *love* women. I go out of my way for women. But here Adrienne Rich is saying that men go around forcing women to like them. To me, it sounds like she's just a really bitter person. I know lots of women who like men and nobody's forcing them."

"We've been talking for a long time this semester about male privilege," Claire said patiently. It was a failure of pedagogical nerve, she reminded herself, to give up on a student. "All Rich is suggesting is that women grow up under an intense, even overwhelming cultural pressure to identify not with other women but with men. To be heterosexual, in other words. And she wants us to ask the question, Can heterosexuality be called natural if it's the product of a powerfully enforced cultural hegemony?"

Talk like that made Tim's eyes glaze over, and seeing her chance, Claire took it. "I'd really like to discuss this further," she said, "but I'm afraid I do have to go. My husband's hosting a reception at his school, and I need to be there."

"What school?" Tim asked her, always eager to turn from the political to the personal.

"The Forge School," she told him.

"Fancy," he said appreciatively. "Very fancy."

Instantly she regretted having divulged that bit of information, innocuous as it might be. The headmaster's wife. Now he would know her for exactly what she was.

She began to gather her papers, her books, and stuff them into her satchel, but the signal was lost on the young man. He remained seated in his chair, nervously tapping one foot on the floor. She stood to leave.

"Did you get my card?" he asked hopefully. She looked at him and forced herself to remain expressionless.

"I did," she said evenly. It had come in the mail the day before, a Happy Hanukkah card inscribed, in his tiny, tortured script, *Hey—you never know!* But what did one never know? She didn't think that asking him would be a particularly good idea.

"I should tell you honestly, Tim," she said, "these cards are not really, well, appropriate. I mean, I appreciate your thoughtfulness, but I think I'd prefer that you not send me any more cards."

He hadn't stood up; he sat, his legs sprawled before him, and looked down at the floor. She told herself she should have mentioned something after the very first card; she should never have ignored the problem and hoped it would go away. Still, it was only lately that she had actually admitted to herself the repellent, altogether ridiculous possibility: that Tim Veeder, in his clumsy way, had a crush—and on the enemy, no less.

He ran a hand through his hair. "Sorry, sorry," he told her. "I'm always saying the wrong thing. Doing the wrong thing. Looking at people the wrong way when I don't even know I'm looking. People take a dislike to me. Ms. Tremper, I don't get it."

She had noticed his return address on all those cards: Pancake Hollow Road. His mother, he'd told her once, ran a beauty parlor out of the basement of their home. Class, she reminded herself, was the real marker in America.

She spoke carefully, afraid to give too much to this young man from Pancake Hollow. "Tim, you have to pay more attention. You just can't be oblivious."

He did not move.

"Right now, for example," she continued. "I've gathered up my books. I've told you I'm leaving. And there you sit."

She'd flustered him. He looked at her with alarm. "Sorry," he said, leaping to his feet and dropping, in the sudden move, his pen, his notebook, his copy of the Adrienne Rich essay, which glided onto the floor underneath her desk. "Shit," he said. Then, "Sorry," as, on his hands and knees, he felt for the fugitive pages. She watched his threadbare navy blue sweater ride up on his back as he stretched to reach the essay, the beltless jeans low on his haunches, the swath of pale skin coming into view. With distaste she looked away.

"Got it," he told her, brandishing "Compulsory Heterosexuality" triumphantly in case she didn't believe him. "Now I'm out of here. Thanks for speaking with me."

"Certainly," she said, realizing he had not heard a word.

Whatever had he been thinking, sending her all those cards?

Low, coppery sun slanted through the tall windows of this, the most pleasing and historic of the Forge School's buildings. Constructed in the middle of the nineteenth century from local bluestone, Washington Irving Hall, as it was now known, had housed a military academy for three-quarters of a century before falling on hard times. After the war, Jack Emmerich had rescued it from dilapidation and made the renovated edifice the centerpiece of his fledgling campus. Around it, over the years, had sprung up the half-dozen other, mostly unexceptional halls, modern, no-frills boxes of brick and glass.

The large central foyer, with its double staircase and antique Venetian chandelier, throbbed with the pulse of conversation. Waiters moved through the throng, balancing on their shiny platters an array of vivid hors d'oeuvres or trembling flutes of champagne. Looking grown-up and elegant in their dark blue blazers and red ties, those boys whose parents had been able to come to this end-of-the-semester gathering mingled comfortably with the adults in the room. Louis, who was usually such a curmudgeon about public events, nonetheless managed to rise so well to occasions such as this that Claire had to suspect his ordinary misanthropy was just a guise, some armor of self-protection he donned to combat his various professional anxieties. And as for guises, she had assumed her own for the occasion as well. For the space of two hours, she would be the Headmaster's Wife.

But it was only a role (she had put on her conservative blue dress and necklace of pearls). Surveying the crowded reception from the second-floor gallery, she relished the idea that no one there—with the possible exception of her husband—had any idea who she really was. Just yesterday she had received in the mail the offprints from her latest published essay: an extended meditation, in a well-respected journal of women's history, on the meaning— the semiotics, as she called it—of Pocahontas's sojourn in the England of King James I. What had particularly seized her imagination was the historical fact of the Native American's attendance at a court masque meant to cele- brate the triumph of civilization over savagery. At the end of the masque, the bower of Zephyrus had opened to expose, to the monarch's delighted gaze, his beloved Duke of Buckingham, a long-legged and, as far as Claire could tell from the historical record, entirely fatuous young man who was James's current favorite. But what had Pocahontas seen? About that, the historical record was silent. Nevertheless, this intersection of two worlds— the colonizer and the colonized, the fondly gazed upon and the silenced— was rich with inflection, and Claire had attempted to tease out, in fifteen pages of carefully argued speculation, its somber ironies.

She had no illusions about her general importance as a scholar. She was a humble foot soldier in the trenches. But such work pleased and engaged her. And no one could have been more surprised by her gradual evolution than she. After years of her own silence, she had learned to ask questions, not flippantly, the way she had at Barnard, but with increasing acuity. No longer believing most of the things she had been brought up to believe, she saw clearly the extent to which her education had been little more than a skillful indoctrination. Only last week, Tim Veeder had raised his hand and said, in response to certain doubts she had expressed about current events on the world stage, "But Ms. Tremper, the simple fact is, capitalism works."

She had startled them all—herself included—by answering, without blinking an eye, "Yes, but for whom does capitalism work? It may work for you, but ask a homeless person how well capitalism is working, and they might not think it's working very well at all."

Perhaps she made them uncomfortable, this feminist who looked like nothing so much as their safe and gentle grandmothers, but more and more she found herself *trying* to provoke them into intellectual discomfort. "You have to examine what kind of privilege informs your view of the so-called facts," she told them. "Depending on where you stand, the facts can look very different."

At such moments, Claire was acutely conscious of Sharia Washington's alert, famished presence in the overcrowded classroom. Sharia nodded eagerly, her eyes alive with approval, and sometimes Claire had to wonder: was she perhaps creating a monster? The day might well come when Sharia would lead a revolution—not with a machete, but with the tools Claire had given her. Someday Sharia would put everybody in this elegant old reception room, parents and students and teachers alike, up against a wall.

Including, Claire thought ruefully, that tired old white lady Ms. Tremper. For she knew there was a sense in which Sharia had her teacher's number. Claire's attempts to bridge the gap, to forge an alliance across race and class, had failed. Had she tried too hard? Had a white woman's privileged eagerness been all too off-putting for a black woman who cleaned toilets by night in order to attend school by day?

She had wanted a connection there; she had failed. Nonetheless, it was for the Sharia Washingtons that she would continue to teach, whatever the cost. It was not about her own satisfaction, she reminded herself.

From her vantage point in the relatively uncrowded gallery, Claire could see her husband intent in conversation. Looking up, as if he could feel her gaze on him, with a nearly imperceptible nod of the head he indicated that she should come join him where he stood, champagne flute in hand, in the company of a father and his son.

The son was not one of the boys she happened to know. She had to some extent, in recent years, withdrawn herself from the life of the school, allowing her place to be filled by Douglas Brill's energetic young wife (she nodded to Mary Ann Brill as she passed her on the stairs). They were a couple straight out of the fifties, so uncomplicated, so dreary, in many ways perfect for the school. Meat and Potatoes, Louis called the Brills privately, on the rare occasions when he found it necessary to refer to them at all. But then, that was what he presumably liked about them: that they rarely ever needed referring to one way or another; that they ran themselves, so to speak.

"My dear," Louis said smoothly as she interjected herself into their circle of conversation, "I'd like you to meet Mr. Noah Lathrop. His son, Noah the Third, is doing quite splendidly with us." She recognized that tone, but hardly considered Louis's sleek, discreetly managed fawning any kind of hypocrisy. A headmaster who failed to be alert to the presence before him of wealth and privilege would, after all, be sorely neglecting the interests of his school.

The senior Noah Lathrop was striking, if not exactly handsome. His shock of glossy black hair, his sparkling, ambitious eyes, a deep tan, all seemed to murmur Riviera, Costa del Sol, Morocco. She could tell at once he sailed yachts, drank pastis in the afternoon, basked on secluded beaches when the rest of the world lay buried in winter. He had gambled in casinos and raced expensive cars. He had slept with countless women, all of them beautiful. He had broken hearts. He had reached the stage where hunger for money had turned into jaded indifference. He was not a nice man, probably he was soulless—but in the right circumstances, he could no doubt be absolutely compelling.

As recently as a decade ago she might have been stirred by him. Given her upbringing, her motion through the world, she would have had little choice in her response. Now her dislike of men like him was instant and powerful. Though of course she was perfectly capable of keeping her dislike entirely to herself.

Pityingly, she turned her gaze on his son. "Hello," the younger Noah said. His voice was flat, inflectionless. His light hair had been cut very short, and despite his name, there was something in his features, some steeliness or severity, that seemed vaguely slavic to her. She saw him as a boy gunner in some desperate World War II battle in the snow. He was sad but headstrong. His blue-gray eyes were lusterless. He shook her hand with the requisite firmness—he'd been well trained—but that firm grasp unsuccessfully concealed a deeper indifference. He really did not care to be meeting her. He really didn't care to be here at all. He was deeply miserable; powerfully, even dangerously, volatile. Then he released his grip. But she already thought she knew him. She would have to ask Louis about him later.

"And how were your classes this semester?" Louis prompted.

The younger Noah shrugged. "I like my English class," he said.

This was a boy, she imagined, who didn't smile a lot. But she thought she might like him. If he was at the Forge School, it was almost certainly because he'd failed somewhere else.

"That would be Tracy Parker," Louis said. "He's one of our finer teachers."

"Was he the one you were telling me about?" Noah Senior asked his son. He was an information man. Information was power.

The son was naturally evasive. "He might have been," he said, clearly regretting *anything* he might have said. "He's pretty cool. Doesn't put up with bullshit."

"Then I'm surprised he's not on your case all the time," said the father—who was, along with everything else, a bully.

"Maybe he is," the son told his father.

"Oh," he replied. "Then I'd like to meet the guy."

"Unfortunately," Louis said with barely concealed annoyance, "he couldn't be with us this afternoon."

Claire was surprised. She'd thought they were supposed to go to Tracy's for dinner after the reception; it had been on the calendar for weeks and weeks, a fixed date of some importance. Tracy had been strangely insistent.

In response to her quizzical look, Louis took her sleeve and said, sotto voce, "He had to make an unexpected run to the train station. It seems this mystery guest we've been hearing so much about went and missed the train he was supposed to catch."

That promise of a mystery guest had had Louis agitated all week. "I think you'll be pleasantly surprised," was all Tracy would say by way of explanation, and though she'd wanted to take him aside and tell him that Louis was seldom pleasantly surprised, that there was nothing he hated more than a mystery, she decided it was best not to meddle.

They were late, as she'd phoned Tracy to warn they might be. The reception had lingered long past seven, but Louis was always loath to disappoint any of those parents who might want to chat with him. Long after everyone else had drifted off, as the caterer carted away the remains of the reception and the waiters tidied up, a small, neurotic mother—her son nowhere in evidence—continued to pour her torrent of anxieties down on a surprisingly patient and sympathetic headmaster's head.

"I thought that would never end," Claire told him by way of sympathy as they walked along the snowy path toward Tracy's.

"Our students didn't used to come from such damaged families," Louis mused. "It's true what they say. This country really is coming apart at the seams."

Snow had come early to the Hudson Valley: mid-December, and already the ground had been solidly blanketed for two weeks. It had caught her unawares: no chance to mound the roses, and the poor lilacs, their brown leaves unshed, had splintered under the weight of that first wet snowfall. Still, the campus looked resplendent all in white. Under a clear, star-pricked sky into which a half moon was climbing, the ground actually seemed to glow.

"Perhaps we should have brought wine," she said as they mounted the front steps to the white frame house.

"Don't be ridiculous," Louis muttered. He'd always thought that a reprehensibly bohemian habit, but she rather liked the gesture, especially when, as tonight, there might be some question about their host's choice of wine.

Did young people know anything about vineyards and vintages these days? Her students at the community college—her colleagues too, if the truth be told—seemed ignorant of anything but the most appalling jug wines. One plastic cupful at the departmental Christmas party had left her the next morning with the worst headache.

In his sock feet, Tracy greeted them at the door. They paused on the threshold, clumsily, to remove their snowboots. Accommodatingly, he'd put out two pairs of slippers for their feet. Louis seemed a bit startled—she'd forgotten to warn him that Tracy kept Japanese house. Nonetheless, he submitted to the eccentricity with more good grace than she might have expected. Far from wearing him down, the reception seemed to have cheered him.

On the living room's white sofa—a new sofa, she remarked, flanked by new end tables—sat a gaunt-faced young man. He looked up languidly from the magazine he had been reading. She did not recognize him but he, clearly, recognized her. He wore khaki trousers and a loose-fitting white shirt half open down a chest so skinny she could see the bone of his breastbone, his ribs. His copper-colored hair was slicked back from a high forehead. Looking for some cue, she glanced at Louis and was surprised to see an unmistakable look of perturbation on his face. Hand extended, an unreadable smile flickering across his thin lips, the young man moved unerringly toward her husband. Louis stepped half a step back, seemed to steady himself, then took a step forward.

"You do remember me," said the young man. After a barely perceptible hesitation in which Claire thought it possible her husband might actually turn on his heel and leave the room, Louis tepidly held out his hand.

"Oh, quite, quite," he said, his manner formidable and aloof. "You underestimate yourself."

Then it all came back to her. It wasn't so much that Arthur Branson was older; rather, he was like an elegant building an earthquake has weakened: still standing, but undermined, fragile.

"Claire," he said warmly. "So lovely to see you." He took her hand in both of his. He'd always shaken hands with her that way. What she remembered, absurdly, was how, as a schoolboy, he used to bite his nails—discreetly, as if no one would notice. That had endeared him to her. She remembered how he'd seemed both winningly bold and frightfully shy. "I told Tracy not to keep me a secret," he went on. "I don't know what he was thinking. I feel like the showgirl who comes bursting out of the cake. Surprise! But you're both looking very well, I have to say."

She wished she could say the same—but since she couldn't, she didn't. Presumably he was used to that. Her brain scrambled to sort out all the various pieces, but however she put them together, the solution to the puzzle was dark and disquieting. Arthur looked sick. He looked like someone who might be dying.

"It's been a very long time," she told him, trusting her voice to convey the right note of regret.

"Hasn't it?" he said. "We'll never get all caught up. I was just saying to Tracy—the train ride up, it was like a dream. I have to say, the trains are much, much better now than they used to be. Have you noticed?" He'd never been inarticulate, but his speech had always had a fractured quality to it. That had not changed. She tried, unsuccessfully, to remember what color his hair had been when he was a student at the Forge School.

Louis, who had not ridden the train in a decade, spoke carefully. He was trapped and making the best of it. "I hear they've made quite a few improvements over the years. I hear they even run more or less on schedule now. I wish Claire and I could say the same." He turned to Tracy as if seeking refuge. "We're terribly late. I apologize."

"No problem," Tracy told him. "How'd the reception go? I'm sorry I couldn't make it, but, as you can see, I had to go pick this character up."

"Silly me," Arthur said. "Who knew the train would be on time."

But Louis paid him no attention. He seemed reluctant even to look Arthur's way. They had not spoken, by Claire's count, in more than a decade. "I had a rather interesting chat with the father of your man there," Louis told Tracy. "What's his name?"

Tracy only looked baffled.

"Lathrop," Louis prompted.

"Oh, Noah," Tracy said. "Yeah, I hear his father's a real trip."

Louis pretended not to hear the irony. "Quite the successful businessman," he said. "He just happened to be in New York for the week. His base these days is Tashkent in Central Asia. It appears he either owns or intends to own half of the former Soviet Union. More power to him, I suppose. It was very generous of him to drop by. He seems genuinely interested in his son's progress. Your name, by the way, came up."

Her husband was trolling for something—Claire had seen that strategy too often not to recognize it—but for what, she hadn't a clue. Turning to Arthur, she said, pleasantly, "So how do you know our Tracy?"

Instantly she was aware that Louis had stopped his own conversation in order to listen to hers.

"Oh, we met through mutual friends," Arthur told her. He looked Tracy's way, as if gauging what or how much he should say. For the first time since their arrival, Tracy looked uncomfortable. Arthur refused to be fazed. "You know," he said. "Some people dabble in mutual funds; others invest in mutual friends. We took a shine to one another, as my grandmother used to say."

"We've known one another for a number of years," Tracy added hastily.

"But we should come to the table. The soup's all ready, and then I'll disappear for a bit and finish up the next course."

Pasta with squash and walnuts in a dark, peppery sauce followed the creamy potato soup. While Louis ate with a concentration the food did not exactly warrant, she struggled to keep the conversation afloat. Seldom had she seen her husband so skittish. In his acute panic, it was all he could do to refrain from bolting for the door.

The wine, a Merlot from Chile, wasn't terrible, and she said something polite to that effect.

"Chilean Merlots are the only real Merlots," said Tracy authoritatively.

That was news to her. "How so?" she asked, uncomfortably conscious of trying to make conversation.

"Only Chilean Merlots are ungrafted," he explained. "Meaning original rootstock. The French vines were all killed in a blight around the turn of the century. But the Chilean vineyards were so isolated, they never got the disease."

"I knew I loved that General Pinochet," Arthur broke in cheerfully. "I should have moved there when I had the chance. Did you know my mother actually married a Chilean? My senior year in college. His name was Gunther, of all things. I think he might have immigrated there after the Second World War. You know: a little bit of trouble back home in the fatherland. Just speculation. But I'm sorry. We were talking Chilean Merlots. So all the other Merlots are grafted? How very interesting. I didn't know that."

Many years ago Louis had told her earnestly, "Arthur Branson is the real thing." He had meant, by that, the perfect student, the kind of young mind he believed in: eager, quick, and receptive. Trustingly, even guilelessly, Arthur had allowed himself to be led into the cathedral-like stillness where all of Louis's jealously hoarded treasures lay waiting to be richly bestowed upon the acolyte. Together, mentor and disciple, they had sat up late into the night, musical scores spread open before them, to work their way through the *Ring of the Nibelungen*, the *German Requiem*, the songs of Wolf and Schubert. They had read aloud to one another passages of Pater and Ruskin; on more ambitious evenings Louis teased his pupil's struggling German with Hölderlin and Stefan George. Often she'd fallen asleep to the drowsy music of their talk filtering up from downstairs. Regularly on weekends the two of them had taken the train to New York to visit the Frick, the Met, the Guggenheim—the latter, she suspected, so that Louis could give educational vent to his loathings as well as his loves. Those were the years when she had been busy commuting to Albany to complete her dissertation, happy to leave Louis to his own devices, secretly pleased that he could devote himself, after all these years, to the real thing.

In answer to her inevitable question, the young man who had been the real thing spoke dismissively of his current work in advertising. He was a graphics designer; it was stupid work. At the Forge School he'd been a painter of uncommon promise; his essays, many of which Louis had proudly passed on to her, had glowed with a sensitive intelligence. Had time coarsened him? The more he talked, the more he seemed a bittersweet caricature of the gentle, inquisitive boy they'd once known. He was more amusing these days, more sharp-tongued and, to use a word she greatly disliked, bitchy—but sadly he lacked substance, as if he'd consciously rejected that quality, thrown it recklessly away. As if Louis's fond tutelege had, in the end, come to nothing. No wonder her husband seemed barely able to look his way across the table.

Though it wasn't that alone. Louis had had a number of fine students down through the years, students for whom he had nursed high hopes, but none had engineered quite so unforgiveable a break as Arthur. Toward the end of his freshman year at Brown—he'd enrolled there despite Louis's lobbying for his own beloved Cornell—he'd written his friend and mentor a long and altogether unwelcome letter. She never saw the contents of that document, though she would never forget the change that registered in Louis's face as he read it through—the way, in Schubert, the music can sometimes, in an instant, darken from joy to despair. "We've lost him," Louis announced with a terrible, heart-stopping finality as he folded the letter and returned it, fastidiously, to its envelope. But what news might have provoked such a judgment? "I don't understand," she'd told him. "What has Arthur written to you?" For a long time Louis sat in silence. When he spoke, it was with distaste and shame. "He fancies that he's—how do they say it?—that he's come out of the closet. He throws that in our face." Louis was a man capable of inflicting great pain—on himself no less than on others. But he was resolute, a man of great and unswerving principle, a man whose faith had been shattered. She saw him later, down by the compost heap in the garden, lighting a match to three or four pages he held by his fingertips. They had not spoken of Arthur since.

"I'm wondering what the students are like these days," Arthur said as Tracy served them salad from a large yellow bowl. "My only source of information about the younger generation is what I read in the newspaper, and I have to say, it's not encouraging. Tracy promises I can meet one or two of them tomorrow."

Tracy handed around the salad plates. "Well, perhaps," he said cautiously.

"He thinks it'll allay my fears."

"Our student body," Louis said tersely, his salad untouched, "has, if anything, improved over the years. I think Tracy can attest to the fine young men we teach here."

If Louis's glacial reserve perturbed his hosts, they did their best to carry on as if nothing were amiss. With each other they tried to be playful and at ease. Wisely abandoning the subject of the Forge School, they spoke about

Arthur's desire to afford a house in the country one day. "But you're such a city person," Tracy exclaimed. "You'd go crazy up here. Stark raving mad." They laughed about Tracy's recent spree of furniture purchases. "Oh my God, he's finally turning into an adult," Arthur kidded. Occasionally he would tap Tracy affectionately on the wrist, or touch his arm. What exactly those gestures meant, she couldn't tell.

Her own repertory of conversational gambits exhausted, in desperation she excused herself to the bathroom. The face she saw in the mirror over the washbasin startled her—she looked so old, so haggard. Daubing a needless touch of powder on her nose and patting down her graying hair, she let her eyes roam over the various domestic items scattered around. On the shelf next to the washbasin, Arthur had stowed his shaving kit. She counted nine prescription bottles, all neatly lined up on the counter beside the kit's old leather. Perhaps his father had given him that kit as a present once, years ago, when Arthur set out into the world, perhaps, even, when he first came to the Forge School as a boy with all the world ahead of him. He had traveled farther than anyone might have predicted. Picking up the plastic bottles, she read the strange, exotic names: Rescriptor, Crixivan, Zerit, Zovirax, Zithromax, Diflucan, Marinol, Lorazepam, Oxandrin, a throng of characters from some bad science-fiction novel, only this was not science fiction, this was the reality against which, since her first glimpse of Arthur's thin frame, his wasted face and hectic, too-bright eyes, she had been hoping against hope.

Inside the desecrated temple of his body battles raged, losing skirmishes and other desperate rearguard actions she could not begin to imagine. She found herself surprisingly affected, as if the bad news from the front were somehow her own as well. And what about Tracy? Was he in a position to get sick too? Had he been tested? All the pleasant time they had spent together this past fall, his mood easy, carefree, she had envied him his youth, his bright prospects. And not to know any of this. Every day he must live with such horrible anxieties. What hadn't he told his friends?

Or perhaps, the thought occurred to her, he had told his friends, only she and Louis were not the kind of friends in whom one confided such things. She should have realized he was gay; her obtuseness disappointed her, and she chided herself for having taken him merely at face value. But she was disappointed in him as well, she realized, for having withheld himself. From Louis, that made sense, but she had made an effort, hadn't she, to be his friend? They had talked freely and openly with one another. His graceful evasions had passed her right by. Suffice it to say that everything now added up. "It changes everything," she could hear Louis say, as clearly as if he had actually spoken the words.

Over the years, she had developed a habit of touching things. Where it came from she didn't know, but it comforted her, somehow, to handle objects—photographs, keepsakes, mementos—whose lifelessness people had animated with meaning. She found herself taking Arthur's plastic pill bottles, one by one, and cradling them in the palm of her hand. How old was he? Thirty? Thirty-five? And Tracy still younger. She remembered a boy from her high school who had died in the Pacific; another from college who had been lost in Korea. She simply could not imagine lives ending so soon. Oh, you poor young men, she thought wildly.

When she emerged from the bathroom, feeling herself oddly aged by this ambush of grief, she could not tell if things had changed around the dinner table as well. Arthur was concluding an apparently amusing story about how he had recently met, at a Divas for Life benefit, Jessye Norman—or, as he called her, "Just Enormous."

"As a singer, I think she's rather vulgar," Louis judged dryly. "No matter what part she takes, she's always Jessye Norman, no more, no less. She simply has no idea what it means to get into character."

"But that voice," Arthur said meltingly.

"Soulless. Mere technical proficiency," Louis countered.

"But there's so *much* of it. Resistance is futile."

To Claire's astonishment, Louis actually smiled. He shook his head in what she took as bemusement, or was it simply to measure the distance that separated him from his former student, the impossibility of such conversation anymore? Pushing back his chair and making as if to get up from the table, he announced, with surprising honesty, "I am very fatigued. I've had a most trying day. Tracy, thank you for the evening. Arthur, it's been good to see you." He said it so stiffly that none of them—perhaps including Louis himself—could tell whether he actually meant it.

Without a word they trudged homeward across the snowy campus, their heavy steps unbearable interruptions of the pristine silence. She knew this mood of his, though seldom, if ever, had she seen it anywhere near so pronounced. As if keeping a wary distance, as if terrified that the smallest thing might mortally impinge upon him, Louis moved with great care. At times like these he was so easily breakable. She resisted the temptation to crack him wide open.

Climbing the front steps wearily, he paused, as he always did, to find the house key among all the others on his ring. But then he stopped. "I can't," he said, his voice oddly, painfully constricted. "You open the door."

In the front hall they removed their coats and hung them in the closet. She was like a city in the midst of civil war. Anger and grief vied for control of her heart. She would not try to talk with him, because she knew all too well that he would have nothing to say. Whatever he might have said, he would fold over and over, till it was so small and so concentrated that he could ignore its presence inside him. She had thought, once, that a day might come when those presences might open—either gracefully, the way paper flowers blossom when dropped in water, or with explosive, cathartic force. Now she no longer believed anything would happen at all.

In the kitchen, he took down the bottle of scotch from the cupboard. "Would you care for some?" he said, his voice dusky, distracted.

"No thank you," she told him, regretting her refusal the moment she spoke it. But she would not retrace her steps. "I'm going up to bed," she said.

He sighed, and poured himself a generous portion. "I'll be up shortly," he told her.

She knew that would not be true. He had a long, terrible night ahead of him. Sometimes a clear conscience was the worst of all.

XI

All week he had meant to make the pilgrimage, if that was what it was—but all week, busy with the tedium of Christmas festivities at his sister's house in Richmond, he had found one reason or another to put off his journey. Now, the next-to-last afternoon of the year, a damp cold lay over the tidewater as he sped along the interstate toward the Williamsburg exit.

By odd coincidence, the letter had arrived only a few days before he'd driven down.

Dear Tracy,

I am very sorry to have to write to you with the sad news that Holden Chance has passed away. Perhaps you have heard this news elsewhere, but if not: Holden committed suicide on October 25, at his parents' home in Charleston. I can tell you now what Holden never wanted anybody to know: that he tested positive about a year ago. He was depressed about that, of course, but lately he'd been getting on with his life. He'd just gotten out of rehab for some addictions he'd been struggling with, and we all thought he was doing a lot better. But who can ever know how a person is suffering deep down? I don't have to tell you that being gay was very hard for Holden, and I think he never really came to terms with who he was. I know you and he had been out of touch for quite a while, but I also know he always, always thought the world of you. I would've written sooner, but it took me a while to find your address.

I hope this finds you well. I am still very shaken up, though I try to comfort myself with the thought that our friend is at peace now.

Feel free to call me if you need/want to talk.

Sincerely,

Jake Ross

Holden Beauregard Chance IV. How proud he'd been, both of that pat-
rilineal "IV" and the matrilineal "Beauregard" of Confederate war fame, for
Holden had been one of those aristocratic plantation boys, an all but vanished
species who still, from time to time, emerged from the reclusive cotton fields
of Dixie to attend a school like William and Mary. His voice was languid,
his accent voluptuous. Bourbon flowed in his veins. Already at twenty his
insolent good looks were starting to show a dissolute turn. Like many of the
plantation boys, he never seemed to wear socks, and his naked ankles between black loafers and the cuff of his chinos, especially when he sat in the
coffee shop, legs crossed, smoking a cigarette—which was how Tracy first
glimpsed him—were lovely to behold. Sharp-boned and surrounded with
sparse, fine hair, ankles like that, if you were susceptible, could break your
heart. And twenty-year-old Tracy was highly susceptible. He and Holden
ended up spending much of the autumn of their junior year together, and
even though they had both soon acknowledged, cheerfully and unsentimen-
tally, that they were too different ever to be compatible over the long haul,
Tracy had nonetheless always found some kind of comfort in assuming that
Holden's lovely ankles, as well as everything else that was lovely about him,
would happily continue on the planet for at least a few decades more. For
several days after he got the news he had relived again and again, fondly,
sorrowfully, their moments together—just as now, leaving the interstate, tra-
versing the marshlands and pine glades that made Williamsburg, at least
approached from this direction, seem an isle of Avalon (a garish ring of motels
and pancake houses guarded the other approaches), he found it nearly impossible to believe that such a rich, smart, sassy life had been extinguished
so quickly.

He'd considered calling Devin with the news about Holden, since the two
of them had been friendly, had even tricked together once at a frat party a
few weeks before Devin met Tracy, but he hadn't talked to Devin since
October, when he'd seen him in the city, their silence mutual as the months
slid by, as if, after all this time, their friendship had inexplicably come to
some kind of an end. Funny, he hadn't suspected anything at all was amiss
when he'd said good-bye that Sunday morning—but somehow, somewhere
along the way, something had irrevocably changed.

And in all his relations, he thought as he wended his way through the
town, inexplicable shifts seemed to have occurred, as if it really were possible
for one's stars to be in inauspicious alignment. That unnerving dinner with
Louis and Claire, for instance, after which Louis, especially, had grown markedly more distant and reserved. He now knows I'm gay, Tracy told himself,
trying at the same time to reassure himself that that distinctly unsurprising
revelation could hardly be the sole cause of Louis's withdrawal.

And then there was the Noah situation. Or there had been the Noah
situation—which now, thankfully, was over. Determined to defuse things

before they got any farther out of hand, for the last four weeks of the semester he'd kept his student as gently at bay as possible. It was undoubtedly for the best, and he felt, all in all—when not visited by the occasional pang of wild sorrow that could arrive without warning—relieved that their ill-advised and inappropriate friendship had cooled.

Leaving his car in the visitors' lot by the football stadium, he strolled onto the deserted campus. Only five years had passed since he graduated, hardly any time at all, really, and everything seemed remarkably unchanged: the elegant, ivy-wreathed Georgian buildings; the herringboned brick walks; tall dark magnolias with their waxy, brooding leaves; the allée of crepe myrtle; the sunken garden, where he used to pause on spring afternoons to watch shirtless young men play soccer. All at once, he keenly regretted having given in to his sister's insistence that he kennel Betsy back in Middle Forge; it would have been nice to have his dog frisking alongside him on the sunken garden's expanse of lawn. The campus's emptiness was eerie, unnatural. Of course this was a place ghosts would return to, seeking the paths they had walked and the dorms they had made love in and the classrooms where they had dreamed of the unimaginable future.

Standing all alone in the center of the sunken garden—he was never sure why they'd called it a garden, exactly, since there was nothing but lawn—he felt a shiver of unidentifiable dread so intense it compelled him to say out loud, the way, in an abandoned building, you might try to reassure yourself by whistling, "Holden, you southern queen, you. Stop making me have such gothic thoughts." The sound of his voice startled him in the empty air. But now he knew why he'd come, and where he needed to go.

In the woods behind the sunken garden, a brightly painted Japanese bridge arched gracefully over a quiet pool. William and Mary lore had it that *Playboy* had once ranked the secluded dell the most romantic spot on an American college campus. He and Holden had shared a yummy late-night kiss there early on in their relationship; he'd then led his boy into the bushes for one of the most stirring blow jobs he'd ever given anybody. It was one of the few times in his life he'd ever swallowed. There were, in retrospect, perhaps a million reasons to regret that mouthful, one for each spermatozoon swimming in the warm gooey mix, but now, leaning on the bridge rail and staring into the tranquil pool where orange smudges of goldfish lurked like lesions waiting to surface in as yet unblemished skin, six years after the two of them moved on to other things, Holden to Jake and he to Devin and then Japan, where he'd seen any number of arched bridges and koi-filled ponds, the real things and not imitation, he was glad he'd wanted Holden's seed in his mouth, glad he'd taken it. And if this were to turn out to have been the very spot on earth where the virus had entered him, the most romantic collegiate spot in America, well then, he thought defiantly, so be it.

But his defiance was short-lived. The old panic set in. What if he really did carry the virus in his blood? He felt a strange throb go through his torso. Could you feel its tongue of fire flicking inside you?

He knew from experience that such thoughts could only plunge him farther into panic. The solution was so stupefyingly simple: get the test, be done with it. But his predicament was just as stupefyingly simple: he could not bring himself to do that.

In flight from phantoms there was no fleeing from, he forsook the pond, cut back across the quad, past the Christopher Wren building, and entered into Duke of Gloucester Street. Colonial Williamsburg was surprisingly congested with tourists. He remembered vividly his own first visit to the place: the reconstruction he found so kitschy in his college years had enchanted him utterly as a ten-year-old, and he had vowed then and there that when the time came he would go to college at William and Mary.

In front of Bruton Parish a legion of smiling Japanese tourists stood at attention, waiting for their leader's camcorder to be done with them. Up ahead, on the commons in front of the Governor's Palace, a man in colonial dress tending two oxen yoked to a cart lectured a small, palpably uninterested audience on oxen commands. "Haw means left," he told them, gesturing with his hand. "Gee means right." Somewhere in the distance a musket demonstration was being given. In a fenced-in lot a chestnut horse grazed on a pile of hay. Resting his crossed forearms on the split-rail fence, a boy of thirteen or fourteen watched with a pensive expression on his lean face. He wore cowboy boots, jeans, a spangled denim jacket; beneath that, a fancy black shirt stitched in silver. His hair fell in black bangs over his eyebrows.

The angel descended when you were least expecting it. Tracy felt something quietly go click in his despairing heart. Feigning interest in the chestnut horse, he broke his stride, but as he sauntered over to the fence a man's voice called out, "Git on over here or yer gonna git left."

"Ya'll wait for me," the boy called out to his family, who had walked on ahead, father and mother and two younger brothers, perhaps nine and seven. Their voices were deep country drawls. The father turned to look back, rail thin, his face showing the toll of hard years. He too wore cowboy boots, and a cowboy hat as well. He motioned brusquely with his arm to hurry up, and his son obeyed.

Tracy followed at a little distance. He enjoyed watching the boy's wide buttocks, his gait made ever so slightly precarious by his cowboy boots—the male equivalent, Tracy mused, of walking in high heels. A trucker's wallet, secured by a chain to his belt, bulged in the boy's left back pocket. He kept running his hand through his hair, pushing it back out of his eyes. You cute little tramp from darkest Appalachia, Tracy thought playfully, his mind inventing reckless fantasies, all perfectly harmless of course, a melancholy game to while away an afternoon. He was not particularly eager to get back to Richmond and his sister's house. He had spent the week there in a vaguely disconsolate torpor, sleeping twelve hours at a stretch, eating too much, getting no exercise. It would be a relief, the day after tomorrow, to make the long drive home—if home was what Middle Forge was for him these days.

The family had stopped to peruse the menu posted at one of the taverns. Tracy stationed himself on a bench on the opposite side of the street whose only traffic was pedestrians or the occasional carriage. Disappointingly, he couldn't hear the family's words, only the rural music of their voices, but he had a clear view of the boy absentmindedly scratching his shoulder, a charming gesture to contemplate. And he hadn't noticed the boy's belt buckle before, a bright silver oval boldly embossed with the letters CSA. Splendid, he thought, just splendid.

He and Holden had loved strolling among the out-of-town hordes—boy gazing, Holden had called it. "Oh my Lord, that man pushing the baby stroller just cruised me!" he'd exclaim, or, whenever his companion's attention seemed too obviously caught by some beauty guarded by his watchful entourage of family, he'd playfully slap Tracy's wrist and say, "Stop that, you pervert!"

"I'm just looking," Tracy would complain. "I have no intention of touching."

And he *didn't* have any intention of touching, either then or now. Deciding he did, however, want to hear the southern boy's voice one more time before the family disappeared into the tavern, he got up to move closer—but as he did so, the parents must have decided the tavern was overpriced, or it was too early to eat, or perhaps the authentic-sounding fare, pigeon pie, smoked ham on biscuits, was too like their own country diet, and they preferred to eat somewhere more exotic, perhaps one of the innumerable waffle houses out on the strip. In any event, Tracy was glad his little idyll had been granted a momentary reprieve. What better way to spend a dull winter's afternoon than following a beautiful boy around town? And about white trash youngsters like this, unschooled and volatile, there could be a particular kind of edgy attractiveness.

Look but don't touch, he admonished himself, wondering nonetheless what might happen if he were, in the right circumstances, to touch? There was a friend of Arthur's who hired local boys, sixteen- and seventeen-year-old rednecks, to do miscellaneous chores at his weekend house up in Columbia County. Trim and fit from his Chelsea gym, the very picture of reassuring masculinity, Ron would invite them in after an afternoon's work for a couple of beers, and at some point he'd pop a video into the VCR, "a straight video, mind you." They were happy enough to lean back on the sofa, close their eyes, and pretend. Tracy's response: they're going to find you murdered in that house of yours one of these days. Still, he thought ruefully, everybody had to die sooner or later. At least Ron would go to his grave *knowing* what Tracy only dreamed about.

Admiring the cannons, the coat of arms, the young ladies paid to parade in colonial dress, the family from darkest Appalachia milled about on the grounds of the House of Burgesses, while Tracy, lingering safely on the periphery, reserved all his admiration for the serendipitous combination of genes that had produced, out of such unpromising parents, so remarkable a creature.

"Down this way's the jail," the beautiful fluke of nature called out. Excitedly he pointed to a sign, the cuff of his denim jacket riding up to expose a bony wrist. "Ya'll come this way." As the family flocked eagerly past him, Tracy lowered his eyes as if engrossed by the broken oyster shells that composed the path beneath his feet, wondering what on earth poor Louis would think, were he to glimpse his protégé in his truest element. Perhaps it was for the best that their relations had cooled. It hadn't, after all, been an honest friendship; he'd concealed too much of himself beneath that veneer he'd long ago perfected, while this lone wolf of a self scrambling hungrily down a steep path in pursuit of a ravishing morsel of adolescence was—he thought with a surge of rebelliousness—his purest, most profound self.

Down by the old gaol an enchanting tableau awaited him: the boy's younger brothers had locked him in the stocks and were dancing around him merrily, clapping their hands and singing, "Clay got caught, Clay is a thief." Tracy of the stolen heart drank in the spectacle eagerly. It aroused him to see the young offender on display for all the world to see, his slender wrists shackled, his shapely hands hanging limp, level with his ears, his sheepish grin.

"You look jist like you belong there," his grim-faced mother called out.

"I ain't done nothing to deserve this," Clay said.

"Nothing yit," his father told him. "You jist wait."

While the mother snapped pictures with a throwaway camera, the rest of the family, oblivious to whatever audience they might have, took turns submitting to the stocks' mock humiliation, laughing and pointing at one another as if their various punishments were the funniest thing ever.

"Was you in one of these when you was locked up?" Clay asked his confined father.

"Naw," the careworn man told him, looking out dolefully at the camera. "They don't have these no more."

Clay nodded sagely, but there was a look in his dark eyes, a tinge of sadness, histories Tracy had no clue to, but that filled his heart with longing: if he could somehow befriend Clay, comfort him, make everything all right in his dusky, thwarted world.

But the pleasures of the stocks were soon exhausted, and the family reluctantly moved on. The streets of restored houses seemed to leave them indifferent, but mechanical things called to them. They took their time at the windmill, the brickyard, the shingle-making demonstration. Tracy shadowed them diligently, though he was beginning to lose interest in his game. What, after all, was the point of following around some boy whose only quality, really, was his boyness? Hadn't he already, in a sense, drunk to the full whatever was possible? But at that very moment when he had decided to leave them to the rest of their lives, the backwoods clan passed a public rest room. Tracy could hardly believe what he heard. "I got to pee real bad," Clay announced in a loud, careless voice. "Ya'll keep on walking. I'll catch up."

Tracy's heart practically stopped in his chest. Was it possible the sly little beauty knew perfectly well he was being pursued? Ron always insisted that redneck boys were a whole lot easier than you might think. Stop that, you pervert, he thought, fiercely reining in his galloping imagination. And indeed, the moment quickly asserted its innocence.

"Anybody else need to go?" the father asked his family. "Rory? Taylor?" The two little boys shook their heads. "All right, go ahead, Clay, but don't dawdle. We'll be right up the street."

Heart racing, Tracy hesitated. He'd tailed the family far too long; it was a miracle they hadn't caught on to him. To enter the rest room now, however innocently, would be foolhardy. And yet they paid him no mind, turning their backs and ambling slowly up the street. Aroused, he pushed open the rest-room door.

The dank gloom smelled heavily of disinfectant. Above a line of sinks hung a matching line of mirrors, their light silvery and cold. On the opposite side of the room, Clay stood at the middle urinal in a row of three. No partitions divided the urinals. From the movement of his elbows Tracy could tell Clay was unbuckling his belt. Holding his dick with his right hand, he rested his left against the top of the urinal. Tracy stepped up to the porcelain beside him. The boy had let loose a prodigious stream; evidently he really had needed to pee bad. Taking no note at all of the man who had sidled up on his right, he stared blankly at the concrete block wall in front of him.

Half hard, Tracy worked to free himself, discreetly glancing to his left and down as he did so, and there it was, a modest thing, circumcised, not much bigger, really, than Tracy's middle finger. He didn't dare sustain his gaze more than an instant, but was adept at quickly capturing what he needed: that the boy's thumbnail was bruised dark, the head of his dick silky and reddish, his piss clear as water. Only when the long stream ended did Tracy allow himself a second, slightly longer glance as Clay shook himself dry, then stuffed his secret flesh back into his jeans. Tracy waited for his own flow of piss to begin, but his cock was still half hard, and nothing would happen.

Completely unaware he was the object of such daring study, Clay zipped up, buckled his belt, and flushed. His cowboy boots clicked briskly across the concrete floor as he left without bothering to wash his hands.

Tracy's pulse was still zooming, but his semi-erection had begun to subside. You dirty old man, he told himself as his piss finally began to flow
and his heartbeat returned to normal. He hadn't done anything like that in
a very long time, not since Germany, when he had been nineteen and
abysmally lonely and occasionally found himself stealing quick peeks at the
youngster he'd positioned himself next to in the rest room of a train station
or a youth hostel.

Look but don't touch, he thought wistfully. He carefully washed his hands
at the basin. Look all you want, he explained to Holden Beauregard Chance
IV, who stood at the next basin and, so it would seem, washed his hands as
well. There is nothing wrong with looking, Tracy assured his old companion
of long ago. And what goes on in your head, no one can touch.

Lynn and her brood inhabited a charmless mansionette in an affluent development in Richmond's West End. Two years ago the forty acres had all
been fields, and the new houses squatted stark and uncomfortable in the
bare winter landscape. So this was the price of success, the palpably unsuccessful Tracy thought grimly as he steered his scrappy Toyota into the drive
beside the gleaming new Lexus and Jeep Cherokee.

A big house glowing warmly against the winter's night. A spouse to come
home to. Children to carry on the genetic legacy, that million-year trust he
carried in his traitorous loins. A place blissfully secure in the middle of the
world. I do not want these things, he reminded himself as he mounted the
steps to the front door. Instead I want . . . But what did he want? The forbidden, illusory bliss of Clay from darkest Appalachia? Banish the ridiculous
thought, he instructed himself as, taking a deep breath, he entered his sister's
house.

Sprawled on the sofa watching a football game, his brother-in-law barely
glanced up. Jim Durning worked as a computer software consultant—
though what, exactly, that line of work entailed was something Tracy had
never managed to glean from him. But if the new house, the new cars, the
general air of luxury were any indication, his services did not come cheap.
Tracy had known a dozen Jims in college, fellows of great certitude and
confidence, *big* men, not so much in stature as in presence, in specific
gravity, men who amiably blustered their way through the welcoming
world, never needing, like Tracy and his kind, to scan the horizon constantly for trouble. The Universal Man, Lynn approvingly dubbed her husband. He was good with car engines, leaky faucets, chain saws. He was
building a sailboat in the garage.

From the kitchen came Edison, the two-year-old, his hands excitedly
grasping the air in front of him. The sight of Tracy stopped him in his tracks.
Suddenly shy and uncertain, he grabbed anxiously, through his diapers, at

his little penis. Tracy squatted to confront his nephew on more equal terms. Edison shook his head and wrinkled his nose as if to sneeze, but then said, carefully, hopefully, "Did you bring me a surprise?"

"Oh," Tracy said, showing two empty hands. He'd intended to pick something up at one of the stores in Merchants' Square, really he had, but the episode with Clay had left him tingling and distracted; he'd gone straight to his car without a second thought.

"Don't bother your uncle," Jim said without looking up. As if on cue, Edison began a well-practiced whine. He stomped his little bare foot.

"Edison," Lynn warned firmly, appearing from the kitchen with a frown. "What have I told you?"

Edison looked at the floor and clenched his fists. He stamped his foot again, but more tentatively.

"What have I told you?" Lynn repeated. Edison said nothing, though a fitful cry quivered in the back of his throat.

"Nobody hears you when you whine," his mother told him firmly.

"I wanted," Edison said.

"Nobody hears you," Lynn repeated, though she looked at Tracy with what seemed, if not reproach, then disappointment.

"Sorry," he said, rising and showing once again his empty hands. "I was going to get something. I got busy."

Was he overreacting, or did his sister's look seem to say, as the wail of the six-month-old drifted in from the kitchen to join his older brother's, "*You* were busy?" It was true. His own life, during the last week of holiday idleness, had sometimes seemed very small, nearly worthless in fact; the things he spent his days consumed with, meaningless. Take Noah. How to explain about him? There was not a person in this house who would comprehend, even for an instant; it would be as if he were speaking an unintelligible language. My whole being, he thought in a flare of self-pity, the very heart and soul of my life, makes no sense to them.

Beneath the baby's piercing cry came another sound from the kitchen, at once unidentifiable and strangely familiar. It hissed and clattered malevolently. "What's going on in there?" he asked.

A sudden weariness seemed to overtake his sister. She put her hand on Edison's head as he clutched needily at her leg. "Pressure cooker," she said, and suddenly the sound sorted itself out. "She wouldn't take no for an answer."

From the sofa Jim observed darkly, "That racket is going to drive me bonkers."

"Don't even go there," Lynn warned her husband. The pressure cooker, all shiny and imposing, had been unwrapped with some bewilderment on Christmas morning, but Betty Parker had explained her gift with conviction.

"Raising a family," she'd told Lynn and Jim, "there was no kitchen appliance I appreciated more."

Was there anything quite so painful, so fraught with the possibilities of hurt, as gift giving within a family? The cooker's hiss and clatter took him back to Sunday dinners after church, gray midafternoons of winter in their house in the immaculate suburbs. In retrospect, it seemed, everything had been perfect—but could that really have been the case, given how easily they had faltered and lost their way as a family after his dad had died? Soon enough there'd seemed little reason to come home, and after his mother sold the house in Connecticut and moved to a beach condo in Florida, there'd no longer been any home to come home to anyway.

"Lynn," his mother said. She stood in the doorway, holding the unhappy-looking Nathan. "Can you help me set the table? Dinner'll be ready in no time, and I've got to change this little fellow. Oh hello, Tracy," she said, noticing him in that distracted way she had adopted, as if she ran the risk, in looking at him too closely, of seeing things she could not bear. While in Japan, lulled, some-how, by distance into thinking the news of little import, he had made the mis-take of telling her, in a letter, that he was gay. Since his return, there had been two or three ridiculous scenes between them, devolving into a tense and wary truce. "Did you have a nice afternoon?" she asked politely.

"It was okay," he told her, wondering what she'd think were she to know the real reason he'd gone, and what he had done with himself once he was there. "An old friend of mine died recently," he made himself continue. "I went to school with him. So I just walked around campus and thought about him. He was a very close friend."

He could sense his mother stiffen. Any reference to his personal life made her nervous, as if the smallest detail might open the wound all over again. He realized he would never be able to say what, for a dangerous moment, he had been on the verge of saying: Holden wasn't just a friend, Mom, he was a lover. I swallowed his come. He died of AIDS, you know. Which means I probably have the virus inside of me. And I'm scared to death, Mom. I'm so scared I don't know what to do.

He wouldn't subject her to that. His fears were his alone, middle-of-the-night companions he had to make the best of on his own. Perhaps that was why, mysteriously, he needed Arthur these days: sadly, distressingly, there was no one else among the living with whom he could be honest anymore. Only with the condemned, the walking dead, did he feel safe.

Jumpy and morose, he went upstairs to the guest bedroom his sister had installed him in. For ten minutes he sat on his bed and stared at the cool beige carpet at his feet. The room *felt* like a guest bedroom: unlived in, pristine, soulless. But then the whole house felt that way. He wanted to shout angrily; his afternoon had had that effect on him. But shout at whom?

Where was Noah? he wondered. What was he up to in the lull between Christmas and New Year's? Did he stay with his terrible father, or had his mother, with all her complicated needs, lured him out to Long Island? It upset him, vaguely, to think of his student living whatever life he lived when he was apart from Tracy. But why should that upset him all of a sudden? With a pang, he tried to quell the spasm of jealousy he suddenly found himself ambushed by, only to discover, in place of that pang, a dull emptiness. Deliberately, responsibly, he had banished Noah from his thoughts these last few weeks—and now, unbidden, here he was all over again.

"Traaacy," his sister called up to him. "Dinner's ready."

For an instant he considered feigning illness, or exhaustion. He did, in a sense, feel both; but then, wearily, he rose and descended the stairs to join the rest of the family.

The dining room table was set with his sister's coolly elegant wedding china. There were moments, he had to admit, when her taste was actually fairly superb. Candles flickered, the chandelier's dimmer switch had been turned down low. "I went ahead and put Edison and Nathan to bed," Lynn told him. "They were being impossible. I thought we adults deserved to dine in peace for once."

"Mnn," Tracy said noncommittally, as his mother sailed in from the kitchen, gloved in insulating mitts fashioned like sharks and holding before her a large steaming platter. He didn't like to admit it, but the children, irritating as they might be, at least enabled the adults to get through their meals without much danger of any real conversation.

"Careful," his mother warned them all as she placed the platter triumphantly in the center of the table, "this is hot hot hot." Potatoes, carrots, and onions surrounded a luscious, juice-oozing pot roast of the kind he hadn't laid eyes on in years.

Though technically—and certainly philosophically—a vegetarian, Tracy could be accommodating when he had to. He'd eaten turkey on Christmas Day, catfish at Captain Jack's Seafood Shack, a chicken breast or two. And his sister, he was satisfied, had met him halfway, even concocting for his benefit a pasta and vegetable dish she served not once but twice. But he drew the line at beef.

"Jim," Betty invited, apparently oblivious to her affront, "would you do us the honor of carving?"

Tracy looked at his sister; she only shook her head as if to say, I had nothing to do with this.

The roast, when sliced, was red and succulent inside. Pooled in the serving platter, blood-juice saturated the vegetables. Tracy knew his mother too well. If she could just get him to eat red meat once again, that would be a beginning. Slowly he'd see that it wasn't bad to be like everyone else. Before long, he'd give up entirely on his foolish notion about being gay.

"Pass your plates around," Jim told them. "I'll serve. Ladies first."

"Tracy, your plate," urged his mother, after hers and her daughter's had been heaped high.

"Mom," he said, as delicately as he could, "you know I don't eat red meat."

She tried to look surprised. "Oh," she said, not daring to meet his eyes. "Oh dear. I wasn't even thinking. I was trying to fix something nice. You used to like pot roast so much when you were little."

"That's okay," he told her. "I'm not all that hungry. I'll have some bread and some salad. I think I've gained about five pounds this week."

"You're very thin these days," his mother countered. "And I don't understand why you're suddenly on this vegetarian kick."

"Mom," Lynn warned, "you're picking on him."

All Tracy could do was smile and shake his head. "Mom," he said, "I've been on this vegetarian kick, as you call it, for about five years. It's no big deal. I just don't eat meat, is all."

"Sometimes I don't understand what happened," his mother observed plaintively. "You were such a normal, happy child growing up."

"What do you mean, 'What happened'?" Tracy asked. "I'm perfectly happy. Anyway, who says it's normal to eat the flesh of other animals?"

"You're misinterpreting me," his mother told him. "You always do that." She looked as if she were about to burst into tears, and Tracy felt a strange surge of pity. Florida—or perhaps it was grief, loneliness—had changed her. He could barely imagine her life these days; indeed, was afraid to try too hard. It seemed possible, after all, that he'd not been a good son to her. That he had callously abandoned her for his own pleasures in her hour of direst need.

A skirmish with his mother was the last thing he wanted. "Sorry," he apologized with bemusement. "All I meant was, there's nothing wrong with not eating meat."

With a clatter that startled them all, Jim laid his knife and fork across his plate. "Actually, Tracy," he weighed in, "that's where you're dead wrong." A strange exasperation filled his voice. "Like it or not, human beings are at the top of the food chain. Simple as that. It's our perogative to eat meat."

Tracy considered, for a moment, pointing out the mispronunciation, but then thought better of it. This was hardly the time to play the fussy English teacher. The gauntlet he'd been half waiting for all week had been thrown down, and he realized, without a bit of regret, that he too had been spoiling for a fight.

"Not only is it our perogative," Jim went on grandly, "I'd even say it's our duty. Our biological responsibility to nature."

"I have no idea what nature even is," Tracy challenged.

"See?" Jim said with triumph. "That's exactly the problem. People think they can just go and forget our evolutionary role, do anything they want. But life's not a game. There's harsh reality out there."

If Tracy wasn't exactly sure he knew what Jim was talking about, he nonetheless thought he could recognize code words when he heard them. Arthur, bless his ACT-UP heart, had seen to that.

"What are you talking about?" he asked.

"AIDS, for example," Jim said.

Of the four of them, only Betty had begun to eat. Head down, the sorcerer's startled apprentice, she seemed to want to pretend she'd played no part at all in getting all this started. Was she embarrassed to have unleashed more than she'd planned?

"You go against nature," Jim went on, "you're asking for trouble. Simple as that. Surely I don't have to point that out to somebody with your credentials."

Tracy had to wonder what, exactly, the Universal Man understood. He'd always assumed Lynn had told her husband, at some point or other, "There's something about my brother you should know." He'd always assumed, likewise, a certain degree of tolerance there.

With calm fury he asked, "And what, exactly, *are* my credentials?"

"Haven't we had enough of this conversation?" Lynn wondered mildly, smarter, perhaps, than anyone gave her credit for.

Jim glared at his wife for a moment, then said sharply, "You're right. Let's not get into this."

But as far as Tracy was concerned, they already were into it. "I have friends who are dying of this disease," he told Jim.

"I'm very sorry about that," Jim said. "I was trying to make a philosophical point."

Tracy had had it with philosophical points. He remembered how Louis Tremper had gone out of his way, these past few weeks, to avoid the contagion of a gay colleague. Wounded by the memory—he'd actually thought for a while that Louis was his friend—Tracy found himself saying, in a voice more hysterical than he might have wished, "I don't have to listen to your philosophical points. If anything, gay men are saints because they're not reproducing themselves like rabbits. That's what's killing the planet—straight people who think they have some God-given right to just keep pumping out more and more children."

The whole room seemed to hold its breath. In that moment of great clarity he glared at Jim and Jim glared back. If for no other reason than to defend the memory of Holden Chance, who had left barely a mark on the world, Tracy suddenly saw he had no choice but to hold his ground.

"I'm going to ask you to take that back," Jim said with ominous calm. "You're not getting away with talk like that in my house."

"Then let me say it again." Tracy spoke icily though shakily. "It's not gay people who are the problem. It's heterosexuals who go on breeding like there's no fucking tomorrow, which there won't be if you keep it up. As far as I'm concerned, anybody who's bringing children into the world these days is committing war crimes against the planet."

His mother slammed down her fork. "Tracy, shame on you," she said angrily.

"I can't stand this," Lynn said, and got up from the table.

"I should fucking bash your face in," Jim said with surprising calm.

Tracy couldn't manage quite the same. His voice was trembling, and he felt close to tears. "You'd like that, wouldn't you?" he accused. "You've been waiting to bash the faggot ever since you met me."

"Tracy, stop it," his mother said.

"Because that's what I am," he told her. "A despicable, inconvenient faggot. So you'd better get used to it."

He knew he was irrationally, even dangerously, angry. He knew there was no purpose to this argument except the need on both his part and Jim's to have it out with each other, to do damage. And maybe he'd gone and proved Jim's point after all: here they were, two dogs needing to draw blood in order to establish once and for all who was going to be the alpha male in this pack. It was Jim's den, of course, Jim's brood. Of course he had the advantage. He always would. Nature, after all, was on his side. Nature, and reality, and no doubt God Himself.

"Get out of my house," Jim told him.

"Fine," Tracy said. "I'm going. I'm leaving right now."

"The sooner the better," Jim told him.

"Tracy, you're acting like a spoiled child," his mother accused.

He was precariously close to shouting. "I'm not acting like a spoiled anything," he said. "I'm being demeaned by this homophobe, and you're sitting here letting it happen. He's only saying what you've been thinking ever since I came out. Well I don't have to take it. I don't care who you are."

Rising abruptly, face flushed with rage, he pushed back his chair and stalked out of the room.

"I'm your mother," he heard as he mounted the stairs. "That's who I am. I'm your mother and I love you."

At the top of the stairs, Lynn was waiting for him. She held Nathan, who'd fallen peacefully asleep despite being awakened, momentarily, by all the clamor. Hard to believe such an innocent creature was a planet destroyer. Nonetheless, Tracy thought angrily, he'd meant what he'd said.

"You're way overreacting," his sister told him. "Jim wasn't trying to insult you."

"Don't give me that," Tracy lashed out. "God, I didn't know you were married to such a Neanderthal."

"You're being ridiculous, Tracy."

"I refuse to be an issue," Tracy said. "I'm a person, not an issue."

Shifting Nathan in her arms, Lynn stared at him with what looked remarkably like sadness. "Maybe some people think you've gone and turned yourself into an issue," she said quietly.

"Can't anybody around here get it through their head? This is who I am. Period. And anyway, it's nobody else's fucking business. Why can't you all just leave me alone?"

"Don't get mad at us just because you're not happy," Lynn told him.

"I don't even want to talk about this anymore," Tracy said. "Just let me get my things and I'll be out of here."

"Just remember," Lynn reminded him—it was how she'd spoken to him when they were kids—"once you calm down, you're going to see things differently. You're going to feel ashamed of yourself." His temper in those days had been famous.

"Maybe I will," he told his sister evenly. "But then again, maybe I won't."

"Families," Arthur said, his distant voice soothingly close in Tracy's ear. "What can you expect? The more dysfunctional the better, is what I always say. Though yours does sound like it takes the cake."

"It's not even that my family's so dysfunctional," Tracy complained. He sat on his futon, bare legs out straight, pillows cushioning his back against the wall. "It's like—*I'm* the dysfunction."

"Funny how that is, isn't it? So you stormed right out of there and drove back in the middle of the night. That'll teach them."

There was no doubt he'd behaved badly; and yet, for all his uneasiness, he felt unrepentant, even exultant.

"*What* a grueling drive," he complained. "The New Jersey Turnpike at two o'clock in the morning. All the demon truckers come out."

"Then I hope you made a potty stop at every single rest stop along the way. The Vince Lombardi is my particular fave. Or is it the Joyce Kilmer?"

"That's you, not me," Tracy admonished his friend. "I can't tell you how happy I am to be back in my own house with my own dog and a weather forecast that says we're supposed to get two feet of snow. Is it snowing down there yet?"

He really did want to stay in this beautiful house of his forever, though he knew he'd have to move out next year; the house was meant for families, not single instructors. Doug Brill had already let him know the place was as good as his.

"Well, what do you know?" Arthur said with a flurry of static that meant he was moving around his apartment. "I believe it is snowing. Good golly, is it coming down. Oh, I'm going to go out and scamper about for a while. I love New York in a snowstorm. How much did you say? Two feet?"

"That's what they say. Can you wait a second? I've got another call coming in."

"See," Arthur said cheerfully, "already your family's calling to apologize."

But it wasn't his family, and he hadn't expected it to be. He felt both desolate and strangely relieved. At first he didn't recognize the low, hesitant voice on the other end of the line. "Noah," he said cautiously. "How are you, Noah?"

"I'm at the train station here in Middle Forge. So I guess that means I'm not so well."

It could have been an attempt at a joke, but Tracy wasn't so sure. "What's the matter?" he asked. "What's going on?" He resisted the impulse to say, "Go away, leave me alone."

There was a pause. "Hey Trace," Noah asked, sounding even more uncertain than before, "would you mind to come get me?"

Tracy hesitated. Desperately he cast about for excuses; finding none except for perhaps the weather, he asked, aware how foolish it sounded, "Noah, are you in some kind of trouble?"

Noah sort of laughed, or at least that was how Tracy heard the sound. "Head trouble is all," he said. "Nothing a little heroin wouldn't fix. I don't mean to put you out or anything. I mean, if you're busy with something. I just feel like I sort of could use a friend right now."

The words had their allure. If Noah was perhaps something of a schemer, Tracy thought darkly, he was nonetheless pretty good at it.

"The train station, huh?" No doubt he'd have ample cause to regret all this, whatever *this* turned out to be. And you don't know what it is, he told himself. "Okay," he said. "I'll be there."

"I'll be out front, by the phone booth," Noah said helpfully. "You can't miss me." Then the line was dead. Feeling confused, skeptical, exhilarated, Tracy clicked back to Arthur, who was oddly, sweetly, humming to himself.

"Gee, I thought you'd forgotten me," he said. "The family must have been very, very sorry."

"Aargh," Tracy told him. "Look, I've got to go. I've got to go pick up somebody at the train station."

"Really? Now that sounds mysterious. Were you expecting this person?"

"No," Tracy said. "Definitely I was not expecting this person. I'll tell you all about it later."

The streets were much worse than he'd imagined, the snow thicker, the wind harsher. Traffic was practically nonexistent, New Year's Eve festivities

effectively canceled by the storm. Only the Heidelberg, a dreary little restaurant on Main Street that turned into a dreary little gay bar at night,
hopefully flashed a welcoming Dinkelacker sign in its window. No plows
had come through, and wouldn't, Middle Forge being Middle Forge, till
morning.

It wouldn't have been out of the question for Noah to walk to campus
from the station, but Tracy was glad the boy hadn't come pounding on his
back door without any warning. At least this gave him time to think—but
about what? He really had put Noah almost completely out of his head, he
told himself, though when he rechecked that adamant assertion just to make
sure, he was alarmed to discover how uncertain he actually was.

Despite his care his little Toyota was describing leisurely fishtails back
and forth across lanes. Prudently he slowed to the speed of a strolling boy;
if he went slower and slower he'd never have to arrive, or when he finally
did arrive Noah would be long gone, grown safely into manhood and out of
the reach of hopeless longings.

A spell of strangeness seemed to lie over the slumbering village. There
had been snows like this in the Black Forest the year he lived there, great
blanketing storms that put the whole landscape to enchanted sleep. A word
seemed to surface in his brain, but then sank back, elusive, into the depths
as he turned carefully into the Metro North parking lot only to discover that
the Toyota, sliding in a wide, slow-motion arc, seemed to have other plans.
For a single gorgeously dilating instant he had lost control; he went with the
spin thinking, I could die now. I could fall asleep beneath this snow. I could
wake in the dark forest. With its gables and sharply peaked roof, didn't the
little brick station itself belong in a medieval fairy tale? And there, forlorn
and shivering in the sulphurous light, a bloodred rose amid the field of
deathly white snow—why was he wearing his crimson warm-up sweats from
cross-country?—stood Noah Lathrop.

He looked so terribly young as the car glided safely to a halt in front of
him, and Tracy had forgotten how beautiful he was, how finely etched his
features, how striking his blue gaze. This boy had asked him to come for
him. He had no winter jacket, no luggage, only a knapsack slung over his
shoulder, too small to contain even a change of clothes.

"Spectacular," Noah observed as he slid into the front seat. "Have you
been practicing your counterterrorist driving?"

"You must be freezing," Tracy told him, at the same time silently asking
his hapless student, What on earth were you thinking? What were you planning to do if I wasn't here?

And yet what Tracy felt was not disapproval but elation, startlingly powerful, as if he himself had been rescued from the storm.

Noah, however, seemed a little less than elated. "I hate your town's weather," he complained, clutching thin arms across the Forge School crest that emblazoned his chest.

"Don't you believe in listening to the weather report?" Tracy was conscious of pulling back, restraining himself within irony's safer embrace.

"Actually—no," Noah told him, reaching down to massage his bare ankles. He was wearing no socks with his sneakers. "You could say I believe in trusting to fate. Are the roads bad?"

"The roads are fucking terrible," Tracy said. "As you'll see."

"Fucking terrible," Noah repeated. He seemed to like the epithet; it seemed to relax him. He settled more comfortably into his seat, and it was uncanny, Tracy mused, how little either of them resembled who they really were. They might have been brothers, the older picking up the younger after sports practice; or father and son; even a teacher and his star student; but not who they were, which was none of those things, not even the last, but rather something unmapped, mysterious, dark in its way as Africa.

He'd ask no questions; let Noah, for the time being, volunteer whatever he volunteered. Though for the moment, as Tracy negotiated the empty but treacherous streets of Middle Forge, the refugee from the cité radieuse seemed content to sit in silence, as if their estrangement of the past month and a half had never happened, as if nothing needed any explanation beyond the two of them in a car on a snowy night.

His house was lit and shining like a beacon. He didn't remember leaving so many lights on, but from the road it looked remarkably inviting, as if sense and order and contentment, those elusive household deities, had taken up residence. In the driveway, the tracks the Toyota had left were already disappearing under the relentless onslaught of fresh snow. The towering conifers by the side of the house hung heavy with their gleaming burdens.

"I hope you've got enough food stashed away," Noah joked, his first words since the train station.

"I hope you're not too hungry," Tracy told him.

They stamped the slush off themselves on the back stoop, left footwear in the mudroom. Noah's sneakers were soaked through, his bare feet pink with cold. Betsy nuzzled them with her wet nose. "Hey Bets," he moaned, scratching behind her ears, kneeling to allow her to plunge her face into his. "Long time no see, huh?"

Tracy resisted mightily the temptation to order Noah out of his wet track suit—which, on closer inspection, looked relatively dry. He comforted himself with the thought that at some point, tomorrow perhaps, a change of clothes would still be necessary. Noah in a borrowed shirt and pants lounging around the house while the world beyond lay in the thrall of a different kind of beauty: the idea was positively moving.

In the kitchen he busied himself making hot chocolate for them both while Noah took his time in the bathroom. The fairy tale spell he'd felt on his way to the train station had not entirely left him, the shimmery sense that perhaps he had crashed after all, right through the thin wall separating an ordinary life from an enchanted one, and he found himself checking the mudroom just to reassure himself that those were indeed Noah's sodden sneakers lying there beside the bench and not some trick of the light. And then there was Noah himself, no trick of light either as he stood in the doorway. The past month and a half—their estrangement, their flight from each other—seemed trancelike and unreal. They were friends, soul mates—a bond not to be taken lightly. Why had he ever thought the right thing, the responsible thing, was to flee all that?

"I'm a real pain in the ass, aren't I?" Noah said cheerfully, taking the mug of hot chocolate and settling into a corner of the sofa, where he drew his bare feet up onto the cushions.

"Depends," Tracy told him, refusing to look at those feet, Noah's long toes and shapely nails, looking instead at his own steaming mug. "So what's the story here?" he asked.

But Noah didn't answer. He sat there testing the chocolate's temperature with his lips, blowing across the surface to cool it down. There were moments like this in class when Tracy asked a question and faced total, uncomfortable silence from the room; at first those long empty seconds had unnerved him, till he'd learned to wait them out. Take your time, he told Noah silently. I'll be here. I have nowhere else to go.

As if at some private joke that had formed itself in the steaming chocolate, Noah smiled. He shook his head, dismissing who knew what ghost of a possibility. "You know, Trace," he said bemusedly. "I'm sitting here trying to figure out what to say. And I can't." He looked up, still smiling, but Tracy thought he saw nothing but misery in that smile. "I just don't know that I want to say *anything* right now."

Tracy tried to sound gentle, though he felt a burr of irritation. "You've got to try, Noah. I mean, what's going on? There's some story here that I need to know if I'm going to be your friend." He hesitated for a millisecond over that last word, but decided the circumstances warranted it.

"No," Noah said. "It's not that—it's just . . ." He stopped again, perturbed, frustrated, running once more into some invisible, baffling obstacle. And Tracy thought, Noah, I haven't got a clue. He thought: go ahead, tell me you're sexually confused. Tell me you love me. He thought: I can't stand this. Please go back home and leave me alone. He thought all those things as a single, complicated thought whose strands would not unravel from one another.

"Why did you run away?" he asked Noah point-blank.

"I'm always running away," the boy answered evenly. "Remember?"

"I understand that," Tracy told him. "But this time you're not even wearing a coat."

"I just decided to come up here, okay?" Noah said sullenly. "I didn't know what I was going to do till I was already practically on the train. Trust me."

If this was what it felt like to be a parent, Tracy thought, it wasn't a role he much relished. "I'm not trying to get on your case," he said, riding the case as hard as he could. "I'm just trying to, I don't know, figure out where we are here. Did you get in an argument at home?" With a sudden sense of panic the situation sank in: however noble or base his motives, he was a gay man who'd taken in a runaway kid, who happened to be one of his students, and now they were stuck here together for the night.

"It wasn't an argument," Noah said. "It was just—home. My dad and stepmom. Sometimes they're too much."

"Well, okay," Tracy said. "If it makes you feel any better, I just had a huge fight with my family too."

"Tell me about it," Noah said, though his tone indicated that he did not, in fact, want to be told about it.

"It's the way families are. You fight with them because you love them," Tracy said, chilled to realize how completely indifferent he felt toward both his mother and his sister. "It's part of the package."

"Yeah, yeah, that's what everybody says," Noah said. "Can I tell you? I hate my fucking father. I hate my fucking stepmother. And I hate my fucking mother." He spit the words out bitterly. His flat certitude made Tracy wince as if under a physical blow. Tracy might be indifferent, but he did not hate his mother or his sister, which was perhaps worse.

"What would you have done if I wasn't home?" he asked.

"I guess I took a chance. The bigger question is, what would I have done if you'd just said fuck off?"

The admission—the perspective it put on things—flustered Tracy, nearly brought an unanticipated tear to his eye. "I'm honored," was all he could think of to say. "I didn't quite know what terms we were on."

"I didn't either," Noah said quietly. "Thank you for coming to get me, Trace. You saved my life."

"It wasn't quite *that* dramatic," Tracy told him warily—dangerous emotions lay in wait, after all—"but you're welcome all the same."

As if in answer, from somewhere outside a series of very loud explosions jolted the room. For an alarmed instant he thought the police had burst in, guns blazing, but it was only someone—quite nearby—who had set off a round of midnight fireworks. Betsy roused herself for a few barks in reply, the way she did every day at noon when the fire whistle blew, and Tracy, his heart calming, lifted his mug. "So. Happy New Year," he said. "I think I'm going to take that as my cue and go to bed. I'm totally zonked. Can I tell you? I drove straight through from Virginia in the middle of the night last night."

"Running away," Noah said.

Tracy thought for a moment. "Actually," he said, "what it felt like was coming home." Or an illusion of home, precarious and unreal. But he would not dwell on that now. It was late; there had been enough for one night. Before him lay a future in which anything could happen, good or ill, magic or disaster. He knew there were limits to trusting one's judgment about these things, and that midnight, the turn of the new year, was inauspicious at best. "So let's talk sleeping arrangements here for a second," he said briskly. "I'm going to put you on the sofa, which unfortunately is not a Castro Convertible, and is not long enough to be very comfortable, but it's all I can do. Unless you want to sleep on the floor."

"How about the futon?" Noah asked impishly.

"That's where I'm sleeping, you nut," Tracy told him firmly.

"Okay, the sofa. Better than a snowdrift. Does Betsy get to sleep out here with me?"

"If you wish," Tracy told him.

In all of New York, hadn't there been a single place for Noah to go. With that unhappy thought tugging at him Tracy pulled sheets, blankets, a pillow from the closet and stacked them on the sofa. "Good night, Noah," he said. "I'll see you tomorrow. You know where everything is."

"Yeah, good night, Trace," Noah told him. "I do know where everything is."

Tracy shut the door to the bedroom and took off his clothes. He told himself he felt neither elated nor aroused, only dead tired. If he'd behaved abominably with his family, they'd also, in their way, behaved abominably toward him. But at least his behavior toward Noah had been beyond reproach: generous, charitable, understanding. You're going to grow up to be a great human being one day, he silently addressed his young friend. And I'm going to make sure that happens. It's the least I can do.

But if his noble behavior so impressed him, then why did he feel so dejected?

The memory of Noah's slender fingers massaging frozen ankles came back to him, and then a fragmentary phantasm: Tracy was removing Clay's cowboy boots, tugging them off gently to reveal the boy's sexy, unwashed Tennessee feet. Had it really only been yesterday that he and the ghost of Holden Chance IV had cruised the high street of Colonial Williamsburg? The last thirty hours were so absurdly populated with the living and the dead that what he needed more than anything else, he told himself, was an interval of decent unconsciousness in which to sort everything out.

Outside the window, the snow was still falling thickly, on village and forest and river and castle. *Märchen*. He had tried to think of that word earlier. Fairy tale, diminutive of the word for rumor. Sighing deeply, he lay down on his austere futon and closed his eyes to a darkness in which countless rose-red princes lay dreaming, in thorn-clad bowers, of other, waking princes, and kisses, and warm, warm lips.

He wasn't sure how long he had been asleep when a movement wakened him, a hand on his shoulder, a choked voice close to his ear saying, "I think this is what you want."

XII

The sun, shining more brilliantly than seemed possible, smothered the room in light. He rubbed his eyes in amazement, not remembering, for a moment, where he was or why, till he looked out the window to see acres and acres of snow, snow piled so high, so deep, it would be spring before you ever glimpsed the ground again.

When he'd slipped naked and shivering into the dark bedroom and gently lifted the covers to slide in next to Tracy's recumbent form, he'd had no idea what would happen, but he'd come this far and figured the most Tracy Parker could do was throw him out of his bed. But that hadn't happened; Tracy had not pushed him away. Instead, with a sigh that sounded surprisingly like misery, he'd opened his arms and pulled him close, not saying a word, only holding him tight, the way you might hang on to a life raft if you thought you were drowning.

And after that? He must have fallen asleep right away in the warm lock of that embrace, exhausted by the day's wanderings, passed out on a surfeit of urgently achieved fulfillment, because the next he knew light was flooding the room and beside him, curved protectively away on the other side of the futon and dead to the world, was Tracy Parker. And beneath the both of them, like despair itself, Noah felt the starkly familiar sensation of a cold, urine-soaked sheet.

It couldn't have happened, he couldn't have pissed Tracy's bed, but of course the shaming possibility that haunted all his nights had come true.

"Fuck!" he said, half aloud. "Fuck! Fuck! Fuck!" The incantation, as usual, changed nothing. He'd been so careful, those nights he'd stayed over to house-sit, to bring a plastic undersheet along just in case. He'd always been so prone to accidents of one kind or another, whether breaking bones or losing things or pissing the bed or setting forest fires, that his therapist back at the other school had worried: too many accidents are no accident. Sometimes it seemed like there was some implant in his brain that made him sabotage everything that came his way.

And to think that he had been on the verge of everything. After months inside his head, he'd wanted reality, and that's what he'd gotten, only reality was turning out to be more than he'd bargained for. Shifting onto his side to face Tracy's back—just a bare shoulder, spread with a few freckles, and the curve of his straw-colored head were visible outside the covers—Noah struggled not to weep in frustration. That Tracy Parker was actually lying beside him in the flesh seemed too good to be true. That in a matter of minutes, half an hour—it didn't matter, did it?—Tracy would wake up to find Noah had pissed in his bed seemed too awful to live through. You stupid fucking baby, Noah accused himself. You've ruined it. There was no way Tracy Parker would have anything to do with him after this.

The only thing left—a melancholy, desperate task—was to salvage whatever he could from the wreckage of his dream. Gingerly he scooted himself closer to the sleeping figure, cozying up under the covers till he nuzzled his chest against Tracy's back, his hips against Tracy's boxer-clad buttocks. His hard penis lay pressed up flat against firm flesh. Lightly he kissed that exposed shoulder, then allowed his lips to linger against the papery texture of skin. He draped an arm across the unconscious body, letting his palm rest against Tracy's chest, his fingers splayed among the blond hairs there. Don't wake up, he willed the sleeper. At least not yet. He kissed Tracy's neck, the back of his earlobe; circled a nipple with his thumb. Then he trailed his hand lower, past the navel, the relaxed, slightly convex stomach. Did he dare? His fingers toyed with the waistband of Tracy's boxers, and the sleeper moaned groggily, coming slowly, indolently, out of the depths, then seeming in an instant to bolt fully awake.

"What?" Tracy said in alarm, sitting upright and looking around with a wild, confused look. "Oh yikes," he said. "What a nightmare. Somebody," he added almost as an afterthought, "went and pissed the bed." He stood up and threw the comforter aside. There, like a kidney-shaped swimming pool, was the faint yellow outline of the offending stain.

"I'm really, really sorry," Noah said, all at once conscious of his nakedness, his erection that lay against his stomach.

Tracy looked at him curiously. "Oh Jesus," he said, gazing nonetheless at the arousal Noah defiantly made no effort to conceal, "don't worry about the futon." He laughed nervously, ran a hand through his heroically mussed-up hair. "That's the least of my worries."

By now they should have been totally carried away, surging upstream toward the source of the mysterious river that was love, life, happiness, but Tracy Parker didn't want him, and why should he ever have thought that he did?

"Make yourself decent," the unhaveable Tracy Parker said firmly, though

Noah could feel his naked body thoroughly, even greedily scrutinized. "Go take a shower. We'll sort this all out later. We've got plenty of time." His voice, attempting to sound casual, nonetheless quivered, though whether it was with anxiety or excitement, Noah couldn't tell. "What's it look like out there?" his teacher continued nervously. "Two feet? Two and a half? For better or worse, neither of us is going anywhere today. So let's say I make us some breakfast, and we'll act like civilized human beings here."

Feeling both chastised and bestirred, Noah got up slowly from the futon and forced himself to stretch luxuriously, facing Tracy, allowing the man full view of his slim body, hairless except for its treasure trail and patch of pubic bush that sprouted a penis still as upright as a teapot's curving spout.

What would have been really civilized, Noah thought, but what Tracy Parker unfortunately didn't suggest, would have been an offer to share the shower's hot, healing stream with his rowdy young guest.

The last thing he wanted to think about was his dad, but his dad was exactly the subject Tracy had to bring up. They sat before big bowls of oatmeal topped with sliced bananas and granola—his staple, Tracy bragged, from carpentry days in New York. "Will he be worried?" he asked in an exasperating voice of concern. "Shouldn't you at least give him a call, let him know you're okay?"

Noah shifted uneasily in Tracy's luxurious maroon bathrobe and resented the kindly proffered advice—as if Tracy could possibly know anything about the way it was between him and his dad. He tried to sound indifferent, though he worried, even then, that he might well be inadvertently giving something away. "Oh, he'll be fine," he said. "It might do him some good to worry now and then."

Tracy didn't seem too pleased, but what could he do? He'd gone and dressed himself as if for an ordinary day: jeans, a red flannel shirt, white socks but, of course, since he forbade them indoors, no shoes. Noah liked that his teacher sort of needed a shave. He'd never seen the immaculate Tracy Parker unshaven, and the dark stubble definitely had its appeal.

Sipping his tea and frowning a bit, Tracy said, "So I guess things haven't gotten any better between the two of you."

Noah tried not to talk too much about his dad; he had the distinct feeling that Noah Senior did not like to be described or analyzed behind his back, and he could never get over the paranoid notion—but who said it was paranoid?—that everything would eventually get back to him. "I have my ways" wasn't his dad's favorite sentence for nothing. So maybe, on second thought, Tracy Parker should be worried after all. It was highly unlikely that his dad would go to the trouble of tracking him down—he'd just wait to give him hell or worse later—yet it wouldn't take too much to figure out, if he were so inclined, that if he hadn't gone off to his mom's house, then the Forge was probably the next likeliest destination.

Well, that would certainly be enlightening, wouldn't it, an eye-opener for everybody if his dad came barging onto the Forge campus, making a bee-line—but how could he know?—for Tracy Parker's nice faculty house. You paid for me to get educated up here, Noah challenged the absent but unforgiving figure, so what did you expect? That I wouldn't take advantage of the opportunities? Maybe the possibility never occurred to you that I might be as good at seizing opportunities as you ever were, Mr. Phillips Andover and Dartmouth College.

"You really want to know my dad?" he said to Tracy. "Here's Noah Senior in a nutshell. He tells me I have to be in New York for Christmas, so I go. No big deal. And then he doesn't show up. He's got business. Okay, no big deal either, though I could've gone to see my mom if I'd known, which is probably why he wanted me to be in New York in the first place, so he could fuck with whatever plans she might have made. Because that's all they do, is fuck with each other's heads. I mean, they haven't been married in, like, seven years, and they're still fucking with each other's heads like there's no tomorrow. My dad's worse about it, but she does it too. It's like their way of relating. Or my dad's way of relating; he does the same thing with his other former wife. *And* his fiancée."

"Your dad's working on number three?" Tracy said. "I never knew that. I'm impressed."

"You don't know my dad," Noah told him, feeling, despite himself, a defiant touch of pride. "If he wants something, he goes after it. Like he's going after Central Asia right now. The old Soviet underbelly." It was his dad's phrase, and he was surprised to find himself using it.

"Like father, like son." Tracy laughed.

"No," he corrected Tracy touchily. Why did everyone always have to say that? "Definitely not."

Whatever he thought about that, Tracy knew well enough to take the hint. "So back to your story," he urged. "And have more oatmeal if you want."

But the detour had taken Noah too far afield; he couldn't remember exactly what story he'd wanted to tell, only that under no circumstances did he want to include the part about Chris Tyler and his doctor friend, the threeway that had nearly happened but then, thank God, didn't. Remembering that close call, though, took him back to the broader outlines of his narrative. "Okay," he continued. "So I'm fucked, and my mom's fucked, and my dad's nowhere to be seen, and I'm stuck with Gunila." Should he mention that she was Stolichnaya Spokesperson to the World? He didn't want to get off track again because the tricky part was coming up.

"After a couple of days I make my own plans; I'm supposed to hang out with this guy from school. And a friend of his," he added, thinking, Why not stick as close to the truth as possible? "So then right before I'm supposed to go over there, what does my dad do? He shows up and says he's taking us out to dinner, me and Gunila both, and when I say I've got other plans he says, well cancel them, and when I say no, I've already made these plans, Dad, these are *my* plans . . ."

"It escalates from there," Tracy finished for him. "Well, I still think you should call him. Just for good measure."

Don't press me, Noah thought, though what he said was, "I'll think about it." There was lots of stuff from the holidays Tracy Parker didn't need to know about. He didn't need to know, for example, that Georgiana Baldrick, the coke-fiend wife of his dad's lawyer, had slipped her tongue in his mouth when she unexpectedly kissed him good-bye at the end of a Christmas party. He didn't need to know that a certain not-so-innocent somebody had already had a cock in his mouth as well, albeit briefly and meaninglessly. He certainly didn't need to know just how close, out of desperation, out of hopelessness, that somebody had come to taking up Chris's New Year's Eve proposition, and all because he'd nearly given up (and thank God it hadn't been completely) on the possibility that he and Tracy would ever be together, even if it only meant something so complicatedly simple as their just being the kind of friends it had seemed, for a while during the fall's golden excitement, they had been on the verge of being.

If certain places you came to in your life felt right, then how many others were just as clearly the wrong place to be? It would have been nothing but perversion, pure and simple, to have ended up in bed with Chris and his doctor friend. It would've been no good for anybody. The world, when you got down to it, was disturbingly full of close calls.

"All finished?" Tracy said with a repellent cheerfulness that was utterly beyond Noah. "I tell you what: why don't I do the dishes, and you can dry."

Why don't we just go back to bed and get it over with? Noah thought bitterly. He'd neither washed nor dried a dish in his entire life, but if that was what it took to get Tracy Parker to love him, then he was game for it.

Since there was only the one snow shovel, he and Tracy took turns uncovering the driveway. He hadn't exactly seen the point since the road in front of the house, because it was a dead end with only two other houses on it, would probably remain unplowed till tomorrow. But Tracy wouldn't be dissuaded. "Better sooner than later," he said, a bit hypocritically, Noah thought, given how things were turning out. But what could he do but go along as good-naturedly as possible? Soon his shoulders, unused to the exercise, were aching. His lungs stung with icy air; he exhaled clouds of frosty vapor. But it was great to be outside, to be under a sky so blue it shone like enamel, to see Tracy's house settled into snowbanks like a ship stranded by Arctic ice floes, as if they were explorers armed only with the scantest of provisions, now set out on foot toward some unimaginable discovery just over the horizon.

He never used to like snow, its suffocation of the landscape, till his seventh-grade biology teacher, Mr. Brookner, had said, "Think of it as a protective blanket that's actually keeping all the plants warm." Surprisingly, that had done the trick, and ever since then he'd felt strangely nervous in winters when there wasn't a cover of snow, everything naked and exposed to the killing winds and frozen star-haunted nights.

The Toyota was completely buried; nothing but a hillock marked its secret grave. He shoveled a narrow path toward the driver's side and managed to pry the door open. That dim space, lit only by eerie snow-filtered light, beckoned mysteriously; he couldn't resist sliding into the driver's seat. It was the den of some hibernating animal whose happy plight, slumbering safe from the wild world months at a time, he profoundly envied. Not fifty miles away, under this healing white comforter, his ruined forest likewise slept; in twenty years it would be as if nothing had ever happened there. Twenty years in nature's clock was a catnap, the wink of an eye. Before his eyes, as if caught by time-lapse photography, he saw the hated settlement of Forest Haven collapsing into ruin, the roofless brick shells of the houses strangled by vines, the rooms invaded by shrubs and saplings, grass sprouting through cracks in the asphalt of abandoned roads, great trees surging up, splitting walls, their roots turning under the last evidence that the place had ever been violated.

"Hey, you there," Tracy called. "Back to work. It's not naptime yet."

But he'd had enough. "Your turn," he told Tracy. Reluctantly he forsook his lair and, handing Tracy the shovel, stood aside to survey the meager amount of driveway he'd cleared. Tracy launched into the task with vigor, and Noah liked watching him at work; he could glimpse his fit friend the way he'd been back in his carpentering days. Without warning, Tracy's many years before the Forge fell like a shadow over the present moment. To him I'm just a kid, Noah reminded himself. Tracy had lived ten unimaginable years before he was even born; twenty-five before he'd ever met him. And he thought with sick anxiety of all the people, utterly unknown to him, who had moved through the bright orbit of that life. Arthur, for instance, the teasing voice on the answering machine. He'd been up for a visit in December, Noah knew, but Tracy had kept them far apart. Still, Noah had seen the two of them in the distance once that weekend, not on campus but in town, Arthur a lean, lanky faggot—there was no other word for it—with a yelping laugh that drifted quite clearly across the distance separating Noah from the two friends, or whatever it was they were.

"Hey Trace," he said abruptly. "Do you mind if I ask you a question?"

Tracy stopped his exertions—his progress down the driveway put Noah's feeble attempts to shame—and leaned himself, raptly attentive, on the upright shovel. But now Noah felt stupid. His question would seem strange, out of nowhere. That was what people always said about him: that he was hard to follow. But if they knew all the logical connections in his head they wouldn't think that.

"Who is Arthur?"

Tracy looked either perplexed or evasive, and Noah wondered: had he somehow gotten the name wrong?

"Your friend from New York," he prompted—and on further thought, realized he hadn't gotten the name wrong at all. "You know," he said. "*Arthurina.*"

"Arthurina," Tracy mused, almost as if he'd never encountered such a silly word before. "Why do you ask?"

"He came up to visit you, right?"

"Yes he did," Tracy said. "Arthurina, as you call him, is a very dear friend of mine from way back, when I first lived in New York City. Before I went to Japan. I don't think you'd like him much. He can be a little alarming at first. Unfortunately, these days, he's very sick."

Noah thought grimly, It just keeps coming up, doesn't? Like those heads popping up all around you that used to scare him so much in that game Whack-A-Mole he'd played once out at Coney Island. "You mean AIDS," he said.

"Unfortunately."

"That's terrible," Noah said bravely, even as the strange thought crossed his mind that Arthur, in that single glimpse he'd had of him, had reminded him a little of Chris Tyler, not his physical appearance, because Noah hadn't been that close, but something vaguer, something he couldn't put his finger on. It made his next question, though he tried to make it sound ironic, somewhat harder than he'd anticipated.

"Should I be jealous?"

Tracy seemed genuinely perplexed this time. "What for? Because he's sick?"

"No, no," Noah said quickly. It wasn't what he'd meant at all. He'd have to just come out and say it. "I meant, is he . . . well . . . is he, like, your boyfriend or something?"

Tracy smiled. He had a gorgeous smile, like candlelight, and all at once it occurred to Noah that he knew how to use it as well, putting his interrogator at ease just with that expression of gentle indulgence, tenderness, patience. Before he even said a word.

"He *was* my boyfriend. Ages ago, before he got sick. Now he's just my friend. And no, for your information, I don't have a boyfriend. So there. Actually, you know, Arthur went to the Forge, way before our time of course. In fact . . ." He paused, his smile gone now, replaced by a distinct look of worry. "But that's another story," he said dismissively.

"Tell me," Noah demanded. He hated it when Tracy treated him like that.

Tracy looked not just worried, but grim. "What I was going to say was, he had a little affair with one of his teachers while he was here."

"See? Happens all the time," Noah was quick to point out.

"It was not a happy thing," Tracy said. "Not a happy thing at all." And with that he threw himself back into his mighty shoveling, with what seemed to the unsatisfied Noah like redoubled purposefulness.

An afternoon of monotonous brilliance. Long icicles stabbed down from the gutters—like ice picks made of ice, Noah thought. Ice turned against itself. Sock-footed, he paced the house's bare rooms, Betsy following, her nails clicking hollowly across the floors. "I've got some work I need to do," Tracy had said before disappearing behind the closed door of his study, but Noah had no particular illusions. Tracy Parker was hiding from him, and there was nothing he could do but wait till he came out.

He'd never been any good at filling empty time, entertaining himself while he waited. And most of life, he'd concluded, was about waiting. Waiting for the class period to end, the schoolday to finish, the game to be over, waiting for the train, waiting to grow up, to be old enough, waiting to be done with whatever boring thing he was doing at the moment. For getting rid of boring, empty, useless, depressing time, there was nothing so good as sleep: jump ahead fast-forward, get on with the plot, such as it was. Even the animals knew that.

Out the window he could see the driveway he'd barely started and Tracy had finished, a gleaming ribbon of asphalt going nowhere. Maybe that was the difference between them, and for a moment he thought he could see how wrong he'd been about this man he'd obsessed about for the last three months. Certainly things weren't turning out as he'd planned; the delirious, uncontrollable passion he'd envisioned was showing itself to be tedious, hesitant, all hemmed in. He realized, gazing forlornly at that driveway, how angry he was with Tracy for not wanting the same thing he wanted, and in the same way he wanted it.

Of course he could always run away one more time. He greatly relished the thought of Tracy emerging from his study to find him long gone; then he'd see what he'd missed. Or would he only feel relief at being left alone?

He could run or he could wait. And he was no good at either one.

He wanted to break things, smash dishes against the radiator, throw a lamp against a wall. Let Tracy know how he was feeling, that it wasn't fair. He wanted to kick Betsy, or break an arm by slamming it into a door frame. He wanted to set fire to the house and watch it burn.

No, no, no. He did not want to set fire to the house. He wanted to set fire to time and watch it burn like a candle or, better, a match. He remembered the sensation he sometimes had when he was furiously writing out one of his stories, how he'd look up to find that an hour had consumed itself entirely, and feel stunned but strangely excited that only his scribbles on the page marked its vanishing.

Right there he called a halt to his aimless circumnavigation of the house's finite space. Locating his knapsack, he extracted the notebook he always carried with him and sat himself cross-legged on the sofa. He patted the empty space next to him; alert and eager, Betsy jumped right up. Then he opened to a blank page, paused a moment to let the black torrent rush through him, and began to write.

The Soviet Underbelly
An Adventure Dream (For All Ages)
by Noah Lathrop III

One snowy morning they knock down Noah Lathrop III's door & wake him up out of a really fine sleep (no dreams) & say You're under arrest. Its 2 men dressed in black pants, black turtlenecks, black boots. I think I've seen them somewhere before but I'm still sleepy so I don't quite know.

Who are you? I ask. (innocent me).

We used to work as models, but then the KGB recruited us. It's much more fun being torturers than models, because we're beautiful, & we need to cause pain.

Yes, says the other one.

Oh, I say, I get it. You're the famous Brewer Twins.

Correction, they say. We were the famous Brewer twins. Now I am Kazak, & this is my brother Kergix (sp.???), & like we say, You're under arrest for Crimes.

Uh oh, I say, which one?

Oh, we can tell you're really guilty, Kazak says.

Yes, Kergix says. So it doesn't really matter, now does it.

So come with us, Kazak says.

We go out to their helicopter, & get in & it goes & lands us in this courtyard with four high walls around it, their's no door leading in or out, just these four sky high walls.

Then a door opens in the wall like magic & out steps The Kommisar.

I say, I don't know you, do I?

Of course, says the Kommisar. You have always known me.

We will torture you now, says Kazak.

Yes, says Kergix, getting out a saw from his bag. Its got these tiny razor sharp diamond teeth, & when he starts sawing off my leg I can *hardly feel it. This isn't too bad I think, only now I don't have a leg, which is terrible. Then he saws the other one off, right at the hip, & I'm going Oh shit, now what am I supposed to do. He puts this special goop on them both to heel them right up. Then his brother Kazak takes the saw & goes, Now we'll do your arms, so they cut the right one off & then the left one. & I'm yelling Stop, stop, trying to move my arms & legs but I cant because guess what, their not there. It doesn't hurt, it's just that I need my arms & legs back.*

The Kommisar keeps laughing his head off, & I keep going, Where do I know this guy from?

Then Kazak & Kergix take these special spoons & gouge out my eyes like egg yolks, then they cut out my tongue & stick these special antiseptic ice picks in my ears to pierce my eardrums. So now I can't hear or see & I can't scream or talk or anything, just be there in the dark where theirs no sound & I can't even move.

They just go away & leave me there. Oh, & they put a special tube in my side so liquid food can go in & I won't starve, I'll just stay like this forever.

He stopped writing and closed his eyes. The torture he'd invented pleased him. In its way it was perfect. These days it seemed like he was always writing about torture and never the other thing—but then, believe it or not, he was pretty cautious these days. He censored himself. Not like that first great thing he wrote, back at his other school, starring him and Mr. Brookner in a plane crash in the jungle where they had to live like savages, just the two of them, running around with no clothes and all, and then the part where the snake bit him and Mr. Brookner had to save his life: that was the best part to write, especially when Mr. Brookner massaged his chest and stomach with special ointment, his hand rubbing in circles lower and lower till he said, What's this? and then . . . Well, it had gone on for pages and pages, great stuff, but not meant for anybody ever to read, definitely not for his nosy roommate to read, and excruciatingly not for Mr. Brookner, who of course his roommate took it straight to.

He burned to remember all that. He'd never had a teacher so kind as Mr. Brookner, so understanding, and then try explaining to him how it was all a bad joke (ha ha). Or to the counselor. Or any of the other plenty who got wind of the stupid story and wouldn't let it go.

Except for Mr. Brookner, he hadn't liked that school much, and he hadn't been a bit sorry to leave (though a hot tear, or three or four, appeared out of nowhere when Mr. Brookner shook his hand good-bye).

• • •

Tracy's hand on his shoulder shook him gently awake. Sometime in the late afternoon, drowsy, fretful, disconsolate, he'd given in: curled up in the warm blankets and comforter of Tracy's ruined futon. ("Nonsense—it's not ruined," Tracy had tried to assure him. "What's a little pee anyway?")

Now Noah found himself apologizing once again. "I didn't mean to fall asleep. What time is it?" The light had gone out of the world, and Tracy, for whatever reason, hadn't turned on the lamp; darkness saturated the room.

"It's dinnertime," Tracy said softly. "You must've been exhausted. You slept at least three hours."

"Did you go out?" Noah asked.

"Out?" Tracy wondered.

"To get food."

Tracy laughed. "I just improvised. They still haven't plowed my street. Now come on, it's all ready."

Sluggish, with the thin line of a headache stretching somewhere in the back of his brain, he tried to pull himself together. For half an hour after waking up from a nap he was always an idiot, IQ of fifty at most. He hated that he'd opted out, fallen asleep instead of keeping watch as the long, difficult day had demanded. A test, like shoveling the driveway, and once again he'd failed.

Or perhaps Tracy had failed, by neglecting to join him in his nap, as he'd hoped against hope, when he crawled into the futon's disheveled nest of covers. Our love has died, he said to himself with bitter drama.

Tracy had cooked another one of his stupid, wonderful dinners. "Let's see," he said, gesturing at the feast he'd laid out. "To start, some miso soup. Then, a nice roasted vegetable medley—parsnips, carrots, turnips, and rutabaga."

"Root vegetables rock," Noah deadpanned. Tracy had made an effort for him. Already he was starting to feel better.

"You bet," Tracy told him with serious enthusiasm. "The best. And then some spicy soba noodles. And for dessert, poached pears. Well, one poached pear, half for you and half for me. That's all I had in the refrigerator."

The surprising thing was, it all sounded quite appealing. "You know, you've gone and turned me into a vegetarian," Noah admitted as he seated himself at the table. "All I used to eat was hamburgers and M&M's and shit like that. Now I can't stand the thought of all that stuff."

Tracy only smiled, though so broadly it was clear he felt delighted by the effect he'd had on his student.

Only faggots don't eat red meat, Noah's dad would say.

"I mean, really," Noah went on. "I didn't understand the consequences before. The rain forest and all that. How we make animals suffer."

"There should be more people like you," Tracy said.

"Like us," Noah reminded him, nonetheless pleased that there weren't too many like him, at least in Tracy's eyes. Though he still had to wonder: was Arthur one of them like him?

Oblivious to the pang of jealousy he had unintentionally provoked, Tracy lit candles, even poured them both a glass of red wine. "Cheers," he said. "To us, then."

Noah sipped cautiously, feeling grown-up and responsible, though unable to repress a grimace at the wine's dense afterbite.

"It's really an acquired taste," Tracy assured him. "I hated the stuff for years. Then I went out with Arthur, who's a connoisseur. He taught me everything I know about wine, which is about this much." He gestured with his thumb and forefinger, the same gesture Gary Marks made when he was disparaging the size of someone's penis. "I'm still not what you'd call much of a drinker. Two glasses and my lights go out. I guess I'm what you'd call a cheap date."

Noah laughed uncomfortably, trying to decide exactly how he was sup-posed to take a joke like that, concluding it could really go either way. This was a different Tracy Parker than he'd seen before, as if his teacher had finally decided to take him seriously, to treat him as an equal. So this was how gay men talked. Tracy seemed looser, more at ease. He seemed, in a word, faggier.

"This is really delicious," Noah complimented him. "As always."

"Thanks," Tracy told him. And then it was the oddest thing—as if, with that single word, he dove back into an ocean of silence. Self-consciously, Noah tried to think of something else to say, but suddenly they seemed to have nothing in common. They ate for several minutes in uncomfortable silence, their chopsticks clicking busily against porcelain, their chewing un-naturally, even comically, loud.

"About Arthur," Tracy said, as if he too had long strings of logic that happened all in his head before he got to what he wanted to say. He'd stopped eating and was looking at Noah strangely. "What I told you about—Arthur and one of his teachers."

Was this it? Noah wondered. Fear and anxiety seized him, and he sat motionless. When he realized the chopsticks still poised in his left hand were trembling, he laid them on the table.

"I've been thinking about that," Tracy went on. "I mean, should it have happened or not? And I guess the easy answer is no. It should never happen, under any circumstances. But the harder answer . . . Well, let's just say Ar-thur really wanted it to happen. The teacher was the one who freaked out, and that's when things unfortunately got nasty. But Arthur was old enough to know what he was doing. Maybe it was crazy, but Arthur's always done crazy things. I'm also thinking, when I was your age I had this incredible crush on a guy who was like thirty or something. We were both working in this summer theater program, and we became really good friends. I wanted to be with him more than anything else in my life, and I'm pretty sure he was attracted to me, too. This one afternoon we came really close to doing it. I mean, I actually came out and told him I wanted to sleep with him, and we went back to his place and everything but then at the last minute he freaked out. Or maybe he didn't freak out. Maybe his conscience told him, No, don't do this. I don't know. But he told me I was too young."

"So do you think you were too young?" Noah wanted to know.

"I wish I knew," Tracy said with a pained expression on his face. "I really, really wish I knew. What I do know is, the first time I actually had sex was about a year later, in the back of a car with this creep I'd met in the parking lot of a gay bar I was too young to get into. He had this really enormous dick and he fucked me without a condom. I didn't know any better. Plus he was not gentle at all. It hurt like hell. He knew he was taking advantage of me, and just wanted to get his kicks and get the hell out of there. So I couldn't have done any worse on my first time out if I'd tried. Certainly Eric would have treated me with love and respect. If only I'd been able to convince him. So, no," he concluded resolutely. "I don't think I was too young, as it turned out."

Was Tracy asking Noah to convince him? If that was what it took . . .

"Then I don't see why there's even any question about you and me," Noah said as convincingly as he could. "There's things I need to know, Trace. I'm asking you to teach me. The way you wish somebody taught you."

"I wish I didn't have all these scruples," Tracy said. "Thinking about all the consequences." Noah noticed how he clenched and unclenched his right fist on the table beside his plate. In frustration? In anger or nervousness?

"I wish you didn't either. What is it with you older guys?" Noah kidded, surprised he could find a sense of humor in a situation that was making him so tense. He felt a sharp pain in his gut, he was so tense, but he forged on anyway, wholly serious now. He put everything into what he had to say, looking Tracy straight in the eye with the most serious expression he could manage. "We're soul mates, Trace. You've even said that. We've got this incredible bond." He couldn't quite bring himself to say, You're a faggot and I think maybe I am too. Instead he pleaded, "Do you want me to go off and have my first time with some sleazy guy I don't know who's going to give me AIDS or something?"

Tracy took a deep breath and expelled it in a huge, weary sigh. Nonetheless he continued looking at Noah with an intensity that was actually a little unnerving, Noah so seldom made eye contact with anyone; it was an invisible but undeniable link he'd didn't know quite what to do with, especially when, as now, it went on and on, gathering depth and focus but leading to—what?

That was the great mystery. Where did he think any or all of this was supposed to lead? Try as he might, he couldn't imagine the future whose door he was so desperately trying to open. All he could think of was that sequence of Brewer Twin photos he'd downloaded from the Internet: two picture-perfect brothers joking around, wrestling a bit before getting seriously moody and passionate with each other, hugging and rolling around naked in the ferns and then that beautiful beautiful kiss that made his heart soar into his throat.

Tracy was the one to break the perfect, scary link that bound them. He shifted his stare off toward a far corner of the candlelit room. He unclenched his fist and splayed his fingers, palm down, on the surface of the table. "Let's just say," he mused haltingly. "Let's just say that . . . whatever happens here is special. It's set apart. I mean, from everything else. It's something that happens. Part of a continuum."

Whatever it is, just say it, Noah thought, exhilarated by the direction he thought the words were heading, but also irked that it all seemed up to Tracy now. What if he'd changed *his* mind since this morning? That thought apparently hadn't occurred to Tracy, who seemed more intent on reliving his private past than sharing their present.

"If this happens," Tracy said gravely, assuming they both knew quite clearly—and were perfectly agreed on—what *this* was, "and I'm only talking theoretically here, but if this happens, it has to be like it never happened. You want this and I want this, but the stupid rules say we can't either of us have it. Think of today as a snow day: the rules get suspended, but then you have to go back to how things normally are."

Noah was listening hard, but he still wasn't one hundred percent sure what was being said, exactly. Why were things never spelled out the way you wanted them to be, so there wasn't any doubt?

Then Tracy said the astonishing thing that made it all blazingly clear, like sunlight on snow. "I'm doing this because I love you," he said simply. "And I want to help you. I want you to have what I never had."

In the dream adventure Noah could barely reply, his throat too tight, his eyes about to well up with tears. His answer was the hardest, most brilliant thing he'd ever said. He punched all fifteen parched years of his soul into it. "I want you to fuck me," he said.

"I know," Tracy said. "I want to fuck you. I want this to be something really beautiful, Noah."

It was all Noah could do to nod solemnly. So the dread thing was going to happen after all. Tracy Parker was going to put his penis inside him till Noah whimpered that mysterious amalgam of bliss and agony that had obsessed his imagination for so long.

You don't have to do this, he reminded himself. It's not too late. You don't have to go over to the dark side.

It will be like it never happened, Tracy had said. That was where Tracy Parker, for all his vast and enviable experience, was so dead wrong.

"Come," Tracy beckoned. He held out his hand across the table and Noah accepted it. Together they stood up slowly, eyes locked again, gazing at each other, it seemed, with a tenderness so languorous and melting he'd never imagined such a look possible. Stepping around the edge of the table, Tracy pulled him slowly into a great embrace. "I love you, Noah," he whispered reassuringly, nuzzling his ear, and Noah told him back, though under the circumstances it sounded ridiculous, even vaguely suspect, "I love you too, Trace." Together they swayed a little drunkenly without having had hardly anything to drink, arms locked around one another, not exploratory—he took his lead from Tracy—but just holding tight as if in panic or great relief. Tracy's pelvis pressed assertively against his, and he returned the pressure, feeling his thickening cock, and Tracy's too, mashed between them.

Releasing his grip, Tracy sounded like nothing so much as a stage manager on opening night. "Let's bring the candles to the bedroom." And as Betsy loyally roused herself to follow: "Here, why don't we put you in your cage? I'm really not up for a threeway." He laughed skittishly. "Can you take care of her? I'll go put some nice music on." Noah didn't mind; he liked it that his teacher was taking so much trouble over him. It made him feel wanted, even if the jubilant abandon he'd expecting hadn't quite materialized. Those few afternoons with Chris Tyler had been pure sex—sex talking through them, sex using them like mad puppets. This, on the other hand, was something more considered, deliberate—both disappointing and weirdly arousing. The love feast, he said to himself, unsure where the phrase had come to him from, but struck by its solemnity, and entirely clear about its effect on his dick, which had never in his life felt harder or grander.

Classical piano music began to play softly. He knew nothing about music, was indifferent to it, both the corporate noise his peers listened to and the baffling monotony of the so-called classical.

"My favorite piece," Tracy proclaimed fervently. "Franz Schubert, the B-flat opus posthumous. Do you like it? I think it's so gorgeous."

"Sorry," Noah apologized. "I've got a tin ear."

Though there was something gorgeous, if not about the music itself, then about the music together with the candles lighting the darkened bedroom as to the two of them stood before one another, on the verge of it all happening, finally and at last, just the way it was supposed to.

When Tracy reached out to undo the buttons of Noah's shirt—Tracy's shirt, actually, a too-big blue-and-black flannel he'd lent him—Noah matched his progress button for button, a reflection in a mirror, till they both stood thrillingly bare-chested. Tracy laid an outspread palm on Noah's shallow chest, right in the middle, and Noah reciprocated, flattening his hand over the more heroic, lightly furred cleft of a truly muscular chest. Imperfect twins, alas, though Tracy hardly seemed displeased or disappointed; they moved their hands slowly clockwise, counterclockwise, over nipples, throat, belly, till with a sigh Tracy drew Noah to him and kissed him lusciously, a mouthful—and minute full—of juicy spit and tongue. Hands found the waist of his borrowed chinos, loosened the belt that cinched their extra inches around his hips, and began to mirror-unbutton buttons they had unbuttoned dozens of times before, back in the world before this candle-flickered world. He sprang free, both pants and boxers dropped to his knees, his penis proud and aching as Tracy knelt worshipfully before him and slurped him into his mouth. Hardly had he registered that amazing fact—Tracy Parker was actually sucking his cock—before he said "Oh!" his ejaculation taking him utterly off guard, though Tracy seemed unfazed, pumping him in and out of his mouth as Noah felt three distinct, obliterating spurts spatter the back of that prayerful throat. Taking Tracy's head in his hands, he skewered that mouth on his dick, which did not diminish but stayed agonizingly firm as lips and tongue and throat continued to work him avidly, so avidly in fact that his shaft was suddenly supersensitive, its nerves raw and painful as happened whenever, disappointed that his orgasm had failed to be as all-encompassing as he'd looked forward to, he continued to jack himself vigorously after coming.

"I didn't mean to shoot," he said, pulling himself out of Tracy's mouth, which nonetheless followed his cock an inch or two like a baby after a tit.

"Ah, the spirit of youth," Tracy murmured, looking up with a smirk of rebuke, eyes aglitter, still on his knees and clasping with his big hands the backs of Noah's thighs. He let the tip of Noah's cock brush his closed lips, at the same time reaching one hand around to tug gently at his tender, spent balls. Carefully Noah stepped out of the pants and boxers gathered around his ankles. He let Tracy peel off one white sock and then the other. Sliding out of the rest of his own clothes, Tracy stood and faced him, his big cock standing straight out from him.

The time had come. For one terrible moment Noah quailed at the thought of how much it would probably hurt, the damage it would do; then he pressed resolutely on. "Let's go over to the bed," he suggested.

Tracy followed, and when Noah reached the futon, he moved in close behind him, circling him with his arms, chest to back, his cock pressed up lengthwise against the crack of Noah's ass. "Noah, Noah," Tracy murmured swooningly into his ear. "I want to fuck you."

"Go ahead," Noah said, his voice cracked and hoarse. His heart fluttered in his throat. "Put it in me."

Surprisingly, Tracy released him from his embrace. "Brief intermission," he announced unromantically. "Don't move." Noah's cock had cranked back up, though his stomach felt woozy with dread. When he touched a finger to his asshole to make sure it was clean, the sensation sent shivers through him. The secret to getting fucked, Chris Tyler had told him, is total relaxation. Just open up and let it in.

He tried, not very successfully, to squelch the worrying thought that he wasn't a very relaxed person in general, and this was certainly not a very relaxing situation. Meanwhile, the man who was going to fuck him was back, holding a condom in its square of gold foil and what looked mysteriously like a tube of toothpaste.

"What's that?"

"Lubricant," Tracy explained. He must have still looked puzzled, because Tracy added, "It'll make it easier."

He'd never used anything like that with Chris Tyler, and wondered what other surprises might be in store.

"Lie down on the bed," Tracy commanded him mildly. "On your back. That's good." Noah tried to relax, despite Tracy's rapt scrutiny of his nakedness, his adamant erection pointing due north toward his navel. Looming over him, Tracy lowered his mouth to his belly, his tongue teasing the dimple of his navel, then drifting south to browse in his public hair, to lap at his balls, finally to capture, once again, the whole shaft of his penis. Hands found his ankles and lifted them up, and Tracy's mouth moved toward the nether regions. Noah couldn't believe it: Tracy actually had his tongue there! It flicked lightly around his hole, then settled in for some serious work. Oh my God, Noah thought, unable to help himself, Oh my God, oh my God. He tried very hard to relax, to welcome each foray of Tracy's marauding tongue.

With a great contented sigh Tracy pulled back, gazing down at his captive with that glazed, dreamy expression Noah had seen in Chris's eyes as well. The eyes of a creature completely taken over, possessed by desire. "What a beautiful asshole," Tracy said incoherently, like a madman. Then it struck Noah with the force of a revelation: what if his asshole really did look beautiful when seen through eyes taken over by desire? What if everything you naturally assumed could be overturned in an instant, just like that? It was as if, all along, Tracy had known a secret, been carrying it inside himself without saying a word, and now Noah had caught a glimpse of that other life Tracy lived, the life of desire where a gross thing like an asshole was beautiful and what other unheard-of things might not also be true?

"Just relax," he heard Tracy saying. "I'm going to loosen you up a little here." He dabbed lubricant on his finger and rubbed in cold circles around Noah's asshole. Then he sank his finger in.

Noah hadn't been prepared for that at all. He felt himself clench in panic around the intruder.

"Easy, easy," Tracy soothed. "It hurts at first. You'll get used to it." He pressed in a little more, and Noah, who'd prided himself on his general reticence during sex with Chris, found himself unable to suppress a groan. "We'll just go slow," Tracy coaxed, rotating the finger gingerly in its socket. So far, Noah was not liking this feeling one bit, but he told himself this was only the beginning: the amazing part, or so he hoped, was yet to come.

He tried to put himself on a flat, sun-warmed boulder in the woods, where on summer afternoons he'd lain spread-eagled and naked waiting for something or someone to come upon him, but only blue dragonflies had danced in the sultry air. Now a man was probing him with his finger. "Oof," he said involuntarily as the finger removed itself.

"Good, good," Tracy encouraged. "You're doing great." Then the invader was back, though two fingers, surprisingly, felt better than one, especially when Tracy twisted them slowly inside him, their thickness opening him up, squishing audibly in that slick hole Tracy had called beautiful. "How you doing, gorgeous?" Tracy whispered.

"Fine," Noah whispered back, as if they'd descended so far into something secret neither dared speak it aloud. Poised above him, Tracy stared unflinchingly down into his eyes, an intent, questioning expression on his face. Noah tried to connect those fingers inside him to those serious eyes; tried to imagine what impulses were traveling up the nerves of Tracy's right arm to the dome of his inscrutable brain. And back down to his cock, which loomed as erect as ever.

"I'm going to fuck you," Tracy said clearly, lucidly. His fingers pulled most of the way out, then pushed back in, deeper than before, once, twice, the third time releasing an embarrassing fart Noah hoped Tracy didn't hear. But far from spoiling things, the low note drew a smile from his partner who slowly, even reluctantly withdrew his fingers, saying, "Don't worry. It happens." Wiping his fingers along the inside of Noah's thigh—was there gunk on them? Noah wondered squeamishly; he hadn't really considered that part of it too much—Tracy groped for the condom he'd dropped beside the lube on the mattress. He brought the foil square to his mouth and bit off the corner.

"No condom," Noah said firmly. He reached out to close a fist around that big, stiff, unprotected cock that was finally going to penetrate him. He'd thought about it: he wanted Tracy, not latex. Total connection or nothing.

With a sigh of exasperation, Tracy rocked back on his haunches. "Are you crazy? There's no way I'm going to fuck you without a condom," he said adamantly. "That's lesson number one. Never, never, never fuck without a condom."

Noah rubbed his thumb across the little fish mouth at the tip of Tracy's penis.

"Noah, this is not good," Tracy complained. "This is not a good habit for you to get into."

"Are you afraid I'm going to get AIDS from you?" he asked.

"I'm just not going to fuck you without a condom," Tracy said. "For your own good, okay?"

"Then why'd you swallow?"

"You didn't give me much of a choice there, now did you? Besides, two wrongs don't make a right."

"I'm not happy with this," Noah said.

"Trust me," Tracy told him. "It's the thing to do. Now help me get back in gear. I seem to have lost it." His cock was, in fact, disappointingly flaccid, but Noah stoically seized the opportunity. Shifting himself around, he went at his task with all the resolve he could muster, though he still gagged unappealingly as the big thing poked the back of his throat.

"Easy," Tracy said. "Watch the teeth."

His ineptitude infuriated him. He should've practiced more on Chris; he should've done that threeway and learned everything he needed to know. He hated being the ignorant kid, the one who always got failing grades in everything.

"Use your lips more," Tracy urged. "Use your tongue. That's it. That's great."

Noah relished the murmurs and sighs he was managing to extract, as well as the increasingly satisfying heft and girth that filled his mouth. Relinquishing his catch, he took the condom and rolled it down the length of Tracy's shaft—which hardly seemed diminished by it. The latex stretched nearly to transparency. "Lie back," Tracy prompted. "I'll go easy. I won't hurt you."

"That doesn't matter," Noah told him, the end of the sentence choked off by the sudden, brutal stab of pain. "Oww," he cried in spite of himself. It was more embarrassing even than farting, but he felt sickeningly stuffed, like a big fecal log was lodged up there and he wasn't able to shit it out. The pain grew and grew like a fire lit inside him. So this was the feeling faggots were so greedy for. Now he thought he understood.

Do *you* like to get fucked, Tracy Parker? he wanted to ask, concentrating on formulating that question as clearly as he could in order not to focus on the searing jolt as Tracy pushed deeper.

"I'm inside you. How does it feel?"

"Like hell." Noah grimaced. "Like a pain in the ass," he tried to joke.

"Take a minute to get used to it, beautiful."

So Tracy's cock was in him. At least he'd scaled that fine peak of accomplishment. The idea of it, more than the immediate feeling, made him feel triumphant, since the immediate feeling was just a little short of agony.

Tracy began a few tentative thrusts. Being in him clearly didn't mean being all the way in, as Noah painfully discovered.

People were so stupid. They said, I'm on fire for you. They said, I'm burning up with desire. He wanted Tracy to make him blaze.

But Tracy had become a blind pumping machine. His eyes went vacant with lust. "Uh, uh, uh," he grunted almost dutifully, with each focused piston thrust—or was that Noah's own voice calling out, or even better, the two of them together, locked in this thrilling mortal combat?

Hit me harder, Noah coaxed. I'm a boxer, I'm staggering woozily around the ring, you're landing punch after punch where it really counts, you're punishing me mercilessly, you're knocking the living daylights out of me.

His cock sprang alive at the sweet thought of the pummeling he was taking.

Look at me, Dad, he thought, fisting himself roughly while Tracy methodically made contact with some amazing bright spot located deep in his gut, just look at your stupid faggot son in his burning glory, he hissed as a second load of jism sprayed his heaving stomach.

"Oh fuck," Tracy said sharply. He pushed himself farther in than ever and held there spasming, teeth bared, his face a greedy wolf-snarl of pleasure.

Noah felt a droplet of sweat hit his chest, then another. Tracy bent forward, hair hanging into his eyes, and lowered his lips to Noah's. His tongue entered there gently even as his cock still pulsed in Noah's ass; each flex sent a profound shiver all through Noah's body, and Noah responded by experimentally clenching his sphincter around the buried length of flesh. For several long minutes they lay like that, sharing heavy sour breaths, their bodies signaling back and forth, call and response. Then gently Tracy withdrew himself, like pulling a stopper—*Pock!*—the sound of lips kissing air.

They were in a room flickering with candles. The soft piano music was still playing. Somehow, at least for a few moments, Noah had left all that behind. Maybe he'd even left Tracy behind, because he was startled to hear the voice next to him saying, almost prayerfully, "You're so beautiful, Noah. Do you even know how beautiful you are?"

"Knock it off," Noah told him, half kidding but half serious as well. He'd have loved hearing those words earlier, they'd have made him blush with shy vanity, but now those same words made him uncomfortable, even edgy. Did people always feel like this afterward? Degraded and spent and vaguely *lacking* something?

"No, I mean it," Tracy insisted.

"Let's don't talk, okay?" Noah said. "Let's just go to sleep. I'm really tired."

He hadn't been burned to cinder and ash. There was nothing to it, in fact, this sweat-lathered mingling of bodies. People got fucked all over the world every day and survived, and though he couldn't say he'd come through it untouched, at the same time he was still the same Noah Lathrop III as before.

XIII

The paths between the buildings had been cleared, the parking lots plowed: nice to see that the grounds crew, more often than not a weak link in the school's great chain of being, had proved reliable in his absence. And how happy he was to have missed altogether what people were calling the Great New Year's Eve Blizzard, a Northeaster prominent enough to have made the front page of the *Arizona Daily Star* (WINTER'S ICY GRIP. . .). Seated in his daughter Caroline's comfortable Tucson kitchen over a morning cup of coffee, he had read of its fury. Even now, two weeks later, evidence of the onslaught remained everywhere in mountainous piles of unmelted snow a second blizzard had added to a few days later. Large trees—including several old beauties on campus, he noted sadly—were down. Some outlying areas in the county still lacked electricity. And in his own home, brown water stains spotting the upstairs ceilings told of ice dams along the roof's edges. The weight of snow had brought down a length of front gutter on top of the rhododendrons.

Lux, however, was still alive, and that alone gladdened him greatly. Louis had felt guilty leaving the poor creature behind, though one couldn't very well refuse to visit one's daughter just because an aged and infirm dog occupied a perhaps too-prominent spot in one's emotional life. A kennel, of course, had been out of the question at Lux's age; despite some qualms about giving a comparative stranger free run of his house and its secrets, he had engaged Sandra Robertson, the Forge School's young biology teacher, to house-sit for the holidays. He and Claire were very fond of Sandra, and Claire had even suggested, on more than one occasion, that it might be nice to have her over for dinner sometime when Tracy was also invited. But that had been before Tracy, with motives that still seemed fathomless, had chosen to ambush his unsuspecting friends not only with the unwelcome specter of

Arthur Branson and all his attendant ghosts, but with his own unasked-for revelation as well, an announcement all the more eloquent for its lack of overt articulation, and from whose numinous shock Louis had still not recovered.

Trudging up the salted steps to the administration building, he paused to fumble among several nearly identical keys—he kept intending to mark them, somehow, but never got around to it—and after several unsuccessful attempts managed to let himself in the front door. The air inside had the stale smell of having been held close for a month, like breath in the lungs, though Security had supposedly been around to each of the campus buildings every few days to inspect for any damage—which, campuswide, had mercifully been minimal. It was a good thing he'd gone ahead and had Goethe Hall reroofed in November.

For some years now the start of a new semester had brought a strange heaviness of heart. It had been good to get away to Arizona; the dramatic change of climate, the clear desert air had thrilled him. He'd always scoffed at people who went south for the winter—snowbirds, he'd heard someone call them, a name far too magical for those sagging, liver-spotted fugitives. This year, however, for the first time, strolling around the development where his daughter lived, he understood the allure of warm, dry winters in a landscape beautifully reduced to its bare essentials.

Though the Hudson River Valley under snow, he thought loyally as he entered his office and reencountered, artistically framed through his windows, the impeccable sheet of white covering the quad, had its own essential beauty as well. If only it didn't make ordinary life so difficult.

The red light on his answering machine blinked furiously, and while his first inclination was to leave all that till tomorrow, on second thought, with some sixth sense of dread, he pushed the Play button.

The voice was curt and to the point. "This is the father of one of your students, Noah Lathrop. It seems he's gone off without telling anybody what he was up to, and I have a hunch he may be up there at the Forge School. He's great buddies with one of your teachers, I can't remember his name. So if you could, please get back to me. It's very important." He gave his number, also the date, which was New Year's, a good two weeks ago. The next message, from later that same day, was also from Noah Senior; and the next message and the next, nine in all, each sounding slightly less concerned about the boy and slightly more irritated with Louis. The last message, from the tenth of January, informed him: "Noah Lathrop again. It's fucking ridiculous that no one there seems to want to get back to me. Hello? Is anybody awake behind the goddamned steering wheel?"

Louis felt suitably chastised, reduced to a negligent schoolboy himself. Of course he should have checked his office messages long-distance, that would have been the prudent thing for a headmaster to do, but he could never remember the code he had to punch in to do so, and even when he had the code, as with most wonderful new technology, half the time he couldn't make it work.

Without delay he called the number in New York, only to have the unforgiving voice on that answering machine rebuke him curtly. "I'm out of the country till the end of January. Leave a message. If I deem it important, I'll get back to you." How odd, Louis thought. Had the man found his son? What was going on? He remembered how he'd had an uneasy feeling about Noah's father back in December—a whisper so vague he'd barely admitted it to himself. But it had been there nonetheless, a hint of ruthlessness, a dash of rapacious will that warned one—of what? At the same time he had found himself quietly compelled. Every now and again a parent would induce such a complicated reaction in him—as if they knew that, in the end, the headmaster of a school like the Forge School hardly counted in the scheme of the world.

He found his voice less steady than he would have liked. "Mr. Lathrop," he said. "Louis Tremper here returning your call. I apologize terribly for the delay in getting back to you." He paused, unsure what more to say. He would not grovel; he would be brisk and professional. Nonetheless he was afraid. "Perhaps you could call me at your earliest convenience," he said quickly and then hung up.

In defiance or penance he played the messages through a second time. It was all distinctly worrying. He had no doubt that the faculty member Noah was "buddies" with would be Tracy Parker, and there was no denying that he'd been troubled, ever since that day he'd visited Tracy's class back in the fall, by something in the dynamic between Tracy and that particular student, a tension he couldn't really attribute to anything in particular. As far as Noah was concerned, Louis had learned, over the years, to be cautious about taking an instant dislike to a boy; on closer examination, the dislike all too often concealed other, less easily classifiable currents. But the fact remained that, from the very first, he had felt wary, and given what he now knew about Tracy's particular situation—and sympathetic as he might be—any relationship with the boy, even if it were wholly beneficent and professional, could prove to have its vexing aspects.

Surely, he thought squeamishly, Tracy would have sense enough not to do anything irresponsible; surely he had that much judgment. And yet at the same time Louis could not feel entirely sanguine; he'd witnessed too much in the way of regrettable misjudgment, down through the years, in the halls of this very building.

Hoping to clear up the matter once and for all, he dialed Tracy's number, which he knew by heart, but of course there was no answer on Tracy's end of the line, only his mild recorded voice asking the caller to leave a message. Would some future civilization think it bizarre that humans, at the end of the twentieth century, wasted so much time and energy in a futile attempt just to talk to each other?

"Oh hello," Louis spoke into the machine, suddenly conscious that he and Tracy had had hardly any contact at all, mechanical or otherwise, that final, hectic week of the semester. That he had, in fact, for reasons that now seemed just short of shameful, assiduously avoided his junior colleague. He cleared his throat. "This is Louis Tremper. I've got a bit of school business I need to discuss with you. If you'd be so good as to give me a call when you get this, I'd appreciate it." He hesitated, and then added, "I hope you had a good break, and are looking forward to the start of a new semester."

He hesitated once more, feeling that his message was somehow woefully inadequate, that he'd like to go back and redo it, but of course one couldn't do that with an answering machine, so he concluded by saying "Bye, bye" in a way he hoped sounded fond and conciliatory. For what, after all, had Tracy done? The reasonable answer was, of course, nothing at all—as he had told himself repeatedly during those long, solitary circumambulations of Caroline's neighborhood he'd found himself taking. He thought he understood now that it had been nothing less than panic that had blindsided him that evening. Part of it—indeed, much of it—had no doubt been the shock of seeing Arthur Branson after all these years, seeing him ill and wasting, all that brilliant promise come to nothing. And how much of that, not the dreadful illness of course, but his failure to live up to the luminous future he'd once seemed destined for, was Louis's own fault, either directly or indirectly? What should he have done that he had failed to do? He did not like to think of those dark, compromised times; the years had taught him it did no good to think of them. What had happened had happened, and the dead, as always, kept their own counsel. He had wept tears of remorse that night—he who prided himself on never weeping, except perhaps a tear or two at the end of *Rosenkavalier* or Bruckner's Ninth Symphony. Sequestered in his darkened study, sipping scotch and crying noiselessly, so Claire would not hear, he'd stared out at the moonlit, snow-dusted garden his wife spent so many hours in, a ruin now as the year staggered to a close.

What had Arthur told Tracy? What of the full story, secrets held close for years, did his colleague know?

Perhaps it was precisely because he was certain he wouldn't find Tracy at home that he decided to walk over to his house just to make sure. The day was cloudy, dull, relieved momentarily by the bright flicker of a cardinal alighting in a somber hemlock. In front of Goethe Hall, a taxi from the train station was discharging returning students. He seemed to remember that Noah lived in Goethe Hall; he'd have to call Doug Brill later to find out if the prodigal had returned.

At the edge of the lake, three boys were skating on the ice—an activity strictly forbidden by the school's insurance company. He thought about calling out to them, ordering them in, but the temperatures hadn't been above freezing in days, and what harm could there possibly be? One winter, in Dr. Emmerich's time, they had built a bonfire out on the frozen lake, faculty and students gathering around its inspiriting warmth beneath a clear night sky crowded with constellations Dr. Emmerich picked out for them—Orion and Gemini and Hercules—lifting them all into a great imaginary voyage around the heavens before setting them back down gently on the ice. There were so many ways of living dangerously. That was what he had always liked about boys: their capacity for adventure; their brave questing idealism. It was what he had loved so much in Arthur Branson.

But with that thought, Louis was the one skating on treacherously thin ice. Without another glance in that dangerous direction, he headed back for the safety of solid ground. He refused, these days, to live dangerously—if, indeed, he ever had.

Arthur Branson, on the other hand, had fallen right through the ice. Arthur Branson was drowning in the black viral waters. It was hideous, hideous.

He desperately regretted that he'd behaved so very badly that evening. He'd give anything to be able to rewind the tape and do it over, but life, like the answering machine, didn't offer that option. Which was fortunate, he supposed, for once one started to relive the past, making changes as one went along, where would one ever stop? The very pinprick of conception— was that where one's intervention finally would lead, gently, sorrowfully steer- ing aside the conjunction that would produce the very being who, returning to that moment, knowing what he knew, would have no moral recourse but to firmly, regretfully, say, No, it stops here?

More and more often these days, it seemed, Louis caught himself in the throes of a really despicable self-pity; an encroaching disease, perhaps not unrelated to his somewhat increased indulgence, lately, in the nightly ritual of scotch-sipping. He increased his pace, hoping the crisply articulated air, as sharp in his lungs as the wicked-looking icicles depending from the eaves of the houses he passed, might goad him into a brisker outlook on the pres- ent, anxious situation. He should have called Brill from his office and at least gotten over that particular hurdle, but that was how he seemed to live these days, deferring the resolution of exactly those things he fretted over the most, as if secretly he enjoyed the fretting, the worry, as if at least he knew his way around its disconsolate swamplands.

Tracy's house was at the end of a cul-de-sac, one of a handful of rather stately houses owned by the Forge School but these days mostly rented, for the extra income, to townspeople—or not so much townspeople as the well- to-do young couples from Manhattan who were appearing in ever greater numbers in Middle Forge, and who represented, depending on one's point of view, either hope for the future or a death knell tolling for the past. Louis had always thought Tracy's house the nicest of the bunch, and for that reason—as well as Dr. Emmerich's having lived there when he was head-master—had kept it available for Forge School faculty, particularly those with families. He was secretly glad that Tracy had had the run of it for the year; come September, however, it would be home to Douglas Brill and his burgeoning brood, of which number five was reportedly on the way. How the man managed, on what the Forge School paid him, was beyond Louis's reckoning. The graceful white frame building, with its ample front porch where in fine weather Dr. Emmerich used to host his late afternoon martini hour, stood deserted in its snowy lawn. From the street, where Louis stood, there were no signs of life.

A fluted note of longing or nostalgia stirred in him as he gazed at the dark windows staring vacantly back at him. Someone had shoveled the driveway and the path to the front door after the first storm, but the foot dropped by the second storm had not been cleared away. He made his way awkwardly through the knee-high mess that overwhelmed his low snow boots and clung to his trousers. Feeling very much the detective, he constructed what he could of a chronology—not, of course, that there had been anything remotely resembling a crime. He figured Tracy must have been in Middle Forge around New Year's, but had left before the fifth of January, and now, the day before classes, was nowhere to be found. There was no reason, of course, that Tracy should have let anyone know of his travel plans, but still, under the blank afternoon sky, it felt vaguely ominous.

Deciding it might make sense to pay a visit to Goethe Hall in person, Louis reluctantly turned and trudged back down the driveway and out to the street. He brushed his trouser legs but the damage was already done; he would have to suffer cold, wet calves till he got home. Crows were calling their awful death music back and forth to one another. Another taxi full of boys had pulled up from the train station, and his heart leaped with relief as he thought he recognized, from the distance, Noah Lathrop. But then he saw he was mistaken. These closely cropped heads that were all the rage among some of the boys could make them resemble one another rather remarkably. The unmistakable person he did see, as he approached the steps, was lemon-haired Christian Tyler, looking theatrically elegant if too thin in his black cloth coat and turquoise scarf. Seated nonchalantly on the low brick wall next to the steps, he appeared to be smoking a last forbidden cigarette before surrendering himself to another semester of the Forge School's rules. He cast a sly, defiant look at the other boys as they headed past him into the building, chattering among themselves and ignoring him completely. Seeing Louis, he turned and said, politely, not bothering to hide his cigarette, "Hey, Mr. Tremper. Happy New Year. Hope it's another wet and wild one."

Curious, how Louis's head swam suddenly with images of Arthur Branson, since the two, except for their height and thinness, resembled one another not in the least. Nevertheless, Louis couldn't resist warmly extending his hand to the somewhat startled Christian, who hesitated a moment before accepting. "Welcome back," he told him heartily. "I trust you're well? You must stop by my office soon."

"Oh, I'm just fine and dandy," Christian said, and though it sounded arch, as was his manner, Louis had the impression that he actually meant it. "I'll definitely stop by. Say, early next week, once things get settled down."

"Excellent," Louis told him. Then, on the off chance, he asked, "You haven't seen Noah Lathrop, have you? Sophomore. I believe he lives in this dorm."

For a moment Christian seemed startled. "I just got here myself," he said. "So, no, I have no idea *what* Noah Lathrop may be up to." If Christian sounded vaguely offended that he should be expected to know anything about Noah, Louis reminded himself that Christian was after all not on the best of terms with his hallmates. Boys were a heartless bunch, pack animals who rarely missed the scent of blood. From their perspective Christian was undoubtedly standoffish, eccentric, queer. So naturally they baited him; he in turn refused to take the bait; it inflamed them all the more. Boys, unfortunately, being boys, there had been the occasional unpleasant incident in the dorm last semester, which Louis had made sure Doug Brill attended to promptly and properly.

Brill himself wasn't in. He'd gone into town to buy ice cream and cookies for tonight's dorm gathering, his wife informed Louis. A small, harried-seeming woman—and why shouldn't she be harried?—Mary Ann Brill had always irked Louis, not the least because she insisted on home-schooling the two oldest children, an affront, as Louis saw it, to the Forge School, even though neither of the two children were anywhere near high school age. On her blouse she wore a pin that said MARANATHA: THE LORD IS COMING. For a while, a year or so back, their apartment door had been adorned with a bumper sticker expressing similar sentiments, which he had at last persuaded a reluctant Doug to remove, a frankly authoritarian gesture (Dr. Emmerich had always firmly insisted that the Forge School was *not* a religious academy) for which Mary Ann, he suspected, had not forgiven him, though she would be perfectly content, when her Lord and Master came, to obey *His* every command. Certainly in the privacy of her own apartment she was free to adorn herself however she might; Louis couldn't very well go dictating the private practices of his faculty—as long as they didn't partake of illegality or moral turpitude.

Settling one of her smaller children uneasily onto her hip—she had never seemed to Louis much cut out to be a mother, but looks, apparently, were deceiving—Mary Ann told him, no, she didn't think Noah Lathrop was there yet, but (looking at her watch) he should be soon, since all the boys were supposed to be back at five, as he well knew.

Yes, he supposed he did know that. He supposed, too, that he should prepare himself for a quietly miserable evening of not knowing certain things he desperately needed to know.

Stay calm, he counseled himself. Not till tomorrow would things necessarily be dire.

"Oh yes, Caroline's doing marvelously," he reported in answer to Libby's polite question. They had just seated themselves around the dining room table, and he was uncorking the wine, a promising-looking Australian Syrah the Fallones had brought. "I believe she's very happy out there. Content with her lot. Wouldn't you say so?" He turned to Claire for support.

"I believe Caroline's just fine," Claire said dryly.

Having hoped for a little more encouragement on the subject, Louis felt he should elaborate. "There was a time there, you know, when, frankly, I worried. But I've come to the conclusion that Caroline's simply not interested in marriage. At least not for the moment. Now Susan, on the other hand: the moment she hit adolescence, she was looking for a husband, a family. Caroline's just not that way. She's always been much more career-oriented."

"Women in science," Reid observed. "More power to them. This lamb, by the way, is scrumptious."

"Louis gets credit for the lamb," Claire said. "It was his idea, so I said, it's all yours. He so rarely cooks these days, I jump at the chance whenever he seems the least bit interested."

"I cook," Louis defended himself. "Every morning, I cook you an egg."

"That's true," Claire admitted. "It's a lovely habit."

"Anyway, I hope you aren't sick of lamb," Louis apologized to Reid. "I wasn't thinking." Wandering the supermarket this afternoon with Claire, distracted by thoughts of Tracy, of Noah, all his unsubstantiated fears, he had chanced upon the superb cut at the meat counter and felt vaguely comforted by the prospect of its succulent delights.

"Oh, hardly," Reid told him. "Lamb is one of those essentials. Salt, olive oil, lamb, yogurt, wine." He ticked them off on the fingers of one hand, ending where he had begun, with the pointer finger outstretched. "You could build a whole culture around those things. Come to think of it, the Greeks did just that."

"You need a vegetable or two," Libby mentioned.

"Vegetable shmegetable," Reid told her. "Do you know what the Greeks' favorite vegetable is? It's this thing they call *chorta*, which translates simply as 'bitter weed.' That's exactly what it is. You see old women out in the median strips along the highways collecting the stuff."

"Sounds delightful," Louis said.

"It thrives on exhaust fumes. The busier the highway, the tastier the bitter weed."

"Like life," Libby said.

Reid looked at her, and Louis, seeing his expression, was profoundly shocked: how there was nothing there but an indifference so quiet and settled neither Reid nor Libby even seemed aware of it. "That's good," Reid told her. "That's very good."

Discomfited—he hadn't realized things were half so bad these days at Castel Fallone—Louis seized the wine. "More, anyone?" he asked after refilling his own glass. Libby shook her head, but Reid held out his glass, and so, after a moment, did Claire. Of his latest Athenian exploits—he'd been there a full three weeks—Reid had reported nothing, not even when the two found themselves alone over the martini shaker in the kitchen, and Louis was distressed to discover that his friend's silence, far from relieving him, instead cast a further pall of anxiety over his evening. Never, it seemed, did anything satisfy him: what he heard, he didn't want to hear, and when he needed words, there was only silence.

"And how's the other half of the family?" Libby asked. Louis watched her, wondering if she knew everything, if Reid had told her. She seemed surprisingly at peace, out of reach of her husband's shocking indifference. Perhaps it had indeed done her good to lie low for the holidays, as she had claimed she wanted to do. He always suspected her of binge drinking in Reid's absence—a phrase like "lying low" certainly sounded like code to him—but Claire insisted that her friend did no such thing. Well, he thought, if *he* were Libby, he might consider binge drinking a rather attractive option along about now.

"I think Susan and family are doing quite well," Claire told her. "This was their year to spend Christmas with Greg's parents in Seattle. It's hard when everyone's so far-flung, geographically. I suppose it's equitable, but I admit it's a little disappointing, especially when the little boys are at this age, when they change so quickly. Susan plans to bring them east this summer, though, so we'll see them then."

"Why would anyone choose to live in Alaska?" Libby wondered.

The truly disgraceful thought occurred to Louis that he much preferred Caroline to Susan, whose proposed two-week interruption of their midsummer rhythms he was already beginning to dread. He could see his book, like a little boat that has lost its bearings, drift ever farther out into a sea of blank pages, unwritten words. Unlike her younger sister, Caroline was no beauty; she was hard and direct. And unlike her failure of a father, she had not let distractions stand in the way of her work. She had gotten on with it, and her essays on plate tectonics were highly regarded; in her field she was already, at the age of thirty-five, what they called a "name." Had this, then, been the whole of his destiny: to sire these two daughters, so very different from each other, the one awash in the fecund and chaotic joys of family, the other solitary and focused? Despite what he said publicly about Caroline, he greatly admired her for not having married; it bespoke a certain integrity. And while Susan's life had altered itself, under the pressures of marriage and motherhood—and, he supposed, the bracing rigors of life in Alaska—to the extent that she seemed at times unrecognizable, Caroline had remained admirably herself, intensified rather than diluted by her journey into adulthood. If she had a lover, either male or female (the thought did cross his mind from time to time), she was discreet about it. In their two weeks in her house, he had seen not a trace of cohabitation, and was convinced that she did, as she claimed, live alone with her cats, her fine collection of Indian pottery and blankets, her flowering cactuses, her shelves and shelves of fastidiously organized scientific journals. And yet how lonely it must be, never to have settled with a companion by one's side. What wild and desperate impulses it must on occasion give rise to, what acts of reckless abandon.

But it was not, he realized, about his daughter he was thinking, but about Tracy Parker. Had loneliness driven him to put his arms around a boy in some doomed semblance of love?

"It all sounded terribly frightening," Reid said. "I must say, she handled herself like a real trooper out there."

"We were very fortunate here," Claire replied. "Weren't we, Louis?"

Alarmed, he nodded vaguely. He hadn't a clue what they were talking about.

"I haven't been to the campus yet," Reid said. "What're things like over there?"

How had they gotten from Caroline and Susan to the storm? Had Castel Fallone suffered? He'd have to find a way later, without completely embarrassing himself, to ask Claire about it.

"It wasn't bad," he said, banishing Tracy resolutely from his mind. "We came through intact." All at once he had the clearest image of the Forge School as one of those walled gardens in a medieval Book of Hours, a paradise safe from the savage wilderness beyond. But where did that thought lead, except to the image, equally clear, of two naked figures, a man and a boy, amid the clover and lilies in blissful, forbidden embrace? Even in the garden, wolves were prowling.

Furtively he checked his watch. Was it too late to try calling Tracy again? And perhaps, just for good measure, he should check in with Brill and make sure Noah—and all the other students, of course—had arrived back at the Forge School in one piece.

For a single reckless moment he allowed himself to entertain the remote possibility that Tracy and Noah had run away together, that no one would ever see them again.

Ridiculous, he told himself. Here he had leaped to a conclusion nothing warranted in the least.

"Pardon me," he said, as Claire rose to clear the plates in preparation for dessert. "There's a phone call I need to make."

Claire glanced at him oddly. As if taking his cue from her, Reid surmised, with a chuckle meant to indicate that he wasn't to be taken seriously, "Forgot to call off that midnight tryst?"

"I told Doug Brill I'd give him a call about a little matter that came up earlier today."

"Oh," Reid said knowingly, with a broad wink. *That* little tryst."

"What are you talking about?" Louis asked tensely.

"It's a joke," Reid told him.

"Oh," Louis said, more to reassure himself than anything else. "Of course."

He went into the hallway, where a black rotary phone sat in its immemorial place on the side table. Lux stood patiently at the front door, his forehead pressed against it as if he wanted to go out.

"What's the matter?" Louis asked him.

He opened the door to a surge of cold air. But Lux did not move. He seemed confused. A great sigh came from deep in his lungs, and he turned and lumbered back toward the kitchen.

From the dining room behind Louis came an unnerving silence, as if, in the absence of others, Reid and Libby could find not a single word to say to one another. Surely, Louis thought, this couldn't go on? But of course it could; it could go on indefinitely.

He picked up the receiver and dialed. The cheerful chaos of the Brill household flooded his ear.

"Mary Ann said you stopped by earlier. And what can I do for you, sir?"

He felt foolish, a prying old fussbudget—nevertheless, he was headmaster, and a headmaster was concerned with the well-being of his students.

"Sorry to bother you, but I've had a couple of conflicting messages concerning one of our students, Noah Lathrop. I was just wondering if he got back here without any difficulties."

There was a very brief pause, which nonetheless felt immense. Then Brill said the dreaded thing: "Actually, he's not back yet. But I have a message saying he'll be in first thing tomorrow morning."

"Did you talk to him?"

"Mary Ann did. She's the one who took the message down. It doesn't sound like there's a problem."

"No," Louis said, feeling sick. "I suppose there isn't. Again, sorry to interrupt your evening."

"We were just going to put out some refreshments for the kids. You know, welcome them back."

"That's a fine idea," Louis told him. "I'm sure they'll appreciate it."

He hung up, then stood motionless, staring down at the phone. In the dining room, talk had resumed.

"It looks wonderful," he could hear Reid say of the slice of *tarte Tatin* Claire was presumably presenting him with.

He picked up the receiver and dialed Tracy's number. When he heard Tracy's recorded voice, he hung up.

The stillness was unutterable. In such moments, could one suspend one's heartbeat, it might be possible to hear time itself gliding noiselessly past in the night's plush gloom. For a long time he sat motionless at his desk, staring into the black vacancy held within the window before him—as if the future lay there, obscured but implacably in wait: the future toward which everyone was rushing at the speed of a heartbeat (he could feel the reliable old muscle in his chest pump out its unvarying rhythm, seventy beats to the minute, as it had done without fail for sixty-five years).

His nerves felt shredded, his nightcap of scotch pulsed dully behind his eyeballs and sleep was as far away as ever.

He pulled his notebook from the bottom drawer of his desk and began idly to leaf through its pages. Four decades of notes preparatory to the commencement of his masterwork. Or if not his masterwork, then at least a well-considered tome. Or if not that, a distinguished slender essay. Or if not that, if indeed perhaps nothing . . .

He read at random.

I should not want you and others to have the impression that a mode of feeling which I respect because it is almost necessarily infused with <u>mind</u> *(far more necessarily so, at any rate, than the "normal" mode) should be something that I should want to deny or, insofar as it is accessible to me (and I may say, with few reservations, that it is), wish to disavow.*

You cleverly recognized the <u>artistic</u> *reason why this might seem to be the case. It is inherent in the difference between the Dionysian spirit of lyricism, whose outpouring is irresponsible and individualistic, and the Apollonian, objectively controlled, morally and socially responsible epic. What I was after was an equilibrium of sensuality and morality such as I found perfected in the* <u>Elective Affinities,</u> *which I read five times, if I remember rightly, while working on* <u>Death in Venice</u>. *But that the novella is at its core of a hymnic type, indeed of hymnic origin, cannot have escaped you. Letter of July 4, 1912.*

At even went to the Club. . . . I was absorbed in admiring an elegant young man with a gracefully foolish, boyish face, blond, refined, rather frail German type, somewhat reminiscent of Requadt. Seeing him unquestionably affected me in a way I have not noted in myself for a long time. Was he a guest at the club, or will I meet him again? I readily admit to myself that this could turn into an experience. Diary, Fri. Dec. 20, 1918.

In my exhaustion, forgot to note that yesterday the Hermes-like young dandy who made an impression on me several weeks ago attended my reading. In conjunction with his slight, youthful figure, his face has a prettiness and foolishness that amounts to a nearly classical "godlike" look. I don't know his name, and it doesn't matter. Diary, Sun. Mar. 30, 1919.

Loneliness brings forth what is original, daringly and shockingly beautiful: the poetic. But loneliness also brings forth the perverse, the disproportionate, the absurd, the illicit.

Hofmannsthal's Frau ohne Schatten: *It must be strange and voluptuous to fantasize like that. Diary, Tues. Nov. 25, 1919.*

A nice observer once said of him in company—it was at the time when he fell ill in Vienna in his thirty-fifth year: "You see, Aschenbach has always lived like this"—here the speaker closed the fingers of his left hand to a fist—"never like this"—and he let his open hand hang relaxed from the back of his chair.

Looking up from his notes, Louis gazed out at his reflection in the window. *Closed Fist, Open Palm: Moral Discipline in the Works of Thomas Mann,* that lucid and powerful work of scholarship and speculation, whose tenacious weaving together of rich, varied strands of argument would point out for a grateful generation the possibility of reconciling intellectual license and moral discipline, whose capacity for mustering facts, and, further, whose fluency in their presentation, would lead judicious critics to place the treatise alongside Mann's own great work, some even claiming, in headier moments, that the aspirations of the disciple very nearly superseded the accomplishments of the master. . . .

In the window, where before he had seen only vacancy, his reflection gazed back. He was shocked to see how drawn and weary he looked. How old he had become. Time, indeed, was running out. Soon would come the night in which there was no more work—not the work of the hands, nor the work of the mind, nor the work of the heart. The bitter truth peered back at him unflinchingly. He was a self-deluding old fool. *Closed Fist, Open Palm.* The book he had spent his life preparing to write would never be written.

In a sudden fit of revulsion—or was it revenge?—he turned to the final pages of his notebook and read avidly.

Saturated afternoons, the Tatra Mountains in fullest August. The rains do not stop. It is as if the whole countryside must drown. Inside the great summer house—gabled fantasia of stone and timber and mossy shingles—the cool walls sweat. The room is dark and damp. Somber, intricately flowered wallpaper rises to meet high ceilings. In the center of the room a regal four-poster bed holds court.

No one uses this room. It has the air of having been forgotten, as if disuse has rendered it invisible to the rest of the house. As if it is a dream erased daily by the sturdier realities of waking life.

They undress wordlessly, the two young cousins, the dark-haired boy from the military academy, the blond beauty who is pampered, often kept at home. Thump of shoes, jangle of belts, whispers of cotton or linen. Two neat stacks of shed clothes rise side by side on the chest at the foot of the bed. This useful fiction of an afternoon nap: for some minutes they indeed lie together on the capacious bed as if napping is, after all, their intent. The air is cool but not so cool that they cover themselves. They are young and warm-blooded.

In some far precinct of the great summer house, Schubert is being played. The notes of the piano fall with grave regularity, a meditation not unlike the rain itself. The drumming of the rain is the drumming of their hearts.

Jaschieu is no stranger to either the world or its sorrow. He curls onto his side, facing his younger cousin, but the boy, if he senses this movement, does not respond; rather, he continues to lie supine, arms folded, eyes closed, as if waiting for some visitation or perhaps only the onset of midafternoon slumber. In profile, his eyelashes are long and dark. His beauty, fragile as porcelain, is just as easily broken. Jaschieu knows this. It is the knowledge that aches darkly within him.

Golden-haired Tadzio breathes in once, audibly, the reverse of a sigh, and it is as if the shy deer standing motionless in the thicket has caught, on the breeze, the whisper of a scent. Moving inside some thoughtful dream, Jaschieu's right hand begins slowly to creep toward its prey. His fingertips graze the silky flesh of a boy's thigh. He can feel his cousin tense, then relax as the fingertips rest lightly and unerringly on the smooth surface of the skin. With the greatest care in the world he begins blindly, somnolently, to explore a thigh, the ridge of a pelvis, the taut fine drum of a boy's belly. He meets no resistance, not a whisper. No fingers clutch his wrist. No voice breaks the tremendous drumming of the rain, their heartbeats.

Here is the indentation of a navel whose hollow his thumb traverses. He travels north to finger the hard nub of a nipple, drifts

across a dip of cleavage to its companion, which he rolls between
forefinger and thumb, then begins the long trek south. He has
raised himself on his elbow to conduct this pilgrimage. His fingers
elicit short gasps from Tadzio as he touches here, and here, and
then here.

Here in this room, this rainy afternoon in the mountains:
anything is possible, everything is allowed.

With a spasm of anxiety, Louis closed the notebook. How well he remembered the intoxicated state in which he had first penned those lines—that evening in October, Tracy Parker's sweet, calming spirit still filling the house. Everything had seemed possible that evening, and he had dared dream what he had not allowed himself to dream for years. Gratefully he welcomed the return of the god to his temple. He had not thought the hymnic impulse harmful; it only lived, after all, between the pages of his notebook. But the shameful, even demoralizing thing was this: as the shadows of suspicion had closed in, as the Louis Tremper who walked daily in the world said to himself, with sorrow and pity, Tracy Parker is a homosexual, the Louis Tremper who opened these pages and confided his dreams in ever greater fervor and detail, goaded on, in fact, by events as they unfolded, had come to seek here a last resort from the self it was increasingly necessary for the other—the public, the steady, the esteemed—Louis Tremper to become. Here in these secret pages another Louis Tremper felt only a quiet wonder, an unaccustomed joy.

It took such will to keep so much at bay. Even now he was aware of a host of things that did not bear looking into too closely. How deeply he regretted his panicked avoidance of poor Tracy, but panic, sadly, had been the consistent emotional note of his life. Forty years had gone by, but he still remembered with awful clarity a certain classroom at Cornell, an underpopulated seminar in German literature, a fellow student suffused with such poise, such foolish grace, that Louis could not prevent himself from gazing at him with longing. Longing for what? he'd asked himself, mystified but at the same time enthralled. Admiration, he named it, though in other moments he called it by a more desperate name: adoration. He had lived for a year in Germany, this young man; his accent was impeccable. One day in class that twilight gray gaze met Louis's own, and they held each other's stare for several perilous minutes before Louis, confused and troubled, looked away. But he could not look away for long, and when his will broke down, he found the boy still staring his way. For several reckless weeks of autumn those stares had continued. They had never spoken. Then, after class one day, the boy was waiting for him in the hallway. He took Louis's arm, mysterious and conspiratorial, and steered them out of the building. "Come with me," he said, his voice low, breathless.

Suddenly in a panic, he wanted nothing to do with the boy; his familiarity, his touch, were repellent.

"My dorm room," the boy told him. He seemed to glow with palpable excitement, a shimmer of energy that Louis could see at once, even in his innocence, was darkly sexual in its origin. Roughly he withdrew his arm from the other's grip. "I think you're very mistaken," he said loudly, fiercely, enjoying the look of shock and surprise that crossed the boy's fine features. He did not wait for a reply, but marched off across the arts quad in a fury at being so vilely misunderstood.

He had done, of course, the right thing. What irony that panic so often turned out to be identical with better judgment.

He shuddered, took an especially deep sip of scotch, and was fifteen, the spring of 1945. Newsreels showed Berlin in ruins while the somber strains of Bruckner's Ninth Symphony played. His mother was very ill. She had flare-ups and quiescences, spoke strange, hurtful, incoherent things; had spent several weeks this last winter resting in a hospital north of Poughkeepsie. Out of harm's way one morning he crouched behind the garage and listened as she flung words at his grandfather as if they were handfuls of black cinders. She beat her fists against his chest as the white-haired man stood dumbfounded in the midst of his beloved flowers, letting the blows fall against him without even attempting to deflect their fierce assault. "Don't you think I see with my own two eyes?" his mother had shouted. "Do you think I'm blind? Do you think I'm stone stupid? Oh, I know your secret. I see clearly. My husband, my father. My own son as well. I see through all of you. Filth and abomination. And my own son as well. A pansy like the rest. Don't you think I know that? The three of you are sick, sick, sick!" she shouted, arms flailing, as his grandfather—her father—had finally said, "Whoa, that's enough, little lady. Now simmer down before somebody gets hurt."

Random like all her words, utterly disconnected and mad, they hit dead in the heart that secret target no one should ever have suspected he carried within himself.

He had fled, his own madness shouting silently within, through backyards and alleys, a mile, two miles, till a stitch in his side and a burn in his lungs called a halt to his physical flight though his other, more terrible flight— past that dangerous boy at Cornell, past the shoals of all the other unquiet yearnings—did not stop until, one rainy evening in 1955, worn out with running, he had stumbled into the saving refuge of Claire Anselm. But even after that, truth be told, he had never really stopped running.

He picked up his glass and finished off the last of the scotch. Enough, he told himself. Enough scotch for a single night, enough morbid thoughts. Stashing the notebook safely under its stack of innocuous papers at the bottom of his desk drawer, he saw—as clear as anything, a reality all its own—

Tracy Parker lead Noah Lathrop tenderly and silently to a secret room in an ancient house that had never existed at all save in Louis's worst or bravest imaginings. He could hide the notebook as carefully as he wanted; *that*, on the other hand, would not go away.

Lonely silver light framed a room at first, as always, unfamiliar. He lay stiff and cold on the sofa, his old bones covered only by a thin wool afghan. He hated waking to the discovery that he'd not made it to his bed the previous night—damning evidence of weakness, though Claire, bless her heart, never seemed to take these minor infidelities amiss, and on such mornings, when he contritely brought her breakfast up, would only say—entirely without irony, he'd decided—"Working hard last night?"

Barely dawn; he would creep upstairs, he thought, take a longish shower in the hopes that hot water and vigorous soaping with the washcloth would ease his muscles back into pliancy. Once he'd shaved and dressed it would be time to make breakfast. Afterwards, he wasn't sure what obscure impulse had made him look into the kitchen before ascending the stairs—perhaps some still lingering wisp of spirit, some vestigial energy that had not yet dissipated. Halfway between his pillow and the refrigerator, Lux lay on his side. Louis knew at once. "Oh, Lux," he said, kneeling on creaking knees beside the poor creature and laying his hand on its beautiful fur. The motionless flesh was still warm. A little pool of urine had formed by Lux's back legs; his tail was wet. His dark eyes, so intense when alive, had glazed over.

There was nothing to do. Curling up stiffly beside the inert form on the floor, Louis laid his head on the dog's flank, his ear against the flesh whose warmth he could feel, as he lay there, gradually fade into the cold floor of the kitchen, sublimate into the air, be absorbed into his own sorrowing body.

He did not cry, as he had feared he might whenever he had imagined this eventuality. He hoped it was not cowardice that he felt glad it had ended at home like this, rather than in a veterinarian's office, Lux's eyes alive with sudden terror as loving hands held him down on a steel tabletop, as the kindly killer hovered close with his merciful needle. He could not have borne it. Still, he was so sorry Lux had been alone. He remembered how, earlier in the evening, he'd found him standing by the front door, confused, disoriented. He should have known then that something was wrong, but he himself had been distracted. As clearly as he could, Lux had been trying to tell him something that he, selfishly, had been unable or unwilling to hear.

He stroked the dog's lolling head and peered into those cloudy unseeing eyes. Lux's lips were pulled back, teeth bared, muscles strangely taut, so that he appeared, in death, to be smiling at something.

Without quite knowing why, Louis picked up the heavy form and laid it carefully on the plaid pillow that had been most of Lux's diminished world for the last year or so. Had they needlessly prolonged his suffering by allowing him to live, arthritic and half blind, his ears painful with polyps, his kidneys failing? He gave the dog's great head a final fond pat, then took a wad of paper towels from the dispenser and wiped the cold puddle of urine from the floor. From his arm, also, where some had leaked when he lifted Lux's body.

For a moment he considered saying nothing to Claire, going about the morning's business, bringing her breakfast, leaving for his office as if nothing were amiss. She would find Lux soon enough. Of course that was madness. This truth, too, had to be faced.

He stood in the doorway of the bedroom, feeling as if he should have knocked, as if he were a stranger who did not necessarily deserve to enter. Claire lay on her side of the bed, the comforter on his side undisturbed. Even in sleep there was a certain formality to her. He felt certain she would sleep this way after he was dead, keeping to her side of the mattress, carefully preserving his space, maintaining its inviolability as he had schooled her to do, perhaps too harshly, in the early years of their marriage.

He felt such tenderness for her, lying there as yet untouched by what had happened. If he had not been the best of husbands, it could never be said that she had not been the best of wives.

Sitting down gingerly on the side of the bed, he touched her shoulder.

"Claire," he said gently. They seldom touched anymore, and she looked at him with a hazy expression of concern.

"Did I cry out?" she asked him.

"No," he told her, perplexed, rubbing her shoulder lightly as if to reassure them both of their substance.

"We were coming back from a concert. Do you remember that night? Some animal leaped in front of the car. I was dreaming that. Only this time I couldn't stop. I cried out but I couldn't stop."

"Everything's fine," he reassured her. "It was just a bad dream. But I'm afraid I do have some sad news. Lux is no longer with us."

He paused. Actually saying it made the fact suddenly inescapable, but he forced himself to continue, to put into words and so render irrevocable an event that till now had seemed only temporary, even remediable. "He died sometime last night."

"Oh Louis," Claire said quietly, as if it were more his loss than her own, though he knew she had loved Lux deeply as well, had worried about his end. "I'm so sorry."

"He went peacefully," Louis told her. "In his sleep," he added, realizing that *that* was the real reason he'd carried Lux back to his pillow, so Claire wouldn't have to know that Lux had died in some kind of distress, that something had spooked him, driven him to leave his pillow for a few last—

panicked?—steps as the shadow overtook him. Where had he thought to go, whom had he sought in the middle of the night?

He had seemed to be smiling.

A thought seized Louis with great urgency and would not let go. "We've got to bury him," he said. "We can't let rigor mortis set in."

"Louis," Claire reminded him, "there's three feet of snow. I'm sure the ground under there's frozen solid."

He only shook his head. "No," he said, "We have to do this quickly." In all their proleptic anxiety, they had never properly talked this through, so certain had they been that the painful decision to have him put down would, in the end, be theirs to make. Now Lux had been snatched from them—or had he slipped away, made a clean escape? The thought troubled Louis. An atavistic shudder ran through him. Gripped by this impulse he knew was entirely irrational, he rose from Claire's side.

She reached for him, but he was beyond her grasp. "I'll call the vet," she offered reasonably. "We'll have Lux cremated. We'll bury the ashes in the spring. In the garden, by the lilacs."

"I don't want Lux cremated," he said as he strode from the room, and then, even though he knew how ridiculous it sounded, he continued, "*Lux* didn't want to be cremated."

"Louis," Claire called out behind him. "Please. I know you're upset. But you're not going to make things better by giving yourself a heart attack."

He marched willfully down the stairs. "My heart's fine," he told her, though he referred only to that hardworking material muscle, not the heavy spiritual organ he also carried within. "And frankly," he added over his shoulder, "right now, I don't particularly care."

He stood on the back porch in the dawn's wan light. The day would be overcast, perhaps with snow flurries. No path had been shoveled out to the toolshed; he had to make his slow progress through thigh-deep snow. In dreams he moved this way, his flight from unnameable terrors impeded by some invisible hindrance. Snowdrifts blocked the toolshed door—he could only pry it open a few inches. Wading back to the mudroom, he found Claire waiting for him in her dark robe.

"Really, Louis," she said.

"Let me do this," he told her, though already he was beginning to feel foolish. "You go on inside. You'll catch a cold standing out here."

"What if I told you *I* didn't care?" she said dryly.

They looked at one another. Claire's expression was sad but also wry. Of course it should all end right there—Louis knew that perfectly well. He was being childish, silly, absurd; he was throwing a tantrum. Nevertheless, despite his recognition of all that, a great black current had seized him and was plunging him headlong toward the abyss he had known, even as a child, could open without warning: inchoate, frustrated rage in whose torrential grip, while the flood lasted, he was utterly helpless. It had been years since such rage had carried him off; he had thought, with relief, he'd finally, in his twilight years, outraced its rampage.

With a roar of grief, he grabbed the snow shovel and fought his way back to the shed. Furiously he shoveled at the enemy, the immense undefeatable annihilating power that masqueraded, for the moment, as a snowdrift obstructing the door to the toolshed. He knew this was not about Lux. It was not even about Tracy Parker and Noah Lathrop, or Noah's threatening father, or Reid and Libby's desperate marriage. With a final heave of snow, he wrenched the shed door open just enough to slip inside. It was as if he'd stumbled into a momentary refuge. Almost instantly his rage receded. The light shone dim; there was the surprise of seeing the bare earth of the floor. The lawnmower was hunkered down under plastic to keep field mice from infesting it with their nests. Pruning shears of various shapes and sizes hung from hooks. Empty terra-cotta pots lined the shelves. Against one wall, in Claire's neat alignment, leaned a hoe, a pitchfork, several rakes, the garden spade. He had always held himself aloof from his wife's gardening, praising her efforts with a perfunctory "Very nice, very nice." Why, he wondered, taking the spade down from its hook on the wall, had he always been so ungenerous, so withholding?

With everything hidden under a blanket of white, it was difficult to tell where Claire's flowerbeds began and ended. Choosing a spot near the aged stand of lilacs where he was relatively certain nothing of value had been planted—and what if it had?—he began to dig. Successive thaws and freezes had rendered the snow heavy as clay. He lifted and threw aside leaden shovelfuls. Cold air bristled in his lungs, but soon enough he reached bare earth. He worked steadily, without rage. What would happen would happen, he felt with a sense of doom that was very nearly comforting. Clearing a circle sufficiently wide, he plunged in. The impact shuddered up his arm. He tried again, but Claire had been right. The winter earth was as unyielding as iron.

Or not quite as unyielding. He found, after repeated attempts, that it was possible to make a little progress; he could see, however, that to dig a hole large enough to accommodate Lux would be impossible.

So they would have Lux cremated after all. It was the sensible thing to do. With a sense of resignation he carried the spade back to the toolshed and stowed it next to its useful cousins. His antics now seemed keenly embarrassing; what a wonder Claire put up with him at all. He found her in the kitchen, kneeling beside Lux and peacefully stroking his noble head.

"I'm sorry," he said. "I apologize. I was acting like a fool."

She looked up at him with the same compassionate gaze she had bestowed on Lux. "Are you all right?" she asked forgivingly. "Even last night, you didn't seem to be quite yourself."

Of course she had noticed his agitation. Forty years of marriage made even the most guarded soul transparent. And Reid and Libby, no doubt, had noticed as well, commenting on their host's distraction on their ride home— if, indeed, they even spoke to each other anymore except in the presence of others, so transparent to one another had they become. Even Lux, his senses dimmed but still acute, attuned to currents his human counterparts could not detect, had noticed something amiss. Had seen the coming storm and chosen to escape while there was still time.

He considered for a moment the troubling omen, then rebuked himself sharply. He hated that in himself: committed to shining reason, contemptuous of superstition in all its benighted forms, whether fear of the number thirteen or the adoration of venerable icons—was there anyone, at heart, more cravenly superstitious than he?

"Louis," Claire repeated. "Is something the matter?"

"No, no," he said, startled from his thoughts. He could not bring himself to tell her his fears. He could not confess the haunting sense that he himself was mysteriously responsible for whatever might be unfolding between Tracy Parker and his student; nor could he confess that the esteemed Noah Lathrop Senior spooked him as much as the avenging angel itself. For the time being, hoping against hope (and might it all not turn out to be nothing more than a misunderstanding?), he would maintain the steady course: carry the body back to its pillow, tidy up the mess on the floor, pretend desperately that everything, even as dire shadows flickered all around, was in fact just fine.

Eleanor Osterhoudt gazed out at the world with her usual aspect of profound sourness. She resembled, to a remarkable degree, especially when twin plumes of smoke issued from her nostrils, a gargoyle set up to guard the inner sanctum.

"I trust your holidays were pleasant," Louis said.

"With this weather?" She rolled her eyes and took a long puff. "But you missed all that. Was Arizona nice?"

"Arizona was, in fact, quite nice," he said. "I could even imagine retiring there someday."

"You'll never get me in one of those retirement communities," Eleanor told him with a shudder. "All those old people. How depressing. Give me the younguns any day. Keeps my spirits up."

"There're plenty of young people in Arizona," he reassured her, musing that she did, however, have a point. The sight of all those fresh-faced students as he walked to his office had unmistakably lifted his bleak spirits. The very acknowledgment of that fact, however, cast him down again. The old troubles closed in.

"By the way," he asked, trying his best to sound casual, "You haven't seen Tracy Parker by any chance this morning, have you?"

"He hasn't been in. Reid stopped by looking for you. And Sandra poked her head in to say hello. She's a dear."

"She *is* a dear," Louis agreed, his mind already elsewhere as he entered the inner sanctum of his office. At least his answering machine wasn't blinking angrily.

"But speak of the devil," Eleanor announced from the outer office. Louis turned toward the door, expecting to see the affable, mildly flirtatious Sandra Robertson, to whom he would have to break the news about Lux, but it was not Sandra Robertson. He remembered, with a vividness that took him aback, that first hot afternoon in August when Tracy Parker had walked through that door. Having not laid eyes on him in a month, he was struck again by the young man's charm, the sheer enthusiasm for life he seemed to exude from every pore, as if he stood burnished in a golden halo. He is a homosexual, murmured a thrilling, inflammatory voice somewhere deep inside Louis, and the elder man felt himself, almost palpably, catch fire. "Why Tracy, hello," he exclaimed in surprise and relief.

"Sorry for not getting back to you," Tracy said. "I didn't get your message till last night." Beneath his golden glow, did he seem tense and haggard, or was Louis prepared to see in his expression only what he wanted to see? Then Tracy smiled and said, "It's good to see you, Louis."

No one, Louis thought fleetingly, should be allowed to smile like that. Completely disarmed, he found himself relaying the very message he had been prepared to give Sandra: "I'm afraid I have a bit of very sad news, Tracy. Lux died this morning. He was ancient, of course, nearly as ancient as I am, but I know you cared about him."

Tracy looked genuinely shocked. "That's terrible," he said. "I'm really sorry." Spontaneously reaching out, he touched Louis on the arm, a commiserating gesture, tingling and electric, a touch that clearly, in the right circumstances, could heal. It was all Louis could do not to withdraw from the clasp of that hand.

"That makes me so sad," Tracy continued. "Lux was a really special animal."

Louis couldn't help himself: from the corner of his eye he wiped the tear he had been relieved, earlier, not to have shed. Tracy's hand remained on his upper arm, its grip, once Louis had surrendered to it, firm and reassuring, Tracy's brown-eyed gaze as deep and searching, in its way, as Lux's used to be.

He was embarrassed that Tracy had seen the tear.

"But that was not why I called," he went on briskly, remembering his duty even while a part of himself, grateful and terrifically well disposed toward

Tracy at the moment, hesitated even to bring up the unpleasant business. "I came over to the office yesterday and found quite a number of rather puzzling telephone messages from the father of one of our students, I believe one of your students. Noah Lathrop. There seems to have been some kind of mis-understanding at home, crossed lines of communication, that kind of thing. You know how these broken homes can be, mother and father at cross pur-poses all the time, the poor kid caught in the middle. Anyway, Mr. Lathrop seemed to have some notion that his son had come up here to school early. He mentioned that he might be staying with someone up here. I was just wondering—since you know him—whether, well, whether you knew any-thing at all about this, how shall we say, bit of confusion. . . . Not that you should, necessarily," he added for good measure.

"Well, actually, I don't," Tracy said without missing a beat. "I haven't seen hide nor hair of Noah Lathrop." He paused, thoughtfully, as if deciding how much detail he should go into. "Not that I'd really expect to hear from him. He's a somewhat difficult student, as I think you're aware. I wouldn't say that he and I are on particularly good terms"—he hesitated almost imper-ceptibly—"these days."

"It was my impression you had become rather good pals," Louis probed gingerly.

Tracy laughed. "Oh," he said. "That's news to me."

But hadn't they been pals? Was it possible he'd misread everything from the very beginning? He wasn't sure whether that possibility elated or un-nerved him.

"I thought," he said, "I mean, I seemed to remember, when I visited your class, there was, well, you seemed to have a good relationship with him outside the classroom."

"I'm not sure Noah Lathrop has a good relationship with anybody," Tracy said. "I did try, though. It's not like there's a problem there. He's taking English Two from me this semester—later this morning, in fact. But I wouldn't say I know him particularly well. No better than I do any of the other boys."

"I see," Louis said. "Well, I was just wondering. It's a big mystery to me what those phone calls were about. The father's out of the country right now."

"I get the feeling," Tracy said, "that he's almost always out of the country. That is, when he's not out of his mind."

The bluntness of the observation was a little shocking. "Is that what Noah tells you?" Louis asked.

"He did tell me that," Tracy said. "Yes he did." He glanced at his watch, then said, "I'm going to be late for my first class if I don't run."

"Well, welcome back to the old grindstone," Louis told him, noting, from the clock on the wall, that Tracy was, as usual, being prudent: he had ample time to make his class.

"Again, I'm really sorry about Lux," the thoughtful young man commiserated on his way through the door.

With a sigh of relief, Louis sank onto the sofa and leaned back, his arms loose, the tension clenched there since yesterday emptying from him in a long-sustained gesture of thanks. If he hadn't gotten around to asking where Tracy had been for the past week, that was because it hardly seemed necessary anymore. Whatever else he might be, Tracy Parker was clearly a consummate professional when it came to his work. In that, Louis had complete faith, and he regretted that he had ever doubted it.

For a single moment he considered the possibility of resuming old times. How easy it would be to seek the young man out later in the day, invite him over for an evening of music, a nip of scotch. There was some Schumann he'd been longing to play for his eager listener. But then in the next moment such a plan seemed completely impossible. With that sense of missed opportunity that had dogged him throughout his life, he realized sadly that, despite the morning's reassuring news, far too much had changed for them ever to go back to the innocent terms of those days of autumn, before Tracy Parker's regrettable liabilities had muddied the clear waters of their great, promising friendship.

XIV

These days of January you could feel, were you so inclined, in something of a state of siege. If, by temperament, Claire was not so inclined, she nevertheless found herself anticipating with some dread the onslaught of the next winter storm, the third in as many weeks. A foot, a foot and a half, was being forecast, and a fourth blizzard was said to be hard on the heels of the current threat. She'd never been one to batten down the hatches, but the cautiousness of old age was perhaps beginning to catch up with her. Why else would she have ventured out to the Grand Union on an afternoon when half the population of Middle Forge seemed intent on laying in supplies?

Unable to find a cart at the entrance, or even a handbasket, she wandered the jostling aisles on the off chance that an abandoned cart might be adrift among the throngs. Instead, her eye was caught by a young man in the produce aisle who was inspecting a head of romaine lettuce. He'd filled the child's seat of his cart with a festive assortment of kale, collard greens, red-leafed lettuce—a garden on wheels. When he turned around to add the romaine to his collection she found herself looking Tracy Parker in the face.

Her heart quickened nervously; she felt a blush come over her. "Well, hello stranger," she said with a cheerfulness she hoped might cover her surprise. She had not seen him in six weeks, and though she had thought of him—with concern, with pity, and yes, she might as well admit it, a certain longing (she *missed* him)—she had done nothing at all to be in touch. Not that Louis had instructed her one way or another. As if it never had happened, they'd not mentioned that dinner party again; a ridiculous pretense, of course, since it had so palpably happened, and with such consequences. In the blink of an eye, the young man they'd seen sometimes as many as three times a week for the past two months had simply disappeared from their lives. Had Tracy known, instinctively, that he would have to wait for

Louis to summon him to the house again—and, receiving no summons, had not pressed the point? How fragile relationships were between people, how easily upset—especially friendship, that delicate alliance bereft of the formal bonds that at least gave marriages a fighting chance.

And yet, as if there had been no awkwardness or estrangement, Tracy greeted her warmly, confiding, "I'd never have come out here if I'd known this place was going to be so mobbed. Did we declare war or something?"

"On the television," Claire told him, remembering he didn't have a television, "they're saying we're in for another big storm."

"Oh great. Like we're all going to be snowed in for three weeks. What're these people thinking?"

"It's panic," she said, feeling like a conspirator, though she too, she reminded herself, had come here out of her own version of panic. But now she had stepped to the other side, Tracy's side, a place of humor and common sense. It felt a rather enjoyable place to be.

"Well, panic or not," he told her, "the romaine here sucks. But I get what I deserve. I was too lazy to drive out to the health-food store."

She tried to think of some gallant retort, but the surprise of seeing him again had taken her wit away. He looked at her sympathetically. "I was very sorry to hear about Lux," he said quietly. "Lux was a great, wise dog."

It made a tear, for a moment, come to her eye. They would never see Lux again. That era of their lives was gone. "We'd been so worried," she told this kind young man whom Lux had seemed to take to. "We knew his time was coming, but the thought of putting him down . . ." Even now, she found herself choking up to talk of it. "In the end, he was very considerate. He folded his tent and moved on quietly. He died in his sleep, on his favorite pillow in the kitchen."

"Louis told me," Tracy said.

It took a second to sink in.

Of course, she thought. Her husband and Tracy would have to talk. They worked together, after all. There were all sorts of reasons for them to talk. Nonetheless, Louis had said not a word about any conversation with Tracy Parker during these long weeks of supposed estrangement, and she found herself suddenly resenting her husband's unilateral ways. Tracy had, after all, been her friend as well.

"How's Betsy?" she asked, eager to move herself away from the brooding she knew she was doomed to return to later.

"Betsy is just great. And I was thinking just the other day about when you and I went to the pound to get her. That was a fun morning."

It had been great fun, in fact (but what had ever happened to the gray cat, the one without hope?). And what did it matter that Tracy Parker was gay? Their connection, immediate and frank, had been the connection of friends drawn together through common sympathies, shared interest. Too bad they now found themselves stranded in the shoals of polite banter, while the deep intimate ocean beckoned.

He seemed to have similar thoughts, but, unlike her, he acted on them. "Do you know what?" he said. "I do *not* feel like coping with this madding crowd right now. Let's say we ditch our shopping carts and go get a cup of coffee somewhere. Would you be up for that?"

That was what had struck her about him from the start: his youthful, refreshing spontaneity, the sense that the world was ripe with enchanting possibilities. When was the last time she'd ditched, as he put it, her shopping cart—or anything else?

"Why not?" she said, feeling twenty years younger and, against all odds, attractive again—and not just to the likes of a Tim Veeder.

"Where did you leave yours?" Tracy asked.

"Actually," she told him, "I never even got that far. I came down the vegetable aisle looking for a stray cart and I found you instead."

"Then we were both in luck," he said with a smile so sympathetic, so warming, that for an instant she found herself falling for him the way she had that long-ago morning in the animal shelter. "Let me put my lettuces back," he continued, "and we'll get out of here."

That rare thing, she thought: a free spirit with a sense of responsibility. A conscience.

Besides the Grand Union, Middle Forge Plaza was home to a number of smaller stores staked out bravely among the vacant ones: Eagle Eyeglass Emporium, Palumbo's Wine and Spirits, a tai kwon do studio, and a recently opened venture called Chamonix, which sold gourmet coffees and European chocolates. Claire stopped there from time to time with Libby, who regularly treated herself, after their yoga class and healthy lunch, to a box or two of chocolate consolation. This afternoon, as always, Chamonix was desperately empty. It felt delicious, though, to seat herself with Tracy at a small table at the window and sip rich Tanzanian coffee, all caution thrown to the winter winds, while the rest of Middle Forge busily hunkered down for the coming storm.

"So tell me," he said. "How've you been? How was your trip to . . . where was it?"

"Arizona," she said. "Tucson. We were visiting out daughter Caroline."

"And how was that?"

She considered the polite response, then decided to go ahead and tell the truth. "Difficult," she said. "It's very bleak out there—the landscape, I mean. Depressing. It made me want to cry with frustration. Does a landscape ever do that to you? Louis thinks I'm crazy, but I could simply never live in a place like that. I need my garden, my flowers. Though it's always nice to see one's child, you know, the adult they've grown into. But I worry about her, Tracy. She's thirty-four years old; she lives alone. She says, 'Thank God there's no one in my life right now,' and I think she means it, just as I think she means it when she tells me that she's quite happy, utterly devoted to her work. But I do worry. She's my daughter, after all. It's not good for people to live without love, whatever they may tell themselves. It's not healthy."

The intensity of Tracy's response took her by surprise. "Tell me love matters," he said plaintively, looking at her with a shockingly disconsolate expression on his handsome face. "It does, doesn't it?"

"Of course it does," Claire told him firmly. In so many ways he was just a boy who needed mothering. And where was his own mother, his family? What were they like? She knew so little about him, really, beyond the charm and assurance he usually projected, that she had to remind herself there was undoubtedly more to him—perhaps much more—than those pleasant surfaces might indicate. "Absolutely, love matters," she reiterated for the sake of that other Tracy whose loves and fears she knew nothing about. "We forget that at our own risk."

"I guess I'm glad to hear you say that," he said dejectedly, shredding a paper napkin and ignoring his cappuccino. "Sometimes I just don't know. I've been thinking a lot about love these last few weeks." He seemed far away, preoccupied, as if this talk had propelled him into precisely those private regions inaccessible to a casual acquaintance such as herself. Was it Arthur he was in love with, a dying man?

"It was very good to see Arthur Branson again," she offered bravely.

Tracy looked at her blankly.

"Oh," he said. "*That* was a real disaster, wasn't it? I mortally offended Louis, didn't I?"

"No, I wouldn't say that," Claire lied impulsively. "It's just that—"

Tracy finished bluntly for her. "It's just that the last person on earth Louis wanted to see was Arthur. Plus he finally figured out I was gay. Aren't I right? Two home runs in one evening. And now he's gone and crossed me off his list."

She dropped a curling zest of lemon into her espresso and wished he hadn't put it quite so accurately.

"I hope you know this doesn't change anything between you and me," she said awkwardly. "Whatever issues Louis may have, as far as I'm concerned, your being gay is just another aspect of who you are."

He smiled miserably. "Thanks, Claire. I appreciate that. And I guess with Louis, well, there's nothing I can do about that."

"He's very conservative," Claire said. "He gets anxious when people go about flaunting their sexuality. That's where the trouble with Arthur comes from. After he left the Forge School he changed. He became more, well, flamboyant. You didn't know Arthur back in those days. He was very different, very quiet and studious. I'm afraid Louis took it personally when Arthur came out of the closet with such a bang."

Claire had never seen the slightest trace of anger in Tracy, so she was surprised at the sudden flare of rage. "He made Arthur cry," Tracy said, so fiercely that the proprietress of Chamonix, trying to keep herself busy behind the display counter, looked their way in alarm. "After the two of you left, he just sat there and wept. Arthur feels such great loyalty to Louis, after everything he did. He can't understand why Louis turned his back on him. After going to such lengths for him. After single-handedly rescuing him from a living hell the way he did."

"That's very generous of Arthur. Louis was certainly very fond of him, very supportive—but then, everyone was fond of Arthur. He was really the Forge School's great dazzling hope when he was a student."

"Some, I guess, were fonder than others," Tracy said with a hint of sarcasm.

"Oh, Louis was quite fond," Claire defended. "He thought Arthur was the real thing."

"I wasn't thinking of Louis."

"Oh," Claire said, a bit puzzled.

"I was thinking of Dr. Emmerich."

She thought for a moment, but failed to see the connection. "I'm not sure I know what you mean," she told him.

He looked at her as if, for some reason, he didn't quite believe her. He patted down the little pyramid of napkin he'd shredded onto the table, then spoke cautiously but mysteriously. "All I know is what Arthur told me."

"About . . . ?" she prodded, genuinely curious now.

"You really don't know what I'm talking about," Tracy told her in a tone of mild surprise.

"I haven't a clue," she said honestly. "You've got to fill me in."

Tracy pulled another napkin from the dispenser and began to add its shreds to the pile. "I don't even know if I should go into all this. It's ancient history. And all I've got is what Arthur told me, and Arthur does have an extravagant imagination. But I don't know why he would make something like this up."

"Now you've *got* to tell me," Claire urged, even as she reflected to herself how many troubles began with just such an innocent demand.

Tracy took a deep breath. "Okay," he said. "About Dr. Emmerich, and how he used to, you know, invite his favorite students out to his farm, and it was a real honor to get invited out there."

"This is all true," Claire told him, though it was odd how an almost infinitesimal kernel of dread appeared in her heart.

"Well, I guess Arthur got invited out there quite a bit his senior year. He'd never felt the experience of being so . . . *appreciated* by somebody, and I think it gave him this tremendous sense of security. He said it felt like finding his balance in the world."

"Jack Emmerich was very charismatic that way," Claire said.

"Only things went bad. Dr. Emmerich weirded out on him, pulled the rug out from under their relationship. He was very cruel."

"Tracy," she said, feeling hot and flushed. She pushed her espresso cup aside and stared intently at her young interlocutor. "Are you trying to tell me there was something sexual between Arthur and Jack Emmerich, of all people?"

He nodded gravely. "Intellectual, emotional, physical. It was a romance. Only Dr. Emmerich panicked and decided he wanted out. That's when it got ugly. And that's when Louis stepped in."

He spoke with such arid certainty that Claire listened with an ache in her heart as dull and gray as the parking lot beyond Chamonix's plate-glass window. For a panicked moment she thought she saw Libby get out of a beige BMW—what better time for Libby to decide to stock up on chocolates, and what worse time to run into her friend?—but fortunately it wasn't Libby, only another large-hipped woman who occupied too much sad and baffled space in the world.

She had never heard any of this that Tracy was telling her, and surely, if it had happened as he said, she would have known about it. Her husband was a man of many secrets, but that he would have kept something like this from her seemed impossible to believe. How many years ago would it have been? Fourteen? Fifteen? All that time in their life seemed so very distant: Louis was not yet headmaster; she had not yet returned to school; Lux, gentle, faithful, gone-forever Lux, was not yet in their lives (he'd been such a mouthy little puppy when they first got him, she remembered with a pang). Had they been good times or bad? She honestly couldn't say, so intermixed were her memories.

"From what I understand," Tracy continued, "it must've taken a huge amount of courage to stand up to Dr. Emmerich. You knew him pretty well: is that right?"

She had indeed known him, though no one, with the possible exception of her husband, had ever known him "pretty well," as Tracy so casually put it. She found herself resisting the young man's blithe incursion into the complex terrain of her past. Knowing Jack Emmerich even to the limited extent she had known him had been neither simple nor easy. All of them—she and Louis, Reid and Libby, the only four still left from those years—had lived in some varying degree of awe and fear. She remembered Jack's invariable courtliness toward her, and how, beneath it, she had felt a force like steel. He had mesmerized Louis, and why not, with his encyclopedic knowledge of Wagner, his command of German that Louis could only envy, his manly and forthright sense of mission in the world? But she liked to think he had never succeeded—quite—in mesmerizing her.

"I hardly know what to say," she told Tracy, shaking her head in consternation. "I've never heard a whisper of any of this. I find it very difficult to believe." Or rather, she found—to her distress—that she could not immediately discount Tracy's tale. They had all known, through the years, about Jack's utter devotion to certain of his boys. That was what made him, they unanimously agreed, such an extraordinary educator. And he *had* been an extraordinary educator. But she had harbored, even then, doubts she could never voice: how there was something slightly troubling about some of Jack's infatuations, how he could praise endlessly the virtues of boys who turned out, when you met them, to be rather dull, who certainly did not blaze with the bright flame he claimed to detect in their souls. But as far as she knew— and she'd know, wouldn't she?—there had never been the slightest whiff of scandal, not even a stray rumor through all these years.

Wouldn't it be strangely, even tragically, fitting if that extraordinary man had succumbed, in the end, to those very qualities that had made him extraordinary?

Nonsense, she thought warily.

"Louis never said anything to you?" Tracy asked.

She shook her head. "And what does Arthur say my husband did, exactly?"

Tracy shook his head in return. "He made Dr. Emmerich back off. What else can I say? I'm not sure even Arthur ever knew the details of that confrontation. Just that he did manage to graduate, which Dr. Emmerich had given him cause to doubt, and, even more surprising to Arthur, that Brown never rescinded his admission, which Dr. Emmerich had also threatened. So he went off to Brown in the fall, and I guess he came out of the closet there. And then—isn't this right?—Dr. Emmerich died not too long after."

"Yes, there was a car accident," Claire said. She had never seen anyone so devastated as Louis; she had feared for him, his sense of loss was so immense. Seen through the lens of that grief, still so vivid to her, Tracy's story seemed utterly implausible, schoolyard gossip at best. Perhaps Arthur Branson had indeed become unreliable; perhaps AIDS had begun to affect his once-remarkable brain.

She wished she knew if they were lovers, he and Tracy. She wished she knew how to ask that simple question of a young man. It might explain Tracy's motives in telling her this story. But he, apparently, wanted to dwell a bit longer in the past.

"It's a funny thing," he said, "about Arthur and Dr. Emmerich. It didn't have to turn out badly. That's the sad thing. It could have been this incredibly positive experience for Arthur."

The wistfulness in his tone struck her. "Tracy," she advised, "I wouldn't romanticize. Relations between teachers and students are inherently volatile. I don't think any of these affairs end well. I think they do terrible damage to the kids involved."

"You don't think there're any exceptions?" he wondered.

She considered for a moment. When she'd been in college, several of her professors were married to women who had once been their students. But that was different, somehow, though she wasn't sure, when she thought about those marriages, that they had been particularly advisable or, in the end, especially for the wives, very happy. She respected power and its differentials, but she also understood the insidious damage it could wreak, quietly and over time, on a relationship. "No, I don't really know that there are exceptions. Certainly there's no way a sixteen- or seventeen-year-old can possibly know what he or she is getting into with an adult ten, twenty, however many years older. I think it's a flat-out abuse of power, and I think in those circumstances the teacher's always the one to blame."

"I guess there has to be blame," Tracy said. "Plus it's against the law. Unlawful sexual activity with a minor. It's a felony in New York state."

"Well, there you have it," she told him.

"Which means a fairly severe penalty," he went on. "Like ten years in prison. It would pretty much ruin your life."

"I should think so," Claire said.

Tracy looked troubled.

"You're not saying that Arthur was thinking of bringing charges against Jack Emmerich, are you?" she said darkly. She steadfastly refused to believe the car accident could have been anything more than what it was.

Her words seemed to startle him. "Oh no," he said. "Not at all. I was just thinking. I wonder what kind of evidence. I mean, it seems to me a student could invent a story, if they wanted to get back at a teacher. I wonder what happens when it's one person's word against another."

"I honestly have no idea," Claire told him. He could be like this, she'd noticed; he'd get an idea in his head and obsess over it for quite some time.

"You and I"—she patted his arm fondly—"have nothing to worry about. Let's leave it to the criminals and the police to work all that out."

Beyond Chamonix's plate-glass window, the sky looked pregnant with threat; a light snow had begun to fall and it occurred to her that she should get home. Louis would worry.

"I think the blizzard's upon us," she said. "And we're provisionless as ever." She noticed he'd barely touched his cappuccino; the cinnamon-flecked foam head was still intact. "Do you want to finish your coffee before we go?"

"It wasn't very good," he said, reaching in his pocket for his wallet.

"No, no," she told him. "This is on me." She took from her purse a ten and, perhaps defiantly—the cappuccino had been perfectly good the few times she'd tried it—folded the bill under her saucer, a one hundred percent tip, the kind that would make Louis fume. And perhaps Tracy as well. But she liked Chamonix; against very long odds, she wanted it to succeed. She wanted all noble ventures to succeed.

"Thank you," she told the proprietress, wishing she could remember her name. Was it Ann Marie? Marie Therese? Something that sounded Swiss.

"Bye-bye," said Ann Marie or Marie Therese.

"Bye," Tracy echoed.

"Well," she told him in the parking lot. "I'm very glad I ran into you. It's been too long. And remember what I said. Louis doesn't dictate my life. Let's get together again sometime soon. Perhaps lunch?" Dinners, of course, remained out of the question. What would she say to Louis: I'm going over to Tracy's for dinner?

"That would be nice," Tracy said. He seemed sad, subdued.

Uncertain how to make better whatever it was that was wrong, she told him, "I'm very sorry Arthur's feelings got hurt. You've given me much to think about this afternoon."

"Don't worry over it too much," he said. "The past is the past. It's the present we should worry about."

She was about to shake his hand good-bye when he clasped both her shoulders and pulled her to him, planted a dry kiss lightly on her cheek. "I consider you my friend," he told her with what sounded more like desperation than affection. "I could really use lunch with a friend from time to time."

"Our power's out," Libby said in an aggrieved tone. "How about yours?" Claire cradled the phone between ear and shoulder and peered out the window. In the cone of light cast by the street lamp thousands of snowflakes swirled about like avid moths drawn to their doom. The television weatherman had been right: this third storm was proving just as mighty as its predecessors.

"We're fine here," Claire reported. "We're holding tight. Louis is outside shoveling the driveway right now."

"Isn't that a little optimistic of him?"

"You know Louis. He has this theory that if he shovels the drive every hour while it's snowing, then it's not that onerous. By the time the snow's through falling, the driveway's all clear. And guess who gets to feel virtuous?"

"He's going to have to stay up all night," Libby observed.

"Oh," Claire told her friend, "these days he does that anyway."

"Well, you're lucky, I suppose. Two shovelfuls and *my* husband would die of a heart attack."

Claire felt herself stiffen. What whisper or shadow in her friend's voice provoked such a sudden ache of dread? "Libby," she said warily. "Is everything all right?"

Libby laughed mirthlessly. "What's the bright side of being without electricity?" she asked. Then, in that brittle, too-bright voice Claire hadn't heard in years, Libby answered her own question. "You don't have to see your situation quite so clearly."

Claire had always known that her friend's black river had only plunged underground, that it still seethed beneath the apparent calm of the landscape, unseen but hardly vanquished. She had always known that, one day, in the middle of some placid field of flowers, its dangerous torrent would burst forth to the surface.

"Is Reid there with you?" she asked in alarm.

"Oh, Reid," Libby said carelessly. "Reid hasn't been here in two days. No, three days. Three days and counting."

She paused, and Claire was aware, in the sudden silence, of her own heart knocking breathlessly in her chest. "What's happened?" she asked.

"Haven't you heard? I thought everybody had heard except me. It's love, Claire. That ridiculous emotion. After all these years of playing at one romance or another, now he tells me it's finally happened. He's fallen in love. Devastating, don't you think?"

"But he always imagines he's in love," Claire said desperately, repulsed, as always, by Reid's priapic unruliness. "What makes us think this is any different? Weren't we laughing about it just last month?"

"This time I've lost him," Libby said with such certainty that Claire, despite everything, knew it might indeed be true. "What he said was, 'The night before Constantinople fell to the Turks, the Virgin appeared to the emperor on the walls of the city and asked him to return to her her icon, the most sacred icon of the empire. Why? the emperor asked her. Because, the Virgin told him, the spirit of God has forsaken the city.' How's that for announcing the end of a marriage?"

Claire refrained from mentioning that she thought Reid Fallone was a pompous ass.

"Don't ask me if I understand," Libby went on. "Because I don't. All I know is this: that I'm in love too. Have been all along. With *him*. It never mattered much before, when I knew I had him, but now it's all that matters. And I can't stand it."

"You and Reid will outlast all the rest of us," Claire assured her, but even she could hear how that old truism had lost its luster.

"The demons never go away," Libby said in a voice gone icy and remote.

"Libby," Claire commanded sternly, though she felt herself gone shivery inside. "Don't talk like that."

"You never had demons," Libby told her. "You're the only person I know who never had demons."

"You'll get through this," Claire rallied her friend. "I'm there for you. Remember? You have me always." But she was aware, even as she said those words, that she was no longer talking to Libby Fallone. The phone line had suddenly gone dead. "Hello?" she said. "Libby?"

Surely it was only the storm—a limb down across the lines, a power outage somewhere that mattered. Dialing the Fallones' number, she realized she was trembling. Please don't let this happen, she thought. As a girl she had once watched, with wonder and anxiety, acrobats from a traveling circus entertain the crowd from on high. Take your eyes off them for an instant, she had warned herself, and they will plummet to the ground. But she had not looked away. She had kept them aloft—and Libby as well. For all these years, her watchfulness had looked very much like love.

A recorded voice informed her, politely, that all circuits were busy, and that she should please try her call again later. That meant the storm was indeed to blame, didn't it? And yet she was not reassured. All evening she had felt unsettled, the result, she'd told herself, of her conversation with Tracy Parker. But she had known, deep down, that those revelations alone could not account for the pervasive unease she'd felt, really, ever since Lux's death. She hardly believed in omens; still, it disturbed her how Lux had slipped away in the middle of the night when no one was watching.

She dialed Libby's number again, and once more the pleasant recorded voice asked her to try later. Later, she wanted to explain in frustration, might well mean too late. But of course one did not explain life and death to a machine. Resolute in what she must do, she pulled on winter boots, an overcoat, her gloves, the woollen hat she'd knitted years and years ago, back when she still tried to fill her life with the more obvious tasks.

The automatic garage door rose to reveal Louis and his snow shovel at the bottom of the driveway; already a half inch of snow had retaken the asphalt nearest the garage. In the rearview mirror she saw him look up in surprise as the Audi backed toward him. "Claire," he said as she came to a stop beside him. He'd stepped off onto the ridge of shoveled snow that lined the asphalt. "What on earth are you doing?"

"I think Libby's in trouble," she told him. "I have to go out there. I'll explain later."

He leaned in close, grimacing. He'd never liked Libby. Some wounds, Claire supposed, simply never healed. She spoke as authoritatively as possible, the way she might announce a lecture at which attendance was mandatory. "You know how she gets sometimes. Her power's out, and that's spooked her."

"The roads will be quite impassable," he said. "And where's Reid? Isn't he out there with her?"

"Reid," she improvised, though she had not the slightest idea where he might be, "is stuck in New York. With this weather, he called to say he'd decided to spend the night."

"At least someone's got some sense. Now Libby will be all right, I'm sure. It's madness to try to drive in this."

"Louis," she said impatiently, "the Audi's fine in the snow. I'll drive carefully. I'm sure the main roads aren't even that bad yet. I'll call when I get there."

"I don't like this," he told her. "I'm coming with you."

"No," she said, releasing the brakes and easing the car into the street. "Just keep the driveway clear for me," she called out the open window before raising it with the touch of a button. Shovel in hand, he followed her several steps down the driveway but saw it was no use. His foolish, impetuous wife. He stood watching her, this sad anxious man she loved. Cautiously she depressed the accelerator; the wheels balked for an instant, then seized the road, and in absurd slow motion she began her journey down the snow-padded street.

You never had demons, Libby had said. The only person I know who never had demons. Was it possible she might have meant the observation to sting exactly as much as it had? *You* were once my demon, Claire told her absent friend, but the confession fell surprisingly flat. Once, perhaps, that had been true—but no longer. Not, in fact, for a very long time. With a shock Claire saw how the exquisite flame had flickered and gone out. How she had allowed it to go out.

For years she had refused to let herself feel a thing.

But surely that wasn't true? she thought fiercely. The possibility ate at her as she steered the car onto Academy Avenue. Beneath her mildness, her civility, was it possible there was simply nothing? For years she had told herself she kept them all afloat: husband, friends, even her students. Had she neglected, in the process, something vital to her own soul? Had she allowed the flame to burn so low it was now in danger of complete extinction?

Louis had been right about the main roads. No plows had been through, and in the intersections the stoplights flashed red. Power was out all over— only their block, for some reason, had been spared. Still, she would not turn back. You have me always, she had told her friend, and she meant, now more than ever, to keep her word. Razor blade, rope, Reid's pistol, beautiful blue pills. There were so many lethal possibilities. Libby could be deep into the woods by now. Coatless, in only her bath slippers and thin robe, she could be settling, at this very moment, into a patch of scrub, behind the camouflage of a fallen log, seeking and finding the warm, inviting, gently numbing bed of snow.

She had let her guard down; she had not been alert to the creeping darkness.

"Tell me love matters," Tracy Parker had urged her forlornly, and from her vantage point on the sidelines she had willingly obliged him. But what did she know of all that tumult? Life, happening all around her, had in the end left her oddly untouched. But how had that happened? All at once, the ordinary years of her life, on whose quiet steadiness she had secretly congratulated herself, looked like nothing so much as a series of small surrenders, each so negligible as to have counted for nothing at the time, but all leading here, to this rather unnerving absence of demons.

The storm demanded the utmost from car and driver alike, but the Audi drove like a dream. Fierce winds buffeted the car, gusts of snow spilled across the road, but nothing could touch her. She had left the edges of Middle Forge's lamentable sprawl, and was heading into the bleak countryside. For company, she switched on the radio. It took her only a moment to realize that the desolate melody was Schubert. Some wag at the classical radio station had seen fit to reinforce the blizzard with *Die Winterreise*, or at least its opening song. How her husband loved this music, Claire told herself wistfully; though it was a young man's music in so many ways, it spoke to him still.

She, on the other hand, had never exactly tramped through the snow for anyone. The duties of friendship hardly approached a young man's passionate love-grief, and she felt a shameful pang of resentment that she had been called out into a night like this when everyone else, supplies prudently laid in, remained snugly at home.

Like a weathervane, the mood of the music shifted. The piano asserted itself in fitful strokes. And suddenly, without warning, in the road ahead, a great white presence loomed. Had wind and snow intensified into something palpable, a great leaping beast? Before she could even think, it flared and was upon her. She drove her foot hard into the brake pedal. The tires locked, the car continued straight ahead just as the road curved inopportunely to the left. She looked past her headlights for the stationary tree rushing out of the darkness to meet her but found only a sudden dip, a jolting bank of snow, the shallow resting place of the ditch that ran alongside the road. Then everything was completely still. It took her an instant to realize that the radio was still playing Schubert, the motor still humming, the car and herself superbly intact. Of the apparition in the darkness that had so startled her there was not a trace. Or had it been nothing more before her than a fierce squall of snow punching across the road?

She flicked off the radio; the piano's clatter, that lovelorn voice, only made her bad nerves worse. Putting the car in reverse, she tried to urge it back up the gentle slope, but the tires only spun. She turned on the hazard lights and climbed out of the car to survey her predicament. Auto Maintenance for Women hadn't quite prepared her for this. Off in the distance she saw what might be the lights of a house. She figured she was about midway between home and Libby's: six of one, half a dozen of the other, as her mother used to say. She considered heading out toward the light flickering in the distance but could hear Louis saying, "Don't be ridiculous." It was best, she imagined, to stay with the car, keep the heater running, and wait for help.

Well, Libby, she told her friend as she eased herself back into the Audi's snug compartment, looks like you're on your own tonight. For once, it seemed, everybody would be on their own. She was surprised to find how easy it was to relinquish them all. Let Libby go, wherever her doom called her, let Louis go (and yet she worried about him out there shoveling; she worried about his heart, that magnificent muscle that one day must stop in its tracks). Reid Fallone and Tracy Parker and Arthur Branson. Let them all go. She turned the radio back on; the lullaby of *"Der Lindenbaum"* had commenced. She closed her eyes and breathed deeply, as her yoga class had taught her. My body is a temple, she told herself. My body is the dwelling place of God. She continued to breathe deeply, slowly, evenly. It could be hours before help arrived. Why hadn't she ever gotten around to buying a car phone, as she'd long intended? But then there was so much she'd never gotten around to doing (she had earned a Ph.D., she reminded herself; a prestigious journal had published "Pocahontas at the Masque"). Still, for all that, her life had lacked passion. The demons had never come for her, and she had mistakenly been glad of that. That was what, in the end, she would stand accused of.

"Der Lindenbaum's" sweet suggestive song faded in and out of her consciousness. She felt, suddenly, quite exhausted, and, leaning her head against the headrest, she closed her eyes. All day Tracy Parker's tale of events long past had haunted her. How much of what he had told her was true? The thought of Louis keeping from everyone, for all those years, Jack Emmerich's secret shame both stirred and depressed her. Oh Louis, she thought. And poor Arthur Branson, too, whose whole subsequent life, she could not help but think, had been set in motion by that sad episode. What might have happened had Louis not then turned his back—in shame or repugnance or regret—on the boy he had rescued? She tried to comprehend her husband's long-ago actions, no doubt undertaken with the best of motives, and yet what unforeseen consequences might they not have had? The damage love does when love goes astray. And did it ever, given half a chance, fail to wander?

She had closed her eyes for only a moment, she thought, but then she must have opened them again because she found herself staring intently— for how long now, she wasn't sure—at a most curious sight. Beyond her windshield, a splendid creature sat on its haunches and stared back at her. "Lux," she said, for though his fur had gone snow white and his eyes glowed gold, she knew with certainty that it was he. She must have fallen asleep, she thought—and for hours rather than minutes. The dark was beginning to lift; a pale dawn was on its way. The forecasters, she saw, had been entirely wrong. The snow had stopped; indeed, it had melted nearly away. Lux sat in a field blooming with delicate white wildflowers, their blossoms like tiny pricks of starlight. She had the urge to reach out and lay her palm soothingly on the top of the noble creature's head, but her arm felt so heavy, and motionlessness so sweet, that she could not bring herself to stir a muscle. In the gray distance she saw a building of some kind, much closer than she'd thought the lights of the farmhouse had been through the storm; for a moment she thought it must be a power substation, perhaps the very one that had caused the lights of Middle Forge and Castel Fallone to fail, but then she saw that it was no power substation at all. It was a temple. Stony, austere columns rose skyward. There seemed to be an altar in there, and figures moving about. Was that Louis? And Tracy Parker? And it was impossible, wasn't it? For there, dressed in that black blazer he always used to wear, and smiling that charming, dangerous smile, stood Jack Emmerich. For many years he had lived here in seclusion, in this ruined temple on the edge of town. And no one told me, she thought—but that omission did not so much irritate as quietly awe her. They had all known, and out of deference or pity or sadness had kept it from her. But now she understood. She watched from a distance as Louis and Tracy and Jack, never glancing once in her direction, began to dance, slowly and formally, to the music of Schubert, a grave and courtly masque as snow or flower petals or stars fell all around them. And it was incredible—she would not have believed it had she not seen with her own eyes—but snow-white, golden-eyed Lux danced the masque as well.

So, she thought with some degree of satisfaction. But what, exactly, had been solved that her heart hadn't solved years ago? she wondered as she became aware of a persistent knocking next to her ear, a voice saying, "Hey, Ms. Tremper."

For a moment she did not remember where she was. A figure stood outside the car window peering in. She had been stranded; she had been waiting for help. She lowered the window. "Ms. Tremper," Tim Veeder asked with concern, "are you okay in there?"

"I'm fine," she said. "I must have, I don't know . . . I must have dozed off. What are you doing out here?"

"I could ask you the same thing. I plow for the town." She could see his pickup truck, the lowered blade of its snowplow. "You could have gotten yourself in real trouble," he told her seriously. "It's a good thing I came along. But don't worry. We'll get you out of there in no time."

"What do I do?" she asked him.

"Nothing," he told her. "With me, you're in excellent hands."

She had to grant him that. With admirable efficiency he went about hooking the slack cable from his winch to her bumper, and in no time had pulled the Audi from the ditch. "I'm very obliged to you," she told him, though the irony was hardly lost on her.

"Where were you coming from?" he asked. "Were you trying to get home?"

"Yes," she said, still a bit disoriented from it all, "trying to get home."

"Isn't home that way?" He pointed in the direction from which she had come.

"Yes," she agreed, "it is."

"I'm going that way," he said. "You should follow behind me. I'll clear a way."

He would lead her directly to her driveway, she thought; he knew exactly where she lived. How many times had he cruised past, watching, longing in whatever way someone like Tim Veeder longed? But he eased her mind immediately. "The famous Forge School," he told her. "Everybody knows where that is. Are you close by?"

"Off Academy Avenue," she told him as the realization sank in. What she'd fervently hoped for all fall had indeed come to pass: he'd lost interest in her, as mysteriously as he'd been afflicted in the first place.

And why not? She should feel relieved, she thought, to set that little episode behind her. And she did, she told herself. She did feel relieved.

She followed his truck in silence. Had her little vision in the snow been a touch of carbon monoxide, perhaps? She wondered if she should have the exhaust checked out. And in any event, the music to a courtly masque would have sounded nothing like Schubert. How, in fact, did one even begin to dance to the remarkably un-dance-like rhythms of a *Lied*? The whole thing had been preposterous, dull, absurd.

She had to admit it made her feel safer to be following in the wake of Tim's snowplow. What had he thought of the C-minus she'd given him for the course? Even now she wasn't sure whether she'd been punitive or generous.

He had turned on his blinker, indicating Academy Avenue. She followed suit, and he gave her a thumbs-up out the window of his truck cab. It was just like him, wasn't it, to be driving in a blizzard with the window down.

Having made one full sweep of the driveway, Louis had begun another. The sight of her Audi elicited a joyous wave. He planted his snow shovel in a drift and motioned her into the drive while Tim idled his truck alongside the curb.

"Well?" he said as she pulled up beside him.

She wanted to tell him how very happy she was to see him, but instead observed, with a sigh, "You were right. The roads are impassable. I didn't make it much past the edge of town."

"I shouldn't have let you go," he told her. "I don't know what I was thinking."

"All's well that ends well," she assured him, aware with a surge of icy anxiety that she did not, in fact, know whether all had ended well. Even now Libby was lying unconscious in a pool of vomit, basking in the warm embrace of hypothermia, submerged in a bath crimson with her own blood. "Has Libby called, by any chance?" she asked her husband.

"I've been out here the entire time," Louis told her apologetically. "I won't have heard a thing."

For an instant she had to stifle a sense of peevish frustration, but then she reminded herself how Louis, dutifully keeping the drive clear, could have no idea how dire things really might be. Easing the Audi up the drive and into the garage, she hurried into the house. In the hallway the answering machine was ablaze with messages. She punched the Play button with some trepidation, but her relief was instant, the way an unresolved cadence, cruelly suspended in the orchestra, will suddenly melt into the bliss of the tonic. "Claire, where are you?" Libby's voice asked anxiously. "I'm worried. Our phone went out for a bit. Please call me as soon as you get this." One after another the messages streamed forth, each echoing the first. Claire took several deep, deep breaths. There had been no reason to charge forth into the storm after all. Libby was fine. The demons—hadn't she proved it conclusively?—were entirely in her own head this evening.

Lifting the receiver, she dialed. Libby answered at once.

"Oh, Claire," she said, "I'm so glad it's you. I was starting to panic. Where were you?"

"Not to worry," Claire told her friend. "I was outside with Louis. I couldn't hear the phone. But I take it you're reconnected."

"We've even got power," Libby said. "Things are looking up all around."

"That's good. You sounded very . . ." But she could not find the word—or was she afraid that by naming whatever baleful possibilities had seemed, for a moment, to shimmer in Libby's voice, she might draw her friend back into their clutches?

"I had a bad moment there," Libby confirmed. "I hope I didn't cause alarm. Really, I'm doing okay. There are times when I even think I can make out the future, and it doesn't look that bleak at all."

Through the window, half obscured by blizzard, Claire could see Louis down at the curb, where Tim's truck still waited. She had forgotten him entirely—and really, she thought, she should invite her former student in for a cup of tea. She should at the very least thank him properly. He had, after all, saved her, if rousing her from such strange thoughts might be said to have saved her.

"I should go," she told Libby. "You take a hot bath; relax. Have yourself a glass of port. You deserve it. Tomorrow we'll talk. We'll make plans."

"Thank you," Libby told her, "just for being there for me. Once again."

If only you knew, Claire thought. But Libby never would know. She would make certain of that.

With a bit of annoyance she saw she'd tracked snow onto the hallway's old oriental carpet. What she wanted herself was a hot bath and a nice glass of port; instead, after rummaging for a moment in her purse, she made herself venture back outside. The storm had not subsided in the least. Borne on gusts of wind, the snow tore down in sheets, body blows any one of which could knock a person down if she wasn't on her guard.

"What a lucky coincidence," Louis told her as she joined him at the bottom of the driveway. "This young man was just telling me he was your student at the college last semester. He's saying highly complimentary things about you."

Tim stood by the cab of his truck, smoking a cigarette. "Sorry, Ms. Tremper," he said ashamedly, holding up the offending article. "I know it's a bad habit."

Would she ever have the heart to tell him she really couldn't care less?

"I have to thank you," she told him, holding out the twenty-dollar bill she had brought down with her. "Please accept this small token."

He eyed the money hungrily. "I can't," he told her politely. "I'm just doing my job. But I do have a favor to ask."

She waited, wondering whether that meant he'd received his grade from last semester.

Tim shifted awkwardly. He picked at a scab on his thumb. "Do you think, by any chance, maybe, you could be my adviser?" he asked.

"I have to say," Louis mused, sipping from his scotch, "that was quite nice of him, offering to plow our drive like that." They sat in the living room, snug against the storm that rattled, now and again, the windowpanes. Louis seemed quite pleased with himself, as if Tim Veeder had been a messenger sent to reward him for his efforts with the snow shovel. Claire wondered how much she should tell her husband.

"If only he could think half as well as he drives a snowplow," she said, feeling stingy even as she said it.

"That bad?"

"Dreadful," she confirmed. "The bane of my existence last semester. He was the one who kept sending me all those cards."

"Cards?" Louis said.

"Surely you must have noticed."

"I suppose I did," he said vaguely. "Yes, as a matter of fact. I did wonder who your new pen pal was."

"Pen pal." She laughed. "If only." But then she added, on reflection, "I think he had a certain crush on me at some point."

It was Louis's turn to laugh. "He seemed gallant enough, in his way. Rather rough-hewn."

"That's not the half of it," she told him. "It was all a lot of bother."

"And now you're stuck with him. Heroic, I'd say, agreeing to be his adviser after all that."

"What could I do?" she wondered.

"I'm sure that's why you're a very, very good teacher," Louis told her. He'd finished his scotch and, stretching, rose to fetch himself another. He gestured toward her own empty port glass, but she shook her head. She felt pleasantly drowsy, fatigued by the day's long unfolding. Now that it was over, it seemed very nearly fantastical in its way. From Tracy Parker she had heard an aston-ishing tale, hardly to be believed and yet ringing, sorrowfully, of the truth. To save Libby Fallone she had braved the storm (she was quite certain now that her venturing out had indeed tipped the invisible scales, shunted aside the threat that had marked her friend out). Through it all, she had preserved her equanimity.

"One feels," Louis said, returning from the kitchen with his scotch re-newed, "one could put on a bit of music before bed. What do you say to that?"

"That would be nice," she agreed, thinking of the ruined temple on the outskirts of town, how she had seen Jack Emmerich looking fit and treach-erous as ever, how he and Louis and Tracy had moved together in ancient, immemorial dance.

"I have a hankering after Sibelius," Louis confessed.

"It's all this snow," she told him, remembering snow-white Lux in a meadow of wildflowers.

Louis laughed appreciatively. "Winter music. Something strong and clean, I think. We haven't heard the Seventh Symphony in ages."

She would not tell her husband what she had seen. She would not tell him what she knew.

XV

Darkness was fast overtaking the lawn, the bare trees. The snow glowed blue in the fading light. There had been moments in the last few weeks, Tracy told himself, sitting before his computer and staring out the window of his study, when joy had seized him—when he had been able, for a snatched moment here or there, to give his circumstances the slip, to forget the fix he'd gotten them both into and simply float in the liquid suspension of the present. As a teenager he'd had a recurrent fantasy: how one night, unbeknownst to anyone, he'd just slip away. In his hand-me-down Chevy he'd head west, no map, no destination in mind, simply let the miles carry him, through the lonely hills of New York state and on out into the continent's dawning heartland, the lost little one-stoplight towns, the empty flowing fields of grain, till finally, after days, weeks, perhaps months, he'd reach the Pacific's glittering rim. He wasn't, in those daydreams, so much running away from something as toward something, some bright and blessed future where he would be bolder, braver, where love—sometimes in the guise of Eric the costume designer, but more often the beautiful stranger he had not yet met—would greet him with open arms. He had had an inkling, even then, that only by losing himself, the well-behaved Connecticut boy he'd always been, might he ever hope to find his other, truer self.

Actually it had been Noah's idea, not his, to forsake Middle Forge the morning after, but in the boy's suggestion Tracy had recognized fate's signature, the god's ironic hand. With Betsy in the backseat, they'd journeyed all day across the Empire State's snow-buried southern tier, and it was extraordinary how two hundred or so miles seemed to put them beyond the grasp of everything that threatened. As dusk touched its rusty light to the steep hills, they found themselves in a hamlet of such fierce poetry, or so it seemed to Tracy at the time, that he once again accepted it as fate. Two convenience stores competed with one another across Main Street; an aluminum diner gleamed like an abandoned toy; the scattering of old clapboard houses badly needed a carpenter's sure hand. And the sign on the low-slung, distinctly ordinary Magic Pines Motel promised both VACANCY and PETS WELLCOME.

He felt numb with the enormity of his transgression; at the same time he thrilled at the prospect that it was all to be repeated, elaborated, improved upon in this little town far, far from home. "Come here," he'd commanded Noah as soon as they were safely locked in their little room, and as if it were all a dream of his own making, the boy came. He was neither docile nor shy. He had a will and desire entirely of his own. All desire, Tracy had had occasion since to think, is to some degree monstrous.

For five days they had stayed there, lost to everyone but themselves. They made love, and then showered, and for a while watched the mesmerizing idiocy of television, and then made love again. Afterwards they walked Betsy along streets hemmed in by snow, the margins of the highway, in plowed parking lots. At the diner they ate bread and salad and spicy beets, the vegetable of the day for days on end.

"So what about the rest of our lives?" Tracy did not dare ask. Instead he said, with a smile, "Cut it out," when Noah tried to play footsie with him in the booth. Back at the motel, the boy sat cross-legged on the bed, a pillow behind his back, and wrote stories in his notebook Tracy dared not ask to read. Instead he studied the beauty of his student's bare feet, his perfect ankles, the classical grace of his calves.

"There's nothing for us," he wanted to cry out in panic, but in that charmed motel room there was, in a sense, everything for him, as he discovered yet again, reaching out to touch with wonder Noah's calf, his thigh, pausing as Noah laid down his notebook and pen and looked at him from under eyelids half-shut with the heaviness of desire.

There would be nothing to show for any of this except punishment. So he did the holiest thing he could imagine, which was to touch his tongue reverently and hopelessly to the dusky rosebud of Noah's anus, that secret site of wonder and repulsion, surprised at how the phrase came to him unbidden: greater love hath no man.

And then on the fifth day they had returned, as they must, to the ordinary world—the nightmare routine of school, all the unconsoling habits of home.

Even though he had been expecting it, the soft knock at the back door made him jump. He remained seated at his computer, listening to the clatter of Noah's boots as the boy discarded them by the door in the kitchen, the moan of pure pleasure as Betsy greeted their guest, the prolonged rattle of dog biscuits tumbling from the box as Noah fed her not one, as he was supposed to, but many, many. Had there been a time when Tracy's heart had lifted at the prospect of a visit from this person? Now he felt nothing but dread, a sick ache in the pit of his stomach.

"Hey Trace," said that voice, nonchalant, unfathomable.

"I'm in here," Tracy answered almost reluctantly, at the same time relieved to have Noah once again within the safety of these four walls where he could keep track of him, where at least he could entertain the delusion of being in control of the uncontrollable.

He didn't look up from his computer screen when Noah appeared in the doorway.

"What's that?" Noah asked, coming over to the desk and laying his hands on Tracy's shoulders. Tracy willed himself not to flinch, and after a moment reached up with one hand and touched Noah's, their fingers interlocking, caressing—and why couldn't this be possible between them? "A modem," Noah went on. "Cool."

Tracy would not allow himself to seem distraught. "I think I've finally got it working," he said. "So what're you up to?"

"Same old same old," Noah told him. "Is school as much a drag for the teachers as it is for us kids?"

Tracy attempted mock dismay. "You're calling school a drag?"

"Except for your class, of course," Noah said. "Your class is definitely not a drag."

"Well, that's good," Tracy told him, wondering if his student could tell how, these days, the teacher was just going through the motions. How the teacher's mind, even in the doldrums of a class discussion about *Romeo and Juliet,* was constantly unfurling its own outlandish scenarios. How, whenever Noah spoke in class—which wasn't, thankfully, that often—the teacher half expected him to say, "Speaking as somebody you fucked the other day . . ." Uncanny, the evil tricks his imagination could play. But Noah seemed, for the moment, blissfully unaware of the absolute power he had so suddenly acquired, the quiet terrorism he could wield were he so inclined.

What unnerved Tracy the most was the simple fact that, despite all his better judgment and best intentions—in fact, as if in blatant mockery of them—he had allowed to happen between himself and his student exactly what he had known must never happen. Or was it that simple? He had not counted on Noah's own tenacious will. He had never thought of his student as passive, exactly—for hadn't that strange gift of a roll of toilet paper been the initial volley in what he had not suspected at the time would be a pro-tracted siege, leading in the end to the fall of the city itself?—but neither had he been prepared for the boy's quietly aggressive needs. And then there had been his own mood of defiance as well, his willful surrender that first night to a hunger he no longer, at least for that single moment of his undoing, cared to restrain. Was it a form of madness, no longer to be able to trust your sense of things? To be betrayed by decisions apparently arrived at carefully and through reason, but really no more than marauding appetites cunningly tricked out as reasonable choices? He had once—sentimentally, no doubt, even recklessly—imagined Noah as a temple inhabited by the beautiful god, all the while failing to see that another, craftier god had erected his temple within the hapless Tracy Parker as well.

And now none of it could be undone. That was the exquisite irony: the act that had undone everything could not itself be undone. Unlawful sexual activity with a minor. The law was the law, unambiguous, unimpeachable, unforgiving.

"Hey Trace," asked the minor with whom he'd had more unlawful sexual activity than he dared calculate, "can we make a fire? You said we could. I'll bring up the wood." Tracy had noticed the stack in the basement when he'd moved in, but then had completely forgotten about it till a blown fuse had sent them down, a few days earlier, to investigate.

"A fire," he said, all too certain what a roaring, romantic blaze in the hearth would eventually lead to. "I guess so. Why not?" Soon they would have to talk. Soon things would have to come to an end. But not tonight, he realized with disgust and arousal.

He let Noah take the lead, following him down into the musty basement, unused since he scarcely had anything he needed to store down there. It had taken him some time—until Arthur's visit, in fact—to fathom that Dr. Emmerich had once lived in this very house, that those crude shelves that at one time had held home-canned tomatoes and beans and corn from the farm in Sullivan County had been built by Dr. Emmerich's own hands. Had the headmaster laid in supplies as a hedge against the same war that had prompted the bomb shelters beneath the dorms? And the dry quarters of wood Noah stacked in his arms, how long had that cache sat untouched down here? Had it come from the back acres of the farm as well? He hardly believed the house was haunted, and yet what else was it but the guilty ghost of Jack Emmerich that lingered with increasing insistence in his thoughts these days?

"Now we're both going to have black feet," Noah said, clearly in a cheerful mood, as he so often seemed this bleak February, as if in inverse proportion to the misery his teacher was reluctant to let him see. He balanced on one leg to show Tracy a white sock's soiled bottom. Was he feeling cocky because he really did realize the powerful position he was in, for perhaps the first time in his life? Or was he just happy, like any other adolescent, to be getting laid? Tracy could no longer count the number of times they'd had sex, but each time it happened he caught himself storing away each detail, each sensation like a man preparing for years of penance in the desert. Never again in his life would he be blessed with such merciful bounty, and the real sin, the unforgivable sin, it seemed to him, was to fail in his appreciation of the great, forbidden gift he had been given.

That first night he had lain awake, scarcely able to contain his euphoria and desolation, and studied, in the clear, lonely moonlight that filled the room, the prostrate, sleeping form beside him. Noah snored lightly, almost imperceptibly. Tracy watched the boy's unblemished back, his tight adolescent buttocks, the backs of his thighs and felt consumed with sadness and pity. He had expected Noah's body to astonish, and he had not been disappointed, though it was, all in all, a somewhat melancholy astonishment, the final much-deferred fruition of dozens and dozens of boys glimpsed, dreamed of, yearned after, a decade or more of boys he assumed he had lost forever only to rediscover them here, transmuted into this single, slim, eager young body that had wanted to get fucked. You don't know how much I love you, he thought to himself. Because if it was true, as he suspected at least once an hour these days, that he really was dying, then what did it matter that he flung caution to the winds and watched it exhilaratingly scatter? In his short, desperate time on earth he had known the love of a boy. At least, he mused as he followed Noah upstairs from the basement, arms loaded down with wood, his eyes on those shapely buttocks before him, at least he had seized that chance. At least, of the legions of wistful things that haunted his brain, he had made one thing real.

"All right," Noah said, spilling his armful of wood onto the fireplace's apron of bluestone, "let's get this show on the road."

"I think we need kindling, don't we?"

"Forget it," Noah told him. From the kitchen he fetched matches and a stack of old newspapers whose sheets he wadded into loose balls. "Kindling's for sissies. I know all about making fires. My dad taught me."

"Well, okay," Tracy said amicably. "We wouldn't want to be sissies here."

"No sissies," Noah proclaimed as he stuffed the wadded paper into the grate. "No faggots, no sissies, no queers," he iterated with each wad.

There was a violence to Noah's humor that worried Tracy. "Just us chickens," he sparred back cautiously while Noah built up a pyre of logs with a meticulous delicacy that seemed, Tracy thought cruelly, like nothing so much as a sissy's.

"You got it," Noah said. "Chickens and chicken hawks." He smiled ambiguously and dusted his hands on the front of his pants. "Now give me those matches."

"Chicken hawks?" Tracy bantered with profound unease.

"Just something I heard," Noah said, striking the match on the side of the box—*zip*, like a boy's trousers opening. He reached in to the paper and lit, and lit again, and soon the paper had taken all around. Flames licked eagerly along the logs. Tracy stood over Noah's crouched form, enjoying the sight of the boy's ass crack as it disappeared into his jeans. He'd been inside Noah but not inside his mystery. That was what still unnerved him every time he looked at the boy: his unknown quantities, the scope of his volatility, the depth of what Dr. Maurer in the counseling office no doubt diagnosed as his emotional disturbance, below whose surface agitation, Tracy hoped fervently, the deeper waters were calm, the bottom smooth and sandy and no monsters lurked.

The fire was not taking. The papers had burned to ash, and now the flames that had so confidently attacked the logs withdrew into the nothing from whence they'd come.

"Fuck," Noah said.

"Maybe we do need kindling after all," Tracy suggested, but Noah was not amused. Don't do this, Tracy thought, but already it was too late. He'd seen this before: how Noah would set himself some unreasonable challenge, then blame himself for failing.

"I've started plenty of fires before," he said. "There's nothing to it when you know what you're doing."

"It's no big deal," Tracy tried to assure him, though he knew that the problem was exactly that. It had, instantly, become a big deal. Oh Noah, he thought. Do we have to do this?

But Noah was furiously wadding up more newspaper. "Ow," he said, shoving his hand into the ash, grazing the hot metal of the grate.

"Careful," Tracy told him, aware how depressingly like a parent he sounded. "Don't burn yourself."

Once again Noah lit a match and set the paper on fire. "You have to want it not to burn," the boy said with a note of desperation, "and then it'll burn for sure."

"What *is* this?" Tracy asked, once again nonplussed by the intensity of Noah's response. "The Fire Sermon?"

"You'll see." Noah knelt silently in front of the resurgent flames, which, after a minute, flickered and started to die down again.

Tracy said, tentatively, "I take it you're wishing for it to go out."

But Noah didn't answer. A single small ghost of a flame clung tenaciously to a log. Noah stuffed more paper in, and the whole blazed up again. But this time it didn't falter. The wood had taken.

"No fair," Tracy said. "You helped. You put more paper in."

"I was trying to smother it," Noah told him. "And see, it didn't work."

Secretly Tracy was glad. He desperately wanted Noah to succeed—at anything.

"Do you do this often? I mean, hope things won't happen so that they will."

"All the time," Noah said over the roar of the fire, enjoying some quiet triumph Tracy was no part of. "Isn't this great? I wish we'd found the wood before."

"It's very romantic," Tracy said with a pang of self-disgust. Seating himself on the sofa, he patted the cushion beside him. "Now come here, pyromeister."

Thinking he meant her, Betsy ambled over but then, attracted by the novelty of the fire, folded herself contentedly in front of its warmth.

"Pyromeister," Noah repeated kiddingly as he settled in next to Tracy. "I'd say this is just picture perfect." The blaze was prodigious, its sound fierce, like wind rushing in the pines, and as Noah leaned his head against Tracy's shoulder, it seemed to the haunted young man that fire had always cast a magic circle within whose light everyone was safe, whether from prowling saber-toothed tigers or the equally vicious phantoms of the mind. For the first time in days he lost that sense of precariousness that so dogged him. It was as if, for one protected moment, they had been transported back to that motel in the wilds of western New York. We shouldn't have stopped, he thought. We should have just kept going, made a run for it. Their great mistake had been to return to all this, to pretend they were still ordinary citizens and not the luminous criminals they had become. We two together, he thought as Noah's hand rested comfortably, affectionately, on his thigh.

"You mustn't romanticize," Claire had told him that afternoon at Chamonix, before he had revealed to her the full extent of his fall. "These affairs always end badly," and though he had since unburdened himself of everything in half a dozen clandestine meetings they had snatched here and there as if *theirs* were the improbable affair, he nonetheless retained, despite all her richly textured sympathy for his and Noah's plight, those first chilling words she had uttered when the issue was wholly one of principle, unmuddied by the particular circumstances her friend found himself in.

Had he been wrong to confide in her, to enlist her aid as accomplice? Louis, no doubt, would be furious to know his wife was keeping secret counsel with the enemy, and in any other circumstances he would have left her out of it, but the one person whose wisdom he keenly longed for was the very person whose experience and suffering and, yes, damage he had shamelessly betrayed. He dreaded the day when he would confess to Arthur what he had been guilty of.

The hand resting on his thigh slipped boldly between his legs; Claire and Arthur alike vanished like ghosts. Sliding his arm around Noah's shoulder, Tracy kissed him lightly on the lips, lingering there for a moment in a series of chaste pecks (Noah had demurely closed his eyes), then slipping his tongue into Noah's accepting mouth. The boy sighed, a sound gratifyingly like pure contentment. In the fireplace the fire he had started roared and roared; Tracy could feel its heartbeat, the flush it brought to his face, and he basked in the double warmth, feasting on the long wet kiss, a late-summer wasp lazily enjoying the sweetness of a ripe, fallen peach.

Slipping off the sofa to kneel before him, Noah tugged at Tracy's pants and Tracy lifted his hips to let them slide down his thighs. As if to prolong the quiver of anticipation, Noah gazed up at him, eyes lustrous with desire. His lips had parted slightly; he worked his jaw to call up extra saliva for the task ahead. Somehow Tracy hadn't quite expected Noah to be so enthusiastic a cocksucker, a born natural, in his way, no skittish and reluctant prize but a little faggot from the get-go just like Tracy himself had been all those years ago when he'd first bent, panting and faint, over Eric the costume designer's entrancing erection.

Though it was funny, he thought as Noah's lips closed around the head of his cock and the boy's pliable tongue began its teasing, there was a peculiar sense in which such moments felt somehow wasted. He found it hard to explain to himself; it was as if his only real desire was to worship this boy whose beauty was inextricable from his boyness. *He* should be the one on his knees. His should be the tongue paying homage to that young beauty's loose sac of balls, the seam of skin beneath them, the secret funky hole.

"Come on up here, beautiful," he coaxed, pulling from his shirt pocket one of the condoms he kept handy these days, since he'd learned how impetuous their urges could be. To propel Noah, writhing, to that state where suffering and bliss were indistinguishable; it was another form of worship, perhaps the highest, and if there was a tinge of cruelty in the pleasure, it was because the god he worshiped demanded to suffer, at least a little, in return for the abjection of his faithful. Only once had they reversed the sacrament of their usual roles—one night at the Magic Pines when, in the middle of their bedplay, Noah had matter-of-factly announced, "Okay, now I fuck you," and Tracy had spontaneously ventured, "You're right. It might be interesting to try something different." But the episode had proven clumsy, unsatisfactory—even unnatural in their private scheme of things—and they had thereafter reverted to the classic formula of the *pederastia*.

Stripped of his pants but retaining, in his haste, his socks and shirt, Noah clambered up onto Tracy, straddling him, face to face, and even as they kissed Noah was lowering himself onto Tracy. The young man felt the tip of his sheathed penis begin to ease into the boy's rectum.

He loved the involuntary animal groan in the back of Noah's throat. Despite everything—the insane danger, the hopelessness—his heart still beat like mad with exhilaration, knocking and knocking in the cage of his ribs.

And at the back door, he realized, someone was hammering with great urgency as well, a series of staccato thumps coming in groups of four like some dire coded message.

Noah leaped off him as if he'd been stung. "What's that?" he said as Betsy charged frantically into the kitchen.

"I can't imagine," Tracy told him, nonetheless imagining a dozen frightful possibilities all in a heartbeat as he struggled to remedy his disarray, stuffing his shirttails, his abruptly crestfallen erection, back into his pants. "You stay there," he commanded.

On the back door stoop, looking like an Arctic explorer in his hooded, fur-fringed parka, stood Doug Brill. "Quick," he said, rapping against the glass, breathless with fear or excitement. "Call off your dog and let me in. I need to use your phone. We've got an emergency here."

"What're you talking about?" Tracy said, irked and relieved and shaken as Doug shouldered his way past him into the kitchen. "Betsy," he urged ineffectually. "Calm down now." But Betsy, with her keen instincts, had taken an instant dislike to their uninvited guest. She would not be silenced.

"I can't find your phone," Doug Brill was shouting. "Where's the damn phone? You've got yourself a serious chimney fire out there."

"What?" Tracy asked. Realizing he still held the condom rolled in the palm of his hand—and what other traces were on him as well?—he deposited it in his pants pocket, to mingle with his keys and spare change.

"I said, your damn chimney's on fire," Doug Brill repeated. "Now where's the phone?"

"There on the wall," Tracy directed, feeling strangely aloof from the actual emergency at hand, noting, in fact, with cool amusement, that he had never heard Doug Brill use a word like "damn" before even as he ran through a mental checklist: yes, the shades had been down; no, you couldn't see the living room from the back door.

Leaving his upstanding colleague to parley with 911, Tracy returned to the living room. Noah sat on the sofa, reassembled and looking, thank God, entirely decent. With a dazed expression he stared into the fire, which was roaring as if a freight train had gotten lodged in the chimney's throat. Tracy wondered grimly: could they both have been so distracted they hadn't noticed how loud it had grown? Because hadn't that been the whole problem all along?

"There's a chimney fire," he observed, for lack of anything better.

"I heard," Noah said without looking up.

"Let's go take a look. Mr. Brill's called the fire department."

"I said I heard," Noah said petulantly.

"We should probably go outside," Tracy coaxed.

"That's okay. I'll wait here."

But Tracy didn't want him just to wait there. He resisted mightily the urge to suggest that Noah might want to make a discreet exit by the front door while there was still time. Only there wasn't still time. Doug stood in the doorway, the hood of his parka still over his head, a scientist about to make some terrible discovery in the ice: a crashed saucer, a dinosaur in suspended animation. As a kid, Tracy had loved those films on rainy Saturday afternoons.

"The fire department's on their way over," Doug reported, his wary attention focused entirely on the disheveled boy on the sofa. "Mr. Lathrop." He spoke sharply over Tracy's shoulder. "I thought you were going into the city this weekend. Didn't I see your name on the sign-out sheet?"

Noah rose to the challenge. He hardly missed a beat. "I did sign out, yeah. I didn't make my train. Taxi was late. Tracy here's going to take me to the next one."

Doug squinted with skepticism. It occurred to him, finally, to push his hood back. He had made his discovery. "You went all the way to the station and then came back here?"

"Kind of dumb, huh?" Noah said blithely. Tracy had to admire his composure, though it bothered him to see his accomplice so skilled at lying. Be careful, Tracy warned silently, you'll get us both in trouble.

"I'd say Mr. Parker's being extremely generous," Doug said. "Way beyond the call of duty." His eyes darted to the fireplace, then back to Noah, but it was Tracy he addressed. "That's some fire you've got going there. I hope you weren't planning to go off to the train station and leave it burning like that."

His tone stung, and for an instant Tracy glimpsed his colleague as he must appear to his students. No wonder they hated him. No wonder they called him the Brill.

From the distance came a siren's blur. "Well that was quick," the Brill said approvingly. "Let's go outside. I sure hope the roof's not on fire. These flue fires are tricky. They can burn right through the mortar and be inside the attic before you know it." He seemed pleased to be able to take charge, to treat both Noah and Tracy as irresponsible children caught in the midst of some prank. Caught, as it were, with their pants down—and their shoes off. Tracy glanced down at the trail of slush Doug had tracked in behind him, his boots casually defiling the cleanliness of Tracy's housekeeping. But it made sense, Brill's proprietary behavior; this house was as good as his. He and his family and the miniature railroad were set to move in the first of July, and though that date seemed infinitely distant, Doug was already looking out for his own.

Guiltily Tracy sat on the bench in the mudroom and pulled on his shoes, then followed his colleague outdoors onto the snowy lawn. Sparks spit from the roaring chimney, beautiful in their way, rising into the dark sky then vanishing. Tracy's heart was roaring as well, and he tried to follow the fate of this or that bright bit of fire as it was borne aloft toward Orion, the only constellation he could ever recognize. He and Noah had stood out here only nights ago, contemplating the shivery infinity of space, a moment that seemed, in retrospect, somehow rapturous, as if they too might have soared away.

Lights flashing but its siren mercifully stilled—the less attention the better, Tracy prayed—the fire engine pulled into the cul-de-sac. Men spilled from the cab and Doug waved to them, then pointed at the chimney.

"You know," he said meditatively, as if it needed to be said before all the commotion began, "with all that environmental mumbo jumbo you pitch to the kids, I'd have thought you'd be against building fireplace fires. Air pollution and all that."

It was a knife discreetly slipped between the ribs while no one else was looking. Tracy had understood, in principle, that the man despised him; it was nonetheless something of a shock to hear his words. He knew he should say nothing, let it pass, but he couldn't help himself. "I'm not the threat to this planet," he spat out tersely as the firemen approached. "The threat that's going to kill us is people having kids and more kids. As far as I'm concerned, those are the real criminals."

Doug looked at him and said simply, "I pity you. I really do." Then, turning to the firemen trundling up the snowy lawn, he called out, "Over there. See that smoke? I hope the roof's not on fire."

With practiced calm, the firemen threw a ladder up against the chimney, and one man climbed up to lower a set of chains down the creosote-coated shaft. Other men carried tubs of sand into the house.

Silent as a shark, the Forge's one security car pulled over to the curb a discreet distance behind the fire truck. From the passenger side, looking surprisingly frail and distressed, emerged Louis Tremper. Tracy watched the headmaster pick his way up the driveway with an old man's exaggerated care. He forced himself to saunter down, as if nothing were amiss, to meet Louis halfway.

"I came right over when I heard," Louis said. "Security called me. Is everything all right?" On the headmaster's condensing breath Tracy thought he could catch the hint of scotch. Was that what he was doing with himself these days, sitting in a darkened living room with a half-full tumbler beside him while Dietrich Fischer-Dieskau sang of wandering and lost love?

Materializing at Tracy's side, Doug answered for him. "I think we have everything under control here, sir," he assured Louis. "The firemen are inside taking the fire out. It's a good thing somebody noticed before the situation got out of control." He narrated with relish, rocking back and forth on his heels and rubbing his hands together excitedly. "See, I was out taking my after-dinner walk, getting my exercise, enjoying the chance to collect my thoughts. I was coming from over yonder. Going this way." As if it mattered, he gestured with military precision. "And I noticed a lot of smoke coming from Tracy's chimney here. Then, when I got closer, I could see sparks shooting out. Oh my gosh, I thought, he's going to burn the house down. I thought the fireplace in this house was never supposed to be used. I thought there was a strict prohibition against that."

"No one told me," Tracy said, thinking of all the richly useless things Louis had told him instead.

"Dear me," Louis said. "Perhaps I forgot. There's no permanent damage done, is there?" he asked querulously.

"You'd have to put that to the fire marshal," Doug said officiously. "Let's just hope the Lord was with us tonight."

And perhaps He had been. Already, Tracy could see, the sparks were vastly diminished. The roar in the chimney's throat had subsided, and the firemen were carrying out the embers. They set the tubs in the snow and stood around as if to warm themselves over the fading coals. Had their presence even been necessary? Tracy was under the distinct impression that chimney fires usually burned themselves out on their own. "We could well have had a catastrophe on our hands," Doug went on, the possibility seeming to titillate as much as alarm him. He was waiting for the Second Coming, after all. "I'd suggest we should get someone in pronto to clean the chimney so this doesn't happen again."

Back off, already, Tracy yearned to tell him. Chastened, though, he kept his silence.

"Yes, yes," Louis said. "Excellent idea. In the meantime"—he wagged a finger at Tracy in what almost seemed a vein of humorous rebuke (was it possible the old man was more than a little drunk this evening?)—"no more fires. We want to be cautious. We don't want to live dangerously. Now do we?"

"No we do not," Tracy agreed, even as he saw Louis's gaze settle upon Noah. The boy stood apart from the commotion, coatless and thoughtfully holding Betsy on her leash; he seemed to be contemplating that same Orion he and Tracy had gazed at a few nights before.

Like a timpani roll that swells ominously and then subsides, Tracy could feel the perturbation go through Louis's system. The older man frowned, made a bitter expression with his lips, an expression of distaste—or even disgust. So now he knew everything; now he knew he had been lied to. For Tracy even to try to explain it away would be an insult. And Louis, it seemed, did not expect him to. He did not say a word, but with a gesture of great weariness turned away. Doug Brill cast a smiling glance Tracy's way to show that, although he did not entirely understand, he nonetheless could intuit that something noteworthy had just happened; then, ever solicitous, he took Louis's arm to lead him back down the treacherous driveway to the waiting security car.

Tracy breathed a grim sigh and slid his cold hands into his pockets, finding, in the warmth of his right one, the hastily stashed-away condom. His fingers worried the ring of latex as he watched the security car whisk Louis and Doug Brill away. So it had struck at last. More than anything, he felt relief—the way any fugitive must when finally he admits the game is up and emerges from his makeshift hiding place, hands raised in quiet, even grateful, surrender.

The snowy crunch of footsteps coming up behind made him turn around.

"Well, young man," the fire marshal told him, "looks like she's gone and burned herself out." Tracy stared at that flushed face and realized, with a flicker of disdain, that Louis was not the only one who had been called away from his liquor this evening.

"I'd definitely take your friend's suggestion," the fire marshal continued, "and get that flue cleaned out as soon as possible."

"Yes, sir," Tracy told him. "Thank you very much."

"All in a night's work. It's what we're here for." The marshal held out his right hand, and Tracy reluctantly grasped it with his own. If only he knew, Tracy thought. But the irony that might once have pleased him gave Tracy no pleasure at all, only a sick feeling in his belly. "You just call if you have any other problems," the fire marshal said. "Only—there's one thing we don't do." He leaned in close, and Tracy made himself breathe in the hot stink of the good man's breath. "We don't do cats in trees. Everybody thinks we do, but we don't. You have a cat in a tree, don't call us." With a wink he released Tracy from his grip. "You got that, now?"

"I'll try not to forget," Tracy told him, his guilty hand retreating to his pocket to worry, once again, the slick texture of the condom that betrayed him utterly, though not a soul could see.

He watched as the fire engine pulled away—it seemed ungrateful, after all, to turn his back on his rescuers. One by one the curious neighbors faded back into whatever domestic tranquillity or desperation the fire had diverted them from. Only then did Noah come forward. Had he stayed aloof out of discretion, or had he simply withdrawn from trouble once it appeared? He won't stand by me, Tracy thought with sudden, frigid certainty. If it comes to that, I'm on my own.

"Sorry about all the to-do," Tracy apologized, not exactly sure why he thought he owed the boy an apology.

"Excitement's fun, I guess," Noah told him. "Bets certainly thought so. Right, Bets?" He nodded vigorously, the beagle's impromptu spokesman.

"Noah." Tracy interrupted the comic interlude. He spoke with seriousness and urgency. "I think we'd better get you to the station now."

The boy looked at him uncomprehendingly, as if he'd suggested they take the next rocket to Orion.

"The train station," Tracy told him. "Aren't you going to New York?"

Noah continued to regard him blankly. He shook his head, said "No," emphatically drawing out the "o" as if offended by the very suggestion. "I thought I was staying with you."

"Well, I . . ." Tracy started and then stopped. "Let's go inside," he said. "It's freezing out here."

The chill, however, would not be so easily shaken off. Firemen had trampled their way through the kitchen to the living room, the mud and ice of their footprints amplifying the trail Doug Brill had first blazed. All traces of the fire—logs, coals, ashes—had been removed from the fireplace, as if it had never been. Only the acrid odor of smoke lacing the air gave any hint of the mishap.

"This is very bad," Tracy said, all too aware there were other mishaps whose traces no amount of wishing could remove. "It's exactly what I was afraid was going to happen."

"So we don't use the fireplace anymore," Noah said with a shrug.

"That's not what I meant," Tracy told him. Was it possible, he thought with alarm, that Noah could be so naive? But as if he expected their evening to resume exactly where it had left off, the boy planted himself on the sofa. With an eager yelp, Betsy joined him.

"Betsy," Tracy said sharply. "You know you're not supposed to be up there."

"Oh, she's just excited," Noah said.

"Betsy, down!" Tracy commanded, startled at the anger suddenly erupting in him.

Noah seemed startled as well. "Trace," he said in a tone of hurt and alarm. "What's wrong?"

"Noah, you don't seem to understand. I'm not talking about the fireplace. What just happened was exactly what I was afraid was going to happen. I mean, you being over here. You and me together like this. It doesn't look so good."

"Trace, you're being paranoid," Noah said with a huff of exasperation.

"I am not," Tracy insisted. "This is not a joke. If people find out—"

"It's none of their business," Noah said reasonably.

"That's not how they'll see it. You could get expelled. I could get fired. I could—"

He stopped. He had never discussed any of this on purpose. To speak such fears, it had always seemed, was to beckon them. Or was it because he had always been afraid of giving Noah ideas? The realization chilled him: what did it mean—for everything—if it turned out he didn't, couldn't, trust this boy he loved more than he was supposed to?

Only this morning a small article in the newspaper had pointed its accusing finger. A thirty-five-year-old Long Island dentist was charged with sexually abusing a fourteen-year-old boy from New Jersey. According to the *Middle Forge Record,* they had met in an on-line chat room, then in person several times. On at least four occasions the dentist had sodomized the boy. *Sodomized*: all day the stark, Old Testament word had hung heavily in his mind, like a battered body left to dangle from a tree limb. The smallest thing had betrayed them, a minor traffic accident: the boy was driving the car and the dentist, to whom the car belonged, was in the passenger seat. When the police questioned the boy, he'd talked freely about their relationship, insisting it was entirely consensual. The dentist was being held on $100,000 bond.

Thank God Noah had had the sense, earlier, to keep clear of the commotion on the front lawn. What if the day came when, unaware of the consequences, he talked freely?

Gazing down at the boy he'd sodomized, consensually, he said firmly, too little far too late, "You can't stay here tonight. I'm sorry. I'm either taking you to the train station or you're going back to your dorm room. It's too risky for you to stay here." He would do it, he thought; he would end it here. But then he remembered a terrible thing. Hadn't Arthur told him that everything had been okay till Dr. Emmerich had freaked out? He'd thought he understood that; he'd thought he could negotiate the tricky path to the clearing where everything would somehow be fine. But how, under the circumstances, *not* to freak out?

I'm dead, he thought. I'm already as dead as Jack Emmerich.

But Noah remained undaunted. And wasn't that exactly what Tracy had always loved about boys—the shining recklessness, their vigorous disregard of danger? Now that the god had him completely, it would calmly destroy him. Slowly, deliberately, as if the world were no match for his beautiful youth, Noah pulled the rugger shirt he wore over his head and tossed it to the floor. "Just relax," he coaxed, "and come on over here." He patted the sofa and half lowered his eyelids in langorous anticipation of pleasure. Tracy stood transfixed—but not by the boy's smoothly dimpled chest and ruddy nipples. Something else held the whole of his attention: a mark on Noah's upper left arm, just under his vaccination scar, not a bruise or a cut, but as if someone with a felt-tipped pen had drawn on him an intricate design.

"Noah," he said, "what's that on your arm?" He took a couple of steps closer, the better to make it out, and then he was reading the words uncomprehendingly, reading them over and over without their coalescing into any kind of sense even as some other part of his consciousness registered the design, and the words that were part of it, with such perfect clarity that the shock was already flooding his system before he could begin to say what he was seeing.

Beneath a line of black barbed wire that was twined about a series of small pink triangles, seeming in fact to grow out of the barbed wire, a tangled and grotesque extension of it, was the phrase, rendered in precise lowercase letters, *hiv positive*.

He felt his heart clench, a sensation eerily like implosion.

"I got a tattoo," he heard Noah say. The boy held out his arm to display the grim handiwork. "What do you think? I wanted to make a statement."

Tracy recovered himself just enough to utter, "What on earth kind of a statement is that? And who would agree to do that to you?"

"New York City," Noah said. "Don't you love it? There's always somebody willing to do anything you want them to."

The words chilled Tracy, opening up, as they did, the unwelcome image of Noah wandering the streets of Manhattan, not only vulnerable to but somehow welcoming whatever trouble might come his way. Had Noah been drunk when he'd let this be done to him? Had he taken drugs? What other mortal things about Noah Lathrop III didn't he know?

"I was out with my friend Chris," Noah continued, "and we both decided to get one."

"Chris," Tracy said numbly, aware he had no idea, in his selfishness, who Noah's friends might be. Certainly he had never considered them a threat, though to have overlooked that possibility, it was now clear, had been a terrible mistake.

"We decided 'HIV positive' would really get people's attention. You know, wake them up with a jolt." Noah turned his arm this way and that to admire the jolt now forever inscribed in his flesh. "In Chris's case," he said, "he really is positive. I'm not supposed to tell anybody, but I can tell you."

"Wait," Tracy said desperately, his heart squeezed to a tiny, dense knot and threatening to disappear altogether, stressed into another dimension that might well be the dimension of hell. "Are you saying there's a student at the Forge who's HIV positive? Are you making this up? Does anybody else know about this?"

"Dr. Tremper knows. I think he's the only one." He flexed his arm and the thorns, for that was what they were, rippled as if a breeze had blown through them. Like roses, the pink triangles nodded. The terrible words pulsed as if a whisper of life stirred there. "And some of the guys on my hall," he went on. "I mean, they don't *know*. It's hard to explain. They have . . . suspicions."

Tracy felt dizzy and sick. He hated the way panic could completely master him. He hated the unsteadiness in his voice as he asked, "And how do you know this Chris . . . what's his last name?"

"Tyler," Noah said. "The guys on my hall call him the Fatwa, don't ask me why. But I got to know him. He's pretty strange, and aloof, but he's got this, I don't know, this attractiveness. Sometimes I wish I was more like him."

"I wish you'd told me you were considering this move," Tracy scolded, stroking the violated flesh with his thumb, peering into the abyss of this boy's dangers. The thought that, after all these years, he'd gone and fallen in love with another Arthur Branson positively m..de him want to shout with despair.

"I *wasn't* considering it," Noah said. "At the time it just seemed like a good idea. Now, maybe . . . I don't know. Chris can be very convincing when he wants to be. Very charismatic. Haven't you ever gotten carried away and done something totally spur of the moment like that?"

"Everybody gets carried away from time to time," Tracy told the boy who had carried him away.

"I should tell you," Noah said, his voice carrying a note of warning so subtle only a lover fully attuned to the growing certainty of complete disaster could have heard it. Tracy held his breath and waited. "Not to freak you out or anything. But Chris and I fooled around some. Don't worry, it was back in the fall. I just thought you should know."

It could have been worse, Tracy thought, even as Noah forged on. "I got carried away one night. I told him about you and me. I couldn't help it."

Tracy dropped Noah's arm as if those thorns had stung him. "You didn't," he said sternly.

"I had to tell somebody. And like I said, Chris is cool. What I mean is, he's the Fatwa. Nobody talks to him, and he doesn't talk to them either. He hates this place. Dr. Tremper's the only person on campus he'll speak to. I mean, Chris practically doesn't even speak to *me* except when we see each other in New York. Up here it's like we don't even know each other. It's like, protection."

Tracy hardly even listened. He wanted to laugh out loud—perhaps in a kind of relief. Why not simply surrender to one's doom, since one was so clearly, so spectacularly, doomed? For as long as he could remember they had been partying on the sinking ship, scarcely acknowledging that with each passing day or week or month the orchestra was playing more urgently, the deck tilting more alarmingly toward the bow, the stern rising higher from the water. And who were *they*? Why, all the gay men he knew, from whose ranks he had vainly thought to escape. All his life he had wanted to make love to a boy, and now he had; didn't that mean the end was coming? A truly treacherous desire stoked its fires in him, a violence that both thrilled and surprised him. He wanted to throw Noah on the floor and fuck him till he whimpered with sweet abandon. He wanted them both to writhe and sob. He wanted them to hurt. He wanted never, never, never to have fucked him. Never to have touched him. Never even to have met him.

"I'm taking you to the station," he said brutally. Responsibly. Dishonestly. "Or you're going back to the dorm. It's up to you." He stood up abruptly from the sofa as if that might force Noah to follow.

"Trace," Noah pleaded. Obstinate, he crossed his arms over his chest and pouted. Tracy watched him with desolate pity.

"Don't freak on me," Noah warned.

And don't try to manipulate me, Tracy returned the warning, albeit in silence. "You've got to go," he said aloud. "Don't you see? At least for tonight."

But Noah didn't see. And why should he? No doubt this disappointing adult's actions seemed baffling, even vengeful. He's in love too, Tracy realized with a sorrow more searing than he could have imagined.

"I'm sorry," he said. "I love you so much, but this is just too crazy." Then, to his utter surprise, he knelt in front of Noah and in complete renunciation—or was it absolution he was seeking?—rested his forehead against the boy's bony kneecaps. His sob, involuntary, followed by bitter silent tears, surprised him painfully.

The way he often did when Betsy sat herself loyally at his feet, Noah laid his palm on the top of Tracy's head and laced his fingers through strands of hair. "You're crying," he said with a strained note of wonder.

How else to take it but as the god's blessing?

"This is the end," Tracy said, though he was no longer crying. His tears had come and gone, a brief surrender brutally stanched.

He rose to his feet, reached out his hand to help Noah off the sofa. But the boy refused to register the change. Tracy stood at a complete loss.

"This isn't what I want to happen," Noah said sullenly.

"It's not what I want to happen either," Tracy said. "We've got no choice."

But the move was still Noah's. In a single motion he curled himself up onto the sofa, fetal, withdrawn, and into his mouth, childishly, distressingly, he stuck his thumb.

"Noah, Noah," Tracy coaxed wearily. "You can't stay here. Do you hear what I'm saying?"

But Noah, if he heard, made no sign. He had shut himself away; he was inviolable. Tracy could do no more with him. Angrily he left him there on the sofa and went to the kitchen—as if anywhere in this haunted house could offer any refuge. With envy he gazed at Betsy, who had slunk away from the drama to doze peaceably on her cushion.

Remembering the practically untouched bottle of vodka in the freezer—Stolichnaya, a house-warming gift from Arthur, who liked his vodka and tonic before dinner—he reached into the otherwise empty chamber and took a dissolute swig straight from the bottle. The icy liquid burned bracingly as it went down. A comforting warmth spread through his stomach. He'd always wondered what, exactly, drove people to drink. He took another gulp and then, with a spasm of loathing, stashed the bottle back in the freezer. This was despicable, he thought, but how did one go about evicting a recalcitrant boy from one's home? He could practically read the newspaper copy: "When the police arrived they questioned the boy, who spoke freely about their relationship, insisting it was entirely consensual."

Feeling grimly resolute, he returned to the living room. Noah lay as he had left him, curled up on the sofa, though his thumb had slipped out of his mouth. He seemed to be lightly snoring, as if pretending to be asleep—or perhaps, even more perversely, he actually had fallen asleep. And the longer Tracy stood and stared at this boy he had once convinced himself in was in love with, the more likely it began to seem that the second possibility was actually the case.

• • •

The silvered image floated before him: two blond boys, perhaps eighteen, perhaps not yet, in what appeared to be some kind of rustic summer house. Both were shirtless but wearing faded, beltless jeans slung very low on slim hips. One boy had turned away; the other gazed at his brother's bare back with an expression of moody, wistful longing. Facing the camera full on, he'd thrust his left hand deep into his front pocket, while with his right he cupped his crotch, just to one side of the zipper, as if clasping his partially erect penis through the fabric of his jeans. The quality of the light in the room suggested that beyond the windows it might be raining, the two boys bored and aroused on a thundery afternoon. Their haircuts were identical: short in back, longer in front, a sunbleached blond that revealed darker roots. He could not see the face of the boy who had turned away, but his twin brother possessed, or was possessed by, a grave, heart-breaking beauty.

In the next room Noah slept beneath the blue blanket Tracy had carefully draped over his unconscious form. Though he had certainly not bought a modem for the specific purpose of tracking down the Brewer Twins, it was nonetheless to a site called the Brewer Shrine that Tracy had experimentally made his way—and with a feeling of great urgency, as if those images before his eyes came not from some ghostly electronic matrix but from the troubled depths of Noah's imagination itself, a secret key, perhaps, to the boy's volatility, his capacity for betrayal, for self-destructiveness, for sheerly wanton acts of sabotage.

The rains, in the next image, had stopped; the twins had moved outside into the sunlight. A fringe of woods loomed in the background as they faced each other. Brewer I—who could tell which was which? A predicament both uncanny and alluring—had reached out playfully or provocatively to unsnap his brother's jeans. Chin tucked down, grinning, Brewer II watched those transgressive hands, then he too joined in the horseplay, the two of them over the next several stills sliding each other out of their jeans, laughing sunnily at their crazy antics, wrestling each other into nakedness. On the ground, they grappled together in close embrace, rolling amid cool ferns, seeming both to beckon and resist each other, their penises sublimely limpid throughout, till in the final image—the luminous crucifixion capping these stations of the cross—the brothers surrendered to their mirror selves, kissed and were kissed, perfect beauties, perfect twins.

So these were the images Noah had found his way to some solitary afternoon or evening as he poked around in the dark of cyberspace looking for phantoms to inflame him. This was the double-dream of eros that had so seized his imagination, and which he had called forth that night he'd jumped Tracy in the kitchen with his hapless cry, "This is how the Brewer Twins do it!" Now Tracy knew how the Brewer Twins did it, and he felt both aroused and profoundly sad. Oh Noah, he thought. No one is like this in real life.

For that was what it came down to, finally: real life. The world as one finds it, peopled by norms and policed by laws. And what were the Brewer Twins, their beauty a kind of vacancy that could bear any amount of dreaming, if not a perfect invitation to the impossibly-dreamed and never-to-be-had, the excruciating predicament of those whose desires were still—and no doubt always would be—defined as criminal?

Had Noah jerked off to these cool, studied inducements to desire? Had he sought, in real life, to re-create this lovely fever dream, concocted by a cunning photographer and his compliant models, of perfect, infallible communion? Tracy felt a pang of unadulterated tenderness toward the impossible boy whose life he had clearly done his share, under the guise of help, to ruin.

With a resounding conviction of his own imminent ruin, he disconnected himself from the World Wide Web and turned off the computer. He had tried calling Arthur earlier, but the line was busy; Arthur was like a spider at the center of his own worldwide web, sustained by friends near and far with whom he chatted nightly. Even before he'd gotten sick, in those tumultuous weeks when he and Tracy had been together, a time Tracy remembered now as positively halcyon, Arthur's phone bills had been astronomical.

"Ah," Tracy told his friend when the other picked up after barely half a ring. "So I'm the lucky one who got through."

"And I was just going to call my mother," Arthur said. "So I'm the lucky one too. What's up, gorgeous?"

"Arthur," Tracy said, pausing a moment before taking the plunge. "I need to talk to you. I've done something pretty terrible, and you're not going to like it."

"You didn't go and get yourself a Prince Albert too, did you? Copycat."

"I'm being serious, Arthur. I've totally fucked up my life. I fell in love with one of my students. A sophomore. He's fifteen. I really thought I could manage things and be cool about it, but I didn't. It all got away from me. I've been messing around with him for the last month, and now everything's quite majestically fucked."

On the other end of the line was a long silence, broken only by a siren that rose and fell in the background—as if, by some transposition, the police were converging on Arthur instead of him.

"Oh. Well," Arthur said finally, when the siren's moan had subsided. He laughed a nervous laugh.

"I feel like I've betrayed a lot of people here," Tracy told him. "But especially you. I mean, after everything . . ."

"History *will* repeat itself," Arthur said, perhaps a bit tartly.

"You're my closest friend," Tracy confessed. "You tried to warn me, in your way. I have absolutely no excuse for what I've done. What I'm doing."

He heard Arthur inhale and then exhale heavily. His friend spoke slowly and sorrowfully. "How old am I? Thirty-two, thirty-three? I no longer keep track. But do you want to know what conclusion I've come to at my greatly advanced age? I'll put it to you simply: love is the enemy. That's my conclusion. We should all live in our little monk cells and never venture out—which, come to think of it, is what I do these days. But you know what the problem with that fine solution is? We're not made to live like that. We're born starving for love, and almost by definition it's what we can't have. Not the way we want it. At least, homosexually speaking. Maybe for straight people it's different. I wouldn't know, and frankly don't care to. So what can I tell you? If you want to know the truth—if I were you, I'd be totally unrepentant. Fuck the system. It certainly never helped me when I was fifteen and starving. Jack Emmerich and all his moral scruples can go straight to hell, which I presume they did."

Tracy was listening hard. Arthur, of course, had been on the other side of things. He hadn't had to face Tracy's particular predicament. Only Jack Emmerich had done that, and of course Jack Emmerich was the lucky one right now. Jack Emmerich was safely out of it all.

"What I'm doing," Tracy said. "It's not sustainable. You see that, don't you? My God, fifteen years old, Arthur. Anything could happen, and if it does, I'm looking at serious jail time. Years and years. Who knows? The rest of my life, maybe."

"Then keep loving him," Arthur said simply. "You have to have faith in that."

"But it's not going to work," Tracy cried.

"Probably not. But it's what you've got to do. Better to burn than to rot. Isn't that what somebody in some Conrad novel says? The instant you stop loving him because you're scared is the instant it's all over."

But Tracy had to wonder, even as he heard Arthur's words: how could he be sure that something like that hadn't in fact already happened? That fear hadn't killed whatever mad dream had once burned there?

Arthur, it seemed, knew his thoughts exactly. "Tracy," he said. "Trust me. Love him. I don't have any other advice than that."

"Except to get a good lawyer," Tracy said despondently.

"Well, it can't hurt," Arthur told him. "Just don't give Noah any reason to hate you. Then keep your fingers crossed. For a very long time."

A shiver of alarm went through him, as if he stood naked and exposed for all the world to see. "How did you know it was Noah?"

"The way you talked about him when I was up there."

"But I didn't even know myself then," Tracy countered.

"Of course you did. You knew all along. That's why you can't be regretful. You knew from the start and still couldn't resist."

"A lot of help that argument's going to be."

"It's the truth," Arthur said with certainty. "Love takes us over. It ruins us and never looks back. The Greeks had it right when they said all you could do was obey the gods' demands, no matter how terrible they might be. Jack Emmerich, bless his unlovely soul, taught me that—and you know what? It turned out to be true. Poor Louis could never understand that one thing, and it's why he's had such a respectable, meaningless life. But don't even get me started on that. The more I talk the less help I'll be. My brain sort of fades in and out these days. But remember—if you ever need a place to come to, my apartment's always here. It's so small it almost doesn't exist. They'll never think of looking for you here. There's just one thing I should tell you, though."

"I'm listening," Tracy said, though he had stopped listening some time before.

"I talked to my doctor today. He gave me some not-so-good news. Seems I've failed the Crixivan regimen. My viral load's way high, rumor has it my T cells have gone south for the winter. There are other drugs he can try and put me on, so it's not hopeless. I asked him, Should I be despondent? Tell me honestly. And he said, No, not yet. He said, I'll let you know when you should be despondent. So, I don't know why I'm telling you this except to say, it looks like we all have our little problems these days."

"I'm dying," Tracy told his handsome twin in the mirror, but his twin, implacable, only returned his gaze, a young man who did not look at all as if he were dying. The truly difficult thing, after all, was to live.

He took a deep breath and opened his bedroom door. On the sofa, the blue blanket had been folded neatly into a square. Tracy went from room to room, but the rooms of his house were all empty. What he had wished for earlier appeared to have happened. Noah had vanished.

And so, it seemed, had Betsy as well.

XVI

Walking Middle Forge's deserted streets, past heaps of snow gone gray, or standing on the otherwise empty, heavily salted Metro North platform, or boarding the night's last Grand Central–bound train, where he and Betsy sat alone in the Washington Irving car and his reflection stared moodily back at him from the black window, he thought he might have discovered, with great clarity, a truth that went something like this:

Once there was a boy who was nothing special, a boy accidents seemed to cling to like metal filings to a magnet. A boy who was, literally, a walking disaster, who'd been told that by everybody in the world who might know: his dad, his teachers, his counselors, the few friends he'd managed for a time before losing them, the various doctors who'd set his several broken bones down through the years.

He told himself:

I am the boy who set the woods on fire.

I am the boy who cannot concentrate.

I am the boy who wets his bed.

I am the boy my teacher fell in love with.

I am the boy with the tattoo.

The boy who is HIV positive.

There was a certain logic—wasn't there?—to that last part. A kind of harmony sounding out of all those different random noises. So he would have AIDS. It was like the end of a story where you reveal the truth. And the truth was, he mused as a bridge spanned the black gulf, the scattered lights of a town blazed on the other side of the wide river, the truth was that AIDS was just a different way of proclaiming yourself. He could never be someone like the Fatwa, aloof and defiant and stupendously indifferent; that took too much courage. But he could be who he was.

He could be the boy who would burn brightly.

It seemed like a relatively hopeful conclusion, given everything, to come to at one A.M. on a Friday night—or did you call it Saturday morning already? "Hey Betsy," he said to the dog curled on the floor under his seat, "is it Friday or Saturday? What is it in dog time?"

He had no idea why he'd taken her. Maybe he hadn't expected to go for anything more than a walk around the frozen lake and then bring her back. Maybe he'd just wanted to scare Tracy Parker. But what was the good of that? Tracy Parker was scared enough already, and it wasn't fear Noah had ever wanted from him. No, it was the opposite, some proud bravery his teacher had failed to deliver.

Tracy Parker, you're irrelevant, he told himself angrily. But what did that mean?

When he was ten he'd had a best friend named Liam; for an entire year they were inseparable at that Upper East Side academy he'd gone to for a couple of years before his dad, in one of his fits of mysterious disappointment, yanked him out. A short, spunky kid with a crew cut and ice-blue eyes, Liam enchanted him. He wasn't just another ten-year-old: he had a whole history to him. The summer before they met, he'd been abducted by aliens from his family's weekend house in upstate New York; little gray men had lifted him through the roof of the house and into their spaceship.

"Did they do experiments on you?"

"Yes, of course."

"Like what?"

"Like—they put their hands inside me. They touched my heart and my lungs and my kidneys."

"No way."

"Their hands went all inside my body like it was Jell-O. Honest to God, I'm not shitting you, Noah. Oh man, it was this weird feeling when they stuck their hands inside me."

Was that the first time he'd wondered, though of course he'd been way too young to know anything about it, what it would be like to get fucked? He'd look at Liam and think, Aliens put their hands inside you, and it was like something magic had happened to Liam, and he wanted it to happen to him as well. He wanted Liam's hands to go through him like he was Jell-O.

But then at the end of the school year Liam's family moved away—to Chicago, Cleveland, somewhere in the Midwest. He hadn't really taken it in till the last day of school. They were in the little fenced-in recess yard, standing by the sandbox under the sycamore tree and talking in a way that felt very serious and grown-up. He'd loved that feeling, even though there was grief in it. "I'll write you a letter," Liam told him. "And then you write me back."

Why did he do what he did? Without saying a word, he reached down into the sandbox and scooped a handful of sand and flung it in Liam's face.

So is that where we are, Trace? he asked himself, remembering with a stab of regret that innocent joke Tracy had made: like father, like son. The evil part was, it wasn't a joke. One of his dad's favorite expressions had always been "Fuck the world." And Chris Tyler had warned him, in that conspiratorial way he had: "Once you get fucked, sweetie, that's it—you won't be able to stop." So there he was: he'd wanted to get fucked ever since Liam, and now he'd done it, he was even getting used to it the way you got used to every great or terrible thing. And there was no stopping him. It was all very clear. Like father, like son—only in the mirror. Which was of course why his dad hated him so much. And of course why he'd thrown sand in Liam's eyes. And of course why Tracy Parker didn't want him anymore. Of course, of course.

But just when he thought it all made perfect sense, none of it made any sense. He was too tired, or too stupid—and it didn't matter. Deep in the bowels of Manhattan, the Metro North train was pulling into Grand Central Station. The lights flickered and went out, then came back on, and the train jerked to a halt. At this hour the subterranean hive, usually swarming, was a graveyard of stilled trains, desolate platforms. Even the high-ceilinged main hall, its walls draped for renovation, looked disquietingly vacant, as if it had been hurriedly abandoned by its inhabitants.

"Well, Betsy," Noah said aloud. "Looks like we're here. Got any bright ideas?" Instead of helping, talking to a dog only made him feel lonelier. He could go to his dad's apartment; all he had to do was scoot around the corner to Fifth and head thirty blocks north. But that was the last place he wanted to go, especially with Tracy Parker's beagle in tow. No, the person he really wanted to see, of all people, was the Fatwa.

You could hardly say they were friends. He even suspected, sometimes, that Chris didn't like him that much, that he had his own reasons for hanging around with Noah that had little to do with anything so simple as friendship. But that had always been part of Noah's fascination with Chris: his unreadable attitudes, his inscrutable choices.

When Chris had told him he was positive, his first reaction hadn't been to feel scared. It was so strange—almost like something you'd dream—how in a completely unconscious way he'd known all along the Fatwa must have AIDS.

"It's the nineties," had been his brave response. This was somebody he'd stuck his unprotected dick in. He spoke for both of them. "Anybody who doesn't use a condom—"

"It's not that simple," Chris had countered, but Noah hadn't wanted to talk about it anymore.

"It is for me," he'd said in a way that ended the conversation right there. Later it broke over him like a cold sweat. Still, he didn't blame the Fatwa. He knew what it was like to want something so much you were willing to forget the inconvenient little things that might get in the way of your having it. Be honest, he told himself: you'd have used any lie to get Tracy Parker to fuck you.

He'd written the number of Chris's doctor friend on a slip of paper, which, fortunately, hadn't disappeared from his wallet like most things did. When he dialed from a phone booth on Forty-second, the phone rang seven or eight times, then just when he expected an answering machine someone said, "Yup?"

There was something so unexpectedly intimidating in that adult voice that he almost hung up. "Is, uh, Christian Tyler there?" he asked diffidently.

"Do you know what time it is?" the voice accused.

"Sorry," he said. "It's just that I really need to talk to him."

"Well, he's not feeling well," the voice told him. "He had a headache. He went to bed early. Not that it's early anymore."

How could he help but feel deserted? He thought about mentioning that he was the guy Chris had wanted to have over for a threeway sometime, but decided not to. No telling what Chris had really told his doctor friend.

"Do you want to leave a message?" the voice asked.

"That's okay," he said. "It's nothing too urgent."

"Well," the voice said. "Next time don't call so late. Jesus. I was sound asleep. Made me jump out of my skin."

"Sorry," Noah said again. He knew it wasn't Chris's fault, but he felt a sudden spike of annoyance. Despite his bravado, he secretly wished he hadn't gotten that tattoo, that he hadn't let Chris sweep him along. Chris didn't do gym; he didn't have a roommate or shower with the others; he didn't have to remember to put a Band-Aid over the tattoo so Tim or Gary or Kevin wouldn't ask inconvenient questions. Mostly Noah was just pissed at himself for not having thought all that stuff through beforehand, and now he was stuck with it, the story of his life. But he was pissed with Tracy Parker as well.

They could have been so great together, the two of them. "Let's get out of here," Tracy had said that bright winter's morning, and just like that they'd gone, driving off into the great unknown like the adventurers they really were. It had seemed, in fact, there was nothing in the whole country that could stop them, sea to shining sea. And then that little town, the motel, the feeling that finally what he'd dreamed had come true after all: he really did have Tracy Parker all to himself. What fun that had been, what a long fantastic joyride with another warm, breathing, hugely responsive human body. And in the midst of all that, was it possible, just once or twice or so, that their souls had touched as well?

Then why, all of a sudden, had Tracy gone weird on him? I can keep a secret, he thought angrily. I keep lots of secrets if that's what you're so worried about. But he knew, with a squeamish feeling that settled around his heart, that keeping a secret wasn't anything like the real problem, because the real problem was the same problem that had been there all along. Nobody was strong enough or brave enough or smart enough. They had all these amazing chances in front of them and they just let them go. One night at Tracy's they'd stood out on the front lawn and gazed at the stars. Why they'd done that, he couldn't remember. But the night had been so cold and clear, and the stars so icy and and perfect, and Tracy had said, "There's no end to it. That's the thing I just can't get my mind around. It goes on forever and then some more. Think about it." And he did think about it, though it was spooky to contemplate. Space and space and space. And there they were, standing there, just about as infinitesmal as the universe was infinite, and why the fuck should you care about anything when your insignificance was so incredible, but the thing was you did care, in spite of it all, and that was the thing, he thought, that could really fucking break your heart.

Maybe it was just the cold, but his eyes stung as if tears had forced their way out. He wiped the back of his hand across his face and realized that, in the oblivious fury of his thinking, he and Betsy had wandered all the way to Central Park. They stood at the busy corner where the Plaza Hotel blazed its lights amid the flags of the world, each flag—this was what his dad had told him once—representing the nationality of someone who was staying at the hotel that night.

So many times he'd stood on his dad's balcony and gazed out over the mysterious park at night, but never had he ventured into its wilderness so late. A cold wind seemed to blow down from Harlem, though it was warmer here in the city than in Middle Forge, and the snow, still a foot high up there, had disappeared entirely from the city's streets. Crossing Fifty-ninth, he and Betsy entered the park's shadows. Alert, excited, she led him. He wondered, Was she was as cold as he was? Was she thirsty or hungry? Was he tormenting her, or was this all a great adventure?

He knelt for a moment to cup her wet, frigid nose in his hands. "I'm sorry, girl," he told her. "I don't know what the fuck I'm doing. And I need a friend." In the air before him his breath coalesced like the balloons in comic strips that hold the words. Betsy stared at him soulfully; she wagged her tail. In a comic book, she would have a question mark above her head. How he wished he could take back that impulse that had sent him fleeing into the night— but Tracy had turned his back on him, and he had his pride, that stupid potent Lathrop pride no amount of betrayal could wash his system clean of.

Up ahead was the little zoo, where he sometimes came on dull afternoons to watch the shy arctic fox caged with—and seemingly terrified of—the great sea lions who sent frothing waves up onto the gravel shore where the little fox waited forlornly, day after day—for what? Or the solitary monkey who regularly sat exiled from his brothers on the farthest stone in a series of stones that trailed into the pond that surrounded monkey island. From his childhood a schoolyard litany long forgotten came back to him: The freaks come out at night. In the fifth grade he and his classmates had repeated that line to one another, sniggering as if they knew what it meant, and they *had* known what it meant. It had been a warning they voiced to one another: stay away from that shit. Stay away from lonely streets. Don't go into the park after dark. Once a freak puts his hands on you you'll never stop. It was the same litany he heard in his dorm room night after night as Tim and Kevin and especially Gary Marks tried to keep the Fatwa inside themselves at bay.

Here and there a figure, bandaged from head to toe in filthy blankets or folded cardboard, lay on a bench, sometimes under a bench, those zombie creatures that seemed to wash up on New York sidewalks from out of nowhere. He picked his way among them carefully, the homeless, remembering how he'd thought, when he slipped into bed with Tracy New Year's Eve—*Finally!* As if he really had arrived somewhere at last, a home, a refuge. But there was no *finally*—that's what he was finding out; you got to a place you really wanted to be, and no sooner were you there than you had to move on.

So he was moving on, even if he had no idea where he was going.

Like gray whales, huge boulders broke the undulating lawn. On this stone or that, if not here then elsewhere, some other woods, he had lain in the warm sun waiting for someone to come. For Liam to put his hands inside him. For a man like Tracy Parker to love him.

It hadn't happened. Not even after all those years it hadn't happened. The Tracy Parker he'd thought would fold him close and hold him tight turned out to be as skittish as those bright blue dragonflies that had danced around him as he lay waiting.

In all the low places of the park, water gathered into frozen lakes and ponds. Past the shuttered boathouse, its boats in storage for the winter, he entered wilder terrain. Here brush had been allowed to grow up, fallen trees had not been removed. From the asphalt path that climbed steeply up a hill, worn dirt trails led off in every direction. Lampposts grew scarcer; on all sides a tangle of shadows thronged. It was wilderness untouched, the secret heart of the city that the wall of bright towers to the south and east and west was meant to contain.

Out of the shadows a man approached. He stopped several paces away and stood looking hungrily at Noah, as if not quite trusting his eyes. All he sees is a boy, Noah told himself. That's all I am to him, a boy. And he felt the cruel, merciless power of that simple fact.

I don't have to do any more than look at you and you're mine, he thought exultantly. Had he known that about Tracy Parker from the beginning? Had he merely been flexing his muscles when he brought his teacher to his knees?

But no, he cried to himself, it had been love. Tracy Parker had been his first and only love ever since he walked into English II that sweltering day in September and flashed his melting smile—for Noah alone, or so it had seemed, incredibly, at the time.

The man's tone was edgy, sarcastic. "So what's a sweet twink like you doing, wandering around a place like this? And what's with the beagle? Or am I just way off the mark here?"

"I don't know about the dog," Noah mumbled, hating now that he'd been spoken to. He felt stupid, trailing Betsy on her leash.

The man looked him up and down. He wasn't that old—only a little older, probably, than Tracy Parker. Underneath his black wool overcoat he wore a business suit, but he seemed at the same time disheveled, hectic, as if he'd been crying, or drunk. His face was chiseled and, in its way, handsome, a face that could sell clothes or liquor in a magazine. "Don't tell me you trained her to sniff the johns out," the man said, seeming to find it very funny. "Don't tell me you bring your sex-sniffing dog to the Ramble. That beats all. That's just fucking great."

"Forget about the dog," Noah said.

It sent the man off into another prolonged fit of laughing.

"Hey, I'm serious," Noah told him.

"About what?"

But he didn't know. He shrugged. He hadn't come here to meet some stranger. He'd come here because—well, he had no reason except the panic he felt at the thought that he was, at the moment, totally alone, and if this man, who just might be crazy, decided to kill him he'd vanish off the face of the earth. It happened in New York all the time, kids sawed up, their body parts dumped in the East River or kept in freezers in the apartments of lonely lunatic men.

But what if this stranger with the brittle laugh wasn't crazy? What if he was just another Tracy Parker who had the good luck to live in a great anonymous city where nobody scrutinized your every move, where nobody cared what you did?

"Want to see something?" Noah said to the man who, even in his overcoat, looked like he was freezing. "I got something to show you."

With a peremptory nod, he motioned for the man to follow him. He walked toward a street lamp that cast its circle of light on the path, but when he looked back his catch had not moved. The man shook his head. He pointed toward the bushes, the shadows. Noah stood firm. "Sit," he commanded Betsy, and she sat, loyally looking up at him, content like no one else in the world to be by his side. Noah took off his jacket and laid it on the bench. Then he pushed up the sleeve of his shirt as far as it would go.

"Come here," he coaxed. "Take a look."

Curiosity had gotten the better of his prey. The man joined him, squinting at the arm he offered for inspection.

"There," Noah said, pointing to the tattoo.

The man reached out to steady Noah's arm for a better look. "So?" he said at last, holding his arm in an icy grip. "Do you think I care? I'm a wolf. I'll do anything. I'll fuck your brains out if that's what you want. I'll come inside you if that's what turns you on. How about it?"

He hadn't seen the wolf, but now he glimpsed the grinning teeth, the hunger rooted deep in the bone. This wasn't Tracy Parker. It wasn't even his dad.

"No," Noah cried out, twisting his arm free of the man's death grip. "Leave me alone."

The man laughed and laughed. Noah ran. Icy air tore at his throat, his lungs. His eyes stung. The pavement was hard and unyielding beneath the cold soles of his feet. He ran, and Betsy should have been running too, running by his side, her leash trailing her, but she wasn't; she was running but in another direction, set free in this forest in the middle of the city, wild with her own excitement or fear. He stopped, breathing hard, and looked around. She was nowhere. "Betsy!" he shouted, firm and commanding, but there was nothing. "Betsy!" he cried again, and then again, his voice rising in panic.

"Hey!" the man shouted. He had not moved; he stood, no longer terrible, a small, lit figure where the path curved into the dark. "Your dog went that way," he shouted and pointed.

Forsaking the path, Noah cut through the bushes. Bare branches whipped at his face. The thick rope of a root caught his foot. "Betsy!" he cried. "Here, Betsy! Come here. Please."

But by now he himself was lost, and she could be anywhere. Occasionally, at the Forge, he'd let her off the leash so she could run, and she'd taken off like a shot. The first time it happened—that first weekend he'd house-sat for Tracy—he'd spent several anxious minutes before she came loping back with a silly, satisfied grin on her beagly face. She was good about coming back. If he hadn't lost his head, if he'd just stayed where he was, she'd be at his side by now, panting excitedly, nuzzling his calves with his nose. But he'd made a bad situation even worse. Now there was nowhere to come back to. He doubled back as best he could, reemerging onto a path, but was it the same one? He couldn't tell. He hadn't noticed that figure sleeping in the cardboard box before. And the man with the laugh, the wolf who wanted him, had either walked on or simply vanished.

His coat lay where he had left it on the bench. So this *was* the place. Wrapping himself in its meager warmth, he sat down to wait. It seemed impossible, what had just happened, but there was always, he'd learned, that sense of disbelief, as if you could return to an instant before the fire leaped out of control or you lost your footing and began to fall. He'd spent a life trying desperately to burrow into those moments, to avert the consequences, but always it was already too late for that, already the accident had begun to happen and he was inescapably inside it.

How long did he sit there? From Manhattan's upper reaches came the steady, echoing roar of traffic, hardly diminished even now. New York was never, ever quiet. He hated that; loved the stillness of the Forge's night where only legitimate creatures stirred in the forest. He could barely feel his toes inside his boots, the tip of his nose, his cheeks. He was so cold the breath from his lungs no longer condensed in the air before him. Slowly he was turning to ice. They would find him frozen solid. With a pickax they'd shatter him to bits, disperse his body at random. They, whoever they were.

A policeman—could it be?—was walking his way. He found that very surprising. Almost ludicrous, in fact. A policeman in the middle of the night.

He spoke first, before the officer was even upon him.

"Have you seen my dog?" he said. "I lost my dog."

The policeman frowned. In the dark, his uniform looked pitch black. He was a husky young man with a mustache. Like any carpenter or telephone repairman, he wore the tools of his trade heavily on his belt. One hand clasped the knob of his nightstick, the other a radio.

"It's awfully late for you to be out like this, don't you think?"

"My dog ran away," Noah said.

"You got some ID on you?"

Noah nodded. He pulled his wallet from his pocket and found his Forge School student ID. While the policeman studied the ID, Noah picked up the scrap of paper that had fluttered from his wallet: the Fatwa's phone number. If only, he thought. But there were too many if-onlys. If only he had never met Tracy Parker, if only he'd never come to the Forge in the first place, if only he'd never been born.

"Where are you supposed to be right now, Noah? It's three o'clock in the morning, you know."

He hadn't known, and somehow felt disappointed it wasn't later. He'd figured it should be near dawn. His vigil, far from being nearly over, was only beginning.

"I live right up on Fifth. In the seventies. My dad's Noah Lathrop, if that means anything to you."

"Actually," said the policeman, "it doesn't. Now tell me again what you're doing here."

"I came down here to walk my dog and she ran away. Like I told you. I'm waiting for her to come back." Noah hated policemen; he hated everything they stood for—everything that had scared Tracy off from him.

"What kind of dog?" the policeman asked.

"Just a beagle. A little beagle."

"And how long you been waiting here?"

"I don't know. A while."

The policeman made a grimace. He wrote in his notebook. "I don't like the looks of this," he ventured. "I don't see any evidence of a dog around here. Was she on a leash?"

Noah nodded bleakly. "She ran off with the leash still on."

"Does she have a collar? Any ID?"

Again Noah nodded, though he wasn't one hundred percent sure about the ID. There had been a couple of metal tags jingling from Betsy's collar but he'd never looked at them; just one more thing he should have done. Like a sharp pain the fact that she was lost because of him bore in on him.

"This is not a good place for you to be at this hour," said the policeman as he handed back Noah's ID card. "I'm going to have to ask you to go on home. Your parents must be worried. But I'll tell you what. I'll keep an eye out. Then, first thing tomorrow, come back and put some signs up. A beagle. That shouldn't be too hard to find. She'll turn up. Why don't you tell your doorman to be on the lookout? Dogs're smarter than you might think. Sometimes they know to head back to their owner's building. We'll call you if we find anything. Okay? I just don't want you sitting here any longer. You look like you're freezing."

"I'm going to sit here just a little longer and wait," Noah said.

"No," the policeman told him, "no, you're not. You're going to get yourself home. Now I don't want to see you out here again. Understand? You'll be in trouble if I find you still out here."

What could he do? Certainly not curl up on the bench in resistance. That trick wouldn't work out here. He thought about telling the cop he'd set a fire in the woods. On purpose. Arson. That he'd tried to burn his dad's house down. Or had he? Did he only wish he had had the courage to have done that? It sure would have made Noah Senior sit up and take note.

"Please find my dog," he said. "Her name's Betsy." Saying her name made hot tears stream from his eyes.

With a heavy, heavy heart he stepped uneasily from the elevator into the apartment. Dawn's bleary light illuminated the aftermath of a long evening. Half-empty wineglasses and overflowing ashtrays decorated various flat surfaces. The big mirror had been taken down and laid across the coffee table. Catching his reflection through smears of white powder, he was shocked by how tired and red-eyed he looked.

He hadn't come straight home as he'd promised the cop. Leaving the park, he'd wandered till he found a diner on Lexington where he could warm up and refuel with a cup of acid, unconsoling coffee; then he'd resumed his search, this time on city streets, though he knew if Betsy had left the park she'd be dead by now, run down as she blithely crossed the street.

Betsy, he called out inwardly, as if imploring the row of serene antique Buddhas that gazed at him from their perches on the wall. But of course there was no answer. The Buddhas, who knew where Betsy was, who knew everything and weren't telling, smiled their enigmatic smiles.

He needed desperately to eat; he would make himself breakfast. He would crash in his bed for a few hours. Then he would try to figure out what to do next.

And who knew? Maybe the cop was right, maybe Betsy would turn up at his dad's building, only he suddenly realized, with a sick feeling, that that was impossible; she'd never been to his dad's building. He was so stupid, so stupid. He didn't deserve to live.

In the kitchen, the green marble countertop was a thicket of empty wine and Stolichnaya bottles. A bowl holding traces of inky Beluga floated in a larger bowl of melted ice. Caviar and cocaine and Stoli. His dad must have been in a pretty good mood. Once long ago—he was five or six—his mom had come into his bedroom and awakened him from sleep. "Come," she'd said, and taken him by the hand. A reception was under way. There were dozens of adults standing in groups, talking and laughing and, as always, drinking. On the dining room table a great crystalline bird had alighted. "A firebird," his mom whispered, "carved out of ice." He'd never beheld anything so beautiful. Its glassy neck arched; its translucent wings were poised for magnificent flight. A black mound of beady caviar filled the hollow in its back, and he was allowed a taste from a tiny spoon.

In the morning it was gone—and not too many months later, his mother as well.

The refrigerator held bacon, eggs, orange juice, the kind of breakfast his dad loved. Missing Tracy Parker acutely, Noah searched the cabinets for oatmeal, granola, but found only a box of Lucky Charms left over, presumably, from the summer—before Tracy Parker, when he'd actually eaten such rubbish. But now Lucky Charms, with all their evil sugar, would just have to do. He had just begun to pour the cereal into a bowl when he suddenly sensed he was being watched.

His father stood, arms crossed, in the doorway. He wore a white bathrobe open down his broad, furry chest. His face was dark with stubble.

"You don't just walk in," Noah Senior said in the flat, neutral tone Noah most feared. "What the fuck are you doing?"

"Having breakfast," Noah said.

"I don't mean that," his dad told him.

He hadn't planned what he was going to say; he'd intended to sleep and then work something out. He didn't have the presence of mind, as he so often did, to formulate a reasonable lie.

"I'm in a lot of trouble," he blurted out.

Noah Senior said nothing. He walked over to the refrigerator and pulled out a bottle of beer, popped the cap off with an opener, then took a long, long swallow.

"I lost my teacher's dog," Noah said.

Noah Senior took the bottle from his lips and looked at him blankly.

"I'm fucked," Noah went on. "I got mad about some stuff. I sort of lost my head. I thought I had to get away from all the shit up at school, so Betsy and I hopped a train down here—"

"Who the fuck is Betsy?" his dad asked in that same flat voice. He had the terrible post-coke look in his eyes, half wild, half dead. A couple of beers in the morning usually worked wonders for him.

"Tracy Parker's dog," Noah said.

"She 'came down' with you," his dad said mercilessly. Coke, or at least its aftereffects, made him hyperprecise.

"I mean, I *brought* her down," Noah corrected himself. "I made her come with me. And then, I don't know. She was on a leash and, I don't know, she just got loose and ran away. I looked everywhere. I couldn't find her. It was in Central Park. I don't know what to do."

He refused to cry in front of his dad, but a tear nonetheless spilled down his cheek.

Noah Senior paid no heed. With another long swig he finished his beer. "When did all this happen?"

"Right now. I mean, like, two or three hours ago."

Noah Senior set his empty beer bottle down carefully on the counter. He was never hungover the next morning, but he could be very careful in his movements for a few hours.

"What on earth were you doing in Central Park?"

"Like I said, I don't know," Noah told him, with at least a degree of candor.

"Noah," said his dad. "What do you mean you don't know? What the hell is really going on with you?"

As if to betray him with the truth, Noah's hungry stomach growled, a long low rumble that filled the silence.

"I just don't know what's going on," he repeated clumsily. "I'm starving, Dad. Can I eat?"

"Talk to me," Noah Senior commanded sharply. "I don't want bullshit. I don't have time for it. Tell me the truth here."

Could he honestly say he didn't have a clue what the truth was, or even where the lies should begin? He occurred to him that, if he wanted, he could hurt Tracy Parker. He could destroy him. Make all hell break loose.

"There's this teacher," he said as his dad reached into the fridge for another beer.

"This had better not be another Mr. Brookner story," Noah Senior said ominously.

"No," he said in hasty retreat. "It's nothing like that." But the accusation hit him like a body blow. It *was* the Mr. Brookner story all over again, wasn't it? How could he have failed to realize such a simple, obvious thing? He had no power over Tracy Parker at all. Whatever power he had had already been used up a long time ago. "If I could just start over somewhere new," he'd told his counselor. And moving to a new school actually had made a difference for a while. He'd worked very hard to fit in, so hard that he'd managed to convince himself he'd never written those stories about his teacher, that his stupid spying roommate had never found them, that Mr. Brookner had never had to see any of those embarrassing fantasies scrawled in a script he was already quite familiar with. He had really come to believe, after a year and a half, that the boy who had gotten caught red-handed in a scandal so minor but so personally devastating that he still burned to think of it—that that boy was someone completely unrelated to Noah Lathrop III.

"Then what is it about this teacher?" Noah Senior drilled him.

"I was friends with him, Dad. He was helping me. I think I fucked everything up."

"Helping you, how?"

"With everything. My schoolwork. My self-esteem." Once again his stomach complained, a sound like a low moan. For a single moment there he had wanted revenge, but now, thwarted, a strange loyalty kicked in. Whatever happened, he wasn't going to let Tracy Parker take the shit when it had all been *his* fault they were in this mess in the first place. He wasn't going to be the little faggot, he had told himself; he wasn't going to write stupid sex stories like that anymore. He was going to squelch those ghosts dead away.

Now here he was all over again.

"I don't like this, Noah. You're not telling me everything."

"I *am*," Noah pleaded. "I took Tracy Parker's dog and the dog ran away. Aren't you listening to me?"

Noah Senior reached in the fridge and took out a third beer. "I don't have time for this," he said disgustedly. "When am I going to stop picking up the pieces for you, Noah? I'm sick of picking up the pieces."

It left Noah with nothing to say.

"You want to know what I think sometimes?" his dad went on, even as Noah struggled to consider the possibility that what his dad said was true, that despite everything he thought, he actually did rely on his dad again and again to do exactly that: to pick up the pieces of whatever it was he'd broken this time. "I think you're your mother's fucking revenge on me," Noah Senior said fiercely. "Everything she did was a royal fuckup. Sound familiar? And she never could understand why somebody like me didn't have the time for that. But I'll tell you why I didn't. I know I have my faults. My worst? I'm impatient. I'm ruthless in the pursuit of my goals. I do not brook fools or idiots. See, I don't think people like you or your mother understand me at all. I don't think you've ever taken the trouble to. You're too busy living off the things you claim to despise about me. I work hard to make the money I've made. I don't sit around on my ass. I work hard and I play hard, and I do not apologize. Have you ever seen me hungover? Even once?

"You don't know half the things I do. You can't even seem to fucking remember the name of the country I have perhaps unwisely invested a quarter of my capital in. You don't bother to know that I am not just the capitalist exploiter it's so convenient for you to see me as. Who do you think is paying for the restoration of the Golden Mosque? Who donates thousands of dollars in medical supplies to the children's hospital in Bukhara? Who supports practically a harem of ex-wives and girlfriends? I do those things." He jabbed himself in the breastbone with his pointer finger and continued to jab. "Who has sent you to the best schools? Paid for the best fucking therapists on the block? Who took you to London and you spent the whole time sitting in the hotel moping? Like I said, I'm a busy man and an impatient man. I'm a haunted man, Noah. The Lathrops are not long-lived. Maybe you should think about that. We drop dead around age sixty. I don't have time in my life to put up with bullshit, my own or anyone else's. And neither should you."

His dad spoke passionately but not angrily. By the end his voice was calm, even mild. "Some people matter, Noah, and other people don't. I think, in this life, you choose whether you matter or not, and it's up to you and you alone. I know you think I'm a hard man. Well, guess what, Noah: it's a hard world. It's a world that knocks you down and then kicks you a couple times when you're down for good measure, and as soon as you pull yourself back up, be prepared for one thing: The world can't wait to kick your teeth in all over again."

He'd finished his third beer, and set the bottle on the counter beside the two other empties. He took a deep, defiant breath. After an uncompromising night, Noah Senior was up and running.

"Now," he said. "I'll shower and put on some clothes. We'll rouse Gunila and A. J.—you didn't peek in your room, by any chance? I think you'll find our friend passed out on your bed. The world was spinning a little fast last night. You make yourself some breakfast before that stomach of yours declares civil war. Then let's go find that fucking dog. What's its name? Betsy? What a stupid fucking-ass name for a dog."

· · ·

It was the last thing he'd expected: that his dad would marshal the troops like this on a frigid Saturday morning to rescue his ass once again. But then he grudgingly had to admit that his dad had a flair for the unexpected.

"If you think she's still in the park, then the park's where we look," said the perfectly sober man. "We'll start where you lost her."

There was of course no reason for Betsy to stay in the park; it was only Noah's hunch. But she knew nothing of cities, he reasoned, only the bucolic grounds of the Forge School, and so he hoped she would stick with what she knew. What he knew, on the other hand, and with a dark clot in his heart, was what an adventurous little dog she was, capable of anything.

With some trepidation he steered them as best he could to the Ramble. If his dad was aware of the significance of a boy—or anyone else—wandering that territory alone after dark, he made no mention of it. But then maybe he already knew everything and no longer cared. Maybe, ever since Mr. Brookner, he had known, and Noah, the little faggot, had only been pretending to himself there too.

"If I see one beagle I'll see a pack," A. J. announced. He carried a silver flask of bourbon to ward off the morning's demons. Gunila, as always, seemed icily imperturbable. As far as Noah could tell, a firebird of ice herself, she did not begrudge his dad's nocturnal excesses, but neither did she partake beyond her capacity—probably not a bad sign for marriage number three. The Stolichnaya Spokesperson to the World was not one to let herself get too swept away by anything, even Noah Benjamin Lathrop II.

The beauty of women never, as a rule, haunted Noah, but this morning Gunila, dressed in tight black ski pants and black leather jacket against which her platinum hair shown dazzlingly, seemed strangely possessed of an uncomplicated, straightforward beauty. Not for the first time he found himself wildly desiring to desire her. What was there, after all, for somebody like him? He could go straight—fat chance, ha ha—he could heroically fall in love with the man of his dreams, only to be shunted aside at the first sign of inconvenience; he could get AIDS and leave early through that door. What was he supposed to do? Proclaim to Gary and Tim and Kevin and the rest of the Forge's pathetic band, "Hey, you know the Fatwa? Well, I'm a Fatwa too. And I limbo dance. So watch out"?

Under the metallic gray morning sky halfheartedly spitting snow, the park showed an altogether different aspect. Gone was the dark side he had so disastrously courted. Joggers were out, their uniforms flashing incandescent. Luckier people than he leisurely walked their dogs on a leash, and he went up to them disconsolately to ask had they seen a stray beagle, had such a creature come nosing around their own dogs seeking comfort or play? But no one had seen a thing. Stalwart on their benches or reclusive in the underbrush, the homeless, the drunk, the derelict, slept on, oblivious. From time to time his dad stopped to shake one of them awake, wave a ten-dollar bill for encouragement, but again, no one had seen a thing.

They trooped up the park as far as the museum and then back down, fanning out and regrouping like those flocks of pigeons that flew off in a great agitation at their approach only to settle back in once they had passed.

That he had done what he had done to Betsy was unforgivable. He had not, had not, had *not*, he told himself, done it out of malice or ill will. He had done it like he did everything in life: because he was addle-brained, because he hadn't been taking his Ritalin, because he got frustrated so easily, upset when he didn't get his way, because even under the best of circumstances he was not to be trusted.

At every trafficked cross street his eyes squeamishly searched the gutters. Once, a brown form lying in the middle of Seventy-second, where it cut through the park south of the lake, made his heart stop, but when he ventured closer it turned out to be nothing more than a discarded half-full garbage bag.

"Betsy, Betsy," echoed the call in A. J.'s capacious South Carolina slur and Gunila's Swedish lilt, voices without the audible anxiety of his own. His dad cupped his hands together and shouted with an authority sure to make every Betsy within range, whether animal or human, come running.

But it was all to no avail, and by midmorning, tired and cold and disheartened, they decided to call off the search.

XVII

Nothing, it seemed, was too cruel or disheartening for the mellifluous newsreader from the BBC. "In Sarajevo today," he reported urbanely, "the exodus of Serbs from their homes continued, despite UN assurances that they would be treated fairly after the Muslim-dominated government takes control. Caravans of trucks and overloaded automobiles clog the icy roads from Vogosca to Pale. Some Serbs have reportedly vandalized or set fire to their homes before beginning the trek—" Switching off the little short-wave radio, a Christmas gift from Claire, Louis resumed his fastidious slicing of a kiwi. He supposed the news should please him. The tide had turned; now the Serbs, who had caused so much suffering, were themselves suffering. But it gave him no pleasure. Indeed, it only confirmed his secret fear: Life was war, nothing more or less. Morality was a farce, compassion a luxury. The less-powerful struggled to overthrow the more-powerful; the more-powerful fought desperately to cling to what was theirs.

He had been thinking, both last night and this morning, about Jack Emmerich—thoughts no doubt provoked by the sight of Noah Lathrop standing in the snow, holding Tracy Parker's little beagle on its leash as angry sparks darted from the chimney of Jack's old house. So he had been lied to. Tracy Parker had betrayed him, as Jack Emmerich had betrayed him. Once again everything came together uncannily, as if one's secret fears proved to be the very structure of the world itself, its pattern, its inevitability.

Was one drawn to such recurrences, or did one, in one's way, engineer them? A midwinter afternoon, luminous with a sudden snow flurry bursting from the peach-colored sky; Main Street, outside the Heidelberg; the head-master, a charismatic visionary to whom one had devoted oneself with un-flagging allegiance for twenty years; a student whom one knew as well, knew quite well, in fact, having spent any number of evenings in his company during the last six months, enchanted by Wagner, conversation, even—in those long ago, less strict days—a sip of wine. One presumed headmaster and student had been enjoying a late lunch off campus, hardly a sin but nonetheless an exception; by sheer accident one had emerged from the stationer's store across the street, unseen but nonetheless seeing an affectionate touch that lingered half an instant too long and could easily have been nothing more than a trick of the changeable light. But instinctively, against all reason, one suddenly knew. And then a month later a distraught Arthur Branson was in one's office and everything—the grand adventure gone mad, the threats and coercion, a great man unhinged by passion's darker currents—spilled into plain view, never again to be unseen.

Had Jack been guilty of such abuse before? There had always been stray rumors about goings-on at the farm, easily discounted at the time as envy, overheated imaginings—absurd stuff, really. He could see now how, in a sense, all Jack's affections had been dubious, whether for Stefan George and other things German, or for Arthur Branson, or all the sundry infatuations in between. Jack had been a master of many things great and small. He had been superb. Only with Arthur something had gone terribly wrong, and to this day Louis could still not account for it, except that in such relationships it was surely inevitable, was it not, that something—even everything—go terribly wrong?

Claire's egg, tumbling in its turbulent bath, boiled briskly. The tea steeped. Spring-loaded, the toast popped up in the toaster. Louis dropped the thin wafers of kiwi into the fruit bowl, added a spoonful of brandy, then another for good measure. Pouring himself a finger's width in a juice glass, he drank it down.

Last night's confirmation of all his suspicions had unnerved him. And if that was not enough, he'd dreamed once again that strange dream of a large snow-white dog, and though the creature did not physically resemble Lux, or resembled him only insofar as a supple wolf might resemble an aged and arthritic German shepherd, Louis knew that it was he. Lost in a snowstorm, Louis stumbled about in a cathedral-like forest of conifers reminiscent of nothing so much as those Wagnerian stands of fir he and Claire used to hike through in the Black Forest. Then, unexpectedly, he came to a clearing where there was no snow. Wildflowers bloomed. The magnificent snow-white spirit dog, Lux and not Lux, sat calmly on its haunches and waited patiently for him.

He had awakened in a sweat, his heart thumping like a dog's friendly tail. An omen, he had thought edgily, he who did not believe in omens. Perhaps it meant that soon he would die. That Lux was beckoning him to the other side.

But that was ridiculous. He'd been to the doctor only weeks ago. His heart was fine, his constitution hardy. His outlook on life—well, they had not discussed that particular malady.

In the dream, the creature's eyes, Lux's eyes, had shown like gold.

On Claire's tray Louis set her bowl of macédoine, her boiled egg, her toast, her tea. What caused him, at that moment, to glance out the window? His heart leaped in fear and disbelief; he could not have been more alarmed had he glimpsed a resurrected Lux waiting patiently for him on the front lawn. He glanced at the clock. Ten after seven on a Saturday morning, and Tracy Parker was walking up the neatly plowed drive toward his door.

Caught in the headlights of what was almost certainly an approaching crash, he stood motionless and waited for the sound of Tracy's knock. When it came, a series of crisp assured raps, he resisted the urge to fling the door open at once and meet the moment head-on. He cleared his throat, counted to fifteen—at last it was going to happen, the confrontation he had so shamefully avoided—and then, with great deliberation, he unlocked and opened the door.

"Tracy," he said in a voice as studiously civil, he hoped, as that of the newsreader for the BBC. "At this early hour. Is everything all right?"

"I'm really sorry to bother you," Tracy apologized. He looked awful: unshaven, red-eyed, his radiance gone.

"Not at all," Louis told him. "Won't you come in?"

"I will," Tracy said. "I think we need to talk."

Something terrible had happened, Louis knew at once—something beyond the ordinary distress of being caught out in a lie. For a mad instant he considered offering his guest a brandy. But Tracy was wasting no time; without hesitation he launched into sentences he must have rehearsed on his way over, speaking rapidly as if afraid that, given half a chance, he might reconsider.

"You know I've been lying to you," he said. "I'm not going to insult you by pretending you don't know what's going on."

Louis breathed an inward sigh of relief. If Tracy intended to crash in flames, at least he could be heroic about it. "I assume you mean that student," he told Tracy, all at once surprised to discover he felt such unreasoning enmity toward Noah Lathrop that he could not even bring himself to say the name aloud. If he was angry with Tracy for having allowed himself to be ensnared, he was furious with Noah Lathrop for having taken advantage of his teacher's good nature, his generosity, his all-too-human weakness.

For many years he had not been able to say Arthur Branson's name aloud.

"That student," Tracy said with a nervous laugh.

"Well then," Louis told him ruthlessly. "Be frank with me."

"We've been having a relationship," Tracy admitted.

It was a disappointing word.

"Sexual?" Louis probed.

"Intimate," Tracy said with an air of wonderment. "Loving. Yes. Sexual. Everything. You've suspected that, haven't you?"

"I suspected," Louis said. "I didn't know." Strange how he had longed for this moment as much as he had feared it. A dreadful excitement stirred in him. For years he had kept a sheaf of newspaper articles, a priest here, a high school teacher there, sad relics of human disaster, reminders of what might happen should one ever dream of turning poetic phantoms into reality. He felt a certain awe that Tracy had actually dared. That he had touched with the hands of love a living boy. That he was here to tell about it.

"And I'm afraid that's not even the worst of it, Louis," Tracy went on. "Now it's all gone and blown sky high. I mean, I thought I could . . . I don't know, contain things. But they got away from me. It's out of my control."

Louis longed desperately for that drink. He wanted to toast mad idealism, forbidden desires, the dreams that drove one to criminal acts. He wanted, quite starkly, oblivion.

"Last night," Tracy said, "after all the fire trucks left, and you left, well, it was so clear to me how we couldn't go on. The secrecy and everything. The sneaking around. I tried to tell Noah that. Explain to him how a bad idea from the start was just getting worse and worse."

He stopped, agitated, and Louis seized the chance. "Here," he said, moving with resolve to the cabinet and taking down the bottle. He poured a generous dose into two glasses and handed one to his suffering friend.

"No," Tracy said. "None for me." But he took the glass nonetheless, even as he spoke, and tilted it back in a single swallow. "I guess it can't hurt," he said miserably. "Do you mind if I sit down?"

"Please," Louis told him, sitting as well and gratefully nursing his own share of the brandy's warm comfort.

Tracy ran his hands through his hair, the very image of desolation—nothing less, perhaps, than the wandering figure from *Die Winterreise*. "Noah's a hugely scrambled kid," he continued. "Volatile. I'm afraid he didn't take what I was saying very well. He got upset. I wasn't trying to hurt him or make him angry, just explain to him how impossible everything was. All the reasons. And then he just left. He stormed out. I presume he went to New York. But this is the bad part." He leaped to his feet and paced the kitchen like a prisoner in a cage. His voice broke in distress. "He took Betsy with him."

"Your dog?" Louis asked, suppressing a desperate laugh at this unexpected element of farce.

"I don't know what it means," Tracy said. "At first I thought it meant he'd just gone out for a little, you know, a walk around the lake to cool off, something like that, but then he never came back. I checked his dorm—he's not there. And anyway, he'd signed out to go to New York for the weekend.

See, that was our cover. He'd sign out to go home, but then he'd spend the weekend at my place. Not good. Sordid, in fact."

"And how long has this been going on?" Louis asked.

"Since New Year's," Tracy admitted.

So Noah had been up here New Year's after all, while the headmaster was off neglecting the helm in sunny Arizona. Louis recognized, however, a thrill of satisfaction. He had known since November; he had known their secret even before they themselves did. But hard on the heels of that bitter satisfaction, squeamishness overtook him. Could it be that he had wished exactly this upon the two of them? This passion, this suffering. Had he not wished it, in his way, upon himself as well?

"I really thought I could help him out," Tracy continued remorsefully. "I really did what I thought was best at the time. But I guess I was confused. I guess what I've learned is that I can't trust myself to make the right decision. Because I really thought I had. And then when I realized I was wrong, that the whole thing was wrong, was impossible—then I was in it and I couldn't find a way out. I tried. It's not easy."

But Louis was no longer listening. With stinging clarity he all at once saw something that had completely eluded him, a small matter, really, but devastating in its way. The enmity he felt toward Noah Lathrop—it was nothing other than jealousy. There had been no other reason at all for him to dislike the boy. Why had he not seen that, when it now seemed so excruciatingly obvious? He'd been jealous of Noah Lathrop the same way he'd been jealous of Arthur Branson. The same way he'd once been jealous—did he dare even admit it?—of Libby Davis. Of all those innocent souls, in fact, whom he had perceived as taking from him what he could never admit to himself that he might have wanted, in the first place, to have.

"He seemed very special to me," Tracy went on. "Very damaged but very gifted. The quintessential Forge School student, right? I thought I could rescue him. Isn't that what we all feel? I was in love with the idea of being able to help him. I think my own loneliness got the better of me."

Bleakly Louis understood how little he had ever meant in Tracy's scheme of things. He had loved Tracy. That was the strangest thing of all. He had loved him but could only imagine that love, could only enter its dream, inside the black notebook—a darkened room in an ancient summer house in the mountains where two figures, Tracy and Noah, Tracy and Arthur and Jack and Bobby Wainmark and Christian Tyler and who else besides struggled wordlessly together on a big four-poster bed while the rain rained and Schubert played, and it was strange: listening to Tracy's litany of misery, he found himself secretly disappointed in this young man who, having dared make of his own errant dreaming a reality, now grew so quickly frightened of the beautiful disaster he had created for himself. Such love as this, tragic, criminal, impossible, a dream meant only to be dreamed and never, never to be lived, such love, once undertaken in the flesh, should burn more brightly, should march proudly toward its own magnificent extinction, not quiver in fear at the very taboos it had sought to break asunder.

Perhaps he only expected of Tracy exactly that defiant courage he himself had always lacked. In the shadow-world of the dead, was Jack Emmerich laughing even now, as he had perhaps laughed that rainy evening as he aimed his car straight ahead on a road that curved left?

Tracy's voice brought him back. "I'm prepared to resign from the school," he said defeatedly. "I guess that's what I came here this morning to do. It's all in his hands, you know. Unlawful sexual activity with a minor. Third-degree sodomy. Statutory rape. Endangering the welfare of a minor. I could get hit with all of those things, couldn't I? And all I was trying to do was show some love to another human being. I've been so stupid," he said vehemently.

Beyond the kitchen door, a movement caught Louis's eye. Wondering, no doubt, what had become of breakfast and hearing voices in the kitchen quite different from the usual soothing tones of the BBC, Claire had come quietly down the stairs. Tracy could not see her from where he sat, but Louis gave his wife a look of silent warning. She seemed at once to understand. In any event, he realized, she had heard enough; she might as well have heard everything. Not this time would he succeed in cloaking the truth in silence, as he had managed so superbly long ago. Claire nodded, a stricken look on her face, and withdrew as silently as she had come. So ancient fish rise calmly to the surface of still pools in the forest and then fade back into their depths, Louis thought distractedly, heart filled to the brim with love for the wife who had kept him from just such an abyss as this these many terrible years.

"I don't know what to do," Tracy went on, shifting from recrimination to a more pragmatic tone. "I don't know whether I should try calling his dad in New York or what. I don't even have the number."

"I think I should handle this," Louis said firmly. Whatever other vast scope his reaction might encompass, he was nevertheless the headmaster, and it was to him that the responsibility for the school fell. "I think it would be a grave mistake for you to contact the boy's father."

"I guess you're right," Tracy said. "But I should warn you. Be careful. Noah's dad's a loose cannon if there ever was one."

"What are you thinking?" Louis asked.

"Litigation. The last thing I want is to get the school embroiled."

"How thoughtful," Louis said.

It must have sounded even more ironic than he had intended. "I know how much I must have disappointed you," Tracy exclaimed with something like a sob.

The truth, of course, could never be said, though Louis came perilously close. But he restrained himself. For Tracy now he felt, officially at least, only pity—but also a certain wonder (he would test this out on Claire) that all that charm and assurance had come, in the end, to nothing more than a sordid little episode, an ugly scandal it was his business, now, to avert as best he could.

"Obviously I cannot condone for an instant what you've done," he heard himself say sternly. "But I also do not want to see anyone's life ruined over this." The thought did occur to him, however: why shouldn't Tracy's life be ruined? He had, after all, committed a crime. And who was to say that Noah hadn't been hurt, much as Arthur Branson had been hurt? Once again, he felt an uncanny shiver run through him at the thought that Tracy and Arthur knew each other. That he had even assumed, for a moment, that they must be lovers. Surely Arthur had told him about Jack Emmerich, and even knowing that, Tracy had charged on in. Looked at that way, there was no excuse for the young man. No excuse at all. Leniency must be out of the question.

His tone, despite his cascading thoughts, remained businesslike. "We have to think this through clearly. Right now, we don't have enough information. We don't know where your student is. We don't know what his father knows. We should proceed with caution—which, I might add, is what I wish you had done in the first place. More than you know. But what is done is done." He tipped his glass back and swallowed the rest of his brandy, then poured them both another. Without allowing himself second thoughts he said briskly, "I'll ask you to put your resignation in writing and deliver it to me this afternoon. Then perhaps I'll know more. I'll decide at that time whether to accept it."

"I can't thank you enough," Tracy said. "For everything you've done for me."

Louis felt a tinge of annoyance at that improbable bit of gratitude, but brushed it aside. "Try to stay calm," he told the young man. "I'll be in touch with you when I know more." With that, he ushered Tracy Parker to the door. "I hope, by the way, that your dog will be all right."

"I do too," Tracy said. "Right now, that's what I'm most worried about."

How badly I have bungled things, Louis thought as he shut the door behind his fallen colleague. He had not said what was in his heart to say. But what, exactly, would that have been? That he was not, despite appearances, completely unsympathetic? That he had nonetheless, in spite of all that, lived an exemplary life?

He found himself still thinking about Arthur and Jack. He had loved Jack, of course. And it was at least partly to punish Jack for that circumstance, hardly of Jack's own making, that he had given Arthur refuge when the confused and hurting boy had come to him for help. Unquestionably, under the circumstances, it had been the right thing to do—Louis had never for a moment doubted that. Arthur was frightened as well as wounded, and Louis had known all too well himself what it felt like to bear the brunt of Jack Emmerich's displeasure. Nevertheless, the question had haunted him for years: is a moral act any less moral because the motive is corrupt?

He had always known his path would be difficult. He went back into the kitchen and gathered up Claire's breakfast—as well as what remained of his own disarray—and mounted the stairs. Always the trooper, his wife sat up in bed, propped on pillows, her writing board across her knees. She was grading student papers. To temper the luxury of "Introduction to Writing by Women" in the fall, the school always asked her to teach "The Joy of Business English" in the spring, a task she rose to with grim cheerfulness.

"I'm very sorry about your breakfast," he told her. "It's all stone cold."

"Never mind that," she said. "Tell me what's happening."

His first impulse, as always, was to keep quiet. But Claire was right; whatever she'd heard, it was already too much for him to protect her from the truth of the situation.

"Our young man," he said bitterly. "The news goes from bad to worse. He's been having an affair with one of his students."

Claire looked at him gravely. He met her gaze with an expression of defiant triumph that said, See? No matter his charm, his attentiveness. I was right to distance us from Tracy Parker.

It was a moment before his wife spoke. "Yes," she said quietly, "I've known about all that for some time now."

Louis stared at her dumbfounded. "What do you mean, you've known about it?"

"I suppose it's a despicable thing," Claire told him, "the secrets we keep from each other. But you must remember: Tracy Parker became my friend as well as yours. Furthermore, he has remained my friend."

"I . . ." Louis said, but stopped. This was difficult to fathom.

"We've had lunch together several times," Claire explained. "We've talked. He's been quite candid with me."

"You knew about this all along and you never said anything? That's aiding and abetting."

"Louis, I've been his friend," she said, stressing that noun more than he might have wished. "He needed somebody. I was there."

As you were not. Had she actually uttered those words aloud, she could not, he thought, have accused him more pointedly of failing at something.

"You never told me," Louis repeated, at once stung and furious. "You knew something immoral, illegal, potentially ruinous for everyone involved was going on, under everybody's nose, and you did nothing?" You may have been his friend, but you were also supposed to be my wife, he thought fiercely—though under the circumstances the thought had the potential to be more shaming than anything else.

Carefully Claire laid aside her writing board and papers. She put her green felt-tipped pen on the nightstand beside her and spoke with firm resignation. "I did what I thought best, Louis. I don't regret that. You're not the only person in the world who's allowed to keep certain things private. Did it ever occur to you, when you banished Tracy from your life, meaning *our* life, that I may have had some stake in the friendship as well? Or were you so concerned with managing the situation, making certain that Louis Tremper was not in any way compromised, that you forgot that the people around you, namely me, might have some agency in their lives as well?"

He profoundly mistrusted words like *agency*, words Claire would never have used before she'd started commuting to Albany in order to become a feminist. His sudden bitterness took him by surprise, and he remembered yet another unsettling coincidence: all those nights he and Arthur Branson had sat on the sofa and listened to Wagner, his wife had been learning words like *agency*.

"I know certain things make you nervous," his wife the professor continued, "but that doesn't necessarily mean they make me nervous."

What was she talking about? They never had arguments, and this, certainly, couldn't be called an argument. She hadn't raised her voice. She spoke reasonably, almost as she might to a student who was having difficulties with the material.

With some consternation he realized that he was, in fact, having difficulties with the material. "I'm at a loss as to what to do," he confessed.

She looked at him curiously. "Do you have to do anything?" she asked.

"Yes," he said darkly, "as a matter of fact I do. All hell is about to break loose. And if Tracy Parker must pay, then Tracy Parker must pay." He had been in these circumstances before; there was no other choice. Knowing what he now knew, anything less would be criminal.

He would not call Noah Senior yet. He would wait till a reasonable hour—as if any of the twenty-four hours in the day might be reasonable for such a task. And what, in any event, would he say? Nice to speak to you? I understand one of my teachers has been romancing your son? Has had carnal and unlawful knowledge of? Is guilty of criminal sodomy with?

If Noah Senior struck back with everything at his disposal, who could reasonably blame him? A father had the right, after all, to protect his son from predation, especially when the school he had entrusted with his son's well-being had failed so miserably in that task. Had even, one might argue, assisted in the predation by turning a blind eye to the situation once that situation had first begun to make itself clear.

But he had not known for certain, Louis argued with the invisible court convened in his head. How could he have known?

Of course you knew, accused the court. You watched with great fascination, even a perverse joy. Your misery fed your joy: a young man and a boy in illicit, forbidden congress with each other. It secretly intoxicated you. Deny that if you dare. Your words on paper prove it.

Picking up the phone, he dialed Reid's number.

"Hello, Libby," he said, realizing, when she answered, that it was still scarcely past eight o'clock, and the Fallones might well be slumbering peacefully, no cares such as his on their heads. "I hope I didn't wake you. I wonder if I could I speak to Reid."

Libby spoke with that veneer of brittle cheer that had always made Louis suspicious. "Reid's not here," she said.

"Well, when he gets in, would you ask him to give me a call?"

"There's been a change of address. He doesn't live here anymore."

He waited for her to say more, and when she didn't, he prompted, "Libby, are you all right? I really don't know what you're talking about."

"He's gone. Moved out. Or, I should say, I threw him out. How's that?" There was a tone of eerie satisfaction in her voice. He had never liked her.

"But where is he?" he asked.

There was a silence on the other end.

"Libby?" What, he wondered, was she doing? Opening another bottle? Loading a firearm? Then she spoke. "I've got the number here. It's the King's Arms. On Broadway."

"He's staying in a motel? Why didn't I know this?"

"I don't know why you don't. I assumed my husband always told you everything. Maybe he's embarrassed. He *should* be, you know—and about more than just getting kicked out of the house."

Louis had never known Reid to be embarrassed by anything. Secretive, yes, but never embarrassed. And then it occurred to him: for whatever reason, Reid had withdrawn his confidence in him. No longer was he entrusting his secrets to his collaborator of so many reckless years. Louis stood, phone in hand, a line of sweat breaking out across his brow, and felt a quiet devastation settle in. He had fretted, had writhed with compunction, and in the end had come to depend absolutely on those confidences of Reid's; they had been his lifeline to the greater world. They had kept him alive.

He knew it was hardly appropriate, but all he could do was utter a hysterical chirp of a laugh at his realization.

"What's so funny?" Libby asked him suspiciously.

"Nothing," he told her. "That's what's so funny. That nothing is."

"I don't understand," she said, "but frankly, Louis, and I feel free to tell you this, there's a lot about you that I've never understood."

"The feeling," he told her without acrimony, "is mutual. Now good day to you. I'm sure all of this will get sorted out in the fullness of time."

He hung up, but not before hearing, from Libby's end, her own snort of mirth. He felt—but what did he feel? Nothing that he felt seemed to have any correlation with what was happening around him. He felt an odd elation. An inexplicable whiff of *Schadenfreude*. Things had come crashing down all around him, the shards splintering, the damage considerable. And yet he stood untouched in its midst.

At least for now.

"I'm going out for a bit," he said, looking in on Claire, who still lay in bed but was in the process of dialing the telephone. "I've got to get all this sorted out."

"Do you need me to drive you anywhere?" she asked, putting down the phone—and who was it she'd been calling at this hour? Her life, he knew now, moved beyond him in ways he had never bothered to imagine.

Feeling suddenly helpless and not wanting her help, or anyone's, he told her, "I'm fine walking."

"Louis," she said. "Talk to me. You're not angry, are you?"

"I'm mystified," he told her, and turned abruptly away. At the head of the stairs he paused for a moment before descending, half expecting her to call him back, but she didn't, and so he went on down.

The King's Arms couldn't be more than a mile, just past the Heidelberg, and though he might easily ring up the motel's front desk and be instantly connected to Reid's room, he thought the exertion would do him good. He had managed to walk off nearly every emotional upset life had dealt him.

The brandy sat in his stomach, warm and slightly burning. He wrapped his coat around him, draped his neck in his long wool scarf, settled his earmuffs around his ears.

February had been a month of endlessly overcast skies, and this Saturday was no exception. Snow—lingering, dismal-looking snow—lay everywhere except on roads and sidewalks, where incessant labor had temporarily beat it back, and even on the sidewalks there was the occasional icy patch he skirted carefully. This early on a Saturday morning, Middle Forge looked particularly moribund. No one was stirring, only a miserable-looking dog, a black retriever mix of some sort that followed for five blocks before abandoning him, and he thought of Tracy's clumsy, excitable dog whose fate was now unknown.

The Heidelberg was of course shut tight, the neon Dinkelacker sign in the window turned off. Some vandal, it annoyed him to see, had pasted a pink triangle on the front door. Some vandal or gay activist; he was not unaware of the symbol's significance. Nevertheless, this misguided anti-German sentiment saddened him. If only one could separate the Nazis from the Germans. But that was it, over and over again, wasn't it? The best and the worst, commingled inextricably in a single body, the one inseparable from the other. In the snowy cemetery of the Dutch Reformed Church across the street, which did not beckon, Jack Emmerich's grave was indistinguishable from its fellows. There had been the time he and Claire had made a pilgrimage to Rommel's grave at Herrlingen; in the little churchyard, a simple iron cross, emblem of the old Kaiserreich, marked the site. Several dozen white roses had recently been left, probably that same morning; their buds still tight and virginal, they had covered the grave like new-fallen snow.

There was a sense, he told himself without regret or anger, in which Tracy Parker had magnificently fulfilled every expectation he'd had of him when he'd first crossed the threshold that sweltering day in August.

By the time he reached the King's Arms, an unprepossessing L-shaped structure erected in the early 1970s on a lot carved out of what had once been a pleasing row of brownstones, it was a quarter to nine. He had never particularly cared for the hollow pomposity of Castel Fallone, but this, on the other hand, was desperate indeed. The man in the motel office, a bleary-eyed, bestubbled fellow with the distinct smell of whiskey and sickness about him, somewhat reluctantly directed Louis to Room 2D.

"There better not be no drug-dealing going on up there," he said ominously.

"Sir," Louis told him, "what do I look like?"

"You could've had a shave. You could've just put on them clothes. How'm I supposed to know who you are? You could be anybody. All I'm saying is, I'm warning you." And with that he turned his attention to rearranging the dusty plastic flowers in a vase on the counter.

At 2D Louis knocked and waited, then knocked again. He stood for some minutes, unwilling to concede that his half-hour walk had been in vain. Down on the sidewalk, an ancient woman bundled in rags picked through a waste can, retrieving several cans and bottles, which she carefully, as though they were holy relics, tucked into the half-full garbage bag in her shopping cart. He knocked once more, a last futile rap, and as if by magic the door opened instantly. Wet hair standing up in points, naked except for the bath towel he clutched around his waist and the gold Greek cross that hung in the hairy cleft of his chest, Reid Fallone stood before him in all his fallen glory.

"You," said Reid. "I hope you're not trying to sell something."

"I should have called before coming by," Louis told him. "Libby said you were here."

"Someone actually did come by the other day," Reid said, "and wanted to sell me a set of encyclopedias. Can you believe it? No one ever offered to sell me a set of encyclopedias when I might have considered buying them."

Greedily, warily, Louis's gaze canvassed the small, extremely messy room.

"Here," Reid offered, "entrez vous into my very humble abode, my hermitage in the desert where I am struggling with my demons and worshipping my God." He pulled a wad of clothes from the room's only chair and threw them negligently across the unmade bed. The painting above the bed, an apple orchard in bloom, surely was never intended to seem surreal, though its colors, explosive pinks and whites amid a haze of pastel green, inadvertently made it so. On the dresser sat a half-empty bottle of ouzo and a Greek icon of the Virgin and child, in front of which several votive candles were burning.

"The Panagia Hodegetria," Reid explained. "The faithful believe icons are the actual presence of God. It's been a comfort to me, I must say. Though the manager's been giving me hell about the candles."

Louis couldn't resist. "I hope God's paying his share of the rent," he said, then immediately regretted it. "I'm sorry," he apologized. He had not come to start a fight.

"I accept," Reid told him. "So tell me what brings you here to my penitential exile." Unself-consciously he removed the towel from his waist and began to dry his hair. The simple gesture took Louis by surprise. He had never, in all his years of friendship with Reid, seen his friend naked. The Reid who, at twenty-five, had cut a such a romantic figure was at sixty-five a hairy, sagging old beast. With a faint repulsion Louis stole a glance at the thick, well-used penis swinging beneath his old friend's bloated stomach. Then he looked guiltily away, into the sad, hypnotic, perhaps slightly mad eyes of the Panagia Hodegetria, saying, as much to the Virgin in whom he did not believe as to Reid in whom he believed only slightly more strongly, "I need your advice. Something very distressing has come to my attention." Even now he hesitated to say it plainly; with each person he told, Tracy's predicament become more substantial, more irrevocable. "It turns out that Tracy Parker has been carrying on an affair with one of our students."

Reid stopped toweling his hair. Without going into irrelevant detail, Louis rehearsed the events of the morning and also of the previous night.

Reid looked appropriately grim. "Well this is a fine mess," he said. "And he was working out so well, didn't you think? The students were all crazy about him—and I guess he was crazy about them as well. It's such a pity." He pulled on a pair of boxers, then rummaged distractedly for some pants; finding a rumpled pair of corduroys, he shook them out, stepped first into one leg, then the other. He sat on the side of the bed as he buttoned his shirt.

"The question is," Louis said, "what do you think I should do? As you can see, the situation is very delicate. I've asked him to resign, of course."

"Such a shame," Reid said.

"I don't see any way around it. As it is, there could well be legal ramifications."

Reid looked perplexed. "You're not saying he could be charged with a crime, are you? But then, I suppose he could be, couldn't he?"

"It happens more often than you might think," Louis told him, all too bleakly conscious of the hoard of newspaper articles he kept in his desk drawer at home.

"I suppose it does," Reid said. "One never really pays attention to these things."

"The law is quite specific," Louis said. "And the penalties are extraordinarily harsh."

Reid shook his head. "I don't like it," he said vehemently. "This was a consensual relationship, right? This sort of thing goes on all the time. It's just a question of whether or not you get caught, isn't that what it is?"

That line of argument made Louis acutely nervous. Did he regret the immense pains he had taken to keep the truth about Jack Emmerich and Arthur Branson from his colleague? Would shared knowledge of that sad affair have helped them now? "I'd say this is a special case," he said.

"But is it?" Reid countered. "I taught Noah Lathrop last year. I'd say he's bright, capable, a little unfocused, but which of them isn't? Certainly capable of making decisions for himself Certainly bright enough to know he's in love."

"I would really question whether he's been in love," Louis said testily, "or only thinks he has." Had he come to Reid to be talked into leniency? But what was done was done. No leniency was possible. "A relationship like that could be any number of things," he continued vociferously. "Hero worship, need for attention. We both know that. The boy's undoubtedly caught up in the glamor of something he's far too young to understand. And that's where our Tracy Parker has blundered so badly. He's broken the law, true enough, but he's broken something far more precious. He's broken a sacred trust, the bond between a teacher and a student. That's the damage that can't be undone."

"Louis, you're always so dire," Reid said. "It's not the end of the world, and the institution of education will undoubtedly survive. Look at the Greeks. They certainly knew all about education in a way that would make a conventional moralist's hair stand on end."

"For better or worse," Louis said, "we are not the ancient Greeks. So that's neither here nor there."

"I'm not so sure," Reid told him. "Certainly our old friend Jack Emmerich was not so sure."

A chill seized Louis's heart. He did not want Jack Emmerich here in this tawdry motel room with them. They never talked about him; for fifteen years Jack had lain peacefully in his grave, and Louis had always been certain—as certain as the circumstances allowed—that he had managed to keep from Reid, as well as from everyone else, the darkest depths of their former headmaster's plunge. Indeed, that had been nothing less than his greatest feat: to stand alone against his friend and mentor, to contain the damage, to preserve the institution Jack had built and then so recklessly endangered.

"What are you implying about Jack Emmerich?" he asked cautiously, waiting for Reid finally to say, after fifteen years, that he'd known all along what went on out there at the farm.

But Reid was smiling broadly—generously, if that were possible. He did not look like a man about to rend the veil of silence. "Only what you and I have always known, Louis," he said. "That Eros goes a long way in anything. You don't devote your entire life to boys without having a passion for them."

Louis pondered, for a moment, the perilous implication of those words. "Then, if I may ask, what does that say about you?"

Reid only laughed. "My good friend, I may have spent my life teaching boys, but I have not *devoted* my life to them. As my presence in this motel room sadly suggests."

"Yes," said Louis drearily. "We need to talk about that too, I suppose. Do you want to tell me exactly what is going on here?"

"I was going to apprise you of everything," Reid told him. "Down to the last sordid detail. But I wanted to wait while I finalized my plans. This gives both Libby and myself a great opportunity, you know. And I fully intend to seize it. But I'll wait to talk till I'm ready. Which will be soon, I promise. But now, back to our problem at hand." He rose from the bed and paced grandly the room's confined space. "These are my thoughts. Does Tracy Parker have to go? Sadly, yes. Can we protect him from his fate? Sadly, no. But I think it's a damned shame that such a promising teacher has to come to an end like this. I'd like to think there's a way, somehow, to avert catastrophe."

"It's his own fault," Louis said bitterly.

"I know, I know," Reid agreed. "But it's one of those things. What I mean is, we say we're all for love, then we hem it in on all sides, we prescribe what's allowed and not allowed, we tax it to death, so to speak. But you know what? And this is the great secret we all fool ourselves into trying not to know: more than anything else, Love loves anarchy. It loves to wreak havoc. It loves to dance atop the ruins." He'd folded his arms across his chest and stood looking defiantly Louis's way.

"Oh, stop it," Louis said, suddenly impatient, even angry. It was simply not true. Look at his love for Claire: that was love, no doubt about it, and it had certainly never been havoc or anarchy. But then it occurred to him, a terrible thought indeed, that that was perhaps the very reason things had gone so wrong. The pages from his notebook shone in his mind. He had thought thoughts that should not be thought. He had entertained anarchic, havoc-wreaking notions and failed to banish them promptly. Indeed, he had welcomed their revels and rampages. He had allowed himself to be secretly intoxicated.

"I must call the boy's father," Louis said abruptly. "I must face all this out."

"You know you've got my support," Reid told him. "Whatever difficult decisions you need to make. All I would ask is that you be alert to . . ." For a moment he seemed at a loss.

"To what?" Louis said impatiently.

Reid picked up a votive candle from the dresser top and observed its flickering light. "The shimmer of things," he said. "The spirit and not the letter."

It made sense, Louis thought, to place the call from his office; he needed the bolster and support of its authority. But when he arrived there he was unnerved to discover the red light blinking furiously on his answering machine. At eleven o'clock on a Saturday morning it could mean only one thing. Life, meaningless life, was at times fraught with fearful symmetries.

With great trepidation he punched the Play button and prepared himself for whatever message poised ready to strike him in the heart.

"This is Noah Lathrop," announced the terse, assured voice. "My son is one of your students. As you may well know by now, we've had an unfortunate episode regarding one of your colleagues' dogs, which my son the brilliant fuckup seems to have brought to New York and, I am desperately sorry to say, managed to lose. We've searched everywhere, but I think, unfortunately, there is little to hope for. My son is entirely to blame. I am bringing him back to the Forge School this afternoon. I suggest he and I meet you and—I believe his name is Mr. Parker. Your office. Three o'clock. Again, I desperately regret this."

Tracy's dog. In the midst of the breaking storm he had somehow managed to forget about her altogether, and yet Betsy seemed to be the whole of the dreaded message on his machine. How strange that news that in other circumstances would be terrible now came as nothing short of relief. Scarcely daring to believe he hadn't missed something, he played the message again, and then a third time—but there seemed not even a hint of anything more serious than a lost dog. It barely seemed possible. Unless, of course, Noah Senior had laid a trap that he and Tracy were meant to walk right into.

But that was too dazzlingly dark even to contemplate, and he did his best to quell its whisper in his brain. He did not even consider calling Tracy on the telephone. He must bear this sad news of Betsy's disappearance in person. He had never been particularly taken with the animal—beagles were rather poor excuses for dogs. Nevertheless, he felt a surge of fury toward Noah's criminal carelessness. What happened to poor creatures lost in the unforgiving labyrinth of Manhattan? Surely they didn't last very long. He found himself hoping that her demise was quick and merciful. He remembered how Claire had gone with Tracy that day to the pound—it was when they barely knew the young man—and he'd wondered, at the time, why she hadn't steered him toward some choice of animal more in keeping with his character, or what had seemed to be his character: something noble and affectionate, a golden retriever, perhaps, or a Labrador. Of course he now saw that Claire and Tracy had had more between them—an innate sympathy, a shared understanding—than he'd ever guessed. As he left the building, he wondered if he should perhaps check in with his wife, let her know his whereabouts, his progress through the morning's tangled skein, but something in him rebelled, as if his silence, his absence, might be counted on to dramatize his distress. He supposed, in the midst of all this, that he wanted her to worry about him just a little.

It wasn't that he felt angry with Claire; he didn't believe she had been disloyal or even irresponsible. Rather, it was as if he had discovered that he'd never really known her—though that was nonsense, of course; he had known her very well indeed, as only husband and wife could. But he had chosen to register about her only those things that were pertinent to his purpose.

The campus was quiet and empty; usually about half the boys left for the weekend. More than ever, the Forge School seemed a walled garden protected from the rough and treacherous world, a park in which roamed, without fear, graceful and innocent creatures. Had that not always been its lure? Was that not why he had temporarily dropped anchor at the school in the first place, only to remain for forty years within its safe harbor? Why else would a man elect to spend his life in the company of boys, if not out of fear of the adults they all one day became? Was that not the secret in every teacher's heart?

He realized how greatly he dreaded the prospect of a face-to-face encounter with Noah Lathrop's father. For such men he felt the keenest admiration tempered by the stark knowledge that they could sweep him and his kind off the face of the earth with a single careless gesture. Those few sentences on the answering machine—pared down, declarative, to the point—showed the man exactly as he was: powerful, persuasive, in his way perhaps quite mad. As Jack Emmerich had been. As the vastly powerful, the psychotically assured, the indispensibly bold always were.

Approaching the cluster of houses on the cul-de-sac, he saw with a disappointment unmixed with any relief that Tracy's Toyota wasn't in the drive. His walk had been for nothing. But where could the young man have gone? Instantly Louis was thrown back into the apprehension that had managed, somewhat, to abate itself with Noah Senior's message. Once again all the possibilities loomed dark. Surely Tracy wasn't the kind of person to do himself harm? Had he perhaps fled in panic? Or simply gone out to get milk or, perhaps more to the point, a bottle of whiskey? But that would be his own solution to the predicament, not Tracy's. The young man was not much of a drinker, which had no doubt been the reason Louis had always felt a stir of excitement whenever Tracy accepted his offer of liquor: as if the door had opened onto some kind of possibility. That it—whatever intangible thing "it" was—remained only a possibility was more than compensated for by the simple awareness of its shimmer, its dangerous allure.

Was it possible, Louis asked himself, that he might actually, under the right circumstances, consider throwing Noah Lathrop to the wolves in order to save Tracy's skin? As he turned to leave the porch with that scandalous thought in mind, he suddenly felt light-headed. He'd eaten nothing all day, his macédoine left untouched on the kitchen counter, his toast untoasted in the toaster, those few swallows of brandy long since soured in his stomach and fanned out through his veins. Still, he did not want to return home. Foolish, yes; like insisting that Lux must be buried in the frozen ground of the garden. But now as then, he felt estranged, utterly alone.

His watch said 11:30. An idea occurred to him: He would eat among the boys in the cafeteria. It was good, occasionally, for the headmaster to make an appearance. But first, he had one more errand to run. He set off for Academy Avenue, walking briskly but feeling, as cars shot past, the agonizingly slow pace of even a briskly walking man. He might as well be crawling on his hands and knees, as he did in certain unbearable dreams that seemed to last the entire night.

He seldom entered the little liquor store on the corner of Academy and Broadway. The selection was much better at Palumbo's Wine and Spirits out in the Middle Forge Plaza. Broadway Liquor catered to a more desperate clientele: no French wines here, just jugs that practically had headache written on the label, and no-nonsense, anonymous brands of vodka and gin. What he wanted, *pace* the morning's radio news, was a nice little pint bottle of Slivovitz he could slip into his overcoat pocket, but of course there was none to be had. "Never even heard of it," said the middle-aged desperado behind the counter.

"What kind of brandy do you have in pints?" Louis asked.

"Hiram Walker," the man said. "Blackberry. Apricot. That's about it."

"No plum?" Louis asked hopefully.

"No plum," said the man. "Nope. What you see here is what we got."

"Well then, apricot I suppose," Louis told him, aware once again, as he had been back at the motel desk, how in that moment he could well be anybody. The headmaster of the Forge School or just another drunk in for his Saturday start-me-up. The thought actually soothed him. He understood Tracy's impulse to flee—if that had ever been Tracy's impulse rather than his own. He even considered, for a moment, heading back down Broadway to the cemetery where Jack Emmerich slumbered peacefully, perhaps to sit cross-legged in the snow and contemplate the sweetness of death, the warm embrace of oblivion, the welcoming shade of the linden tree.

Reluctantly he began his trek back to the campus.

• • •

In the cafeteria, Doug Brill sat with his family at the head table. Louis had forgotten: of course the Brills would be there. It was one of the perks the dorm advisers got. And Doug, unfortunately, had sighted him, and with a wave of his hand was gesturing the headmaster over to his table. Sighing inwardly, Louis passed among the sparsely populated tables of boys. At least he had been wise in refraining from more than the merest sip of brandy; he planned to reserve stiffer fortification until right before his meeting with the Lathrops.

"To what do we owe this honor?" Doug greeted him. Louis wondered if a note of sarcasm lurked somewhere there, though he had long ago decided that Doug Brill lacked anything but the most earnest sense of the world. Louis supposed he should thank him for his attentiveness last night: without his vigilance, Tracy's house might have burned to the ground. Perhaps, all in all, that would not have been the worst thing to happen. Houses could always be rebuilt.

"It seemed like a good day to inspect the troops," Louis said. "I suppose I was feeling a little stir crazy."

"Last night's excitement," Doug diagnosed. "I know *my* adrenaline's still pumping."

"Yes," Louis said reluctantly. "I do want to thank you; we all want to thank you for your quick thinking." Irked that he'd been coaxed into this public gratitude, he turned to Mary Ann, who was trying, without much success, to divide her attention between the children and her husband's colloquy with the boss (how much, he wondered, did it cost the school to feed the Brill clan each year?). "You've heard about our little drama, I presume."

"Oh yes," she said. "Doug gave me a full report. Thank the Lord he happened by when he did."

He hated to think what Doug might know. The man was not stupid, unfortunately, and Louis could tell that he had taken a dislike to Tracy Parker from the beginning.

"Yes," Louis said. "I suppose the Lord should be thanked."

"For that and many blessings," Mary Ann said.

Louis cautioned himself to keep his tone in check. Perhaps apricot brandy on an empty stomach had been a less than brilliant idea. "Speaking of blessings," he said, "what are we blessed with on the menu today?"

"Well," Doug informed him, mustering an enthusiasm that would be comic were it not genuine, "the choice today is fish sticks or spaghetti with meatballs. I guess you can tell how the Brills voted." And indeed, without exception, the Brills were feasting on fish sticks.

Then he would be sure to have the spaghetti, he told himself as he laid his coat, his scarf, his earmuffs on an empty chair and proceeded to the cafeteria line. Four boys who had just come in stood ahead of him. With a combination of interest and sadness he watched them, envying their unself-conscious grace, their barely containable high spirits. He tried to discern what they were bantering about, but couldn't.

"Hello, Dr. Tremper," said one of them. It startled Louis; he wondered if he had been caught staring.

"Oh, hello," he said, trying to sound distracted, as if he had in fact been oblivious to their presence. He realized with dismay that the boy who had spoken was Tim Vaughn—the roommate, if he was not mistaken, of Noah Lathrop. It hadn't even occurred to him to worry that news of Tracy's and Noah's goings-on might circulate among the boys; that they might, in fact, have been the first to know. But surely he would have heard something. As far as he knew they were decent, respectable, conventional boys, and hadn't Reid reported to him just this morning the high esteem in which Tracy was held by precisely these boys, all of whom—Gary Marks, Kevin Motes, Patrick Varga—he had observed in Tracy's classroom the day he had sat in on English II? Such boys could be trusted not to tolerate the slightest whiff of scandal.

He was glad to see—though he knew it was entirely petty, even meaningless—that all four of the boys chose, without hesitation, the spaghetti and meatballs, revolting and messy though it looked. He followed suit, smiling to the black woman who served him and whose name he didn't know. "It all looks very good today," he complimented cheerfully, though it was clear, from the look she gave him—friendly but blank—that she really had no idea who he was. "The spaghetti," he said stoically, "looks particularly good."

He had always hated waiting. Hell—in which, as opposed to heaven, he perhaps still believed—was no doubt an immense waiting room before an ominous appointment to which one was never called. Occasionally he paced back and forth, or looked out the window at the crows scavenging on the snowy quad, but mostly he took turns sitting in one chair or another, testing how the room would appear from each perspective. He regarded the sofa, still covered in stacks of papers, and decided there were enough chairs already; no further seating would be necessary. Now and then he would surrender to the need to retreat behind his desk, where he would draw the pint of apricot brandy from his desk drawer, take a cautious swallow, then slide his shameful secret back into its hiding place. He knew he should not be drinking before a meeting as important as this; already the fact that he had done so—and continued to do so as three o'clock came and went and no one appeared—made him feel cowardly, despicable. He was conscious of walking a very fine line, and that the line would undoubtedly grow finer as the afternoon progressed.

The knock on his door, though he had been expecting it for the last half hour, nonetheless startled him. Wishing he had time for one more swig but deciding he'd better not chance it, he positioned himself behind his desk, in a pose to suggest he'd been working, and said in a less-than-assured voice, "Come in."

Noah Senior ushered his son into the office with a casual brusqueness meant to indicate that he, and he alone, was in charge. The younger Noah looked shell-shocked. It took little to imagine the temperature of the car ride up from the city.

Louis rose and extended his hand. Noah Senior's tough grip was brief and to the point, as if the necessary gesture of physical contact repelled him. "I appreciate your coming all this way," Louis said politely.

"Yes, well," Noah Senior replied, casting his gaze around the room as if expecting to find Tracy Parker stashed away in some corner.

"I'm afraid my colleague isn't here," Louis apologized nervously. "I've left messages for him all day but I don't seem to have gotten through." Above all else, he wished to avoid the appearance that he might be hiding something.

Noah Senior looked briefly annoyed. "You have no idea where he is?" he asked, as though to say that he, for one, kept tabs on his employees.

"None," Louis admitted.

"That's a shame. I've primarily brought my son to apologize to Mr. Parker. And to consult on an appropriate punishment, of course."

"Of course," said Louis warily. Punishment for whom, and for what?

"I do not wish expulsion for him," Noah Senior went on, "though, understandably, this is what you may seek. I ask your leniency in that regard."

Louis nodded thoughtfully. He kept waiting for the depth charge to detonate, but it did not. "This is all most unfortunate, dreadfully so, but I don't think expulsion is in order," he said, aware, at the same time, that expelling Noah would, in a sense, solve everything. But now it was no longer an option. And of course, he reminded himself, it would solve nothing. Noah was not the problem.

"My sense is that the Forge School has served Noah well," Noah Senior said. "His grades have improved markedly since he arrived here. I have been pleased. I would even say that his outlook on his studies has somewhat improved. And that, I take it, is due in large part to Mr. Parker. From what Noah has told me, you have a remarkable teacher in him."

"Yes," Louis said uncomfortably. "I think he is generally much admired."

Noah Senior nodded his assent. He was a man who liked for reasonable people to agree. "As for Noah, however," he said, "there remains a question of character. I will speak openly here. You are aware of certain difficulties my son has had in the past, at his previous school. Other difficulties you may not be so aware of. Let me put it to you bluntly. He has a tendency to idealize certain of his teachers in ways that are not particularly appropriate. His imagination is unruly, and that gets him into difficulties from time to time. I will not embarrass him by elaborating further. But Mr. Parker should be made aware that my son can develop morbid attachments to adults who show him what he misinterprets to be special attention."

It was an exercise in the grotesque far beyond anything Louis could have imagined. He watched the boy carefully, trying to detect what effect his father's words must be having. But Noah simply sat there. Knowing what he knew, was this perhaps a secret victory for him, the only kind he was allowed? For the first time in this whole sordid episode, Louis felt compassion. Against his father this son had not a single weapon. Not even Tracy Parker, as it turned out.

"I am distressed at the pain my son has caused," said Noah Senior, sublimely clueless to the abuse of power his son had suffered. But of course that was perfect: abuses of power were not something Noah Senior would be particularly primed to see. His son, to use a phrase of Reid's, was doubly screwed. He would have no advocate whatsoever—unless, that is, Louis were to be his advocate. "I wish to make remuneration," Noah Senior continued. "I have written out a check for ten thousand dollars, for the school to use as it sees fit." From his sports jacket he pulled a yellow slip of paper and brandished it in the air between them.

This could only be a test, Louis thought wildly. The moment to speak the truth was now. He watched the younger Noah, trying to discover something, anything, but the boy's face was inscrutable. It could not possibly be so easy as this.

"This is generosity far beyond—" he found himself saying when the knock on the door interrupted him. With the same grace and assurance he had possessed that day back in August, Tracy Parker walked into the office. His present straits had scarcely dimmed him at all. His smile remained clear and winning. He had decided, apparently, to face all this down as heroically as possible. For an instant Louis felt nothing but alarm. Go away, he wanted to tell the young man. It's all settled. You'll ruin everything.

"I'm terribly sorry I'm late," Tracy said. "Hello, Noah. Mr. Lathrop."

Noah wouldn't look at his teacher. His *lover*, Louis told himself, gazing in a kind of wonder at these two who had touched and kissed . . . and what else his imagination could scarcely contain the joy and panic of?

"Mr. Parker," said Noah Senior, rising to shake Tracy's hand in a move that clearly took the young man by complete surprise. Tracy looked at Louis with an expression of sheer terror, and Louis wished he could somehow signal him—but what look could possibly convey the absurd miracle that seemed to have occurred? For really, there was no other explanation than that. Even as they spoke, the angel of havoc and disgrace was passing silently over the school—whose lintels had been marked, no doubt, with poor Betsy's blood.

"Please be seated," Louis said, gesturing to the available chair whose particular perspective on the room he had tried out several times.

Tracy took a deep breath. "I know we're here to discuss serious business," he said while Louis waited for the fragile flame of hope-against-hope to be doused by a single ill-advised sentence. "But first I have to tell everybody the excellent news."

In the second before Tracy continued Louis had to wonder whether, despite his brave demeanor, the poor young man hadn't cracked under the pressure after all.

Beaming broadly, he announced, with a flair even the surrounding circumstances could not entirely mute, "Betsy is found."

They all seemed to say "No!" simultaneously, each with his own inflection of surprise or relief—or even, in Louis's case, patent disbelief. How could Betsy possibly be found? He had known, from the instant he played Noah Senior's message, that there was no hope. The dog would be the casualty; the dog would somehow pay for everything else. *See?* he could almost hear Reid Fallone exclaim. The universe is not the abyss of darkness you think it is.

Still, superstitiously, he feared the silent angel's return. Someone, somehow, would have to suffer. Of that he was quite certain.

"Claire's got her back at my house," Tracy said. "She's a little shaken up but otherwise just fine. We just got back from the city."

"Claire?" Louis said.

"It all happened so fast," Tracy explained. "I got this call, this man in New York telling me he had my dog. I couldn't believe it; at first I thought it was some sick prank, but he said he got my phone number off the collar. He said he was there in Central Park when she ran away. He tried to find you, Noah"—Tracy turned to the boy and spoke in a tone remarkably clear of reproach—"but I guess you'd already gone by then."

Noah stared at Tracy as if overwhelmed. "I tried to find her," he said in a small, frightened voice. "I looked everywhere."

"It doesn't matter," Tracy said. "We've got her back. She's safe and sound. Lucky me. I didn't even know she was lost till she was found."

"Well, I'm glad," Noah Senior told him. "You were certainly saved a lot of unnecessary grief."

But Tracy wasn't through. The words poured out in a torrent. "I was so excited," he said, his voice still shaky with relief. "I drove right over to your house, Louis, but you weren't there. Claire said, What're we waiting for? She's amazing that way. We zipped right down to the city and picked Betsy up, simple as that. The man who found her was really sweet. He was so apologetic, and I kept telling him, What's there to apologize for? You did a great thing. He made us hot chocolate and we sat there in this tiny little apartment in Chelsea crammed full of plants and he went on and on about how sorry he was, how he was afraid he freaked you out, Noah."

And by the perturbed expression on Noah's face, Louis decided, he had indeed.

"You didn't mention anything about this fellow," Noah Senior said sternly.

"It was nothing," Noah said. "I thought he was a mugger. I thought he had a knife." Louis could see he was a boy who was used to lying, but who was less good at it than he probably thought.

"Hardly a mugger," Tracy said, seemingly oblivious to Noah's deceit. Was it possible, despite everything, that he knew nothing about the object of his intimate attentions? "I'm sure he didn't want to spook you. He works for the Metropolitan Opera. He's a costume designer."

Having apparently heard enough to satisfy him, Noah Senior rose from his chair. "So," he said. "All's well that ends well. You've been very lucky, Noah." He turned to his son. "Luck like that comes once or twice. Remember that. I hope, Mr. Parker, you won't hold any of this against my son. He's too impulsive for his own good. He develops enthusiasms that should not be encouraged. In the future, I trust you will keep that in mind. We Lathrops have a reputation for being difficult—well earned, I'm afraid. My son is no exception. Though I still expect him to apologize to you."

"Noah." He spoke his son's name with military precision.

Louis watched the boy carefully. Noah who was the key, the linchpin to everything that stood so precarious in that room. Who despite that, Louis saw with savage clarity, was absolutely helpless. Left in the lurch as no one should ever find themselves left in the lurch—by father, by lover, by teacher. All of them.

"I'm sorry, Trace, I mean Mr. Parker," Noah conceded. Bravely he held out his hand.

No one would intervene. No one would save this boy. And neither, Louis realized with a jolt of shame, would he. In this very room he had stood up to Jack Emmerich. In this very room he had said, raising his voice in anger against his friend and mentor, "I will not allow you to damage this boy any more than you already have. I will do whatever I have to to stop you." Now he sat behind Jack Emmerich's desk and allowed the carnage to be wrought unhindered. Never had his admiration for anyone been greater than for this boy, trapped between the demands and desires of adults far more powerful and impossible than he; who waited in stoic silence when he could, by a single word, bring everything crashing down.

"Apology accepted," Tracy said gravely, no doubt mystified but nonetheless acting his part perfectly. He took Noah's hand and they shook. What wild or bitter regrets hid behind the perfectly ordinary-looking gesture? Louis could not tell. No one but Tracy and Noah could tell. They held their handshake only a second longer than necessary, then relinquished each other's grip. But not before the strains had stolen into Louis's head, blazing and sorrowful, of that final trio he loved so much from *Rosenkavalier*, the three sopranos soaring and then falling around the Marschallin's heroic renunciation. *"Um Gottes Willen,"* he breathed silently, sorry never to have played that great music for Tracy, but seeing now that it had not, in fact, been necessary.

Whatever Noah Senior saw or heard just then, he too seemed convinced. "No hard feelings," he said. "I think my son has learned his lesson." To the end he was powerfully, even providentially, clueless. But perhaps that was his stunning secret after all. He had brokered this reconciliation without speaking a word of the language. Uzbekistan, shimmering with oriental deceits, had better beware.

"The contribution to the Forge School remains," Noah Senior concluded. "I thank both of you"—he looked from the grateful Louis to the baffled Tracy—"for your understanding. I am profoundly sorry for this intrusion into your time, and for the anxiety that has been caused. Mr. Tremper. Mr. Parker." He nodded curtly, as if to dismiss them. "Come, Noah," he commanded. "We've been enough of a burden to these gentlemen for a day."

Docile, the boy made to follow, but at the door he turned and looked back at them, and it was not Tracy's eye that he met but Louis's. Despite himself Louis nodded in acknowledgment. But acknowledgment of what? Noah seemed, in his enigmatic way, to be smiling.

The door clicked shut. Father and son had gone. Silence filled the room. He was gratified to find that Tracy was looking at him in astonishment.

"Did what I think just happened actually happen?" Tracy asked.

"We're saved," Louis said. *"You're* saved. Apparently your Noah didn't breathe a word to his father. Perhaps Betsy being lost was a good thing. It let you make your escape."

"My escape," Tracy said sardonically. "My offer of resignation still stands."

"Yes. Of course." From the window Louis could see father and son striding across the quad, the younger lagging a step behind. He still could barely believe the catastrophe had been averted, and yet he knew that nothing was ever ended. For as long as Noah remained at the Forge School, the two of them would know the truth. And even after that. For the rest of their lives. "With deep regret," he told Tracy without taking his eyes off the two retreating figures, "I accept your resignation. Effective immediately."

"I understand," Tracy said with what seemed like reluctance. Was he surprised?

"It would be impossible for you to stay here," Louis reminded him, as if he should need any reminding.

"I know, I know." Tracy sank slowly into his chair and put his head in his hands. Only now did the full measure of his disgrace seem to sink in on him.

"I'm very sorry things had to happen this way," Louis told him gently.

"So am I. It was all going so well here. I thought—I'm finally on track."

Louis did not say, You allowed this to happen. You brought this down on yourself. Instead he thought, for a moment, about putting a fatherly hand on Tracy's shoulder, but decided, given everything that had happened, the gesture would not be appropriate. "What will you do?" he asked his disgraced comrade.

Tracy shrugged. He looked up with a defeat in his eyes that was shocking. "Who knows? I'll go to New York. I'll disappear," he said dramatically. "New York's good for that."

If that were the case, then Louis envied the fortunate citizens of that great anonymous city. Soon enough, among new faces, Tracy's state of grace, his nimbus of charm, would no doubt be entirely restored. Or would this sad escapade follow him and haunt him? Even now he longed to ask the unaskable: What had it felt like to possess, for a moment, the love of a boy for whom one had risked everything? But the unaskable remained just that; he had long ago made his particular choices. They hemmed him in as surely as Tracy's now did. One thing did occur to him. "When you see Arthur Branson," he said. "Will you give him . . ." He had planned to say *regards*, or perhaps *apologies*, but what he said was, "Will you give him my love?"

"Of course," Tracy said.

There should have been more, somehow, but there wasn't. An awkward, even unbearable silence enfolded them.

"Well," said Tracy. "I'd better go make arrangements."

"Yes," Louis agreed. "I suppose you should."

Claire had cooked one of his favorite dinners, a winter feast of pork roast, garlicked potatoes, braised fennel, the sort of meal that anchored one to the earth on unforgiving nights. She had brought out the willowware, her grandmother's silver; she had lit candles that flickered warmly in their brass holders in the center of the table.

She looked as if, at some point during the long day, she had suffered a prolonged spell of tears.

He would not ask. The meal had been warming in the oven for perhaps an hour, awaiting his late arrival. Her attempt to make amends vaguely embarrassed him—as if either of them had done anything wrong. He had not meant to be so late, he told her.

"That's quite all right," she said. "I'm sure you had much to do." He could feel acutely the distance in her; how tentative everything was between them, as between strangers. Even after forty years, a marriage could end in an afternoon—that was how fragile life was.

He had not meant to fall asleep in his office, but the brandy, whose consolations he had rather boldly invoked once the meeting was over, and an extraordinary sense of hollowness within him had led him to stretch out on the seldom-used sofa, whose carpeting of books and papers he swept aside to accommodate his sudden need for unconsciousness. When he awoke, dusk had come and gone and he was in the dark.

As if afraid to speak for fear of what might be said, he and Claire ate in silence. They were usually rather good at silence—comfortable, domestic silences. They did not need to chatter in order to preserve their communion. But tonight the silence of their meal was distinctly that of dangerous estrangement.

Claire, always the braver of the two, was the one to break it at last. "Well," she said, "don't we have anything at all to say?"

"Dinner is very good," Louis told her. "Especially the pork roast."

"I don't mean that."

"I know. I'm sorry. Tracy Parker has resigned."

"Yes," she told him.

"Of course," he said. "You were keeping Betsy. You were waiting for him at his house when he came back from the meeting."

"Louis," she said. "Can you understand why I had to be there?"

She had loved their young man as well. He had not realized that before. The small perception dug at him, and he said, wanting for her sake to sound generous, "You did the right thing. You've been quite a good friend to him, I believe."

"At the expense of . . . ?" Claire said.

"I didn't say that," he told her.

"But I think you implied it."

She knew him too well, but that had never stopped him from pretending she didn't. "Perhaps I did imply it," he admitted. "I wish everything wasn't such a muddle. I wish I didn't feel like something has been allowed to happen that ought not to have happened and which everyone, myself included, has colluded in."

"You think Tracy got away with something. That he didn't get punished. Is that what you're saying?"

"He did get away. You know he did. Unlawful sexual activity with a minor. Criminal acts, and now he's scot free." But who was he to assert such things, he who had imagined those same acts with such secret avidity? Was he not also guilty?

The fact remained, he told himself defiantly: he had not acted; he had only dreamed. There lay all the difference. It was no crime to dream.

Nonetheless, uncomfortably, he felt critically compromised, a judge unworthy to judge.

"Trust me," Claire reassured him. "You did exactly what you should have done. Tracy's not getting off scot free. This will haunt him. He'll never be free of it. Absolutely nothing would have been served by ruining his life any more than it already is."

"It's not Tracy's life that I'm concerned about," Louis said righteously. "It's the boy's. I'm afraid I haven't served *him* well at all."

"But perhaps you did," Claire told him. "He could have spoken, you know. He could have told his father everything. He chose not to. You have to grant him agency in this."

"Agency," Louis said with disgust. "What agency? He's a child. He's fifteen years old. What could he do? It was up to me to allow him to speak, and I could have. I could have asked him if there was anything he had to say. But I didn't. I saw my chance and took it. Noah's father believes about his son exactly what he chooses to believe, and I was willing—no, I was *grateful* to let that stand. Justice was not done here."

"Whose justice, Louis?" Claire asked, and when he did not answer, she continued. "I don't understand why you've come to hate Tracy Parker so much."

"I don't hate him," he told her. "I hate what he did. He betrayed his trust. That's what I find hard to forgive. Though no one else seems to be having much trouble there. Reid, I can understand. He's all passion with no sense of duty. But you, Claire. That's what I find surprising."

She smiled sadly. "I suppose that should tell you something, now shouldn't it? I know this is all very upsetting. Believe me, no one's more upset about betraying his trust, as you call it, than Tracy. If you'd been talking to him for the last month you'd know how upset he's been."

Was it his fault, then, that Tracy had done what he'd done? Because the headmaster had cut him off, left him in the lurch with his sick friend Arthur and his confused student Noah?

"I wash my hands of Tracy Parker," Louis told Claire brutally. "He is no longer my concern. My duty is to the well-being of the students of the Forge School."

"Noah is not just a passive victim here," Claire said. "It's more complicated than you want to make it out to be. Noah wanted for what happened to happen. And he can take care of himself. From everything I know, I'm convinced of that."

"You mean Tracy Parker is convinced of that," Louis countered, "and he's convinced you as well." He was surprised to see her so easily duped—but then, Tracy's charm had duped the lot of them. "I have this terrible fear," he went on, "that Tracy Parker, like the boy's father, believes about Noah only what he chooses to believe. And if that's the case, then where does that leave us?"

"That leaves us with the boy. You've got to keep an eye out for him, Louis.

To be there for him. Tracy tells me Noah's got another two years at the Forge School. Well, you've got to make sure he thrives. You can't let him be another Arthur Branson for you."

But what did she know about Arthur Branson? Louis asked himself with alarm.

It was as if she could intuit his thoughts exactly. "Tracy told me," she admitted. "He told me what Arthur told him. It's true, isn't it, Louis? You saved him all those years ago. And you never told anyone."

Louis flinched to hear a truth so compromised, so undermined as that. Did Arthur really think he'd saved him? "I turned my back on him," Louis said fiercely. "I know that's what he thinks. But I got him through the Forge School. That was all I could do. I couldn't do more than that."

He thought Claire might be close to tears again. It had been a difficult day for her as well. He could see that now. He regretted that he had been harsh with her.

"You can't blame yourself," she said, and he was suddenly shocked to understand that the tears, trembling there but still held back, were not for herself, or for Tracy Parker, or even for Arthur Branson. They were for him. "All those years," she said, "and nobody ever knew. It was heroic, what you did. And how lonely you must have felt."

Even now he could not say, "I was afraid of loving Arthur Branson too much. That was why I had to turn away."

"But now you have to do it again," she said.

She was right; he knew that. This time he must not turn away.

"The trouble is," he confessed, "I don't like the boy very much."

Claire looked at him compassionately. "No one said you had to," she told him.

He dreaded the prospect more than he could say. It would demand of him a courage and discipline greater than he had ever sustained in all his long, unblemished career of teaching boys. Noah was a boy, after all, one might eventually come to love.

He rose, clenching and unclenching his fist, and did what he too rarely did these days. He bent down to where she sat and kissed his wife on the cheek. "Thank you," he said, "for the delicious dinner. And for your wise words. I'll do the dishes in a bit, but there's one piece of business I need to attend to first."

"I'm happy to wash up," she said. She had never much trusted him with the fragile willowware. "Go ahead and do whatever it is you need to do."

"Without you," he told her truthfully, "I would be completely lost."

He went into his study and shut the door. Opening the desk's bottom drawer, he pulled out his notebook of many years—his life, he realized. Such as it had been. Or rather, the life that never was. *Closed Fist, Open Palm.*

All those scrupulous pages of notes, and those other shameful pages as well. A sheaf of clippings fell onto the floor, and he stooped to pick them up. A high school hockey coach had been arrested on Long Island for regularly molesting one of his team members over a six-month period. In the photograph accompanying the article, a handsome boy of fifteen or sixteen sat next to his beaming, nervous-smiled abuser. Louis regarded the clipping, some years old, already yellowed, with detached calm. Lightning would not strike. In his mind he saw Noah Lathrop extend his hand; he saw Tracy Parker take that hand in his and cover it with his own, mortal flesh to mortal flesh. Their secret blazed electric between them, and he could see it clearly. Just as clearly he saw Jack Emmerich put his arm around Arthur Branson one afternoon outside the Heidelberg on Main Street when no one should have been around to observe.

Stuffing the newspaper clippings back in the notebook, he stuck it under his arm and left his study.

In the kitchen, where Claire was rinsing soap from the willowware, he opened and shut several drawers before she asked him, "Louis, what are you looking for?"

"I've found them," he said. He took the box, and when he left the house he could sense that she stood at the kitchen window and watched him, as she did sometimes when he shoveled snow at night and she worried about his heart.

He did not mind that she saw him now. He had nothing to hide. Making his way through the snow into the middle of the garden, he struck the first match along the rough strip on the side of the box. The flame quivered. From far away a police siren rose and fell. And then it ceased. Everything lay perfectly still and silent.

Calmly, with no regret, he tore page after page of his life's work from the notebook and fed them to the cleansing fire. He had expected the doomed, beautiful pages to soar aloft one by one, weightless, glowing against the night sky like the flames from Tracy Parker's chimney. But that did not happen. The pages curled to cinder and ash. They did not fly heavenward, or if they did, black against black, he could not see them in their ascent.

XVIII

She had once said to herself—she remembered it so clearly—that there were certain mornings in spring that felt almost exactly like being in love. She had been so young then, filled to bursting with a bright arc of longing as wide as the sky itself. Nearly half a century ago that had been, when the twin throbs of Frank Sinatra and a boy named Jimmy Wellington pulsed in her young heart—and the marvel was, certain mornings in spring still felt almost exactly like being in love. Of course she had grown old, she had become an ancient creature, not so much undesirable as simply beyond considering. Well, if there would be no more falling in love, there was nonetheless still the spring, its inimitable light, the sheen of ambient desire with which it suffused everything, everything.

With all the impulsive energy of youth, Betsy strained at her leash. Everything about this April morning, it seemed, was worth investigation. "Easy there," Claire reminded the little beagle. Tracy had been right: the confines of an apartment in the city would have been no place for an animal like Betsy, and if Louis had been less than enthusiastic about taking her on, Claire was nonetheless certain she had done the right thing by insisting on it.

"I suspect Louis will miss him far more than I," Libby said. For a moment Claire thought her walking companion meant Tracy, but of course she didn't. Libby knew nothing about any of that.

"I'm certain he will," Claire told her friend. "He's taking it very hard. Though he's convinced Reid won't last more than three months in a monastery. At least that's what he's telling me. He predicts he'll be back among us before summer's over. He's not even hiring a replacement—that's how confident he is." She tried, without much success, to picture Reid Fallone on Mount Athos. She saw him in a burlap robe fastened with a rope belt; he was riding a donkey. There was not a woman in sight.

She had to laugh at the absurdity of it.

Libby said, "If Louis thinks Reid's not completely serious, then he knows my husband far less well than he supposes. Funny, isn't it, that the two of them could have gone on being such friends, and each so completely clueless about the other."

"That was undoubtedly part of the attraction," Claire told her difficult friend of so many years. "When you get right down to it, we don't ever want to know one another too well. We want there to be that mystery. Where there's mystery, there's hope."

"I suppose," Libby said. "I have to say I'm a little tired of both right now. I like living in the present, as they say. One day at a time. Though I can't wait to sell that awful house and move into some place more livable."

"You always hated that house," Claire told her. "It was never you."

"It never was, was it?" Libby admitted. "I'd say marriage does that. After a while you don't even recognize yourself anymore. The you you started out with, I mean. I do wonder, sometimes, what would have happened if I'd never met Reid."

"Then I suppose I would never have met Louis," Claire said.

"And where would we be today? What would we be doing with ourselves?"

"Impossible to imagine," Claire said. "Don't even waste your time trying." And she meant it. This was exactly who they were; their lives couldn't be sloughed off or reinvented or banished as if they never had been. There was no going back for any of them, ever. Libby might feel herself living one day at a time, freed into some exhilarating future, but Claire knew that was just something one said to oneself—an admirable enough mantra, but no one, in the end, lived like that; each was borne forward, as if on a great tide, by the weight of everything that had already happened. Each rode a wave fathoms deep; at every turn the past overtook the present in a great surf-rush of joy and regret.

Ahead of them, for instance, was Tracy Parker's haunted house. Their leisurely stroll across campus had not intentionally brought them this way—unless Betsy had been leading them all along. Did she recognize her old home? Under a spell of tantalizing scents the dog tugged mightily at her leash, zigzagging this way and that along the sidewalk and up onto the ragged lawn.

The building needed sprucing up: new paint, the chimney repointed, the front porch jacked up. You didn't notice such things so much when a place was lived in. Now the vacant windows seemed to cry aloud the house's sad emptiness. Come July, the Brills would move in; life would fill the house once again; the rooms would echo with the laughter of children, though she wasn't sure she had ever heard those dreary children laugh. Perhaps the singing of hymns would echo, then.

Betsy was positively delirious. She rolled in the wet grass, her nose shiny with dew. Should she turn her loose, let her commune to her heart's content with this bit of ground where no doubt dog and master had frisked together on those luminous autumn afternoons when, as Tracy had confided to her once, his life had seemed at last to be starting to make some sense? It had been six weeks since Betsy's adventure in Central Park, but Claire was still cautious. "She does have this tendency to take off like a shot," Tracy had warned. She remembered how he had knelt down and nuzzled the dog's head with his lips; how she had heard him whisper "Bye, sweetie"; how she thought he had brushed away a tear. "Take good care of her," he'd told her, then added, "and yourself too."

This is all I have left of you, she thought with a wistfulness that still had the power to unsettle. Along the front porch, beneath the somber rhododendrons, several bright clumps of daffodils caught her eye. The sight made her heart leap; these bulbs she had given him one afternoon, and that he had actually, bless his heart, taken the time to plant. Bravely they turned their buttery perianths toward the sun. Had she been in love with him? No, she thought, but she had been very fond of him; he had been a thawing sun in the late winter of her long marriage, a brief but much-needed change in seasons.

Libby seemed to sense her thoughts—or perhaps it was only the house that suggested the subject. "I heard about what happened with that new teacher," she said.

Claire's heart quickened. "You did?"

"Reid mentioned it when we talked last. He said the young man just up and quit."

So that was the official explanation Louis was promulgating. Claire had wondered. She herself had mentioned nothing to Libby one way or the other; had told her, in fact, rather than rehearse the real story, that she and Louis had rescued Betsy from the pound—which wasn't, she reminded herself, entirely a lie.

"Yes," she said, surrendering to the party line. "I imagine he just got overwhelmed by things. Being a teacher is harder than one supposes, really. It takes a special commitment." She knew she was being altogether unfair to Tracy, who had, after all, been quite an extraordinary teacher in certain ways—but then it was not with Tracy, finally, that her allegiance must lie. "Louis took over his classes," she continued loyally. "It's been rather a burden on him. He hasn't seen the inside of a classroom in so long. Though I actually think he's rather enjoying the challenge. He used to love teaching. I think this gives him a sense of purpose—which, between you and me, he's been sorely lacking for some time now. And the boys are keeping him very much on his toes. He delights in the boys."

She had stood at the window and watched him burn the manuscript he had labored on for so many years. Had it been in a fit of despair? Or had he finally let go that futile dream that had held him in thrall for so long? These days he seemed possessed, oddly enough, of a new sense of freedom. She knew no other way to put it.

"And are things well between you and Louis?" Libby asked. "Something like that can sometimes put a strain on things. Unsettle the equilibrium."

Was it possible, Claire wondered, that Reid had actually told Libby everything? Marriages were like that, even marriages on the shoals. For a moment she considered telling her friend the whole peculiar story—but to what end? So she said, not untruthfully, "Louis and I will be married forever. It's how we are." Some things, after all, did not need to be spoken, their reality too fragile to survive the telling. But these nights of spring did she not—rather often, in fact—wake to find him nestled against her in the bed, his arm draped across her as they slept? Or other small gestures: a pat on the shoulder, a peck on the cheek. He had never been less than courtly with her, but was she wrong in thinking she detected, to her great surprise, a tenderness she had not—to be truthful—felt from him in years? He had suffered his losses over the last few months: Lux, whose ashes now rested peacefully beneath the old lilacs in the back yard; Tracy Parker, disappeared without a trace into the surging anonymous crowds of New York; and now Reid Fallone, self-exiled to his cliffside monastery perched above a wine-dark sea. But those losses, she felt, hardly told the whole story. No; at night, finding her husband's slumbering body curved into hers, mortal bearer of mortal secrets, she could at times wonder if what Louis Tremper had actually come to miss, after all these years, was none other than Claire herself.

It was enough, given everything that had happened, to bring a rueful smile to her lips. "Okay, Betsy," she said with a firm tug of the leash. "Time to move on." If Libby had noticed the ecstasy Betsy had lavished on the lawn, she did not show it. And Betsy, having paid homage, seemed content. "Shall we loop around the lake?" she asked her friend.

"Fine with me," Libby said. "My morning's certainly wide open. Come to think of it, the rest of my life is wide open."

"Then let's," Claire urged. "It's so beautiful out. And I can't remember a longer winter."

They followed the path from Tracy's cul-de-sac across the campus's great sloping back lawn, down to the water. Drifts of daffodils were blooming there as well, bulbs she had planted years ago, when her daughters were young. Over time, several hundred daffodils had multiplied to several thousand, a field of golden light.

Along the path, coming from the far side of the lake, two boys ambled toward them. One of them she had never seen before: tall and thin, he sported a rather astonishing splash of hair as bright as that lawn of daffodils, though not half so natural. The other boy looked familiar, but then there was a certain type of boy that age among which individuals were difficult to distinguish. His hair was cut very short. She remembered how, in the late sixties and early seventies, the school had once passed through the crisis of long hair; if only Jack Emmerich had been able to know that some thirty years down the line a look of near military austerity would once again be in vogue. For that was how this boy seemed to her, a young combatant in some desperate war—and then she remembered where she knew him from. A reception, back before Christmas; he had been in the company of his father. He was not beautiful, she thought, but there was in his face a haunted expression by which one could conceivably be intrigued. She tried to imagine the ways that face might have intrigued Tracy Parker, but it was nearly impossible, wasn't it, to try to discover in the features of the beloved any real clue to the lover's plight? But this, she was quite certain, was the boy Tracy Parker had lost himself over.

He seemed not to recognize her—and why should he? But as they approached he showed distinct interest in Betsy.

You would never guess, she addressed the boy silently, the things you and I have in common, now would you? She felt as if she knew him too well. Tracy had told her so much during their fugitive meetings at coffee shops and diners during those critical few weeks. He loved you, she wanted to tell the boy. He did the best he could in a situation the world made impossible.

Cherish that, she wanted to say. You can't know what an extraordinary thing that is.

The wonder of it: that she who had always abided so strictly by the law had found herself, in the wisdom of her years, counseling a young man in acts that were strictly forbidden. The world is a miracle, she had found herself telling him. It is also full of terrible danger.

The dangerous boy scrutinized the dog on her leash. Did Betsy recognize him as well? On an impulse he stopped just as they were passing each other on the path. In a quick motion he knelt on the sidewalk and cupped the top of Betsy's head with his open palm. His nails, she saw, were bitten to the quick.

Betsy nuzzled him feverishly, but then she tended to nuzzle just about everyone feverishly.

"Hey, doggie," he said, using both hands to massage behind her ears. The taller boy looked on, expressionless.

"I love beagles," the kneeling boy explained. "What's its name?"

She hesitated, wondering what Louis would have her do.

"Her name's Betsy," she said with a trace of defiance.

He looked up at her; she could see that his face was not one of those faces that registered emotion particularly clearly. Or was that just the young in general? "It really is Betsy, isn't it?" he said. "Are you Mrs. Tremper?"

"We've met before," she told him. "At the Christmas reception."

"Maybe," he said guardedly. "I don't really remember. I'm terrible with people's faces. It's Betsy"—he spoke more to the dog than to her. "I love this dog."

With some shock she realized that he had almost certainly not laid eyes on Betsy since she was lost. He would only have been told that she'd been found. "Hey, Bets," he cooed. "Do you remember me?" She felt, vaguely, that his unself-conscious enthusiasm was somehow callow, given all that had happened. A young man's promising career had been destroyed, and here was the culprit seemingly untouched by it all. And yet, under the circumstances, what should he do but be a boy? It was, after all, exactly what some might argue Tracy Parker had tried to rob him of.

Did he know that she knew? At least he didn't ask, "Have you heard anything from Mr. Parker?" Though perhaps she wished he had, if for no other reason than the chance to talk about the person who had vanished from both their lives. So young, she thought, and yet already he'd learned what to say and what not to say. Already he held his secrets close to his chest. She considered the moment: here she stood, and there he knelt, a multitude of shared secrets unshared between them. What if they actually dared compare notes? But of course one never did. One went through all one's life and never did.

Would it change anything at all to know the whole truth, each side of it, every facet and angle? Or would the result just be flat-out contradiction, like the four Gospels' incompatible accounts of the Crucifixion?

"I wish I had a dog biscuit for you," Noah told Betsy. He stood up and showed his open palms. "I wish I had a whole handful." Betsy barked twice. "Sorry," he said regretfully. Then, without another word, no farewell, not even a look Claire's way, he and his companion sauntered on as if nothing particularly momentous had occurred.

As Devin Shimabukuro stepped through the door of the narrow café, Tracy rose to greet his old friend. It had been with great nervousness that he had finally summoned the will to call. They had not spoken in nearly six months. But on the phone, at least, Devin had not been fazed. Nothing, it seemed, weighed too heavily on him, a trait that Tracy found, at the moment, rather appealing.

"God, it's been forever," said his friend, prolonging their embrace and speaking warmly into Tracy's ear. "You look great."

"As do you," he returned the compliment, which was only the truth, after all. Devin might grow older, but he never seemed to age. Unfathomable that they had fallen into such a silence with each other for so long. Devin was, after all, his oldest friend.

"I've never been here," he said, looking around. "Looks cozy."

"I love this place," Tracy told him. "It's so New York."

And Devin, he realized with nostalgia, was so New York as well. Despite the day's opulent warmth, he wore a white turtleneck and trim black jacket. His new haircut gave him the chance, once or so a minute, to flick back, with a toss of his head, the ebony lock that fell over one eye.

"Well," Devin said once he'd seated himself. "This New Yorker would like a cocktail. What shall we drink?"

"Nothing for me," Tracy said. "I hardly ever drink anymore."

"Oh please," Devin said, tapping him fondly on the wrist. "Country living's gone to your head. It's the city. Have some fun."

Tracy hesitated for a moment, aware he'd let Devin think, over the phone, he was only down for spring break. He was having some difficulty, these days, deciding exactly what his story was supposed to be. "You're right," he said with a sigh. "It's the city. What the hell?"

"Yay," Devin told him, blithe instigator, as ever, of excess. "I personally have decided it's time to bring back the three-martini lunch," he proclaimed. "Who wants to live forever, right?" But having said that, he nonetheless looked at Tracy with a faint flicker of concern. "Oh my God," he said, as if something had dawned on him. "You're not taking me out to lunch to tell me you're sick, are you?"

"Who said I'm taking you out to lunch?" Tracy said. "The fact is, I'm more or less flat broke at the moment."

"I forgot. The impoverished life of the teacher. But think of all the other rewards. How are the sweet young things these days? Now that spring has sprung, have they taken off their shirts on the playing fields? Do they lie around half-naked on the lawn?"

"You have such a perverse imagination," Tracy told him miserably.

"You really have gone all responsible and everything, haven't you?" Devin diagnosed as their waiter approached. "I feel parched just thinking of your life among the ephebes. Now I really do need that martini. Tanqueray," he commanded. "And dry. Very dry. With an olive. Et vous, my dear?"

"Oh hi, Trace," said the waiter. "How's it going?"

"Great," Tracy told him. "I'm great." Charlie of the calm beauty and dimpled smile was perhaps the chief reason he had made this café his haunt. And how odd to be on a first-name basis with the youth who had so stirred him when Arthur had brought him here back in October, back before things had begun to go so wrong. In fact it had been that very weekend—hadn't it? He still had in his possession, somewhere, that inscribed scroll of toilet paper the troubled boy had given him, a bad-luck token if ever there'd been one, unheeded prophecy of disasters he could not, at the time, have even begun to discern. From the storm's vast wreckage, it was the only relic he had saved.

"I think I'll have a glass of red wine," he told Charlie, remembering Louis's warning: A man who starts drinking liquor before five is doomed. Yet another bit of the headmaster's advice he'd smiled at indulgently and then proceeded, despite himself, to absorb.

"Merlot, Beaujolais, or Cabernet Sauvignon?" Charlie said.

"Oh dear. Choices, choices."

"Have the Cabernet," Charlie advised in a stage whisper, touching him affectionately, thrillingly, on the shoulder. It was all Tracy could do to resist reaching up and patting that hand in return. One of these days, he promised himself, he just might.

"By the way," Devin asked, flicking his hair from his eye, "are these ash-trays usable, or just part of the decor?"

"It's actually a real live ashtray," Charlie told him.

"I always ask," Devin said, smiling that winning but artificial smile he reserved for young men who were too good-looking for their own good. Nevertheless, Tracy watched his friend across the table scrutinize Charlie as the young man walked away. He knows I have a crush, he thought, discomfited, as usual, by Devin's acumen, and expecting some affectionate taunt to that effect. But Devin surprised him. He gazed at Tracy with lustrous eyes. Leaning across the table confidentially, touching Tracy's hand, a gesture unaccountably disquieting, he said in a low voice, "You didn't answer my question, sweetie. Is everything okay with you?"

Tracy laughed. He leaned back in his seat and stuck his hands leisurely in the pockets of his khaki trousers. "Is everything okay with me?" he repeated. For months he had lived in unrelieved hell, unable to confide his terror to another living soul. In dreams his father had appeared, telling him cryptically, "You wouldn't believe how beautiful the mountains are over here." It rather shamed him how, after picking up his results at the clinic, he had actually closed his eyes for a moment and silently thanked the God he'd stopped believing in the year his dad had died. "My health, actually, is terrific," he told Devin. "I got tested. I got the results." Then he added heroically, "I'll live to be a hundred and twenty."

"Good," Devin said. "Thank God. I worry about everybody, you know. All the time. We all have to be so very careful."

But Tracy had not been careful. He had thrown caution to the winds. He had loved a boy. No, he had fucked a boy he had loved. A boy who, in his brave and avid way, had very much wanted to be fucked. Not love but unlawful sexual activity: that was the crime he stood accused of. But by whom, exactly? Here he sat, entirely free, and with an absurdly clean bill of health as well. At least I taught him to use a condom, he reassured himself. It's possible I might even have saved his life.

"Rafael and I got tested too," Devin went on. "A few months back. All's clear with us, too. You'll have to meet him the next time you're down. You'll love him. He's only nineteen—going on fourteen, I sometimes think. All dark and Latin. Fabulously passionate."

"And things are going well?" Tracy asked, startled to realize how many times two old friends had ended up in bed together since their college days. He remembered without rancor how Devin had sprung the fact of fabulously passionate Rafael on him that long-ago night in October, how he had felt a pinprick of jealousy even while holding back on his own secret that had already begun to gnaw at his heart. Had his silence been wariness, or simple self-deception?

"We've been looking for an apartment to share," Devin told him. "If that's not serious, then I don't know what is. And how about yourself? Any upstate cuties to brag about?"

Charlie set their drinks before them, then brandished his check pad. My whole life is before me, Tracy reminded himself sternly as Devin scanned the menu—and as if to reassure himself of that miraculous fact, he studied Charlie Morse's shapely hands, his well-tended nails, the thin wrist that disappeared into the cuff of his white shirt.

"How's our friend Arthurina?" the beautiful youth asked after taking down their order. "I haven't seen her for a while."

"She has her ups and downs," Tracy told him. "You know how it is."

"Give her my best," Charlie said. "I do miss her these days."

"I will, most definitely."

"Sounds like you get down here quite a lot," Devin observed when Charlie had left them.

Tracy took a deep breath. "Actually," he admitted, suddenly relieved to be telling the truth, "I'm down here all the time. I left my job up in Middle Forge. Things just weren't working out. So I'm staying with Arthur Branson right now. I know you two never got along."

"A question of style," Devin said generously.

"I know. A piece of work. But frankly, for me, he's been a saint. He's got this tiny, tiny apartment"—Tracy pinched together forefinger and thumb—"but he welcomed me with open arms."

Devin sipped his martini peaceably. "I always sensed you never quite got over him," he said.

It caught Tracy off guard. Recently he'd been thinking much the same thing. "You're probably right," he agreed. "I guess, in a way, I never have gotten over him." But then he had never really gotten over any of them: not

Arthur Branson, not Devin Shimabukuro, not Holden Chance IV. Not Eric whose last name he did not remember. Certainly not Noah Lathrop.

"I'm very worried about Arthur," he confessed to Devin. "He's not doing so well. He keeps losing weight, even though we've got him eating five meals a day. Meat and more meat. Who'd have thought a rabid vegetarian like me would end up specializing in pork roasts? And he never goes out anymore; he's got a modem, so he just works from bed. He says his feet are killing him. His doctor can't find any reason, but it just keeps getting worse. I have this bad feeling *everything's* getting worse with him and there's no stopping it."

Charlie was back with their plates: a cheeseburger for Devin, kale and white bean soup for Tracy. That Devin seemed unruffled by their waiter's astonishing beauty must bode well, Tracy decided with a touch of envy, for his future with Rafael.

"Are you sure it's a good situation for you to be in?" Devin asked. "I mean, taking care of somebody who's so sick."

"It's what I need to do," Tracy said, aware that he perhaps sounded more stoic than he actually felt these days.

Devin picked up his cheeseburger and inspected it. "More meat," he said. "You've always been so pure. I admire that about you. But I want to ask something. You didn't give up your teaching job because of Arthur, did you? You seemed to like it so much. It seemed so perfect for you."

"I didn't exactly give up my job," Tracy told him.

Devin looked, actually, quite shocked. "You mean you got fired? Impossible. *You*, of all people?"

"Let's just say I had to leave. It's a very long story. I fell in love with one of my students."

"Oh my God," Devin exclaimed.

"We joked about that. Remember?" He tried not to sound bitter. He knew he didn't feel bitter, but what it was he felt, exactly, he couldn't begin to say.

"But you actually . . . I mean—what happened? Was it wonderful?"

"Wonderful," Tracy said, turning the word round and round in his mind. "I suppose you could say, in a certain sense, it was wonderful. It was also the stupidest thing I ever did."

"Tell me everything. Was he hot? How young are we talking here?"

Tracy found he could say nothing at all.

"Did you fuck him?" Devin went on. "I don't know why I find all this so fantastic."

"You weren't there," Tracy told his friend wearily. "That's why."

Something in his tone brought Devin to heel. He narrowed his eyes and said, "I'm sorry. This is all very serious, isn't? And here I'm being such a reckless queen about it. I'm so shallow sometimes."

"It's a deep shallowness," Tracy said. "That's what I love about you. Anyway, it's all nothing now. It's just something that happened, and now we all move on."

"Who's we?"

"The people whose trust I betrayed. The ones I let down. The ones I didn't love enough."

"Oh," Devin said somberly. "Does this mean you're in trouble? I'm not going to be reading about you in the newspaper, am I?"

"I could've gone to jail for a long time," he said—he who had been given the chance to burn brightly, to defy the world with the blessed madness of love. Not an hour went by when he didn't understand, with a clarity so sharp it bit, what he had let slip from his grasp. He regretted everything and nothing; his punishment was to have to relinquish it all. "They could've thrown me to the wolves," he went on. "But they didn't. They let me slink away with my hide intact." But he knew it wasn't *they*. It was Noah, who'd been hurt and said nothing; it was Louis, who'd known everything and said nothing. It still left him stunned and slightly disbelieving. He still half expected the police to knock on Arthur's door one day. For the rest of his life he would be waiting for the knock on the door.

No one knew where he was, he comforted himself. His break with the Forge—all of it, every last, loved aspect of its life—was absolute. About him everywhere lay his future. It gleamed in the sunlight washing the busy streets beyond the café's plate-glass window. It burnished the bar from behind which Charlie, lazily stifling a good-natured yawn, sent a friendly look his way. Pushing his empty plate to one side, Devin felt in the pocket of his jacket for his cigarettes.

"Do you mind?" he said.

Tracy shook his head. At this very moment Claire might be walking Betsy, and Louis might be skirmishing futilely with Reid, and Noah . . . but with an ache of vast regret Tracy Parker could not even imagine what Noah—strange, lovely, brilliant, wounded Noah—might be up to on a splendid April day like today.

"That was so weird," Noah said, looking back over his shoulder, watching the two old women and their frisky beagle disappear around a bend in the path.

"It was his dog, wasn't it?" Chris said. "The one that got lost."

"Betsy didn't get lost," Noah corrected him. "*I* lost her. It's like seeing a ghost. I mean, I knew she got found, but . . .." He hesitated. How to say that the whole episode now seemed as unreal as a dream? Not just his flight to New York, his losing Betsy, but everything that had happened since New Year's. Like a bubble, its surface an intricate wonder of iridescence one moment and totally gone the next.

"You mean, you thought she might still be lost and they were just telling you she got found," Chris suggested.

"Something like that," Noah told him. It was just as well he couldn't find the words. Everyone seemed to want to forget that anything had happened, and he gathered that he was meant to forget as well. But he would not forget. He had made love to a man who had loved him. His body had been penetrated. He would never again be the same experience-hungry boy he'd once been, and he held close to his heart the triumphant knowledge he had won.

And yet, every day, a little more escaped. He no longer thought about Tracy Parker every waking minute, no longer yearned in mute frustration for things somehow to reconfigure themselves into the world as he wished it. He no longer felt the constant presence within himself of the rage that had burned so fiercely—against his dad, Dr. Tremper, the universe of school and rules. Against Tracy Parker as well, Tracy who'd shown himself to be a coward rather than the brilliant rebel he liked to pretend he was, who in the end cared more about what other people thought than about the terrific adventure they'd set out to share.

Lately, it seemed, without actively desiring to, without any conscious choice on his part, he'd moved on.

And now here was Betsy bringing that other world back with her, the way Saint Bernards carry brandy flasks for climbers lost in the mountains to remember civilization by. It amazed him, a little, that Tracy had given Betsy up after all that had happened. But then Tracy had given Noah up as well. Were they all expendable, then? Was that how life was?

The lake's expanse glittered silver in the warm sun. A flock of mallards floated near the shore; five or six Canada geese tore at the grass of the lawn. "I think you should probably get tested," Chris had said to him one day. Why did he remember that just now? It had clearly been something the Fatwa was waiting for the right time to say—maybe working up his courage. And then he'd just said it. "I'll go with you," he'd offered. "We'll go down to the city."

Noah had gone all hollow inside; the blood had rushed from his head. Why are you doing this? he'd wanted to ask, but hadn't; had only found himself nodding, unable to speak, as the edges of his vision dimmed for a single scary moment in which he was just stupid Noah Lathrop who was going to die. Expendable. But then the results had come back. The Fatwa had been there with him when he went to get them. Despite the swagger of his tattoo, he'd tested negative. He wasn't the boy with AIDS after all.

"Thank God," had been Chris's reaction—but Noah had wondered, fleetingly, if it was possible his friend felt somehow abandoned by the good news. That had been a fine moment, after all, the afternoon they'd ventured into that Chelsea tattoo parlor.

Against all odds they were still friends. Who could have foretold, that night back in the fall when he'd run into Tracy and Betsy on this very path, that half a year later he'd be walking with, of all people, the Fatwa? As if it were the most natural thing in the world, Chris linked their arms together, the way he'd done when they marched into the tattoo parlor. For only an instant Noah flinched with the old fear. This was the Forge. What if someone saw them? It was the same fear Tracy must have felt all the time, even in his own house. But then the dread thought came to Noah: soon enough, everybody would see them. For this was a momentous day. Was that why he'd been allowed a glimpse of Betsy? Was she meant to signal him that he was allowed to go on wishing, and that everything would be fine?

Leaving the lake behind them, he and Chris walked arm in arm up the path toward the cafeteria.

"Do you feel ready?" Chris asked. Like the tattoos that afternoon, this had been his idea. He was very charismatic that way.

"Frankly, I feel ill," Noah said bravely, "but I'll be okay. The question is, are *they* ready?"

"As ready as they'll ever be," Chris said. He sounded positively jubilant, a boy who had nothing to lose. Noah quailed, then girded himself. He likewise, he told himself, had nothing to lose. Or at the very least he could act as if he had nothing to lose.

Taking a deep breath, he flung open the double doors of the cafeteria. The familiar, depressing odor of ammonia-mopped floors assailed him, and beyond that the greasy smell of meat.

Tables had been set up in the foyer. Every third Friday of the month was Club Day, a pointless event, he'd always thought, at which the various clubs vied for attention and recruits. Today the usual suspects were out in number: David Valentine at the Chess Club table, Mike Choi with the Cyber Club, Brad Delson and Ben Cannon manning the elaborate setup of the Miniature Railroad Club, by dint of Mr. Brill's patronage by far the most popular club at the school.

His heart drummed nervously. He scanned the room. It was now or never, he thought, though *never*, at the moment, had quite an appealing ring to it. He clutched at his knapsack, which held, carefully folded, along with several rubber-banded stacks of flyers Chris had brought up from the city, the banner the two of them, sequestered in the Fatwa lair, had painted on a bedsheet the night before.

"Okay," he said as he set the knapsack on an empty table. "Here goes nothing." Like a magician producing scarves, he unfurled the brightly colored banner. With masking tape they affixed it to the front of the table, and Chris stepped back to check out the effect. "Fabulous," he said, tossing a lemon-yellow lock of hair out of his eye. Then Noah himself dared take a look. The lettering was bold, irrevocable, clearly visible to anyone who walked by.

QUEER FORGE.
Gay/Bisexual/???ing.
Strength in Solidarity. Join Our Coalition.

He'd never done anything even remotely requiring the fortitude it took to calmly, even nonchalantly, seat himself behind that table, a target for all the world. See who I am? his mute presence proclaimed as loudly as if he'd banged on a drum and shouted.

As Chris arranged and rearranged the various pamphlets—AIDS education, *Youth Services in New York City, Twenty Questions You May Have about Coming Out*—Noah dared himself to flee. In spite of his tattoo, which he took pains to hide, he wasn't marked the way Chris Tyler was marked; his camouflage was still intact. But then he remembered the pigeon that had hung from Chris's door.

They settled down to wait. For several minutes nothing at all happened. Preoccupied with setting up their own tables, none of the other boys paid them any attention. Then the double doors burst open and in marched Mr. Brill and his family. They arrived, as always, like pioneers ready to settle a new land, full of an unstoppable confidence he both envied and despised. And count them: four children, and the fecund Mrs. with another on the way; surely a serious war crime against the planet, as Tracy Parker would have said. Even before he knew Tracy, he'd hated the Brill, ever since those days in study hall when that mutant hybrid (one part drill sergeant, two parts lizard) used to humiliate any boy whose mind he suspected of wandering. Well, the Brill would never guess in a million lizard years how far Noah's mind had managed to roam.

As wife and children descended like locusts on the cafeteria line, the object of Noah's scorn paused to survey the tables, especially the Miniature Railroad Club, where an engine and three boxcars traveled around and around a figure-eight of track to nowhere. "Looking good," he told his minions. "Looking real good."

At last he took notice of the newcomers.

"What's this," he said, as if prepared to be pleasantly surprised. But his look quickly darkened.

"We're announcing the formation of a new club," Chris said brightly, teasingly. "Want to join?"

The Brill scrutinized the banner carefully—unable, it seemed, to decipher exactly what its words meant.

"This your idea of a prank, boys?" he asked warily. "Pretty funny, I'd say." He picked up a flyer and, still frowning, perused it as well.

"Nope," Chris said. "It's the real thing. Scary, isn't it?"

"You seem to think you're clever," the Brill told him. "But you're not.

You've got no idea what you're dabbling with here. Do you even know what gay stands for? Well, let me tell you. G-A-Y. Got Aids Yet? Get it? I'm confiscating these." He scooped up the stack of flyers in his hirsute paw. "This club isn't authorized. You've got to take this stuff down. Pronto."

"I believe you'll find that Dr. Tremper authorized it," Chris improvised smoothly.

"Uh-uh," the Brill said. "If I believe that I'll believe pigs can fly."

"Just yesterday," Chris said.

Noah watched with admiration, then chimed in. "We've got as much right to be here as you do, Mr. Brill. So get used to it."

The Brill looked at him the way his dad used to look at him: that mix of contempt, disbelief, plain incomprehension. "You," he warned. "Watch the lip. I've had my eye on you. And you're both in mongo trouble if I walk over to Dr. Tremper's office and find out you've just told me a lie. Do you understand that?"

"We understand," Noah said. "We'll accept the consequences."

The Brill glared at him, then shook his head disgustedly. He was the one Tracy had been most afraid of. And he knew everything. Noah hadn't quite understood at the time. But this was the man who'd caused it all to unravel, the one who'd gotten Tracy fired—he was sure of it. He should hate him, but he only felt a blank dread as he watched that compact, muscular frame push its way out the door. In the end it was the Brills of the world, Noah understood too well, who had everything on their side.

"Okay," he told Chris. "Now we're cooked."

"Maybe," Chris said helpfully, but then Chris didn't mind being cooked. He was the Fatwa. He was beyond all that. "Look on the bright side. At least they've noticed us," he said.

That attention manifested itself, however, as its opposite: the other club boys desperately pretended to arrange the chess pieces or check the battery on a laptop, or follow the train in its pointless journey, all the while casting furtive and titillated glances in the direction of the two self-proclaimed queers who had appeared in their midst. The air in the room was suddenly sultry with expectation. But of what? With a crash the double doors were flung wide and in loped the Goethe Hall Gang—Kevin, Patrick, Gary, Tim. They must have been horsing around: their faces were flushed, their school uniforms in disarray. Kevin sported a grass stain on his left knee. There was a time not long ago when Noah would have been with them. With them but not of them, he reminded himself, regretting only for a bittersweet moment this betrayal of his friends. He faced the fact coldly: they had not known him; they had not ever been his friends.

"Well, well, what do we have here?" Gary said broadly, pausing to scrutinize the banner while Noah held his breath. "Oh my God. You're shitting me." He looked from Noah to Chris and back again, genuinely stunned, Noah was gratified to note. He met Gary's stare without flinching. "Queer Forge," Gary read aloud in high, hysterical disbelief.

"Gary," Tim told him. "Don't get so uptight. It's a joke."

"Uh, guys," said Kevin Motes. "I don't think it is a joke."

"No," affirmed Noah. He stood up and crossed his arms over his chest. "It most definitely is not a joke. Sorry."

"I knew it," Gary said. His whole body twisted away from the table in a slow pantomime of revulsion as he waved his open palms, fingers spread wide, in front of his face to ward off the spectacle. "I knew I smelled something fruity about you all along."

"Knock it off," Tim told him.

"Your roommate's a queer," Gary pointed out. "Did you know that?"

"Grow up," Tim said. Then, to Noah: "So. I guess you and I need to talk. It's not like I didn't sort of know."

"Yeah, we should talk," Noah agreed. He'd known all along Tim was the decent one; his roommate had probably even known about the bed-wetting and never used that knowledge.

"What do you mean, grow up?" Gary protested. "Your roommate's gone over to the freaking Fatwa."

"I beg your pardon?" Chris said. He had remained seated the whole time, making the best of his immense capacity to look bored. "The what?"

"You heard me, Fatwa." Gary shot the word out with the force of a bullet.

Chris just shook his head and smiled. "Are you having a nervous breakdown?" he asked mildly.

A sudden inspiration flashed in Noah. "Come on, Gary," he said. "Join us." For one supersatisfying instant, he caught the glimmer of pure terror that flickered in Gary's eyes.

Smelling blood, Patrick couldn't resist flinging his own taunt. "You know you want to, Gary," he simpered. Noah had always suspected that Patrick, given half a chance, was basically a shark.

"Shut up, you little faggot," Gary instructed his friend. He clenched his fists as if about to lash out.

"Why don't you make me?" Patrick suggested. "Faggot. Takes one to know one."

It was all so dreary, Noah thought. And obvious. And, for once, oddly thrilling, the way a girl must feel to have boys fighting over her. He waited for the inevitable shoving match, the thrown punch, all hell to break loose. But it didn't. The front doors opened again and in strode the Brill with Dr. Tremper in tow. Cowards when push came to shove, the Goethe Hall Gang dispersed to the cafeteria with such practiced alacrity that Noah was sure neither the animated Brill, in whose voice the note of agitation sounded clearly even if the individual words were inaudible, nor the headmaster, who was saying nothing, only nodding now and again with a grim expression on his face, had noticed a thing.

"See?" the Brill said, gesturing to the banner—as if Dr. Tremper had for some reason been disinclined to believe him without physical evidence.

Slowly, deliberately, the headmaster took off the sunglasses he always wore when venturing out of doors. Secret Agent Man, some of the students called him. "Christian. Noah," he addressed them. "Good morning."

Chris spoke up cheerfully—"Good morning, sir"—and Noah mumbled the same. Dr. Tremper's unshielded gaze seemed to take in everything at once. He did not look particularly surprised, or even dismayed. Unreadable, he fascinated Noah. He took up a pamphlet and examined it, then laid it carefully back on the table. "AIDS education," he said in that formal way he had. "Certainly a worthy cause."

The Brill gave a snort of disapproval. Dr. Tremper cast a sidelong glance his way. "You disagree?" he said. Noah registered the gesture with a sense of shock. The Brill might have everything on his side—God, decency, a family—but Dr. Tremper despised the Brill.

"I don't really think, here at the Forge School, for our students, I mean, I don't think . . ." said the Brill before spluttering to a halt before that acid stare. Dr. Tremper had a similar way of looking at you in class when he thought you were embarrassing yourself.

"Your world is very small, Mr. Brill. There are many things you do not know."

"There're a lot of things I don't want to know," the Brill replied.

"I don't doubt that," Dr. Tremper told him. He paused, and wearily wiped his eyes. Then, looking straight at Noah, he announced, in a voice loud enough for everyone in the foyer to hear, "This club has my authorization. Furthermore, it has my support. I do not want to see these students harassed in any way. They are under my protection. You, Mr. Brill, in particular, I entrust with seeing that that is the case. Do I make myself clear?"

The Brill worked hard to master his annoyance. His face contorted its way through various ugly spasms. "I understand," he said. "Though under protest."

"Your protest is noted," Dr. Tremper said icily, and turned away. "Now good day, Christian. Noah." He nodded briskly at them both—but his eyes, Noah could have sworn, glittered with the ironic suggestion of a smile.

So it's true, Noah thought. You had to listen carefully, as he'd done during the six weeks since the headmaster had taken over their English class, but if you did listen you could catch, carefully concealed beneath that dry shell of formality, all that careful diction and arid wit, the shocking soul of a complete anarchist. It was a feeling he'd had, just a suspicion—Tracy Parker had liked Dr. Tremper, after all—but now Noah saw it clearly. He wanted to laugh, but instead exulted to Chris, as the adults moved out of range, "I can't believe it."

"See? I told you," Chris said, as if he'd been in on the secret all along. "He's on our side. He may not be one of us, but in his own way Dr. Tremper's definitely on our side."

It was as if a future opened inside him, wild and radiant and hopeful. He no longer felt angry—not even with Tracy Parker. Why should he be angry? He'd achieved what he'd sought. He'd made somebody want him—only momentarily, it was true, but that was enough. It was his first success in life.

Reaching out his thin arm, the arm with the tattoo, he flexed his muscle— a comic book gesture, he knew, but still. Maybe, just maybe, out of the exhilaration and mess of the last few months, a monster had been created.

Unfettered, inextinguishable, the monster found himself on the verge of everything. This was the dream he dreamed, suddenly, as clearly as if it were real. He clung to a great crag of rock. Below him yawned the dark chasm. From here anything was possible. He could fall; he could soar. He could burst into flame and astonish them all.

"Come on," Noah urged his classmates as they drifted past. "Join up with us. What are you waiting for? The future's here, and it's queer, a whole new way of living. This old earth's sick, it's tired, it wants things to change; besides, the animals are on our side. The forests are on our side, the oceans too. Aren't you fed up with being so loud and stupid and mean? Come dream our dream with us. What I mean is—stop eating meat, stop putting junk in your bodies. That goes for your heads too. Stop sleepwalking. Live for a change." He spoke whatever inspired sentences streamed into his head; if charisma was a spirit that could fill you up, then he overflowed. All his long conversations with Tracy Parker, their feasts of lentils and root vegetables, the Franz Schubert and the candlelight and most of all the love, not just the touch of flesh but that too, penetration's sacred pain and profane joy, the sheer shout of it. "Where the cities are now," he said, "huge forests will grow up. The dams are going to burst and the floodwaters'll wash away the superhighways. Rainbow trout, salmon, catfish—they'll swim upstream. These fabulous beasts you can't even imagine will be roaming right here, where the campus used to be. And all because of love, love, love. Just a few of us at the beginning. So what are you afraid of? We're all gonna die sooner or later."

Beside him, still seated, Chris stirred languidly. He tugged at Noah's sleeve. "Um, you've got an interesting notion of queer," he pointed out.

Noah didn't mind. "I've had the benefit of an excellent teacher," he told his friend and comrade. He had his vision; he would make it come true. Then he did what he would never have dreamed. He bent down and, on impulse, out of a love as pure as spring, he kissed the Fatwa on the lips.

The other boys passing through the foyer respectfully averted their eyes. Word had spread quickly about the table's existence, and the headmaster's strange protection that shielded it from harm. No smirks, no taunts, no jokes came their way. No one so much as dared cast a look in their direction for the whole of the lunch period, so that in the end it was as if the two young queers were not even there at all.